This story is a compelling and amusing tale that gets us to think about questions of life and faith and the existence of God in new and creative ways. It stretches our thinking on theological issues—and while it may not give us the answers, it certainly helps us to explore our thoughts on those matters. It even includes a happy ending that leaves us feeling good!

Thank you, Light family and Gideon and Celeste and all the other characters in this book for doing that and to author, Jeff Hutchins, for pulling it all together!

—Rev. Richard B. Hanna (Presbyterian)

Pisgah Press was established in 2011 to publish and promote works of quality offering original ideas and insight into the human condition, the realm of knowledge, and the world around us.

Published by Pisgah Press, LLC
PO Box 9663, Asheville, NC 28815
www.pisgahpress.com

Cover design: Jack Williams

Library of Congress Cataloging-in-Publication Data
Hutchins, Jeffrey Melvin
Jerome v. God/Hutchins

ISBN: 978-1-942016-98-4
Fiction

First Edition
First Printing
April 2025

Jerome v. God

A Novel

Jeffrey Melvin Hutchins

Pisgah Press, LLC
Asheville, NC
www.pisgahpress.com

ACKNOWLEDGMENTS

You cannot work on a manuscript for more than twenty years, as I have done with Jerome, and not involve many people in its development.

No one was more important in bringing Jerome to life and to the courtroom than Thomas R. Johnson, an extraordinary man and an extraordinary attorney. He is of counsel with K&L Gates LLC, an international law firm. He not only knows the details of legal practice needed for my novel, but he has a heavy background among theologians. He has been a Board member of the Association of Theological Seminaries of the United States and Canada, and is a trustee of the Princeton Theological Seminary.

Tom reviewed all the legal goings-on in the story to ensure their accuracy. (I had to overrule him occasionally for dramatic purposes.) He offered story ideas and insights into my characters that helped keep the story going and the drama flowing. I cannot thank Tom enough for the many hours he put in pro bono.

The first person to read an early draft of Jerome was Lynda Morgenroth, one of the most brilliant and fascinating people I've ever known. Her perceptive critique gave me the ideas and the motivation to steer the novel in a new and more reader-friendly direction.

One of the final people to review the manuscript was Richard B. Hanna, a long-time Presbyterian minister and recently retired as chaplain at Kirkwood by the River in Alabama. Rich's wisdom prevented me from making embarrassing mistakes in my portrayal of Gideon. Where Tom Johnson helped me get the legal stuff right, Rich helped me get the pastoral stuff right.

The two most important editors as I got closer to publication were Mike Czeczot and Andy Reed, both of whom are masters of the written word. Their affection for my story gave me the confidence and the emotional boost I needed to bring it home.

I must thank Dr. Julie J. Exline of Case Western Reserve University's Department of Psychology. She provided valuable feedback on the psychological profile of atheists introduced in the trial by Dr. Keaton Mueller as a witness for the defense.

Several close family members delved into manuscripts at various stages of development, including my wife, Diane, daughters Rachel and Nell, sister Valerie, and Diane's uncle Lee Neuwirth. The feedback from each of them was tremendously helpful.

During nearly a quarter century of writing and rewriting Jerome v. God, I am certain that I got ideas and suggestions from other people as well, but time has dulled my memory. So, if you contributed your wisdom, thank you, and accept my apology for not naming you herein.

Jerome v. God

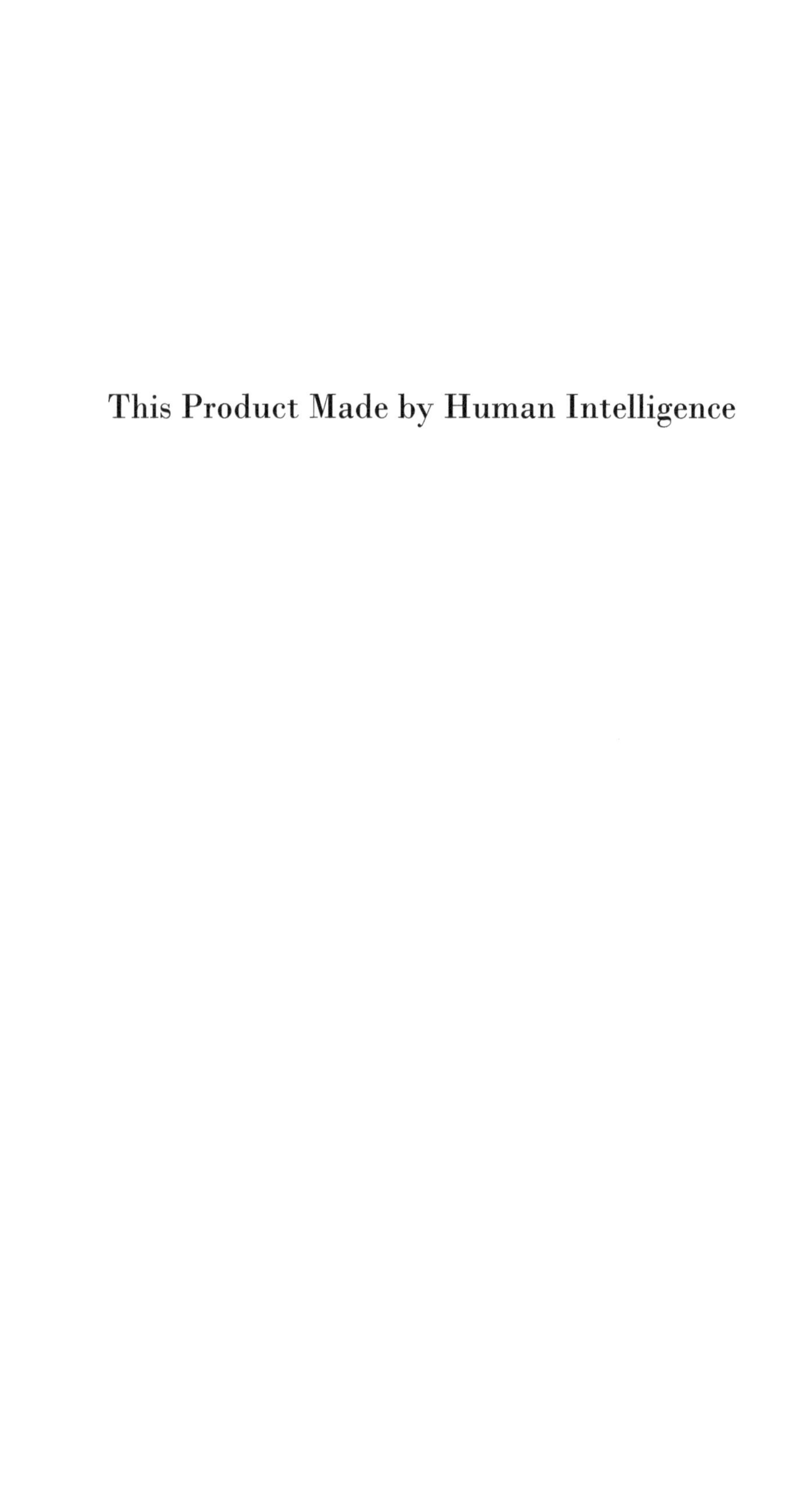

This Product Made by Human Intelligence

Chapter 1

The Day Before Tomorrow

The morning of that memorable day, a jaundiced sky greeted Jerome as he stepped outside, his chest bare, to scoop up the Sunday paper. Jerome Light did not think of himself as ordinary, even before the events of June 9, 2024.

Jerome and Lacy Light had two children, two cars, and three credit cards, one of which Jerome never used. Her parents were alive and in reasonably good health. His father. Abner, had died two years ago, and his mother, Claire, had moved to Scottsdale, Arizona, to be near his sister, Mira. Jerome was average height (5'7"), average weight (170), had brown hair (thinning to the point of insurrection) and all his teeth. He had an IQ of 125 before he had children, who, he felt, tended to limit the new things he learned, mostly pop culture and new snack foods.

Jerome had a good face, mostly oval and white, but not pale. He was clean-shaven, but had such dark facial hair that, even when freshly shaved, his five-o'clock shadow awakened by eleven a.m. There were few lines in his face, since he had always worked indoors.

His nose was sufficiently slender that it had the effect of making his eyes appear too wide apart, an optical illusion not diminished by the heavy eyebrows that seemed to push his eyelids slightly closed. It was, therefore, a somewhat unfriendly visage on an otherwise friendly, well-liked man. Think part Keanu Reeves, part Humphrey Bogart.

The newspaper, the overly provincial *Marshfield Sun-Record*, lay in a clear plastic bag on the sidewalk at the end of the flat driveway of the Lights' house, a two-story colonial with off-white siding and decorative royal-blue shutters. Two crows called to each other. Jerome felt as if they were talking about him, and probably not in a kind way. The yard smelled of grass and daylilies. He tucked the paper under his arm and looked up and down the street at the nearest houses, each on its own 1/3-acre lot, with manicured lawns sporting the glistening dew that picked up the dawn's first rays of sun.

Back inside, Jerome sat in the country kitchen—complete with country-themed gingham wallpaper—reading the news. Without looking up, he said, "There's a story here about a guy who was electrocuted and fell off a roof last year and nobody thought he would ever walk again if he even survived." He paused, mostly to catch his breath after that beastly sentence that he could not figure out how to end. "Well, of course, he's walking again, 'only' eleven months later. And some idiot is calling it a true miracle. Some miracle. The guy's in terrible shape, acute pain, can't do anything normal, and he's working his butt off for eleven months just to stand up with two people holding him. If that's someone's idea of God performing miracles."

Lacy lit a flame under the teakettle and said nothing. Experience had taught her that was her safest option, especially when her non-believing husband got worked up about religion.

Lacy's looks telegraphed her Germanic roots, as well as her Judaism. She had the bone structure of a Semite, but the skin tone of a northern European, and it was a stunning combination, her dark hair framing a pale face with the most endearing touches of her ancestors' noses and cheeks and eyebrows. At age fifty-two, the same as Jerome, she could still turn heads. Jerome once saw a boy no more than twenty checking out his wife.

Another article caught his eye. It was the best news he had heard in a long time, though, he thought, hardly anyone else would notice. "It says that people who do crossword and logic puzzles are less likely to get Alzheimer's." Good Lord, that's what Jerome did for a living. As an editor at Crawley's, the dictionary publishers, he spent all his time dealing with nuances and shades of meaning. It was like spending all day in a mental spa, a place where your mind did the heavy lifting while your body simply went numb. It's the exact opposite, he thought, of the aerobics classes his wife took each week.

Jerome's and Lacy's son Moses appeared in the doorway. "Hey, Dad, can I use your car tonight? I'm going to see a flick at the multiplex with the guys."

Jerome put down the paper and glanced up at the seventeen-year-old boy. The first words in Jerome's mind were, "You're too tall," but he said nothing. Moses's significant advantage in height over Jerome was a constant reminder that his son was not his own. He and Lacy had adopted Moses when the boy was a few months old. The baby had been abandoned in a basket near the Marshfield riverfront, and workers at Child and Family Services had named him Moses. When Jerome and Lacy managed to "win" custody of Moses, the irony of the baby's name had not been wasted on Jerome. It was compounded a year later when Lacy gave birth to a daughter she named Miriam, after Lacy's grandmother.

No one would mistake Moses and Miriam for natural siblings. He was a big kid, athletic, and swarthy. She was petite and fair. In the past year, Moses had matured into a handsome man.

The tea kettle came to a boil, and Lacy rushed to silence its scream. The smell of black tea and peaches filled the room as she sang quietly to herself:

Saturday night at the movies
Who cares what picture you see?
On a blanket with my baby
Is where I'll be.

Jerome said, "Those are two different songs, you know."

"No, they're not," said Lacy.

"You always say you don't pay attention to lyrics. I'm telling you, that's two different songs."

"Dad, what about the car?" asked Moses, as he popped two slices of bread in the toaster.

Lacy said, "You can have the car, Moses, if you'll drop your sister off at Jessica's."

Jerome glanced sideways, his eyes sweeping from Lacy to Moses and back. He wondered when he lost control of his life. *Moses asks me a question, his mother answers instead of me, and I'm all right with that. I've become a wuss!* he thought.

It was nice that Moses had nearly outgrown his most annoying teenage habits. He could still be surly, but he was more likely to try to please Jerome and Lacy. A year ago, Moses had whined and shuffled whenever he had to drive Miriam. He had known, before he got his license at 16, that he would have to help out, but the reality of doing so was worse than he'd anticipated. Now, after a year and a half of breaking him in, and trying to make an adult out of him, Jerome was pleased at how Moses matured. Here, at last, was a friend, not only a responsibility.

Chapter 2

What the Hell Was That?

That evening, Jerome found himself alone at home after dinner. Lacy had a committee meeting at the Temple. Moses was to pick up Miriam from her best friend's house at 9:45.

Jerome sat in front of the TV in his usual spot, leaning on the left arm of his brown-leather recliner with the rectangular cushion that he had put off restuffing for far too long. Late spring was never a good time for TV. Jerome abused the buttons on the remote control, changing channels back and forth. Nothing appeared good enough to pause on for more than a couple of seconds. His mind was restless, not wanting to focus. He expressed his mood through his remote control.

Some kind of animal documentary. Some kind of war documentary. Some cartoon character that would not stand a chance against Bugs Bunny. Some right-wing-fanatical news commentator. A different right-wing-fanatical news commentator. CNN. C-Span. C-Span 2. A Catholic mass. A preacher. "The Gideon Calhoun Hour." This could be funny. Jerome's fingers relaxed a moment.

"God is troubled by this behavior," Gideon intoned. "He is saddened to see his flock led astray."

Oh, he's got the whole act down, thought Jerome, almost admiring the famous TV preacher. Jerome reached for the remote, but before he could find the channel-up button again, Gideon continued.

"I understand God's sadness, and I share it, because I have a personal relationship with God. He has spoken to me and instructed me to be his agent here on Earth."

Jerome said out loud to no one, "What kind of crap is this?" He quickly changed the channel, and then, bored and irritated by all the junk, he turned off the TV and stood up.

The colors in the room began to change as the long-day's sun subsided. The baby blue of the walls seemed greener, and the contemporary dark-red sofa across from his recliner took on an orange hue. Jerome got up to look out the window and was surprised to see yellow stains again splashed across the sky above the houses on Tadpole Lane.

Jerome cocked his head to one side as he looked out the window at the front of the house. He looked like a confused parrot. There was no good reason to bend his head; the window afforded a clear view of the sky. Yet he did, because the color of the sky was so unusual that he was perplexed. The early-June evening was cool, so he cranked the casement window closed, and then slid down to close the other one.

He saw his neighbor, Mike Engelhardt, come out of his house. Jerome trotted out, too. The air smelled like olive oil heating too long on a stove. "Nice evening, eh, Mike?"

"Yeah."

"Isn't that sky amazing?"

Mike was a thirty-nine-year-old plumbing supply salesman. He wore a black toupee atop an urn-shaped body clad in jeans and a sweatshirt. He had not come out to see the sunset, or to check the weather, but to collect the mail that had been delivered while they spent a long weekend at his sister-in-law's. Jerome crossed the street towards Mike as he watched the sky and tried to interest Mike in this marvel.

"Oh, yeah," droned Mike. He gave a token glance towards the western sky, "wow." It was the kind of "wow" that could put a baby to sleep, but it showed sufficient interest for Jerome to carry on in a friendly vein. A flock of birds flew out of a tree and raced south, prompting the leaves and the branches to murmur a breathy sigh.

"Were you and Sandi away?"

"Yeah, just a quick visit up to her sister Tina in Cleveland. Sandi and I are going away in two weeks, so we're trying to . . . What the *hell* was *that?*"

As Mike had spoken, a loud BOOM sounded, startling both men and sending a flock of sparrows fleeing from a tree. "Maybe a sonic boom," said Jerome.

A noisy hiss came from across the street, the ground shook, and they heard what sounded like a groan.

Mike said, "Earthquake?"

"I don't know. I don't think so," said Jerome.

Jerome turned and looked at his house. It seemed to sway for a moment, especially in the center of the roof, which began to sink.

Mike was the first to speak. "Ohmygod!" He inhaled deeply, enough to fill a good-sized balloon. "Did you see that? What the hell is that?"

For a full second it seemed that the world stopped, silent and still. Then, as if some giant fist had hammered the roof, it began to fold itself into the house. The part farthest from the men sank first. The near walls tumbled inward. Finally, Jerome's house began to disappear into the ground with a deafening clatter. Jerome stood looking at the site as if waiting for a bus. He was numb, unfeeling, looking for all the world like a man lost in thought, though there was, momentarily, not a single thought in his mind.

It was Mike who reacted first. Both his hands flew to the sides of his round head. "Holy shit! Your house! Your house is gone!" Both men stood looking at it for a long three seconds, before Mike made a mad dash inside. "I'm calling 9-1-1. Just, I don't know, come with me or something." As he ran away, there was an explosion from beneath the ground where the house had disappeared, and a large plume of smoke and ash rose above the earth.

People started pouring out of the other houses, two or three at a time. Their mouths hung open in such a way that it appeared their jaws had been wired in that position. There was no panic, though, which added to the eeriness of the scene. A few people, of course, were agitated. "Was it terrorists?" one asked. But everyone else was confused, stunned, disbelieving.

Jerome hustled inside the Engelhardt house behind Mike, who made a beeline for the telephone. It struck Jerome that he had no idea what good it would do for him to be standing next to Mike as the 911 operator took the report, but somehow it seemed like the right thing to do. *I should go home,* he thought, and quickly realized that he could not.

That started a flood of practical thoughts racing through Jerome's mind. "Where did Miriam say she was going? Oh, right, she's with Jessica. What are Jessica's parents' names? Oh, right, I have the phone number on the fridge. Uh . . . no. Not anymore. Holy shit, I've got to find Lacy. Crap, my cell phone was in the house."

"The fire trucks'll be here any second," Mike said, almost triumphantly, as he hung up the phone. "What the hell was that?"

Jerome stepped back outside into the warm early-summer night. It was an ideal night. The air was cool, but not cold, and it made one feel alive. There was a slight breeze to keep it from being too still, but not enough to be uncomfortable. The evening sky was clear, except for a few clouds that let the moon illuminate them in deep hues. It would have been a perfect night, except for the fact that Jerome's house was now rubble, and his wallet was buried under much of it. An acrid smell permeated the neighborhood. Black soot began to fall like snow.

Borgin Mindling, the stereotypically Nordic neighbor who lived next door to the Lights, was the first to reach Jerome. "My God, Jerome! You're all right!"

"Of course I'm all right."

"What 'of course?' Your house is gone!!! What happened? How did you get outside? Is anyone else in there? What about Lacy and the kids?" Borgin was frantic, a stark contrast to Jerome.

Jerome looked at Borgin for a moment, compelled to think about Lacy and the kids. *They could have been home when it happened,* he thought, suddenly aware of how afraid he should be. He found his voice. "Jesus, Borgin, you're right! Um, they're okay. They were all out for the evening, and I stepped outside right before it happened."

"What's 'IT'?" Borgin wanted to know. He motioned across the street.

"That's a good question. I have no idea. Mike and I were talking over here, and we heard a boom—"

"Yeah, I heard that, too," interrupted Borgin.

". . . and then a loud hissing sound, and then the ground opened up, and the next thing you know, my house is gone."

"No shit," said Borgin, as other neighbors began to huddle around Jerome, all talking and asking the same questions.

Two fire engines appeared at the far end of the street, rapidly making their way towards the Light house. Behind them, a police cruiser and an ambulance raced to catch up. As the fire engines pulled over towards the now-demolished house, the cruiser pulled into the left lane and stopped. Two officers jumped out and began moving people back.

"It's his house!" said one neighbor to the police, pointing at Jerome. As one officer continued crowd control, the older officer approached Jerome.

"Are you the resident of this house, Sir?" he asked Jerome.

"Yes. I mean, I was."

"What happened, Mister . . .?"

"Light. Jerome Light. I have no idea." And Jerome repeated the story he had told Borgin Mindling. By this time, the firefighters had pulled their hoses, and were hosing down the ground around and inside the sinkhole. Columbia Gas had been notified and had cut the flow to the development. Crews raced to inspect the area.

One of the firefighters came over, whispered something to the police officer, and began walking back towards his truck. The crowd of neighbors seemed to sense that some tidbit of news was about to be shared, so they pressed towards the officer as began moving towards them, his arms extended and waving. "Okay, folks, we need you to back waaay up. We need you to move to the far end of the street." He motioned as if shooting little basketballs with both hands. "If there's gas, it could blow up."

"What's going on?" the crowd murmured as one.

"It's a large sinkhole, and it may grow more. We need you to be as far back as possible, and we're going to move down that way ourselves until the crew gets here. If you have a gas line in your home, do not return there at this time. Wait for my all-clear."

"What caused it?" someone shouted. "Did something explode in the house?"

"C'mon, let's move down the street and we'll all find out soon enough."

"Why can't we go in our houses?" a woman asked.

The officer, a twenty-nine-year veteran of the Marshfield Police, with the beer gut to prove it, was nervous. Trying to be patient and calm, he said, "I don't think that's a good idea until we know what we're dealing with here."

A couple looked anxious. "Should we get our kids up and bring them out of the house?"

"Yeah," he said, contradicting himself, "if you have anyone in your house, go get 'em outta there."

The couple ran to their house two doors down. They disappeared inside. In about thirty seconds, they reappeared, each holding—almost carrying—a sleepy child. Other couples did the same. As people emerged from their houses with pets, children, and, in the arms of one man, a hard-sided suitcase he struggled to carry, the officer shooed them down the street. A few people got in their cars and drove out of the development in the opposite direction from Jerome's smoldering lot.

Jerome thought at first he should stay near his house, but he decided to join the growing mob at the end of the street, afraid to anger the police and firefighters working on his house. Soon, he realized he was at the center of the mob as people pressed him for answers.

"I don't know! I don't know what happened!" Jerome was growing exasperated. "I didn't do anything. I don't even smoke. No, the stove wasn't left on. I was the only one home. I stepped outside about a minute before it exploded."

"It exploded?" someone shouted. "That's not what the cop said."

"I guess 'exploded' is the wrong word, but I honestly don't know. Imploded. Collapsed. Disappeared. What do you want me to say? I didn't do anything." His voice was becoming more and more frustrated. Then, he remembered that he'd been about to call Lacy at the synagogue.

"Does anyone have a cell phone I could use?" Jerome asked the crowd.

Borgin handed his to Jerome, who searched for the number for Temple Beit Or. He dialed it, but no one answered. He walked back towards the police officer, who was less than halfway to Jerome's house. "Officer, I can't reach my wife. She's in the synagogue over on Enterprise Road, and there's no answer."

"I'll send a car around to get her. What's her name?"

"Lacy Light. What about my son and daughter?"

"Where are they, Mr. Light?"

"Um, my son is out driving around. It's a dark blue Camry. Oh, heck, what's the license plate?"

"Is it registered in your name, Mr. Light?" Jerome nodded. "I can find out and put out an APB for you. We'll find him." He reached for the walkie-talkie on his shoulder.

"Oh, wait, he said he was going to the cineplex. And my daughter is Miriam Light. She's at a friend's house. I don't know the girl's parents' names. Her name is Jessica Polsky. They're both in high school."

"Okay, Mr. Light, sir. Don't worry. We'll get your family and bring them here. Please go on back over with the others, all right?" The officer nodded his head in that direction.

"Yeah. Yeah, I'll do that." Jerome retreated.

As he started to walk down the street to join Borgin and Mike and the other neighbors, a strange orange truck pulled into view, emergency lights flashing on its roof. It pulled up beside the fire engines, and six … forms jumped out. It was impossible to know if they were men or women. They all walked the same slightly stiff-legged way, and all wore orange helmets, gloves, and jumpsuits. No skin was exposed anywhere. The policeman who had talked with Jerome quickly got off his radio and went about halfway towards the Hazmat crew to let them see he was on alert. He knew they had no interest in talking with him. The fire chief hustled over to meet the newly arrived crew, exchanged a few words, then withdrew. One Hazmat crew member dangled some sort of device into the hole of what had been Jerome's home.

Jerome saw the genuine deep concern on the faces of Borgin and Mike. It was the first time Mike had ever shown the least personal interest in Jerome, and it was rather flattering, even if the circumstances were extraordinary. Finally, Jerome's mind was beginning to click on all cylinders. The initial shock was wearing off, and he was starting the process of dealing with this tragic mystery.

Both neighbors reached out a hand to Jerome, which added pathos to the bleak and freakish scene. Instead of shaking their hands, which seemed instinctively like the wrong thing to do, Jerome grabbed Borgin's hand with his left hand and Mike's with his right.

"Holy crap, what a situation, eh?" Jerome said, shaking his head. "I can't imagine what happened."

Mike was first to jump in. He pulled his hand away from Jerome. "Well, it could be mine subsidence, I suppose. I didn't think this area was ever mined, but who knows? If a gas line or something exploded under your house, we'd smell it, wouldn't we? Or there'd be some flames." Mike folded his arms across his chest and stuffed both hands under his armpits.

Borgin frowned. "I don't think it's a gas line. It wouldn't have been buried far enough underground to blow a hole like that. It would have created a fire. It would still be burning."

More sirens filled the air as the sky grew nearly dark. It struck Jerome that this was news, that whatever it was that happened, his house was going to be on the news, and he might be photographed. He tried to sneak a peek at his reflection in Borgin's eyeglasses, wondering how horrible he'd look if he were videotaped or photographed. He thought, *How should I look? Distressed? Hysterical? Calm? Philosophical? Goofy?*

One of the sirens headed towards Jerome's group. With all the flashing lights now by his former house, and the darkening sky behind, it was impossible to tell what was coming. A police cruiser pulled up beside Jerome, and Lacy jumped out.

Jerome ran to Lacy, and they hugged. They exchanged a brief kiss, as usual, and then looked at each other for a second before Lacy spoke, her voice nearly breaking.

"What happened, Jerome? What happened to our house? Are the kids all right?"

He drew his left palm down across his left eye. "I think so. They were out, and the cops are going to bring them here."

Lacy was nearly hysterical, but trying hard to hold it together. "Why bring them here? Oh, God, Jerome, I don't want them to see me like this!"

Jerome realized Lacy was not thinking clearly, but he could not help saying, "See you like this? Our house is gone and you're worried what you look like?"

"No," Lacy said in exasperation, and pursed her lips in anger. "That's not what I mean. I mean, this …," she spread both arms wide, "is not where we should meet the kids. We've got to go somewhere besides the middle of the street."

"Okay, you're right," said Jerome calmly. "Where can we go? We'd better stay here until the kids arrive, but then maybe the police can take us somewhere. But, geez, Lace, I want to know what the hell is going on. The Hazmat crew is over there looking at the house." Suddenly, it was "the house," and not "our house." And Jerome was calling his wife by her name, which he did only in serious situations. It worried Lacy more.

"What do you mean 'Hazmat crew'?" she asked. Her eyes shifted to the house and back.

"Well, I don't know what they're looking for, but that's the hazardous materials crew, like a SWAT team of firefighters. They need to know what happened. Maybe this whole area is in danger."

"You mean a bomb?"

"No, not a . . . For God's sake, we don't know. They haven't told us anything."

Lacy had an idea. "How come you're outside? I mean, I'm glad you're alive, but how did you escape?"

"I didn't. I saw an unusual sunset, and I went outside to look at it. I went over to the Engelhardts' house and I was talking to Mike when we heard a boom, and the next thing you know, the house just disintegrated!"

"You mean like it exploded?"

"No, like it just—WHOOSH!—fell into the ground. And then it exploded, I guess." He held out both palms face up. "So, Mike and I ran into his house and he called 9-1-1, and now all these emergency people are here, but they haven't told us anything yet."

"Jesus," she whispered.

"Yeah." He paused. "Well, I asked the cop to get you and he sent the car over to the temple. And he's also trying to locate Miriam and Moses."

"Isn't Miriam at Jessica Polsky's house?"

"I assume so, but I didn't know the phone number there or her parents' names."

"Her father's name is David."

"Oh . . . right! Well, I couldn't think of it, but the cop, the officer, said don't worry, he'd find her."

"I need to call my mother. We're going to have to have somewhere to go tonight," Lacy said. "We better go to her place. At least there might be some clothes there I can borrow."

"What do you need to borrow clothes for?" said Jerome, astonished at this idea.

"Well, I can't go to work like this tomorrow," Lacy replied, as if Jerome were an idiot.

"Work? You think you're going to work? We have no house, no … no bed or . . . I don't know what, no anything, and you think you can just go to work?"

"Well, we still have my car," said Lacy, trying to find some shred of normalcy.

"Oh Christ, yeah, we'll have to find a way to get the car. But anyway, I don't see how either of us can go to work tomorrow. We're going to have to find out what we're supposed to do now."

"Supposed to do?" Lacy's voice raised almost an octave. "Is there something people whose houses disappear are supposed to do?"

"C'mon, you know what I mean." The conversation was pointlessly and uncharacteristically antagonistic, and Jerome knew it. So did Lacy, but neither of them felt like being completely rational at the moment. In fact, it seemed like a pretty good time to be at least a little hysterical. "I mean, if we really lost everything in the house, we're gonna have to do a zillion things, starting with the insurance company. Oh, damn, what company do we use?"

Lacy had an amazing array of data stored in her brain. "Glisson. We'll call them first thing in the morning."

A strange woman, or at least an unfamiliar one, came walking towards them, following the outstretched arm of the police officer. She was around six feet tall, wearing a sleek, knee-length burgundy sheath with a cream cardigan that she had pulled back to reveal her slender torso. At the ends of her long, slim legs, she wore burgundy slingbacks with a medium heel. She appeared to be in her early twenties, probably a recent college graduate. Jerome and Lacy noticed simultaneously the video camera on the shoulder of a man behind the young woman.

"Hi, I'm Angie O'Graham, Action 10 News. The officers tell me this was your house?"

Jerome said, "Do you know what happened?" She was a reporter; maybe she had news.

Angie smiled. "I was going to ask you that question."

Chapter 3

Car Strain

Angie O'Graham was excited to be the first reporter on the scene. The producer would love to get an exclusive. "What are your names?"

"I'm Jerome Light and this is my wife, Lacy."

"What happened here tonight, Mr. and Mrs. Light?"

Lacy looked at Angie, ignoring the camera. "I don't know. I just got home and found out our house is gone." Angie then looked at Jerome. The cameraman panned to Jerome and zoomed in, losing Angie from the shot.

"I was outside our house, I don't know, I guess about 45 minutes ago now, and the sky was kind of a weird yellow color, and then I was talking to my friend Mike." Mike stepped into the shot behind Jerome and raised his left hand as if attendance were being taken. "And we heard a BOOM and then I turned to look at my house and watched it sink into the ground."

Already, in these early stages of the catastrophe that he knew would change his life forever, Jerome was starting to get a certain efficient patter down to explain what happened. Practice was, indeed, making perfect, he thought.

"Why did you turn to look at your house?" asked Angie, in her best Action News manner. "Did you expect something like this?"

"I had no idea. I could hear sounds coming from my house. We thought maybe it was an animal or something."

Angie said, "What kind of animal could make that much noise?"

"Well, I wasn't really thinking about it. I heard a loud noise, like a hiss, and I turned."

"Was there anyone in the house when it sank, Mr. Light?"

"No, I had stepped outside about a minute before. I hate to think what would have happened if I were still in the house." A dog started barking non-stop down the street.

Angie's investigative juices started flowing as her Kent State training kicked in. "Were you doing anything in the house that might have caused an explosion?"

"No! There was no explosion. I was watching TV is all. And then I walked outside."

"So, no one was hurt in the house, as far as you know? Any pets?"

Lacy answered, "No, we don't have any pets. Did you get a good look at the house? We haven't been able to see it since the firefighters arrived."

"There's not much to see, Mrs. Light. The fire department is setting up flood lights now so they can inspect the sinkhole."

Jerome became aware of more emergency vehicles arriving. He guessed that there were more TV news crews, too, because the number of lights going on was incredible. This was obviously the biggest thing to hit his suburban town in a long time, maybe ever.

A phalanx of police officers moved towards the neighbors and Angie O'Graham and her cameraman. One of the officers, a burly, broad-jawed fellow of forty, spoke for the rest of them: "Okay, folks, the immediate danger has passed. We need you all to go to your own homes right now so we can bring in some equipment and take care of things here. Please go home now." He repeated these instructions several times as he moved through the crowd of neighbors and the few gawkers who had begun to arrive.

People began to scatter in all directions. A few called words of encouragement to Jerome and Lacy as they left. A few others lingered for a few extra glances at the attractive Ms. O'Graham. Jerome and Lacy realized that they could not obey the officer's order.

Miriam came walking up to her parents, materializing through the corona of the light atop Angie's camera. She was crying. She ran and threw her arms around her mother, burying her head against Lacy's chest. The camera caught it all, a perfect shot for the 11-o'clock news (*Action 10 at 11*). Miriam was oblivious to the camera and lights and Angie. She couldn't stop sobbing, and no words were exchanged. Moses came striding through, paused a moment in mid-stride as he saw his parents and sister bathed in the eerie light of the camera, a tableau of sadness and loss, then continued forward.

"Dad, what the fuck happened?"

"Hey, watch your mouth, Moses. That's the TV news there behind you. We don't know what happened. Our house is gone. Angie O'Graham says it's something called 'karst terrain'."

Instead of asking about karst, Moses spun to look at Angie, a striking figure nearly his height. "*Cool!*" he thought. Then he brought his attention sharply back to his parents and his distraught sister. "No sh . . . no fooling? Wow! Car strain! Our car did this?"

In other circumstances, Jerome might have laughed as he said, "You have no idea what karst terrain is, do you?" It did not strike him funny at that moment.

Moses looked down. "No, sir."

Other news crews were discovering the Light family gathered in the street, 300 or so feet from the now-famous site, and were coming over to rob Action 10 News of their exclusive coverage. More lights shone in the faces of the four victims, and microphones were jabbed in their general direction. The same questions were repeated again and again, the same answers coming from Jerome and Lacy, Miriam sobbing throughout, and Moses checking out the cameras and the reporters.

Finally, the fire chief, a fiftyish man with a wide, craggy face and a weary expression, appeared alongside a woman, a member of the Hazmat crew, but now with her helmet removed, her hair slightly matted from the heat and sweat it had evoked. "Mr. and Mrs. Light?" she said, "I'm Valerie LePine with the EPA. We need to talk. Is there somewhere we can go?"

Jerome was stunned by the absurdity of the question. "Um, well, I'd invite you into my house, but, well, you know. I can ask my neighbor to let us use his house."

"Good. We'll follow you."

Jerome brushed past the TV news crews and made his way back up the street. Lacy, with Miriam still attached to her, and Moses, trying his best to look cool and with it, followed. As they passed their house lot, they could not help but get their first good look. Bright lights were being aimed everywhere on the property. It looked like Dresden after the bombing in World War II. The lights were so bright, they sucked all the color out of the scene and gave it a peculiar, archival appearance. The homeless family paused a second, gazing wistfully at the scene, trying to take it all in. Then Jerome pushed his legs to keep going, to lead him to Mike's door. *I wonder why I chose Engelhardt's place,* he thought to himself. *We were standing closer to the Mindlings' house, but I guess this is where I wanted to go.* He did not need to knock. Like virtually all the neighbors, Mike and his wife, Sandi, had been watching out the window, unable to tear themselves away from this drama, this excitement in their own front yard. Sandi had begun packing a bag with vital documents and valuables, fearful the hole would grow.

"Come on in, Jerome, Lacy. Come on in, kids," Mike waved them forward.

Jerome motioned Lacy and Moses and Miriam past him, then said, "Mike, this is Valerie LePine from the EPA and Fire Chief, uh …"

"Stephen King," said the Chief. "Yeah, I know. Don't say it."

"Uh, right, this is our neighbor and friend, Mike Engelhardt."

"Pleased to meet you, Mr. Engelhardt," said both officials, not quite in unison.

They all walked into the Engelhardts' front parlor. "Mr. and Mrs. Engelhardt, you're welcome to stay, but please save your questions for the end," said LePine. Now in the living room light, Jerome could see she was a short woman, probably in her late forties. She had short brown hair with a streak of silver over her left ear. Her baggy Hazmat suit disguised her body. "We need to talk first with Mr. and Mrs. Light."

Jerome and Lacy looked awkward. This is not how they envisioned their night would be, sitting in someone else's living room while government officials explained to them why their house no longer existed. Jerome—wanting to make it appear as though he handled disasters like this all the time, despite the fact that his job as a dictionary editor rarely involved anything more disastrous than a dangling participle—decided it was best to sit. He backed towards a sofa, never taking his eyes off the others in the room. Lacy sat next to him, and Moses and Miriam slid in beside them. There was no room on the seat, so Moses leaned on the arm; Miriam sat at her mother's feet and rested her elbows and head on Lacy's knees as Ms. LePine began her briefing.

"The good news is your house is not radioactive. There's no further danger at the site. The crew will be able to remove debris for examination . . . and you should be able to return to the property to see what they are finding. Now, the bad news is that no one will be able to rebuild on the property, and you'll have to negotiate with the town what the property is worth, because you won't be able to sell it for a long time. That's not good news for your neighbors, who are likely to find their property values decrease and their insurance rates increase. However, I should warn you that the authorities are going to need time going over your property before they'll release it to you."

The family looked at her in stunned silence. The agent shifted on her feet, trying to find a comfortable stance. She had hoped by starting with some ray of positive news, the rest would get easier. It didn't.

"Okay, so there's more. Your house is demolished, and I'm sure you want to know why. We know for sure it was not a bomb or an explosion or an earthquake. We're about 98-percent sure the sinkhole was caused by karst terrain, meaning that the basalt bedrock beneath your house dissolved and could no longer support the ground above it, much less the weight of your house."

Jerome shifted nervously and asked, "So, what happens now, tonight?"

LePine said, "Civil engineers and a geologist from the State will be here in the morning to examine the site and give a complete assessment. Remember, we're very early in our investigation here. We know so little and need to know so much. Your local police will be stationed here all night tonight to make sure no one comes near the sinkhole."

"What are we supposed to do, me and my family?"

Mike called from the back of the room, "And what about us? Are we supposed to wait for our houses to collapse? How are we supposed to sleep tonight?"

LePine tried to maintain her composure as she answered Mike first. "If you would feel better going somewhere else tonight, then you should go."

"Go where?" Engelhardt scoffed.

"A hotel, a family member, a friend in a nearby town," LePine said.

"And we have to pay for that ourselves?"

"I'm afraid so," she said. "But you don't have to go. Your house is in no immediate danger. Initial examinations of the sinkhole indicate it's now stabilized. We've seen no signs of any imminent erosion. A team will be here tomorrow to check the stability of the bedrock under the rest of the development. The hole now is only about fifty feet long and maybe thirty feet wide. Your house is at least two hundred feet from the edge. We will know more in the morning. So to be clear . . . there is no evacuation order for the neighborhood."

Then she turned to face the Lights. "I'm afraid you are also on your own tonight, but if you're stuck, we can ask for help from the Red Cross."

"What about FEMA?" Jerome asked, hoping to avoid charity.

She shook her head. "It's not a federal emergency, so they can't help. You probably mean the Ohio EMA, but at this point, it's considered a small, localized emergency."

Mike asked, "So, who's in charge here? You?"

LePine said, "For tonight, anyway, I guess it's me. I'm the top state official here, but you should probably get most of your information from Chief King. This is a local matter for now."

"What's going to happen to us?" Lacy asked.

"Well, you're going to have to find a new home, probably for quite a while. All the debris from your house will be examined, piece by piece. Any of your personal items that are still intact will be returned to you, but from what I've seen, don't expect a lot to be recovered. Fortunately, school is about over for this year, right?" LePine looked positively at Moses and Miriam, thinking they would find some sliver of good news in this fact, but they barely reacted.

Chief King chimed in, "Do you have a place you can go tonight? We've already alerted the Red Cross, and they can put you up somewhere for now if you need that."

"I can call my parents. We'll go over there, I think," said Lacy.

"Fine," said LePine. "Go call them now. Do any of you have questions for me?"

Sandi led Lacy to the phone in the kitchen while Jerome talked to the two officials. "Who do we coordinate with for now? I mean, tomorrow when I get up, who can tell me what's going on? Who can help me recover our stuff? Who's going to pay for this? Didn't you people have any idea this could happen? Is someone at fault here for failing to notify us? Is there anything anyone could have done?"

"I understand you have a lot of questions now, Mr. Light, and we really want to help you. But we can't answer most of those questions yet," the fire chief said.

LePine jumped in, "You're actually pretty lucky that no one was in the house."

The chief said, "If you had been home, you might have been killed. Certainly, you would not be sitting here now."

Lacy returned. "Okay, I reached Mom and Dad, and they're waiting for us. Can we go now?"

Chapter 4

The Night the Lights Went Out

When the Lights got to George and Darcy Day's house—the house where Lacy had grown up—Lacy went immediately to her mother, but it was not clear who was comforting whom. Darcy was upset. They had been about to go to bed when Lacy called. Now, Darcy doubted she'd be able to sleep at all.

While Jerome stayed downstairs with George, Lacy led Moses, Miriam, and Darcy upstairs to get the beds ready. Jerome and Lacy would stay in the guest room with the double bed. They had never slept there before, had never gone to bed together in the same place as Jerome's in-laws, because their homes were so close together. Miriam and Moses would have to share a room for tonight. At least there were twin beds in Lacy's old room she had once shared with her sister Linda. Tomorrow, they could work out the future arrangements. Moses, who normally would have objected to any such intimacy with his sister, knew that tonight was no time for petulance. Besides, he was pretty much in shock himself.

George, a pleasant, barrel-chested seventy-four-year-old with thinning white hair and the complexion of an overripe peach, sat in his maroon bathrobe. He was full of questions about the evening's events, and Jerome patiently went back over everything, knowing already that he'd be telling this story often for years to come.

"You know, I should have realized something was going on when I saw the sky earlier. It was a weird yellow color, almost like the glow of a fire. I don't believe in omens, but. . . ."

"There was nothing about it on the news, though," said George.

"Oh, the news!" Jerome said, almost jumping up. "Can we turn on Channel 10 and watch the local news? Let's see what they have to say now."

George grabbed the remote and tuned to Channel 10. It was not quite eleven, and the story of the Lights' house and the sinkhole did not warrant breaking into prime-time programming. Lacy and the kids came back downstairs; Jerome suggested they all watch the news together.

Moses said, "I'm going to call Marty and Joe and tell them to watch." He ran to call his friends who, it turned out, had just returned from their evening out, the evening that had been interrupted when the cops found Moses's car and scared the bejeebers out of him by asking to "see" him. When he went running off behind them, back to the house, he barely had time to say, "Problems at home; gotta go, guys," before he disappeared.

The sinkhole was the top story, and it was starting when Moses returned to the family room. Moses was glad to see that if they had to lose their house, at least it was spectacular! He was looking forward to school the next day. Miriam started crying again.

The anchor gave the headline, "A massive sinkhole swallows a local house, leaving a family of four homeless, and scaring a Marshfield neighborhood. Here's Angie O'Graham live from the scene."

And suddenly, there was Angie, the rubble of the Light house behind her. The glow of the spotlights made the video appear as if smoke or dust were rising from the rubble, which was a great special effect that Angie would have loved if she could see it. The lights also gave a glow to Angie's hair. (That she had anticipated.) Moses thought she looked wonderful.

"I'm standing here on Tadpole Lane in Marshfield. Behind me is the lot where what used to be the house of Jerome and Lacy Light and their two children stood." The words

"Angie O'Graham

Live from Marshfield"

appeared across the bottom of the screen, blocking Angie's breasts. Then the scene changed, and there was a shot of the four of them hugging. It gave the impression they were still at the scene. It cut back to Angie to reinforce the illusion. "As you can see, Hazmat crews are still poring over the remains of the house, which, authorities say, disappeared at 8:48 this evening." The cameraman zoomed in past Angie's shoulder and adjusted the aperture so the hole would look more massive. Sure enough, as if on cue, a Hazmat worker walked through the scene.

Angie continued her voiceover, "The house, a two-story colonial, was demolished instantly. The first emergency crews on the scene were initially shocked at what they saw and unsure what caused it. They evacuated nearby houses . . ." (*No, they didn't,* thought Jerome, but kept quiet.) ". . . until Hazmat crews could arrive." The scene cut briefly to an earlier shot of the neighbors pacing the far end of the street, and then to a shot following one of the Hazmat trucks as it pulled into Tadpole Lane and up to the former house.

"I spoke with the EPA's Valerie LePine, who was the first government official to inspect the site." Cut to videotape of LePine with her name and title superimposed. "Can you tell us what happened here? Was it an explosion of some kind?"

LePine calmly, almost serenely, explained the devastation. "There was no explosion. The house essentially collapsed on itself. The 'boom' that some people heard was the underground shelf of rock collapsing into an opening."

The image cut again to Angie O'Graham. "The sinkhole destroyed the home of a local family, while miraculously not even breaking a window in nearby houses. Still, the residents of this middle-class suburban neighborhood were on edge."

Borgin Mindling's face filled the screen. "We heard two loud bangs, one after the other. My wife, Dawn, told me not to go outside. She thought it might be terrorists."

It was the first light-hearted moment for the Light family all night. They hooted a little, and clapped at the absurdity of the comment, and it helped relieve some of the tension.

"Jerome Light, an editor at Wexford Press, was fortunate to be alive after the catastrophe," Angie stated soberly. Then, there was Jerome, big as life.

"I was outside our house . . ." The scene suddenly cut to a shot moving around the debris field that was the house. ". . . and we heard a BOOM and then I turned to look at my house and watched it sink into the ground."

"Awright, Dad!" said Moses, helping further break the mood. It was beginning to seem surreal.

Angie continued, "Local and federal authorities will investigate through the night and for the next several days. Meanwhile, shaken residents of this normally quiet community have returned to their homes, all except the Light family, who are said to be staying with relatives. Reporting live for Action 10 News, I'm Angie O'Graham."

"Thanks, Angie," the anchor said. "And back here in the Action 10 News studio, we have Dr. Akaash Sapna, a geologist at Purloyne University. Dr. Sapna, can you tell us . . ."

Jerome switched off the TV. "That's enough. I don't think I can take any more of this tonight. I'm going to bed. We have a million phone calls to make in the morning."

The phone rang. Darcy answered it. "Yes, they're here," she said into the receiver. "Just a minute." She turned to the family. "Jerome, it's someone from your office."

Jerome took the receiver as if it were infected. "Hello, this is Jerome... Oh, hi, Charlie. How did you find me here?... Yeah, I'm sure lots of people are looking for us now. We can't call people now. For one thing, we're exhausted, and for another thing, we lost our address book in the house . . . Yeah. Unbelievable, isn't it? . . . Would you mind calling people and telling them I won't be in in the morning? . . . Right.. . . Right. . . No, we're all fine. Everyone was out of the house. . . I have no idea.... Well, I'll call you sometime tomorrow and let you know. . . Thanks for calling, Charlie. Bye."

He hung up and told Lacy, "That was Charlie Mackles from the office. He saw us on the news, and he's been calling around trying to find us. Fortunately, he remembered your Dad's name and tried us here. Gee, I'll bet lots of people are looking for us, but I can't start calling now. Ohmigod, what about my Mom? We better call her!"

Jerome grabbed the phone and dialed as if he had to decommission a bomb. "Mom! Oh golly, I'm sorry to call you so late. . . So, you were in bed before the news came on, right? . . . Well, we're all safe here, but we have had a problem. . . Umm, well, while we were all out of the house, a, uh, a sinkhole destroyed our house! A sinkhole. . . A giant hole in the ground, Mom! Our house is gone, and everything in it, but we're okay. We're at George and Darcy's place. . . Well, we're going to stay here for a while, until we can figure out what to do. We have to find a new place to live, and we have to get all new furniture and stuff. . . . Yeah, I said we're all okay . . . e-even the kids.. . . Yeah, I know that's good news . . . Thanks, Mom. We'll call you tomorrow after we know more. . . . I love you, too. Bye."

Chapter 5

Meanwhile, Back at the Ranch House

Moses said he was going to stay up and watch some TV. He didn't think he could sleep. Miriam and then Lacy weighed in with the same feeling. Jerome, however, was proud of his ability to sleep through anything, or almost anything. *This,* he thought *will be the true test of how much shit I can take and still go right to sleep.*

"Well, I'm gonna turn in," he announced, and made good on his promise.

For a second, Lacy watched him leave the room, then turned her head, but not her body, towards the kids, and said, "There's no way he's going to sleep through this!" She was wrong.

About 2:00 in the morning, shortly after Lacy and Miriam had given in and gone to bed, Moses was turning off the TV when someone knocked at the door. Moses doubted his ears the first time, but the second knock was a little louder, enough to propel him out of his stupor and towards the front door in his bare feet.

"Are Mr. and Mrs. Jerome S. Light at this address tonight?" the strange man outside asked through a small glass pane to the side of the front door as Moses approached.

"Huh? Oh, yeah, I mean, who are you?" Moses realized he had probably never sounded as dopey.

The stranger seemed to relax ever so slightly. "I'm Magnus Schopenhauer, with Glisson Insurance. Are you their son?"

"Yeah, Jerome's my Dad."

Schopenhauer, a bespectacled skinny man of average height with hunched shoulders and a balding head featuring a few strands of black hair, straightened up and asked, "Could you let me in, please, so I can talk with your folks?"

"Um, I don't think that's a good idea until I get my Dad up, okay? It's not raining, is it? Because I need you to wait there for a minute."

"Okay," Schopenhauer sighed.

Moses ran upstairs to the room where his parents were asleep. "Dad?" he whispered loudly. "Dad?"

Finally an angry "What?" came from the bed. It was not Lacy.

"There's a man outside to see you. He says his name is Mingus Chippendale or something. He's from the insurance company."

Jerome was up like a shot, grabbing his pants and slipping them on as though he had practiced this move a hundred times before. "Where is he, Mo?"

"He's still outside the front door. I didn't want to let him in until you said it was okay."

"Good. That was good thinking. But I think it's okay," said Jerome, as he launched himself off the stairs and towards the front door. "Hello!" he called to the figure standing outside the glass pane. "Can I see your ID, please?"

"Sure, I have it out already. Figured you'd want to see it." Schopenhauer held his driver's license and his Insurance Adjuster card up to the pane. Jerome leaned forward to study the offered evidence, then unlocked the door and nodded him in.

"Mr. Jerome S. Light?" asked Magnus.

"Yes. That's me. I can guess what brings you out here tonight. I wanted to be sure you weren't a news reporter trying to get a scoop."

"Oh, sure, I understand, Mr. Light. No, I've been trying to track you folks down, kinda like a reporter, though. Anyway, Mr. Glisson saw the story on the 11 o'clock news, and recognized your name as one of our accounts, and he called me up right away. And I said, 'Wow, those folks are sure gonna need my help.' But by the time I got over to the office and got your file, and then ran to Tadpole Lane, why, you were already gone, and your mobile phone wasn't answering." Magnus was far too chipper and alive for 2:15 in the morning. "And one of your neighbors was up; I saw the light on. So, I asked if they knew where you'd gone, and they said,

'No,' but they thought the fire chief knew. It took me a little while to find out where the chief was, and then convince him that I'm on the level." Jerome began to get antsy at this overly detailed recounting, but the man never paused a moment as he continued. "And he finally told me that you came here, but I thought I'd come over instead of calling and scaring you and waking up the whole house."

"Well, that was very thoughtful of you, Mr. . . ."

"Schopenhauer. My first name's Magnus." He fairly beamed.

"Magnus, thank you for coming out here. I was planning to call your office first thing in the morning, but this is incredible, you looking for us like this." Jerome was trying to return some of the man's enthusiasm. Then he swayed to his right, and turned slightly away from the annoying man. "I mean, I'm not thrilled you woke me up and all, but I'm impressed with your, uh . . . dedication." Jerome was sincere in his praise, and Magnus glowed with pride.

"Thank you, Mr. Light. We really do try to be like those insurance agents you see on TV, you know, right there in a disaster, when you need us. I know it's kinda corny, but that's what we do. Well, at least, it's what I do."

"Great," said Jerome. "What do you need to know? How fast can we get a check to, you know, get a new place to live?"

"Well, I need to know a few things. I mean, actually, there's a whole lot I need to know, but we don't need to get all of it tonight. Later, I'll have to know everything that was in the house, room by room, and also what you may have taken with you before the house collapsed."

Jerome tossed his head back slightly, and grunted, "Hunh. What we took? We didn't take anything. We didn't know the house was going to collapse!"

"Yes, I know, Mr. Light, but that's not the point. I mean, did you take the cars, or were they crushed, too? What about anything that might have been in the cars, like an appliance on its way to be repaired, that kind of thing."

"Both our cars were out. They're fine."

"That's good, Mr. Light. I'm glad. I think they'd be covered if they'd been damaged."

"Wait a minute," said Jerome. "Of course they'd be covered. I mean, if they'd been in the garage, then they'd have been destroyed, too. And … I guess if the cars were in the garage, then that means Lacy and Moses would have been home, too. Oh, man." Jerome's eyes fell to the floor and his attention drifted off briefly.

"But you're all safe and sound, Mr. Light. I was really pleased to hear that from Mr. Glisson. It's a miracle or something that none of you were in the house when it collapsed."

"You know why it collapsed, don't you?" asked Jerome.

"Wasn't it a gas explosion?"

"Oh, gosh, no. It was a sinkhole. It opened up right under the house." Jerome was proud that the real story was more interesting than another gas explosion.

"Oh, Mr. Glisson failed to tell me that part. Well, that sure changes things." He pushed his plastic glasses back up his nose.

"What?" said Jerome, more alert than he had been in hours. "What are you saying?"

Magnus Schopenhauer swallowed hard. He realized he should not have said anything yet, but he'd been surprised by Jerome's revelation.

"Well, Mr. Light, I'm saying I don't know if your house will be covered for loss by a sinkhole. I've never run into this situation before."

Jerome saw the humor in that remark. "I'd certainly hope not," he scoffed.

Magnus squirmed. "I'm only the adjuster, Mr. Light. I don't make the decisions about claims. In fact, I should probably be going so we can both get some sleep. Then I can see you in the morning. I just wanted to be sure you and your family are okay tonight." He turned away.

"Great. Well, we are, as you can see," Jerome said, almost annoyed at having to make polite conversation after Schopenhauer's bombshell. "Did you say that you checked our file tonight?"

He turned back to face Jerome. "Uh huh. I mean, yes."

"Do you have it with you? Because our copy was probably destroyed with everything else."

"No, I left it back in the office. I copied down basic things, like your address. You'd have to stop by the office if you want to get another copy and discuss it with Mr. Glisson."

"What time should I be at your office? There's no point going by the house, I guess." Jerome felt beaten down for the first time.

"Actually, I want to meet you at your house, I mean, your property at nine a.m. Will that be all right?" At least Schopenhauer was trying to be nice. "Since it's so late, I think you should try to get some rest. I'll see you at nine."

Jerome, beginning to feel the weight of his problem, looked directly at the insurance adjuster. In his most businesslike tone, he said, "Yes, Mr. Schopenhauer, that'll be all right. Thank you for coming. Good night."

Magnus was sharp enough to know he should say no more to Light tonight. Many times before, he had seen the stages of reaction that the Insured goes through when suffering a great loss. He knew exactly what stage Jerome was at now, and that it was time for Magnus to back off. He was pretty sure that Jerome would not sleep much more tonight.

Jerome stared at the back of the door that closed behind the adjuster. Moses, who had kept quiet through the entire exchange, could feel his Dad's withering spirit. He watched until Jerome turned around, sadness in his eyes.

"Damn it, Mo. I know I'm supposed to have all the answers so you and Miriam never have to worry, but right now, I don't have 'em. I don't think there's much left of our house, so that means new clothing for everyone, a new computer, new furniture, a new address, maybe a new school for you and your sister. And all those memories … gone. The photos you and I took on the trip to Oregon, and all your baby pictures and Miriam's, and maybe Great Grandma's jewelry that Mom was saving for Miriam, and our passports, and … Oh my gosh, just everything, Mo!"

Jerome's voice cracked slightly. It was enough to put fear into Moses; he didn't know what to say, so he said nothing as Jerome crossed the room and went back upstairs to bed. Neither of them slept more than a few minutes that night.

Jerome had a peculiar ethos: He wanted never to appear weak in those areas where he could possibly have some hope of being courageous or strong. In grade school, he was puny and non-athletic, and that was, in those days of childhood, the primary measure of a boy. As he grew, he realized there were a thousand daily victories that require different kinds of strength, the victories that come from defying the expected. When people thought Jerome would be unable to do something, that was when he most wanted to persevere. Whenever he overcame the predicted result, it wasn't for the reason everyone thought; it was because that little boy inside him refused to lct the bullies win again. He could be undaunted. He could quit smoking cold turkey. He could marry the pretty girl. He could remain calm in the midst of disaster. He could beat any odds when he set his mind to it.

Chapter 6

Do You Believe in God?

By 6 a.m., the light coming through the bedroom window was bright enough to make further attempts at sleep impossible. Lacy was already awake, but she was lying in bed, trying to comprehend what was about to happen, what kind of day it would be. Jerome looked at her, and their eyes met without speaking. Jerome swung his legs out of bed and, with his back to Lacy, said, "The insurance adjuster came here last night at 2 a.m. He says we may not be covered."

"What!" cried Lacy, sitting up. "Not covered? What do you mean, not covered?"

"It was a sinkhole, Lacc. No one directed it at our house. No one could have stopped it. The adjuster said there's a chance it's not covered. Just a chance, Lacy. So, let's not get upset until we know." He climbed into the same pants he had taken off three hours earlier, the only pants he owned now.

"I don't understand. We've never made a claim. We always pay on time. Now our . . . house and our things are gone, and I don't see how they can say we're not covered!" Lacy was not taking it well.

Jerome switched tactics. "I'm going over to the house at nine to meet Mr. Schopenhauer."

"Mr. Who?"

"Schopenhauer, the adjuster. He was very nice last night. We're going to see what's salvageable. Then we're going to the office to meet with Mr.

Glisson himself."

"I'll go with you." She sprang out of bed, picked up her blouse, and sniffed the armpits. "Maybe the kids will, too; they can help us look for things. Oh no, wait; it's a school day."

Lacy threw on her mother's extra bathrobe and went to the bathroom. Jerome put on his shirt and socks and went downstairs. Darcy Day was already there, fussing nervously with dishes and silverware. "Oh, good morning, Jerome. I guess you all need a good breakfast before you go off. We didn't expect company, so we don't have much in the house, but I think we have enough milk, and I can make oatmeal for everyone."

Darcy, at seventy-two, had taken excellent care of herself. She no longer dyed her hair blond, but the pure white she now sported looked similar. She went to yoga three times a week, and liked to power-walk around the manmade lake in Marshfield Park to help keep her trim figure. She was naturally dark complected, thanks to some Sephardic Jews among her ancestors.

"Hi, Mom," Jerome said. "Oatmeal sounds fine. It looks like we're going to leave here about 8:30 and go over to the house to see if they recovered anything. Then we're going to see about the insurance, and then, I guess, we'll try to figure out where we're going to live."

"You'll stay here with us, won't you? At least for now?"

Jerome puffed his cheeks and blew all the air out quickly. "I suppose, but I haven't even thought about that yet, to be honest."

Darcy lifted her head from the oatmeal preparation and looked at Jerome briefly, then went over and hugged him as tears welled up in her eyes.

"It's okay, Mom, really. We'll figure it out. I can't decide anything right now, not until we've seen the house and found out about the insurance. I know we've got to get back to normal as quickly as we can. I've got to get back to work and so does Lacy. And the kids, well, I don't know. At least they're done with school in a week."

The bright cloudless sky and 60-degree air made an excellent counterpoint to the sober, tired mood of the family. Early June days were never more vibrant and invigorating.

Moses drove Miriam to school with plans to pick her up at the end of the day and return to the Days' house. Miriam said out loud what Moses was thinking: they were both going to be the center of attention at school because something "cool" had happened to them.

Jerome and Lacy, unable to sit around the house a minute longer and make small talk once breakfast was over, took her car and drove to Tadpole Lane. They had given no thought to the scene that awaited them at 7:40 in the morning.

As they pulled into what had been their street, they saw trucks from the gas company, the electric company, the police department, the telephone company, the cable company, the sewer company, the water company, and the ASPCA. And there were three trucks from the different local news programs.

Lacy exclaimed, "Honey, look!" Her jaw dropped as she realized that the loss of their home was being turned into an enormous event.

"I see it! Holy crap!"

Many of the neighbors were standing around, too, watching this amazing sight that they all hoped they'd never see again. There was Borgin Mindling talking with Sandi Engelhardt, standing a respectful distance from the Lights' lot. Jerome realized they could advance no farther down the street, so he pulled over and parked behind the small cable company van. The air smelled like burnt hair, acrid and musty.

It took thirty seconds for the news reporters to realize who had arrived, but as soon as one of them recognized the Lights, they swarmed forward like gnats, half of them holding microphones and half of them holding cameras. It was as frightening to Jerome and Lacy as if they were under attack.

Angie O'Graham stood towards the rear of the swarm. Clearly, she had not been fast enough today, as she was last night. She looked upset, and Jerome decided to help her out, though he later insisted to Lacy that her sexy appearance played no part in his decision. Even in a group of attractive young reporters, Angie stood out. She had a commanding presence that none of the other cookie-cutter youngsters had.

"Ms. O'Graham," he pointed an outstretched arm over the heads of the nearest microphone jabbers and called to her. "Could you please let Ms. O'Graham through?" Jerome asked a perky young brunette and a spiky-haired young man. They parted a few inches, and Angie slithered through and right up to Jerome, with Lacy by her left shoulder.

"Thank you, Mr. and Mrs. Light," Angie began. "Can you tell us what you hope to find here today? How are you coping with this tragedy?"

Jerome replied first, "Thank you for asking, Angie." He knew he was scoring points with her, points that might help them someday. He wanted to give her career a little boost. "We're coping pretty well, and we're here to see what's left of our belongings. It was impossible for us to tell last night . . ." He motioned towards the sinkhole, swinging his outstretched arm. ". . . and it looks like, with all these professionals at work here, it may be hard to find out today, too."

Lacy, who bit a corner of her lip as Jerome talked, chimed in, forcing Angie to swing her mike almost violently in Lacy's direction. "We're a tough family, with good kids and great parents who will see us through. Thank God, we all survived without a scratch."

She knew right away what was coming next. She thought, *Why did I ever say 'thank God'?*

Indeed, Jerome was already building up a head of steam, and he had to release it. "Well, we don't really believe that God had anything to do with this event, with smashing our house or the fact that none of us were in the house at the time."

The spiky-haired dude thrust his microphone towards Jerome. "What part of that don't you believe, Mr. Light? Do you believe in God, Mr. Light?"

No one could tell that Jerome felt himself getting warmer, starting in his chest and working upwards. "I'm not going to answer that question. It has nothing to do with what happened here."

Another reporter shouted from Jerome's left side, "Did you know they've confirmed that it was a karst failure?"

"No, we didn't know that," said Jerome, realizing he'd never thought of turning on the car radio on the way over this morning. "I'm not surprised." Jerome spoke those words a little louder as a kind of reward to the reporter for giving him that news tidbit.

Angie turned her shoulders and microphone back towards Lacy. "Mrs. Light, how are your two children taking this tragedy?"

Lacy later confessed to Jerome that she liked this "Mrs. Light" business. She had expected she would be Lacy to the reporters, as she was to everyone else, and the deference that "Mrs. Light" conveyed made her feel respected for being a victim. That, she realized, was something she desperately needed right now.

"Moses and Miriam are doing fine. They're great kids, and they are pulling together. They've gone to school today so they can try to finish out the school year. I think they're adapting as well as can be expected." Lacy was trying her best to sound like "Supermom," because she figured this would be her only shot at celebrity. Plus, she wanted to give the kids a pat on the back. They were being pretty flexible, all things considered.

While Jerome and Lacy were peppered with more questions, Borgin and Sandi watched, a bit too far away to hear what was said. Imagine! Their neighbors, on TV! And Borgin had been on Channel 10 last night, too! Sandi was kind of hoping for her chance today. She knew that was shameless of her, but she did not care. If her face showed up on the news, she'd have no trouble convincing people that she was a part of this big story! Already, when she'd phoned a girlfriend in another city, her friend had said, "No! C'mon, really? You live right on that street?"

The "Sinkhole Eats Ohio Home" story had gone national. Thanks to the Engelhardts' security camera footage of the collapse, it was a ratings winner. Americans everywhere wanted to see the poor misfortunates whose house was swallowed by the earth! It was a national glad-it-wasn't-me moment.

Jerome and Lacy pushed their way forward through the swarm of reporters towards the property, but Angie O'Graham called out suddenly, "Lacy, would you be willing to be interviewed live in a few minutes by Colleen Tantuli on the *Today* show?"

Lacy stopped dead in her tracks. "Of course!" she smiled, with no hint of embarrassment whatsoever. She loved Colleen Tantuli. She trusted Colleen Tantuli. She knew Colleen would be sympathetic and would not try to make her say anything stupid or self-incriminating. She knew Colleen would let her praise her family on national TV! What more could a mother ask for? Lacy knew that she and Jerome were hip deep in trouble right now, and she felt like her world had been thrown in a clothes dryer. She figured they might need a lot of good will to get out of it, and the best way to generate a lot of good will was through publicity. Being interviewed by Colleen Tantuli would be great publicity.

Angie again pushed through other reporters to get to Lacy. Jerome looked at her. "What about me? Do they just want Lacy?"

"I think so, Mr. Light. It's mostly a question of timing. We won't have much time because they're squeezing this story in during the second hour. They want to do a split-screen with Colleen, and that doesn't work well with two people." Angie scooped Lacy's arm up and walked her towards the property. "Okay, so we want to get a shot of you with the wreckage in the background. I know that sounds terrible, Mrs. Light. I know that's your house back there and not something … impersonal. I'm so sorry for your loss, and I think you're going to find an outpouring of sympathy to help you and your family, so I think, even though this will be difficult for you emotionally, that we're doing the right thing here."

"Will you be interviewing me, Angie?"

"No, Mrs. Light. We're going to hook a headset on you so you can hear the network feed, and Colleen will ask you the questions. I'm field producer for this shoot, and I'll tell you when we're coming to you. Try to relax and answer Colleen as if it were me asking the questions. I'll be right by the camera. You can look at me and pretend you're answering my questions."

"Okay, great," said Lacy, trying to appear calm and professional, yet enthusiastic … and slightly victimized. She looked down at her clothes and realized they were the same clothes she had worn last night, and they were hardly looking crisp. *At least there's no smudge marks or cinders on them,* she thought, about the same time Angie was thinking, *Gee, it would be perfect if her clothes had some smudge marks or cinders on them.* Fortunately, Angie decided against trying to add some at the last moment. "You look great, Mrs. Light," she called, and Lacy relaxed about her appearance after a hasty smoothing of her front with her palms.

Rick, the cameraman working with Angie, managed to swing around and position Lacy directly between himself and the "wreckage" of the Light house. Angie helped Lacy put on the headset and tuck it almost out of view. She clipped a tiny microphone on Lacy's lapel – remembering that it was the same lapel she'd seen in the dark last night – and stepped away. When she returned, she held up a sheet of white paper in front of Lacy. Rick pushed a few buttons, and then nodded to Angie, who took the paper away and stepped back beside the camera lens. "Should be about five more minutes, Mrs. Light."

Jerome watched his wife with fascination. He had never seen her do anything like this before. He was amazed and impressed by her poise. *Wow, maybe this disaster will do some good,* he thought. *The kids are behaving perfectly, we're on national TV, and Lacy is really holding up well.*

Angie spoke up, "Okay, they're wrapping up local weather and going back to the studio now. You'll be the first story after the weather. Colleen will say something about the sinkhole and Marshfield, and then she'll introduce you. As soon as you hear your name, you'll be on the show, so look at the camera and wait for Colleen's greeting, and say 'Hi' or something in return."

Lacy squared her shoulders to the camera. "No, turn back the way you were a second ago," said the cameraman. "If your right shoulder is slightly back, we can see the empty lot better. But keep your face looking at me."

Lacy put on her best Colleen Tantuli face, she thought, and then realized that Colleen had probably had specialists applying her make-up for thirty minutes, while she, Lacy, had given herself all of two-and-a-half minutes this morning to spruce up. As she realized how she probably looked, and was about to ask for a mirror or at least some lipstick, she heard Colleen Tantuli's unmistakable voice.

"Ohio officials say a rogue sinkhole is the reason a Marshfield, Ohio, home collapsed last night. The suburban home belonged to Lacy Light and her husband, Jerome. Lacy is with us live from the property that used to be her home. Good morning, Lacy, welcome to *Today.*"

Chapter 7

An Act of God

Despite her sadness, Lacy's heart leapt at the sound of Colleen Tantuli saying her name. She heard herself say, "Good morning, Colleen."

Jerome could not hear Colleen's questions or see Colleen's reaction. He watched Lacy with awe. He listened to her answers, and tried to surmise the questions. He didn't have to wait long. Colleen asked a grand total of three questions, gave Lacy a respectful amount of time to respond, and before you could say "mine subsidence," Lacy was saying, "Thank you very much," and the interview was over.

Angie went over and hugged Lacy, and that was the first moment at which Lacy began to cry. Not just cry, but sob hysterically, as Miriam had done at nearly the same spot the previous night. Jerome was frozen, watching the two women, not sure what role he should play.

The swarm of reporters, having been amazingly quiet and respectful during the interview with "Today," began to move on the Lights again, snapping Jerome out of his stupor, and prompting Angie to let go of Lacy and resume her professional demeanor.

Jerome rushed forward and grabbed Lacy's hand. "No more questions for now," he threw back over his shoulder at the cameras and microphones. A camera flash went off precisely as he turned to look at the reporters, momentarily blinding him. He shielded his eyes with his left hand, blinking away the spots he saw. Jerome and Lacy moved up the sidewalk towards the sanctuary of the many workers surrounding the property. Then, for the first time, they got a really good look at what was left of their house, and they both stood, staring, stunned, shaken.

They knew they were on familiar ground, a place where they had stood many times. If they looked left, or right, or behind them, the scene was familiar and serene. When they looked straight ahead, it was chaos.

Lacy put her hand to her mouth, then said, "Who can we see about our stuff?"

Angie O'Graham spoke up. "I can introduce you to the fellow from the state Office of Environmental Affairs. He's pretty much the top official here." She ushered Lacy and Jerome up the sidewalk a short way beyond the property. There, a chisel-faced thirty-five-year-old man in a hard hat and jeans was on his cell phone. As soon as he was done, Angie grabbed his attention.

"I'd like to introduce you to Mr. and Mrs. Light, the people who own this house. Lacy, Jerome, this is Douglas Howard from the OEA."

"Pleased to meet you," they all said, exchanging handshakes.

Jerome didn't hesitate asking for help. "We'd like to see if there's anything we can salvage. We have nothing but the clothes on our backs."

"Of course, Mr. Light," said the official. "Follow me. We've already recovered a few things and set them aside. Everything's pretty dirty, though."

Howard led them around sawhorses festooned with yellow tape that cordoned off the Lights' property. The most surprising thing to Jerome was the noise level. He had, without thinking about it, expected the site to be quiet, much like a cemetery, which was how he was beginning to think of Tadpole Lane. Instead, there was noise and activity everywhere. A few workers paused and watched the victimized homeowners.

Lacy stepped in mud. "Dammit, these are the only shoes I have." She realized she would have to rectify that situation as soon as possible. Jerome, she knew, was focused on recovery of things and preserving their financial integrity, but she was thinking, "What will the kids and we wear tomorrow? Or even tonight? Where will we sleep?"

The first pile they saw as they got close to the sinkhole contained silver objects that came from the dining room. "Hey, look, some of our good silver survived!" said Jerome, smiling triumphantly. He knew that would please her.

Howard said, "Can you take some stuff away in your car right now? We really can't protect it here."

Jerome was distracted. "I see our insurance adjuster pulling up right now. He was planning to meet us here. Um, yeah, we can take some stuff with us now. And for the rest, well, I want to talk to Mr. Schopenhauer."

"Mr. Who?" asked Howard.

"Mr. Schopenhauer, the adjuster with our insurance company. He said we might not be covered."

"I kind of thought that might be the case."

Magnus had his ID out and seemed to show it to everyone he passed on his way from the car to where the Lights and Douglas Howard were standing. He showed it to Mason, and then to Lacy, who was meeting him for the first time.

"Um, Lacy, this is Magnus Schopenhauer from Glisson Insurance."

"Well, actually, I'm from the Big Rock Mountain Mutual Insurance Company. Mr. Glisson is an independent agent, but we work with a lot of his clients," said Magnus. "It's nice to meet you, Mrs. Light. I'm sorry it's under these circumstances."

"Me, too, Mr. Schopenhauer," replied Lacy somberly. "But we're pleased to have you here to help us. My husband said you were extremely kind to come out to my parents' house last night."

"Yeah, well, thank you," bumbled Schopenhauer. "I mean, I'm just doing my job." He was solicitous to a fault. He was trying too hard, too sincerely to be kind, and Lacy found it slightly annoying.

Lacy wanted to continue to flatter him, to win him over, in hopes that he might lean their way if there were a tough call he had to make about paying for something. She smiled, though she did not really feel like smiling. "Mr. Schopenhauer, we appreciate how well you are trying to do it. You are clearly on the side of helping people, of really caring about the people you help."

His body gave a little "Aw shucks" move, but he quickly recovered his professional demeanor.

"I never thought about it before," cooed Lacy, pouring her words like syrup, "but having a caring person to help people through tough times like this is so important. I always thought that insurance adjusters were big, uncaring people trying to save their company as much money as possible. But I guess I was wrong." She thought to herself, *When did I get a Southern accent?*

Jerome gave a sideways glance at his wife, surprised at her brazen manipulation, but not wanting to show it, especially because Magnus seemed to be buying this confection. *Don't overdo it, Lacy,* he thought, but aloud he said, "Okay, let's talk about how we recover our stuff from the house."

Schopenhauer went into Insurance Adjuster Mode. "You should work with a company like Disrex. Helping people like you is exactly what they do, and we know they are reputable. We can call them in to do a salvage assessment."

Jerome felt a spark of hope. He raised his eyebrows and asked Magnus, "But you'll pay for whatever they can't recover?"

"It's not my place to say, Mr. Light," said Schopenhauer, trying to be the diplomat.

"I'm sure that's true, Mr. Schopenhauer. I'm sure that's true. I want to talk with someone who can answer that question, either Mr. Glisson, or whoever can tell me what's going on."

Schopenhauer breathed a small sigh of relief. He always hated the rare occasions when someone found out they were not insured. He didn't know for sure that the Lights were not covered, but he had a strong suspicion.

Douglas led the couple and Schopenhauer to a small pile of recognizable goods. "Here's what we've cleared so far. You can take these pieces with you if you want."

They both put on the work gloves and bent down to pick through the pile. It was all dirty, but not as horrible as it apparently had been; someone had brushed each piece off. Lacy fought back tears as she stroked and examined each familiar piece, mostly the good silver. Occasionally, she came across something no longer whole, like some dinner plates broken in half. "There's no point keeping this broken stuff," she said to Jerome.

"Uh huh," nodded Jerome. He began taking the "good" stuff to a small clearing where they could keep an eye on it. Among the pile they found two books of photographs that had been kept near the silver. Although the covers of the albums were in bad shape, the photographs inside seemed relatively unscathed. Then he said, "Look, it's Moses's new tennis racket!" He held up a hoop that barely resembled the professional model they'd given their talented son on his seventeenth birthday. The strings and the grip were gone, but the graphite frame retained its distinctive blue color, if not its shape.

Jerome was growing impatient with the situation. He put his palms on his hips and took ten steps away from the others before he made a wide turn and paced back to where Lacy watched, tears welling up in her eyes. It felt so far beyond his control. His frustration was evident to Lacy, who took his left arm with both hands and clung to it, hoping to distract him a little.

Douglas said, "You're free to go if you want, because it's gonna go pretty slowly here for a while. We'll take care of everything as if it were our own stuff. Things that don't mean much to us might be really important keepsakes to you, so we'll be very careful with everything."

Lacy said, "Could you take especially good care of our photographs, if you find any?"

"Yes, Ma'am, we will. That's what everyone says, so we're on top of it. We'll save every picture we can. You'll be surprised what we can do."

Magnus took over the conversation. "We can make our way over to the office. My car is the green one over here. Do you want to follow me there?"

As they drove away, the scene Jerome and Lacy left behind looked like something from a movie. Lacy looked back at the uniform-clad ants scurrying around the ant-pile that was their home, trying to picture what her house had looked like twenty-four hours ago. She could not. Tadpole Lane disappeared behind them, as did Lacy's memory of living there.

They followed Magnus to the office of the Glisson Insurance Agency. It was in a small, two-story office building. They walked from the parking lot directly into a small reception area. The young, pretty receptionist knew without asking who they were, and she buzzed Mr. Glisson, who said to send them back to his office, which smelled like air freshener.

As Jerome and Lacy entered, they realized Magnus had not followed them back. Jack Glisson, a short, balding man of fifty with a prominent belly, came around the front of his desk and shook both their hands, offering them the only two chairs in his office other than his own. The chairs had bright red seat cushions that matched nothing else in the room except Glisson's garish tie. "Please accept my condolences, Mr. and Mrs. Light. It's nice to see you again, but not under these circumstances. Have a seat."

"Thank you," they replied together, as Glisson, stone-faced, sat down.

"I've gone over your policy, and I've talked with some underwriters at Big Rock Mountain Mutual, and I'm afraid I don't have good news for you." He pressed his ten fingers together like a spring.

"What are you talking about?" asked Jerome, already feeling sick to his stomach.

"We're not going to be able to cover much of your losses, I'm afraid. Your policy didn't cover sinkholes or other geologic phenomena."

Jerome was starting to get angry, but knew that Glisson was not the one pulling the strings here. Maybe he could be nice to Glisson and get the agent on their side. "Well, I'm sure it didn't specify a sinkhole, but, well, I mean, there must be lots of things not specifically named that are covered."

"You'd think so, Mr. and Mrs. Light, but you'd be surprised. There isn't much not listed that we would cover. For example, under 'Loss by Fire,' we don't specify how the fire has to start to be covered, but we do list a few ways that fire would *not* be covered, such as by arson or reckless negligence on the part of the owners. But pretty much, if something's not explicitly in the policy, you're not covered for it." His expression never changed.

"But how could we foresee a sinkhole, for cryin' out loud!" Jerome tried to modulate his voice. "I mean, no one goes out and buys sinkhole coverage, do they?"

"Actually, Mr. Light, some policyholders do, but they're not usually residential customers. High-tech companies with expensive infrastructure, for example, might insure themselves against it. However, that's not really the point here."

"So, what is the point, Mr. Glisson?" said Lacy, as solemn as Jerome had ever seen her.

"The point is that we consider your sinkhole to be an Act of God, and therefore, not covered."

Chapter 8

Accidents Happen

If the insurance agent had wanted to ignite a rocket under Jerome's chair, he could not have done better than to tell Jerome it was an "Act of God" that destroyed his home.

"That was *no* 'Act of God,' Mr. Glisson. It was an act of the universe, an act of bad luck, an act of nature, but it was no act of God," Jerome burst out, both arms waving pointlessly. He could barely stay in his chair.

"Honey," said Lacy. "Calm down."

Glisson tried to remain the voice of reason. He did not know Jerome was an atheist, but he did know that even believers get upset when told their insurance won't cover their losses. "Mr. Light, it's not important what you call it. It's not covered in your policy."

"Oh, no, I don't think that's true at all," said Jerome, his face slowly turning redder. "It may not be covered, but the reason why not is *damned* important. How can it be an act of something that does not exist?"

Glisson was startled. "What do you mean?"

"I mean God. There is no God. There's no God up there who decided to trash my house! There's no God that dug that sinkhole. It . . . just happened. It was an *accident*, and that's why people have goddamned *insurance* in the first place, because accidents happen. We didn't make this thing happen! Is that what you think? That maybe God decided to show us who's boss?"

"Mr. Light, please, I never said anything like that," said Glisson, becoming agitated, gripping the edge of the desk with both hands. "I don't know what God does or why. Yes, I believe in God, and I know that I can never know why He does what He does."

"So, if you don't know anything, then how do you know God is a HE?" Jerome could feel this discussion spinning out of control. He knew he should shut up, but he couldn't help himself now. He was too far gone along this path. "Why not a SHE? Or an IT?"

† † †

"HE . . ." said the Reverend Gideon Calvin Calhoun to his executive assistant, but only because she was in the room. Gideon would have said it even if he were alone. "HE … is such a powerful force in my life! He lifts me up when I am down." The executive assistant, Celeste, did not think it strange at all that the great Gideon Calhoun would talk this way, would open up to anyone about his faith. Nothing about it or her boss seemed insincere to her. That was why she considered working here her dream job.

Celeste Fallow was not young—forty-two, Gideon thought she had said to another woman in the office—and she was not beautiful. But she was wholesome looking, vibrant, energetic, devoted to Christ, and certainly attractive with full breasts and hips, chestnut hair without a hint of gray, and a round face that seemed to glow when she smiled.

"Celeste," Gideon continued, "the Lord has made this day for US! Look how perfect the weather is, how blue the sky! It would be a sin to keep you in the office on a day like this. What do you say we both take the rest of the day off?"

"Oh, Reverend Calhoun, are you joking?" asked Celeste, a tiny finger-wag in her voice.

"Not at all," boomed Gideon, a bit too boisterously, "but you've already been here nearly two weeks, so please call me Gideon."

Celeste was stunned for a moment, looking at the fifty-five-year-old televangelist with the perfect white hair, the radiant flash of perfect teeth, and the cheekbones of a God.

Gideon filled the void. "Do you know what people used to call me when I was a boy? Deon. Like Deion Sanders, or Dion and the Belmonts."

"And the What?" said Celeste, nearly forgetting her place.

"Dion and the Belmonts . . . sang 'Teenager in Love' way back in the 'fifties. Please tell me you know that song."

Celeste breathed a sigh of relief. "Of course I do," she said. She had been so afraid of appearing stupid or immature in front of this man she had worshipped with for ten years.

"No one has called me that in a very long time. My parents (may they rest in peace) always called me 'Gideon.' They couldn't understand why I thought it was cool when the kids started calling me Deon. My mother thought rock 'n' roll was the Devil's music, and she didn't want me preening like some rock star. She said pride was a sin. I didn't understand that at the time, but she was right, you know."

"About rock 'n' roll?" asked Celeste.

"No, about pride. Rock 'n' roll is merely a sound. It's the lyrics that make it good or bad. It can be the Devil's music or the Lord's. But we're burning daylight here, Celeste. What do you say we close up shop?"

"I won't say 'No' to that, Rever—uh, Gideon. It'll be real nice for me to get home early and call my boy in Colorado when he gets home from school," said Celeste. As she spun around to return to her office, her sleeve knocked over an engraved glass penholder on his desk, sending it crashing to the floor, where it broke.

"Oh, my Lord!" Celeste said abruptly, simultaneously startled and worried.

Gideon was quick to intervene. "It's nothing, Celeste. Nothing."

"Oh, I am so sorry, sir. Oh, my goodness, let me clean that up for you. Maybe I can save it or fix it or something, because it was so pretty, and I remember thinking that when I first saw it on your desk, and I can't believe I was so clumsy. I guess I was distracted thinking about those

Belmonts and rock 'n' roll being the Lord's music and all that. I'll buy you a new one, or, or . . . take it out of my pay."

"Nonsense, Celeste. Accidents happen." Gideon continued, "I never used it anyway; it was a decoration, a bauble. We should never be attached to pretty things that serve no function but to build our pride, to assist our vanity. If we cannot let these things go, then it means vanity rules our life, and that's wrong. You know that pride goeth before destruction. And besides, it was a gift from some viewers in Little Rock. I have about ten more that are almost identical from other grateful viewers in other big-hearted cities. So, there's no loss. It'll be our secret."

Celeste smiled at Gideon like he had found her missing cat, and she returned to her desk outside Gideon's expansive and tastefully decorated office, with its large antique wooden desk and ornate six-foot crucifix hanging on the wall his chair faced. He was especially proud of that cross, a gift from his first parishioners on the first anniversary of *The Gideon Calhoun Hour.*

Gideon waited in his office until he heard Celeste leave. He absent-mindedly read over notes for his next broadcast, but his mind was on Celeste. He had been instantly attracted to this woman, and he wanted her to like him. He knew she had been divorced for two years, and that she had a fifteen-year-old son who lived in another state.

The Reverend Calhoun was a widower. He had married when he was much younger and starting to answer his call to ministry. His wife, Julie, had struggled to cope with the burdens of being a minister's wife. She was too young, she said, to have to be perfect all the time. He had loved her deeply, but was unwilling to give up his dream, his mission, in order to take a "normal" job as she wanted him to do. Gideon hoped that, in time, she would learn to handle her role, especially when someday they had children on whom she could focus.

After three years of trying to get pregnant, Julie learned that she had polycystic ovary syndrome (PCOS), worsening her depression. She refused to leave the house. She began gaining weight, triggering a spiral of shame, deepening depression, and increasing obesity. A hundred-twenty pounds at their wedding, Julie weighed 285 when she died of a heart attack two months shy of her forty-fourth birthday. Gideon was overcome with regret and guilt that no matter how much he loved her, he could not save her, even had he left his ministry. The more successful he became, the more she spiraled downward.

Following two years of mourning Julie, Gideon began to enjoy the company of other women, women he knew were attracted to him for his charisma, his vision, his power, even his godliness. Sometimes, he was tempted by women who came to him for pastoral care, women who had been hurt or abandoned or could not cope with life's problems, but he had never allowed himself to take advantage of their vulnerability and his position of power. If he could not resist the temptations of the flesh to serve his God, then what else might he put before God? Nothing could come before God. "We are called to place God above everything else in our life," he remembered always.

Not that he was celibate; far from it. He had had several girlfriends, and had slept with a few women on a regular basis (not at the same time). But he had rules for these affairs:

> Never date a member of his own congregation, for surely it would ruin his ministry and reputation, which was more important to him than anything else in his life.

No one-night stands.

No whores, paid or otherwise.

No fallen women.

No married women.

> No one he did not know and trust, for the Devil was clever and might send Delilah to mislead and betray him.

Of course, with these strict rules, he found it difficult to meet women he could date and romance, and most of the women he did date quickly chafed under his unyielding morals.

His last "date" had been over three years ago, and he had largely put sexual thoughts of women out of his mind. Yet here was Celeste, an angel if ever he'd met one, sitting more on his mind each day. He struggled to understand why, but it was not so difficult to see.

Celeste Fallow was not, technically, a member of his congregation. She knew him only via the television until she answered an ad to be his assistant. She came with impeccable credentials and experience, and was clearly a good, Christian woman, despite her divorce. She liked Gideon; that much was obvious. She was intelligent, thoughtful, efficient, hard-working. By God, she was quite a find!

As he thought about Celeste and pictured her face, he turned off the lights and left his office.

Chapter 9

That Was Lucky, Wasn't It?

Jerome had mostly calmed down—at least outwardly—as he and Lacy hit Pope's Department Store. They had no expectation that they'd be reimbursed for anything they bought, but they knew they couldn't wait to find out for sure; they and the children needed things immediately: clothes and shoes and hairbrushes and cosmetics and basic toiletries.

As they filled a cart with a small wardrobe for Jerome, Lacy's cell phone rang. It was Moses, saying he and Miriam were in the parking lot, and asking where to meet them. While Jerome paid, Lacy went to meet the kids in the Men's Jeans department. It would be easier to grab a few things for Moses, and let Miriam take some time choosing, instead of making Moses wait for what was sure to be an agonizing spree by his sister. While Moses began looking at jeans, Jerome and Lacy stuffed their six bags of loot into two suitcases they'd just bought, and rolled them out to the car. Miriam decided to join them rather than wait for her brother.

"How was school today, Honey?" Lacy asked Miriam as they walked to the car.

"It was *awful.* Do you know how many people came up to me and wanted to talk about our house? It was so annoying."

"Oh, come on," said Jerome. "People are just trying to be helpful, or curious. You're kind of a celebrity, Miriam. Might as well enjoy all the attention. It'll die down soon."

"I don't want to go to school tomorrow, Daddy," begged Miriam. She cast doe eyes at Lacy, hoping one of them would go softhearted.

"I really think you should go, Mir," said Lacy, her face a symphony of sympathy. "What kind of a day are you going to have next week when school is finished and you have nowhere to be? You're going to end up watching TV with Gramma and Grampa, and driving yourself crazy. Why start that routine now? Finish the week with something to do. You'll be out of school soon enough."

Jerome was surprised and pleased by Lacy's clarity. "Your mother's right, Sweetie. It's only a few more days. Maybe by then we can figure something out, get a temporary place of our own."

"I could live at Jessica's house," Miriam said, catching her parents off guard.

"What?" said Lacy.

"Jessica's mom told her I could stay at their house until you find something. She was inviting me to stay, Daddy. I think you should let me." She looked hopeful yet forlorn.

Jerome and Lacy looked at each other. How could they let Miriam go? How did their lives come to this state in a mere eighteen hours? But how could they say no? It made sense. There was not enough room at Lacy's folks' house, not if they all were forced to stay a week or more.

Lacy spoke for them both. "Okay, I'll call Mrs. Polsky and figure out how to do it after we're done here."

With the first batch of purchases safely stashed in the car, the three Lights returned to find Moses trying on a last pair of jeans. Miriam led Lacy to the Juniors Department, while Jerome and Moses grabbed some underwear and Moses picked out half a dozen shirts. Fortunately, early summer meant lightweight clothing was sufficient. They could wait before buying jackets, sweaters, and winter coats—things that would take up much-needed space.

Miriam was beginning to see the upside of having all her stuff destroyed. She had a look on her face as if she had met the Good Fairy. To everyone's surprise, she was picking things out for herself faster than anyone else had. "I'll return what I don't like and try some other stuff!" she explained. She didn't bother trying much on. If she liked the way it looked, size was largely irrelevant, the happy result of a fashion sense among teens that said you could look good in either loose and baggy, or tight fitting and clingy. She wasn't too sure about a particular tank top she wanted to get, so she headed into the "Wardrobe Assistance Room" (as Kleptman's euphemistically called it, and which Lacy once told a girlfriend should be called the "W.A.R. room") to try it on. "I hope it doesn't make me look fat!" Miriam said, as she disappeared.

✝ ✝ ✝

A buzzer went off on the microwave oven at Gideon Calhoun's plantation-style house. Gideon got up from his computer in the old pantry between the enormous kitchen and the everyday dining room. For Gideon, living alone, the oversized pantry with its glass-paneled forest-green cabinets was totally superfluous, but it functioned beautifully as a small office. Food and work a mere fifteen feet apart. It was, Gideon hoped, the way Heaven would be.

As Gideon slid his dinner plate out of the microwave, he mused that he had reached a point in life where he would rather have a great meal than great sex, though, he admitted, either would be quite satisfying.

He took his chicken-and-rice dinner to the dining room, to his place set for one. Then he went back to his computer and clicked on an online Gospel radio station. The site opened and the songs began as he sat down to eat. After a few bites, he got up and took a half-finished bottle of wine out of the refrigerator and uncorked it. He was completely content . . . until his telephone rang.

"Reverend Calhoun?" said a woman's voice, not waiting for him to speak.

"Yes, this is Reverend Calhoun. How can I help you?"

"My name is Louise Baldwin; I'm friends with Celeste Fallow, your assistant?" She posed it as a question, to make sure he would know that she is not another nutcase who got his home number.

"Yes, Celeste, of course. How can I help you, Louise?" His tone was friendly, curious.

"Did you know that Celeste has been in an accident?"

"Oh, my goodness, no! Oh, Dear Lord, what's happened to her?"

Louise changed her tone, realizing that she would have to be the one to tell the famous Reverend Calhoun the bad news. "Um, her car was hit broadside on the passenger side as she was crossing McDaniel, and she was knocked unconscious. The ambulance took her to Mercy Hospital."

Gideon was speechless. This news was too horrible to imagine, even after all the many sad stories that people had brought him for years. But wait! "She's not dead, is she?"

"No, Reverend, as far as I understand, she should be all right, but they don't know yet if she could be paralyzed or something like that."

"I'll go over to the hospital immediately," Gideon announced. "How did you find out about Celeste's accident?"

"The police had her identification, and from their computer they had her home phone number, and when they called, Celeste's sister happened to be visiting and heard the phone call, and she called me from her cell phone, so I think she was on her way to the hospital herself, or maybe she was at the hospital. She happened to see my card on Celeste's refrigerator on her way out the door."

"Well, that was lucky, wasn't it?" asked Gideon.

"Yes, I guess it was. And . . . um, so I decided I'd call you and make sure you were told, in case her sister didn't have your number. I called your office and, well, I told them what happened and that I needed to call you, and they're such good Christian souls that they knew I was not making up a story just to get your home number, so they gave it to me."

Gideon thought silently, *I really must teach them NOT to give out my home phone number, no matter what the story is. They're good Christians, but they're not telephone psychics. That's why I got a pager, doggone it.*

But what he said was, "And I'm very glad you've called me, Louise. I hope I'll get to meet you in person someday. You are obviously a good friend to Celeste. God Bless You, Louise."

The poor woman was nearly overcome. "Oh, THANK you, Reverend Calhoun. Uh, God bless you, too, um, sir. I'm sure I'll see you at Mercy."

"All right, Louise. Thank you again. I'm leaving right now! Bye!"

"Bye."

Gideon snapped himself together. He worried about his appearance. Like it or not, he was fair game anytime he was in public, and there could well be a photographer about. It might even be a page-10 story in the local press. "So, how should I look? A bit more concerned about my assistant than about the dozens of other people I visit each week in a hospital? I think so, but not too concerned. I mean, if I'm grief-stricken or something, they'll suspect a liaison. I can't have a scandal like that."

He went in his closet and looked at the clothes he typically chose for his chaplaincies, then kicked it up a small notch by taking a darker jacket than usual. He liked to have something cheerful on when he went to hospitals and nursing homes, usually by special request, but at least once a week to two different places where he was officially affiliated. He had picked these places carefully to make sure they cultivated the right political and spiritual tone for his public personality. The hospital would do abortions only to save the life of the mother; he could live with that. He also had the nursing home investigated privately, to make sure there were no literal or figurative skeletons in its closets. You can't be too careful when your entire job rests on your credibility.

Gideon thought of himself as a good man, someone who always tried to do the right thing.

He'd been that way since he was a young boy, and that was the reason his mother had pushed him towards ministry. He seemed naturally inclined. He had gifts to share, gifts of patience and goodness and morality. He had the gift of making an agitated person calm, which is no small feat. So what if he mixed a bit of theatre in with his caring now and then? You had to sell whatever good news you were trying to make someone believe. Even if you knew darn well that somebody's loved one wasn't going to make it more than a few days, you held out hope to them, because they needed hope more than they needed the harsh reality. Let the doctors address the scientific; he would address the spiritual.

He grabbed his Bible, and he was off. It wasn't more than twenty minutes at this hour to Mercy, and he knew where he could park that was most convenient.

At the hospital, Gideon went to the Reception Desk. "Hello, Janet, can you tell me where I'll find Celeste Fallow?"

"She's still in the E.R., Reverend. You'll have to ask down there which room she's in."

Gideon wasted not an instant as he turned and headed down the hall.

He was anxious to find out how bad things were, and he said a silent prayer for Celeste as he scooted along. As a familiar face at the hospital, he could move about more easily than most visitors. He went straight to the triage nurse's desk and asked about Celeste. The nurse, a body-builder with a tattoo of Jesus on the side of his neck, would normally have pointed the Reverend in the right direction, but this time, he led him there personally.

Gideon was mightily relieved to see Celeste's eyes open when he entered her room. She did not look at him right away, but as he moved closer to her bed, she moved only her eyes to look his way. A great look of recognition and joy spread over her face, but her head remained immobile.

Chapter 10

Have a Little Faith

Darcy and George Day were traumatized. The sudden invasion of their house had them completely flummoxed. The worst of it was the uncertainty of the situation. Clearly, Lacy and Jerome were not going to be moving back into their old house again, and that meant either that they would be staying here for a long time, or obliged to find a new house or apartment. Darcy did not want to force her own daughter out on the street, but she also did not want to deal with four more people in her house. At seventy-two, she wasn't up for extra food shopping, extra cleaning, competition over what TV show to watch.

Darcy had long felt that the single biggest problem driving families apart was that different TV shows appeal to different generations, and no one wants to give an inch. Every night is a battle, unless they go out. What choice did she have? Leave the house, or fight, or watch some horrible program that's stupid and not funny at all no matter what the grandchildren, whom she otherwise adores, think. Six of them at home each night was unimaginable.

It was with equal parts trepidation and love that Darcy and George heralded the return of the four homeless people back into their house on Aspen Lane.

George finally had to tell Darcy how he felt, and, consequently, how he wanted her to feel. "I don't think I could stand having four of anybody here with us for more than three days. The fact that I love those kids doesn't make it any easier to have our lives disrupted. I've earned some peace and quiet in my final years!"

Darcy failed to agree. "Oh, for goodness' sake, George! Lacy is our daughter, and she needs our help right now. She's your child. How can you turn your back on her?"

George looked both ashamed and hostile at the lack of support.

Darcy said, "I'm no happier than you are about this disruption. I know it won't be easy having four people with us … if it turns into a long stay. But as far as I'm concerned, I'm happy to have them here as long as necessary. I would never tell her she has to get out until she has a proper place to go."

"Well, I didn't put it—"

"So, we'll have to suggest to them that they begin looking for new housing right away, and we'll help them with the payments if they don't have enough cash while waiting for the insurance money."

George looked relieved that Darcy at least shared his desire to keep the intrusion short. He knew she was right; he could never ask Lacy and Jerome and the grandchildren to move out.

As George went to the kitchen to get a drink of water, Jerome pulled up in one car with Moses, followed almost immediately by Lacy and Miriam in the other car. George looked out the kitchen window. "The assault is beginning!" he called to Darcy.

The driveway doorbell rang. George opened the door. He smiled weakly at his daughter, his lips together and the corners of his mouth barely moving, and reached out both arms to her. "Welcome, Sweetheart," he said, and though he meant the words, he could not bring himself to say them with any audible conviction.

"Hi, Dad!" said Lacy, choosing to ignore the signals she had long ago learned to recognize in her father. "Thanks for taking us in. We've had a rough day, and I'm so glad to be with you and Mommy tonight."

Why, thought George, *did she have to call Darcy 'Mommy?' That makes it harder for me to say anything.* Moses sat down to watch TV, while Miriam went to "her" room and closed the door.

Darcy had already guessed that she would have to be the "bad guy" in the house, because she knew that George would not say what he was feeling. She was proud of him for his restraint, but knew that soon he'd be acting cranky to everyone, and picking fights with her when they were alone. She was about to say something to Lacy once Jerome came in and they could get a moment alone.

But Lacy, as clever an observer of one's parents as any woman, spoke first. "We can't possibly stay here with you more than three days, Mom and Dad. It would disrupt our lives too much, because we can't be worrying about you two at the same time as everything else. The kids are out of school come the end of the week, so they'll be looking to do their summer thing, which is not the kind of hours you'll want people coming and going, so . . ."

Darcy could stand no more. Lacy's gambit changed her entire strategy. "You'll do nothing of the kind. You'll stay here as long as you need to, and we'll have to adapt to young people around us again."

Lacy was unsure whether her mother really meant those words. In truth, it didn't matter, because Jerome and Lacy had no choice but to stay here until they found a place. "Oh, Mom, we'll go back over to the insurance company tomorrow and see what they're going to be able to give us for the house, and we'll also get in touch with the government."

"With the government?" squealed Darcy. "How do you plan to do that?"

"Jerome knows someone who knows Nell Shapiro in the governor's office. Maybe we qualify for emergency assistance. The governor could declare it a disaster, and that would trigger automatic actions. If nothing else, they can tell us which agency is most likely to help us, so we don't have to start calling all of them." None of this had occurred to Lacy until this very moment, but the instant she said it, she knew it was the right thing to do.

Jerome caught the tail end of this conversation, and figured out that Lacy was telling her parents that they would move out. He was as anxious as anyone for the current nightmare to end. He went to the phone and called his boss. "There's no way I can come in tomorrow. We've got to find a place to live and we have to see what kind of financial assistance we can get. . . . I will. . . . I will. . . . I'll call you about this time tomorrow to let you know."

"Anyway, Miriam won't be staying here at all," Lacy said. "Oh, my gosh! I forgot that I have to call Mrs. Polsky."

"Who?" asked Darcy.

"Jessica Polsky is Miriam's friend, and she invited Miriam to stay with her for now. I have to call Jessica's mother to work it out. I'll go do that now," she said, and she disappeared into the next room.

Mrs. Polsky offered to come right over and pick up Miriam, so Lacy gave her directions and the phone number there, and asked her to give them thirty minutes to get Miriam's stuff together.

Miriam possessed the astonishing and enviable flexibility that fifteen-year-old girls tend to have, especially about anything to do with their families. One minute she was crying and upset about their house, and the next minute she was begging Gramma Day for a suitcase or bag she could put her new clothes and toiletries in. The whirlwind created by Miriam's flashing about had no discernible impact on Moses's mood. He was as downcast as Jerome had ever seen him.

"Hey, Mo, come on, buddy," said Jerome, putting an arm around Moses's shoulder. "We're a strong family; we'll be okay. You need to have a little faith."

"Faith? Faith in what, Dad?" asked Moses, never expecting to hear that word from his father.

"Well, faith that things will work out all right. Confidence, I guess, would be a better word. Optimism. I know it'll work out. We're all alive, and we've got our cars and cell phones. Ha. What more do we need?"

"Geez, Dad, how can you be so up?" Moses asked.

"I don't know. I, uh, don't want to get down, to let myself be, you know, down." Jerome paused. Then he hugged Moses's shoulder again. "Tomorrow, your mother and I will look for a new place to live and rent some furniture. We'll be fine. You'll see."

✝ ✝ ✝

"I'm sure you're right," said Celeste to Gideon. "I'll be fine. But I will admit I'm scared."

Gideon reached for and held Celeste's cold hand, being careful not to bump the IV. She looked dazed and banged up, but he had faith that she would be fine. He didn't think he could do anything to heal her, but he felt that God was telling him she would soon be out of danger. He drew great comfort from that knowledge, and he figured that if he could impart his positive attitude to Celeste, she would, indeed, heal faster. As it was to turn out, she did heal, but not quickly.

It was great news, indeed, that Celeste was able to talk, though rather feebly, and with obvious fear in her voice. Gideon had often seen accident victims. Many of them looked much worse than Celeste. The question was how quickly she would regain the use of her arms and legs. He was optimistic and wanted her to know. "I've honestly seen people much worse off than you make a full recovery, and the Lord tells me that you will, too, Celeste."

His words were a tremendous comfort to her. Celeste was filled with joy that this great man could talk to the Lord about her. And that she would be fine.

At that moment, an attractive but somewhat harried woman entered the room. "Oh, Cellie, look at you!" she moaned, and raced to Celeste's bedside.

Celeste laughed and cried at the same time. Gideon half expected to see her raise her arms to hug the woman, but, of course, she could not. The dark-haired visitor, looking distraught, bent over and kissed Celeste's cheek, and placed her hands gingerly on Celeste's shoulders so she would not fall on the injured woman, and so she could sustain the kiss.

After a moment, the visitor leaned back and stood upright. Celeste said to her, "Can you get a tissue and wipe my face, please?"

"Of course."

"Where are my manners?" said Celeste after the woman wiped her eyes and nose. "Reverend Calhoun, this is my sister, Elysia Duncan. Elysia, this is Reverend Calhoun, my new boss."

"Of course, Reverend. How nice to meet you. Celeste has told me a lot about you, and, to be honest, I knew who you were as soon as I walked in." Elysia reached out and shook his hand. "I'm sorry I didn't get here sooner, Sis, but I had to make some quick arrangements for the kids. Bobby won't be home till late, and I had to get them some dinner. Maria can watch the others, but I don't want her cooking when I'm not home. She's only fifteen, and not too good around fire, yet."

Celeste gave a weak but sincere laugh.

Elysia took a seat a few feet from the bed. Gideon decided to stay a bit longer until he judged that he had reached the optimum length of his visit: long enough to show that his assistant was not just another sick person, but not so long that his interest in her would be unseemly. Gideon was concerned about his public image to the point of being obsessive. He had to avoid the appearance as well as the reality of any sort of scandal, and having a romantic liaison with his assistant would certainly be a breach of morality. He could not afford for Celeste to suspect his attraction to her.

So, Gideon left her room and went home to sleep after forty-five minutes at the hospital, which was the same amount of time that Miriam Light needed to be ready to go with her friend, Jessica. Calm settled over the Day household and over Calhoun's modest home, and the day after the sinkhole ended for them all.

Chapter 11

And the Evening and the Morning Were the Third Day

Lacy and Jerome were up and busy by 5:30 a.m. so they could shower and use the toilet before getting Moses up for school at 6:00. George and Darcy would usually have slept till at least 7:00, but it was impossible for them to ignore the unaccustomed noises in their home. They remained in bed, awake, till they heard all three guests padding about the house, trying to be quiet, but failing to realize that even the wind their bodies created as they moved to and from the hallway was enough to disturb the normally tranquil equilibrium of the home at that hour.

Moses left for school at 7:00 after a half-hearted plea to stay with his parents that day and help with things. As soon as he left, Lacy said,

"Mom, we need to have a talk with you and Dad."

Darcy lifted her head from setting the breakfast table, and said to her daughter with a quizzical glance, "That sounds ominous, Lacy."

"Well, it's not a good situation, but it's not life or death. We didn't want to talk about it with you last night in front of the kids."

"Okay."

"Jerome and I are going to go to the bank this morning as soon as it opens and see how much they can lend us to get us through, but I think we're going to need to borrow from you and Dad, too."

"Well, of course, Honey. We'll do whatever we can."

"We didn't tell you what happened yesterday at the insurance company. Basically, they say they're not going to pay for much because the sinkhole was an 'Act of God.'"

"What?" said Darcy, as George entered the room in his bathrobe and slippers.

"What's up?" he asked.

Jerome answered, "Lacy was telling Mom that we're probably not going to get any money from the insurance company. They say we weren't covered for sinkhole damage."

"How can they say that?"

"They say we're not covered for any Act of God, and they say that's what this was," said Jerome, barely keeping his composure.

"Sue the bastards," was George's answer.

Jerome said, "Well, I—"

George interrupted him. "No, I mean it. Get a lawyer. Today. Maybe you can sue them. It's worth a try, anyhow."

"I guess you're right, Dad," said Lacy, and Jerome nodded, surprised he had not thought of it himself. "We can call Sumner Stoke. He helped us the last time we needed a lawyer."

Lacy looked up Stoke's number and left a message for him to call her cell phone. She helped her mother clean the breakfast dishes and make the beds, and then she and Jerome headed to the bank. The morning was sunny and clear, with a light breeze that carried the scent of dogwood and iris. As they entered the bank, Stoke returned Lacy's call. They agreed to meet him at his office in one hour.

A loan officer in his twenties wearing a navy-blue suit that made him look like an undertaker came out of his cubicle to greet the Lights. He introduced himself as "Mr. Evan Watts." He had heard about their predicament on the news and treated them like celebrities.

Mustering as sincere an expression as possible, Watts said, "Look, Mr. and Mrs. Light, I'd really like to help you. I mean that. What you've gone through is remarkable, horrible, yet newsworthy. It doesn't also have to be tragic for you. Frankly, you're a high-profile case. People are going to look at how we treat you. But please believe me when I say that we would want to do the right thing no matter how much outside scrutiny we might attract. So, what I'm trying to say is that we cannot simply give you money, but we can loan it to you at below-market rates, as close to free as we are allowed by law to go. And we are prepared to give you up to 6 months' grace period before your first loan payment is due."

Lacy and Jerome exchanged a quick glance. "That would be very generous of you, Mr. Watts," said Jerome, "and we feel sure we're going to have to take you up on that. Even if we get an insurance payment—which seems unlikely—it's going to be a while. We may get a small check at first, while we appeal their initial decision. It seems that some of our losses come under our automobile policy, but it won't be much."

"Well, here's the problem, Mr. and Mrs. Light. You still have a mortgage due on the house. The house itself, of course, is the collateral on that loan. If you stop paying and you cannot pay the mortgage, then normally, we can take your house and your property. But in this case, there is no house to take. The insurance company is not just screwing you for your personal effects; it's screwing this bank for the house itself. As you know, your homeowners' policy pays the mortgage holder first for any loss. When they refuse to pay you, they also refuse to pay us. And that means that you owe us any money the insurance company falls short of your principal. Right now, it would appear you are into us for . . ." He made a pretense of looking at figures on his computer monitor. ". . . about $182,000."

"Oh my God!" said Lacy, who did not see this one coming at all.

"That's before we take your property. And here, again, the bank wants to be generous. Undeveloped property in your neighborhood might typically be worth $75,000 to $100,000 per acre, but your half-acre parcel is now worthless. Despite that, we offer to repossess your property for $10,000. That reduces what you owe us to $172,000. We can renegotiate your homeowners' loan for that amount at the lowest possible interest rate. That should save you enough money to afford to rent some decent housing, maybe a two-bedroom apartment."

"A two-bedroom apartment?" exclaimed Jerome. "And our whole investment, our equity in the house on Tadpole Lane, is gone?"

"Yes, Mr. Light. Unfortunately, you lose that money. That's up to your insurance company. You can't expect the bank to absorb that loss for you."

"Wow!" Jerome barked. "I guess you're right, but I hadn't thought about it until just now. We're really getting fucked, aren't we?"

"I don't blame you, Mr. Light," said Watts, "but it's not by this bank. And we want to do everything we can to help you through this crisis. Your problem is with Big Rock Mountain Mutual. You're smart to get a lawyer to help you at this point."

Lacy's face was grim. "Thank you, Mr. Watts. We appreciate the help you're giving us. We may not need to borrow anything until we find a place to live. We need you to tell us what our monthly payments will be on this $172,000 mortgage on Tadpole Lane, plus the cost if we want to borrow something more. Like, what if we decide to buy another place instead of renting?"

"We could offer to match the lowest rate you can find from a reputable lending institution. That will be a bit higher than the terms of the old mortgage."

"Of course," said Lacy, starting to comprehend the magnitude of what she and Jerome were facing financially if the Big Rock Mountain Mutual Insurance Company didn't come through. "Please draw up the loan papers so we can see the rates you're offering, and we can come back later." She could understand the bank's dilemma, but she was annoyed at the young banker.

"To tell you the truth, Mrs. Light," Watts said, "I've already got those numbers for you. Let me show you." And he spun his computer monitor around so they could all see it. "On the loan, which is actually $172,138, you can see that a three percent rate for fifteen years will yield a monthly payment of almost $1,200, plus I'm sure you'll get a break on your property taxes. You'll still need liability insurance, though. You've been paying $1,524 a month, so you'll have about $324 to spend on your new home. And on the other loan, if you want to buy a house . . . let me just plug in a number that is what you're likely to find . . . and okay, if you bought a $350,000 home or apartment and put down just ten percent, then your monthly payments would be around $2,600, including taxes and insurance. That's a rough estimate, anyhow."

"I'm not sure we can put down that much money, Mr. Watts," said Jerome. "Then what?"

"Then you'll probably be better off renting for now."

"That's really crappy, you know?" sputtered Jerome. He was losing his cool again. "I mean, no matter what happens, if we don't get paid by the insurance company, then you and them, they, uh, are both giving us the finger and saying, 'Too bad.' Isn't that right, Mr. Watts?"

Watts had hoped to avoid this kind of scene. He certainly didn't want the Lights talking to any reporter about how the bank was being unfair to them. "You're missing my point, folks, and I want to stress that it's not the bank's fault. We are prohibited by law from certain activities when it comes to loans. We want to do everything for you we are allowed by law to do."

"Well, I'm sure you're right, Mr. Watts, and I expect my fight is with Big Rock Mountain, but I want you to know that we will ask our attorney to investigate our rights on the mortgage." Jerome was trying to keep his composure. "So, we aren't going to sign any new documents for a few days, until the lawyer tells us to sign."

Jerome and Lacy got up, said their cordial goodbyes to Watts, and headed out to the street. They had a few minutes before their meeting with Stoke. They ran into Reed's Books to get Lacy's favorite coffee and get their heads together.

Jerome took a table while Lacy went up to the counter to order. He saw a small girl, probably about three years old, and her thirty-five-ish father at a table across the way. The little girl was popping on and off her seat as her dad drank his coffee. At one point she disappeared below the table, and he bent to his right, looking under the table to see what she was up to. There was a baby cup on the floor.

The father said, "Is that your cup under the table?"

"Yes."

"Well, pick it up."

The toddler bent her knees slightly and reached her too-short arm under the seat. "I can't reach it," she said. She made no attempt to get on hands and knees, which would let her easily retrieve the cup.

"Okay," said Dad, "I'll get it." And he grabbed the cup without leaving his seat.

Jerome laughed silently. "Smart Dad . . . smarter girl," as Lacy arrived with the drinks.

"So, where are we?" she asked Jerome.

"I'd say we're in the middle of some deep sh—" and then remembering the little girl, "sugar. We could try talking to Glisson again, but I think the next person to talk to him should be our attorney, don't you?"

"Absolutely," said Lacy. "And let's not assume the banker is right, either. I hate to spend the money on a lawyer, but right now, it looks like we'd better at least try to recover something from someone, or we're going to be out a heck of a lot of money. I mean, just when Moses is getting ready to go to college, how can we let this happen?"

"Oh, heck, Mo will be all right. But what about our retirement? What about all those things we had planned for us? We're more than a little screwed right now. I mean, $1,500 a month for the next fifteen years to pay for something we don't even own anymore."

At the high school, Moses's thoughts were on Sylvana Fox, a senior like him. He shared several classes with the slender, pretty blonde who was a good eight inches shorter than he. Moses really liked this girl. It was his first crush on someone his own age, and he didn't want to blow it. Sylvana already liked Moses even before the sinkhole made him almost-famous at school. They had even gone to a movie together a week ago, although Moses told his parents he was at Marty Karlovits' house. Moses planned to tell them about her, and then the house was lost and he couldn't bring it up yet.

Sylvana wanted to meet Moses after school today. They both had their own cars, so they didn't have to worry about rushing off to catch the bus. She'd told him at his locker this morning that it was important. That's the kind of scant information that can ruin a fellow's day.

Joe Block caught up to Moses on the way to lunch. "Hey, wait up, man!" called Joe. He was 5'8" and stocky, with bronze skin and tortoise-shell glasses. Moses stopped and waited for him. "Dude, what's up with your house?"

"Whaddaya mean, 'What's up with it?' It's freakin' *gone*, that's what's up. I can't believe it. It's so . . . unbelievable!"

"No shit," said Joe. "My parents said you can stay at my place if you need to."

"Hey, that's nice of 'em, Joe, but I think I want to stay with my mom and dad right now, 'cause they need a lot of help. It's hard on them, you know, 'cause they're older."

"Yeah, Dude, I know. That sucks. Well, let me know if you change your mind, 'cause you can come over, like, anytime. My mom and dad are cool with it, you know, 'cause they've always, like, liked you."

Moses was not sure why he talked like a moron when he was with Joe and Marty, and otherwise spoke quite well. It's not like Joe and Marty were stupid. True, they weren't the highest peaks in the mountains, but they were sharp enough.

The meeting with Sumner Stoke was short. Stoke was not surprised by the position of Big Rock Mountain Mutual, and it took him little time to come up with various strategies to address it.

Stoke, who looked to be in his late thirties, had unnaturally black hair that he combed straight back from his forehead without a part. His dark brown eyes seemed too big for his pale, clean-shaven face, but he had a boyish charm about him that made Jerome trust him.

"I think," Stoke intoned, "that we may be able to convince them to reverse their opinion. We'll need to prepare a careful appeal."

"What will something like that cost? Can you do it on contingency?" asked Jerome.

"Oh, boy, I'd like to, Mr. Light, but I don't think so. Insurance cases are tricky, because they have lots of legal precedents on their side. Still, people have appealed 'Act of God' provisions before and won."

"Really?" said Lacy.

"Yes, but it's not easy, and I'm not sure whether sinkhole damage has been considered before. If so, our case will be a lot harder to make." Stoke paused, and leaned back in his executive high-back chair. "I'll tell you what, so you're not out a lot of money on a wild goose chase. Let me do a little research this afternoon into damage from sinkholes. I can get an answer pretty quickly and call you later today. If there is a precedent protecting Big Rock Mountain, then I won't charge you a thing."

"And if there is no precedent?" Jerome cocked his chin toward his right shoulder.

"Then I will need a $1,000 retainer to start drawing up an appeal. I charge $300 an hour. I'll probably put in about three hours. My assistant, who will prepare the papers, is $75 per hour, and she will need about four hours. Throw in $100 in expenses, and $1,300 should be enough to get us started."

"Started?"

"Right. After that, we have to see how the insurance company reacts. If they dare us to take them to court, we'll have to look at their case and decide what it will cost us to sue, how much time we'll need, etc. It's only fair to warn you that it could get pretty expensive pretty fast."

"How expensive?"

"$40,000 or $50,000 wouldn't be unusual. There will be lots of depositions of the professionals who investigated your disaster. Plus, Big Rock Mountain Mutual is not headquartered here in Ohio, and your policy says it is under the laws of the State of Connecticut, which is pretty friendly territory for them, not to mention expensive to travel to."

"Well, we could do $1,300 now if we have to," said Jerome, "but check that precedent thing, will you? And let us know."

Sumner Stoke stood and shook hands with both Jerome and Lacy, and they headed out.

Chapter 12

Someone's Out to Get Me

After his last class, Moses headed to the parking lot where Sylvana said to meet him. She was already there. Most of the cars had left. "Hi, Moses," she smiled as he approached. He was excited to see her, but he didn't want it to show. He wanted to look cool, like he was keeping it together.

"Hey, Syl, what's up?"

"I was waiting for you, but . . . I just got here, so no biggie. Aren't you happy to see me?"

"Oh, yeah, definitely." He leaned over and kissed her cheek. He had only kissed her once on the lips, and that had been a quick peck after the movie. Now he delivered the kiss as if he were removing a small tick from her cheek, then straightened back up.

She chose, wisely, to ignore his discomfort and take the lead. She came to him, a head taller than she was, put an arm around his waist, and pulled her head against his chest. It was more intimate than any moment they had shared, and it was the most exquisite horror for Moses. He didn't know whether to push her away, pull her closer, or step back, so he simply stayed put and let her hug thrill him slowly from his skin to his core. After a moment, he put an awkward claw on her shoulder and pulled her ever-so-slightly closer to him. "I'm so sorry, Moses. I'm so sorry you lost your house and all your stuff," she said, never lifting her head.

"Yeah, me, too," said Moses, rendered unable to use more than one-syllable words.

"My parents told me about it yesterday morning when I got up, and I never got a chance to see you yesterday. You should have called me!"

"I really wanted to, Syl. It's, like, too much, you know? How can I be sad about so many things at once? Maybe God's trying to punish me or something."

"For what? You're the sweetest guy I know. Besides, I thought you didn't believe in God."

"That's my Dad. I don't know what I believe anymore. But it sure seems like someone's out to get me or my family."

"Well, speaking of families, that's what I wanted to talk with you about. My mom told me to tell you that you can stay at our house if you need a place to live."

Moses looked surprised at this thought, and it must have registered on his face as some kind of hormonal joy.

"Not in MY room, you dope!"

"Oh, no, I wasn't thinking that!"

"Yeah, right," Sylvana teased. "So, do you think your parents would let you?"

"Wow, I don't know. Maybe. I don't know if I can ask 'em right now, though, 'cause we don't even have a place to live and they're pretty upset."

"If you had a place to live, you wouldn't need to stay with me, dummy!"

"I guess that's true."

"So now is exactly the time to ask. I'd really like to help you out, and I know my mom thinks you're nice . . . and cute, she told me."

Moses wished he were the kind of guy who could hear something like that and not be flustered, but he wasn't. He floundered for words and, when they did not come, he blushed. Anxious to be free of the thought of Mrs. Fox admiring him, he said, "My parents might be out looking at places to live."

"You mean like a new house?"

"Yeah, I suppose so. They didn't tell me. But I'll see them back at my gramma's house for dinner, and I'll find out. Can I call you later?"

"You better!" said Sylvana, as she hugged him again, and then turned and walked to her car.

Moses followed her walk with his eyes. She really was cute, and she had the cutest walk. Why did I have to meet a girl like her now? Why couldn't my life be normal? Why does crap always happen to me? Moses got in his car and headed to his grandparents.

Chapter 13

The Worry Eater

Lacy considered it her job to worry about everyone. Jerome once said to her "I'm going to call you the Worry Eater. You know, like the ancient sin eaters who were paid to eat the sins of rich people. You eat worries. Everyone tells you what's bothering them. They get it off their chest; they sleep great; and you end up awake half the night worrying about their problems."

"I'd better call Jessica Polsky's house and see if Miriam made it over there all right," said Lacy.

"Okay," said Jerome.

"And then I'd better start calling some rental agencies and setting up some appointments for tomorrow."

"Okay," said Jerome.

A four Lights had lost their computers and tablets to the sinkhole, so Lacy had picked up a real-estate flyer at the Double D Foods. She looked through it first, and circled some possibilities. Then, Jerome made another pass of the ads. He circled one or two Lacy had missed, and highlighted the choices she had made that sounded the best to him.

Moses arrived at his grandparents' house.

"Oh, Honey, I'm glad you're here," said Lacy, and she grabbed her son's sides, slightly crinkling the flyer.

"I am too, Mom. I thought you and Dad might be out looking at houses."

"I was about to make some phone calls to set that up. Was everything all right at school?" she asked.

"Uh, yeah, sure. Everything was fine. Maybe something I can talk to you about later."

Lacy rocked backwards, suddenly less anxious to leave. "Is something wrong?"

"Oh, no, nothng's wrong. I want to ask you and Dad something."

"Okay. Jerome? Jerome? Could you come talk with Moses and me for a minute?"

"What's up?" he asked them.

Lacy spoke first, "Moses wants to ask us something."

Moses cleared his throat. "There's this girl I know at school named Sylvana . . ."

Jerome and Lacy's eyes met for a half second. They made what you might call "uh-oh eyes" at each other.

". . . and she said her parents wanted her to invite me to stay at their place until you can find a new house. And I think it's a really good idea, and I want you to say yes."

Jerome started to take a breath in, as if getting ready to speak.

Moses didn't let him. "And I know you probably—I mean, you have to call her parents and clear it with them, but I'm sure it's okay with them, and it doesn't mean anything that she's a girl and I'm not."

"This girl doesn't mean anything to you?" asked Lacy.

"That's not what I said, Mom."

"So, she's special?"

"I didn't say that either, but, I don't know, she could be special. I think she likes me."

"Son," said Jerome, "a girl you like asked you to come live with her, and you only think she likes you? What are you, six?"

"Jerome!" said Lacy, "That's not the point. Oh, Moses, Honey, I don't think you're ready to start living with a girl."

"Mom! I wouldn't be living with her. Well, I mean, yeah, I'd be _living_ with her, but not living with _her_, if you know what I mean."

Jerome was not about to cut Moses any slack here, not out of any parental duty other than a father's job to bust his son's chops once in a while. "No, what do you mean, Mo?" Jerome smirked at Moses.

Moses's words burst out as fast as his mind raced. "Oh, boy. Okay, I like Sylvana, and I went out with her before, and I didn't tell you guys because I knew you'd be all funny about it. Like this, see? But I think it makes a lot of sense to go there for a few days, not like for my whole life, just till you guys find something. And maybe you won't be able to find three bedrooms right away, and then you won't have to because . . . I'll . . . uh." Moses realized that this line of reasoning was going in the wrong direction.

Lacy picked up on it. "Honey, I don't think it's a good idea, especially if you like her like . . . that."

Jerome got serious. "Okay, you have a good point. It's going to take us at least a couple of days to find a place and get some furniture in it. Your grandparents' house is no place for a seventeen-year-old. But what about some of your other friends. What about Marty, or Joe?"

Moses's shoulders slumped. "Joe said his parents invited me to stay there—"

Lacy cut him off. "Well, that's good! Why not do that? You told me you like Joe's mom."

"Yeah, I like his mom, but his dad . . . well, he's hard to take. He's really hard on Joe. I don't like being there when his dad's around."

"So what about Marty?" Lacy suggested. "His parents are nice."

"Mrs. Karlovits' mom just moved in with them. She had a stroke or something last month, and now she's in the spare bedroom. Besides, Marty didn't invite me, and Sylvana's parents did."

Jerome was surprised to hear himself say, "I think you should go stay with this girl, Mo. But . . . you are absolutely right we're going to call her parents first, and you also better understand right now that you and she are going to sleep in separate rooms. If you, or this girl, or her parents think you're going to share her room, then the deal is off, you understand?"

"Yeah, Dad."

"So, you two are in the laboratory phase, eh?" chuckled Jerome.

"What?" Moses replied.

"You know, testing the chemistry." Moses groaned.

Lacy knew she was beaten, so she said, "And when we find a place, I don't want any arguments from you about coming back to OUR house. We only have you for another year, and we mean to keep you with us every day of that year."

"Mom!"

"Okay, maybe not every day, but darn near."

Moses started to leave the room.

"You forgot to tell us how we can talk to this girl's parents," said Lacy.

"I'll write it down for you."

"Mo, you better stick around while we call them—what's their name?" said Jerome.

"Fox. Sylvana's last name is Fox."

The corners of Jerome's mouth twitched slightly, and he nearly made some sarcastic remark, but he, too, could be wisely silent at times. "Okay, while we call the Foxes, stay here in case we have any questions."

Lacy shoved a small piece of paper at Moses, and he wrote down Sylvana's phone number. Lacy began dialing. A voice on the other end of the line said, "Hello?"

"Um, hello, is this Mrs. Fox?"

"No, this is her daughter, Sylvana." Sylvana suspected it might be Moses's mother, and her heart gave a little leap as she waited to find out.

"Hello, Sylvana, this is Mrs. Light, Moses's mother." (Sylvana literally pumped her fist.) "Could I please speak with your mother or father?"

"Uh, sure, Mrs. Light. I'll get her right away."

The phone was silent for fifteen seconds or so, and then Lacy heard a sweet soprano voice say, "Hello, this is Dakota. What may I call you, Ms. Light?"

Lacy was taken by surprise by this request. "My first name is Lacy. Why not call me that?"

"Wonderful, Lacy. Thank you. I'm so glad you called, and I hope you're going to let your handsome son come stay with us during your crisis."

Handsome son? thought Lacy, but she didn't say it. "Oh, well, that's such a nice offer, Mrs. Fox."

"Call me Dakota, please."

"Okay, Dakota. That's awfully nice of you to invite Moses. He just told us about it, and we wanted to talk with you or your husband first before we decide. We want to be sure it's okay with you and that Moses will have his own, um, that he won't be in the way there."

Mrs. Fox understood the unspoken concern. "Sylvana has an older brother who's away at college now, and we wouldn't have let him stay at a girl's house unless he had his own room. In fact, Moses can have Hewitt's room here, because Hewitt is spending the summer at college and working. He's not coming back home until August."

"And you're sure Moses won't be in the way there?"

"Oh, no, we love Moses. We only met him once, but we thought he was really sweet."

Lacy looked at Moses as she heard this report. Moses squirmed, even though he had no idea what Mrs. Fox could be saying to his mother. He knew it was about him, and he wished this conversation were over already.

"He is a nice boy; I'm glad you think so. Well, we're very grateful to you, and we will let Moses stay there with you at least until the weekend. Then school is over and we hope to have found a new place to live by then," said Lacy.

"Oh, yes, I meant to tell you how sorry we are about your house. We saw it on the news, and it broke our hearts. Please let me know if there's anything we can do to help you, besides taking Moses in."

Lacy could not believe how perfect this perfect stranger was being towards her. "We don't even know where you live, Mrs., uh, Dakota. I'd like to come by this evening and meet you, if that's all right."

"Could you come around 8:00 o'clock after we've fed everyone and cleaned up? I'd hate to have you . . . well, wait a minute, why don't you and your husband come for dinner, too! Then you'll be able to feel completely secure about Moses's coming to stay with us."

"That's very nice of you, Dakota. Let me check with my husband. Um, what time would that be?"

"How about seven o'clock?"

"Okay, please hold a moment." Lacy held the phone to her chest and looked at Jerome. "Mrs. Fox is inviting us to dinner with them tonight."

"What time?" asked Jerome.

"Around seven?"

Jerome looked at Moses, who felt his heart sink to his toes, but then quickly realized that he was, surprisingly, getting his way, and he managed to smile at his Dad. "Okay, I think we'll be able to do that. But we need to let your folks know what we're doing," he told his wife.

Lacy put the receiver back to her ear. "Dakota, we'll see you at seven. Is there something we can bring? Perhaps a bottle of wine to toast our . . ." and feeling Moses's eyes about to bore a hole through the side of her head, she said, ". . . whatever! New friends!" She giggled a bit nervously, which struck even Lacy as odd behavior for her.

"That's wonderful, Lacy," enthused Sylvana's mother. "A bottle of wine would be perfect. Moses knows where we live. See you soon."

Chapter 14

Frailties

The Reverend Gideon Calhoun was at the bedside of his injured office assistant, Celeste Fallow, at Mercy Hospital. Often when he visited patients in Intensive Care, he felt more like he was in the way than anything else, as nurses came in and out quickly, and it was those patients who least responded to Gideon. Most of his hospital visits were more in keeping with his status as a celebrity than any religious wisdom he might impart, although as one of the chaplains who volunteered time at Mercy, he was able to recruit many newcomers to his church.

There was something else about hospital chaplaincy that bothered Gideon: he felt guilty whenever he did not feel total compassion and sympathy for a patient. Lately, he confessed to himself, working at the hospitals was less and less satisfying. He was distracted as he went from room to room, from ward to ward. He would listen to anyone, of course, but the things he would say to people had become so rehearsed, so perfunctory, that he found his mind in two places at once. One part of his brain would listen and respond as if by rote, and the other part would be miles away, perhaps thinking about his next sermon, or his next big guest appearance at churches all over the country.

He had never imagined or set out to achieve the celebrity he had acquired. He tried to practice what he preached about humility and service. Gideon was a thoroughly honest and earnest man, and not particularly ambitious. He projected his innocence and faith to all who watched him. No one could fake it that well. That was the key to his success and his transition to television that eluded many others. Unlike rival evangelists who were transformed by practiced hands to look the part on TV—heavy makeup, wigs or hairpieces, shoe lifts—Gideon naturally looked great.

In addition, Gideon had staying power. Here he was, fifty-five years old, and still as popular as ever, probably more so. He barely needed to ask for donations to his different Ministries; people were anxious to give. Yet, he still did things the way he had always done. No fancy, extravagant offices, no large staff. He had enough employees to make sure the mail was handled and that his money was well accounted for. He wanted to keep his personal hand on every piece of his operation so that no one would ever be able to do something to destroy his reputation. He wanted no slip-ups unless they were his own; he was well aware of the many people who were aching for a chance to bring him down.

At times, he would, when talking to colleagues and parishioners, blame Satan for problems he encountered. In his heart, though, he did not believe it. Gideon knew that those rare times he messed up were not because of Satan. The Devil did not make him do it. He believed confidently that his frailties were merely human, not cosmically inspired. If he did not see Satan in his own mistakes, how could he see Him in others'? And if Satan did not control human behavior, then one might reasonably question whether Satan even exists. Yet people expected Gideon to condemn Satan, and he hated to disappoint them. He was not being dishonest, merely accommodating.

His level of success and his managerial style led him into an extraordinarily busy life, and two things did not fit into the time he had left: hospital chaplaincy, and falling in love.

Yet here he was, in Celeste's room, doing both at the same time.

Celeste began to cry. She still did not feel she could move her body and limbs, although she thought there was some sensation there. She was so grateful to be able to talk, but even with words as an outlet for her thoughts, some thoughts must be expressed differently, through tears. Her inner anguish spoke only that language.

Gideon thought his heart would break. He knew already that he wanted to be with Celeste, maybe forsaking all others . . . at least for now. Yet, how could he tell her? His conflict had nothing to do with any vow of celibacy or discomfort with women. It was all about their respective roles, and the impropriety of his taking advantage of her emotional state, not to mention his position as her boss. So many women had told him in confidence of being sexually harassed, and looked to him for guidance. He would lose all his credibility with those women he had helped, and women he could help in the future if they perceived him as a predator. He had to remain above his feelings, or at least to their side.

"What's the matter, Celeste?" he said, taking her hand in the impersonal way he might take the hand of any sick person. "I know you've been hurt, and you're in physical pain, but those tears tell me of a different kind of pain. What is it?"

Her lower lip quivered. "Oh, Reverend Calhoun. I can't believe you can read me so well!" She felt immediately close to him, and managed, with great difficulty, to squeeze his hand ever so slightly.

She needed no other words to convince Gideon that she was too easily deceived, and therefore too vulnerable for him to exploit. He knew he was not "reading" her; he was doing and saying what he would do and say with any patient. Tears are not hard to decipher; they always speak of emotional pain. He had no peculiar insight into her psyche, yet she clearly believed he did. Normally, he was glad for the easy acceptance of his little fortune-teller tricks, but now he felt guilty, for he was not playing only with Celeste's head, but also with her heart.

"I'm so scared," she continued. "I've never been this frightened in all my life. I'm afraid I'm going to die, or be paralyzed. And I want my mother to be here."

Gideon realized how little he knew of Celeste. Was her mother even alive? If so, where did she live? Gideon had not been doing his job.

"Do you have any family nearby besides your sister and brother-in-law?"

"My mother passed away about four years ago," Celeste answered. "My daddy left us when Elysia was just four and I was seven."

"I guess it's been a tough life for you and Elysia then," said Gideon.

Celeste did not answer, but gave a small nod. Gideon put his hand on hers. She tucked her lower lip between her teeth and, without moving her head, rolled her eyes away from him, trying her best to keep control.

Gideon took a deep breath to maintain his own composure. "Would you like me to pray with you, Celeste?"

"Yes," she managed to choke out without shifting her eyes.

At his grandparents' house, Moses jammed his few belongings haphazardly into a bag, which he then flung into the back seat of his mother's car. Lacy got into Jerome's car. Jerome called to Moses, "Let's stop at Dutton's Wine Shoppe to pick up a gift for the Foxes. We'll see you there." They wanted both cars with them in case Moses stayed at the Foxes' house.

They parked outside the store. Lacy was climbing out when Jerome's cell phone rang. He saw the name Sumner Stoke in the caller ID. "Hello, this is Jerome."

Lacy paused outside the car. "What is it?" she asked.

Jerome, however, was listening intently, and lifted one index finger to beg for silence. After about thirty seconds, he said, "Okay, thanks." He hung up and looked at Lacy. "That was Stoke. He said that there's no point arguing the sinkhole was not an 'Act of God' because the courts have already decided that it can be considered an Act of God."

"So, that means—"

Jerome interrupted her, "That means we have to decide whether to appeal the insurance company decision. Stoke wants us in his office at 8:30 tomorrow morning."

"Why not, I guess?" said Lacy.

"Why not appeal?"

"No, why not at least talk to him at 8:30? It will cost us $1,300 to see if there's any chance of getting something. If we don't spend the thousand, then for sure we get nothing, so . . ." Lacy paused and held her hands palms up in front of her shoulders, and shrugged slightly.

"So, why not go ahead," Jerome replied. "You're right. We'll meet with Stoke in the morning and find out what we do next." He looked at his wife. "Lace, why don't you pick out a nice bottle and then ride with Moses. I'll follow you."

It was 6:45. Lacy ran in and selected a nice Alsatian Riesling. Jerome listened to Steve Earle sing "Jerusalem" on the radio as he waited. Lacy jumped in the passenger seat of her car next to Moses. "I bought a liter and a half bottle just in case," she said. With the back of her hand, she swept hair from her face.

"Just in case of what, Mom?"

"Well, just in case we stay a long time, or they're big winos or something." She laughed, and it broke the ice between them.

"So, tell me a little about Sylvana. What's she like? How did you meet her?"

"She's nice. I think you'll like her. She's got a good sense of humor, and she likes a lot of the same stuff I do. I met her in my chemistry class. When we have lab, I get a chance to talk to other kids."

"I was beginning to wonder if you were ever going to start dating."

"Mom! Geez, you don't have to be all weird about it. She's just a friend."

"Oh, Mo, don't be so sensitive. I think it's nice, that's all. If she's 'just a friend,' that's great. And if you want to go out with her, that's fine, too. I'm not ready to buy a wedding dress, you know."

They pulled in front of Sylvana's home, a good-sized Tudor-style house with a three-car garage. Jerome pulled in and parked behind them in a paved guest-parking area. It was exactly 7:00. Jerome jumped out. "Good timing," he said as Moses opened his door and stretched his long legs out of Lacy's car.

Moses saw Sylvana peering out the front window at the sound of the car doors. She quickly ducked back into the house. It appeared she gave a little bounce before disappearing. A moment later, she was opening the front door as the three Lights came up the walk. Moses was afraid she might try to hug him when he got to the door, but she knew instinctively to hold back.

"Uh, Mom, Dad, this is Sylvana. Sylvana, these are my parents."

"Hello, Mr. and Mrs. Light," she said, holding out her hand.

Lacy took her hand and shook it gently. "Hello, Sylvana. How nice to meet you. Thank you for inviting us over."

"Hi, Sylvana," said Jerome, as he also shook her hand. He was already looking beyond her into the house, where jazz music was playing softly. It was clear the Foxes were in a different tax bracket than he was. Sylvana had quickly moved inside, leading the way through a high-ceilinged foyer into a large, warm kitchen. There were two long islands in the kitchen, one with a sink at one end, in addition to the main sink on a counter along the wall. A tall, thin, attractive woman was busy cooking, and the smells of garlic and herbs were tempting.

The woman wiped her hands on her stylish apron adorned with various vegetables and their names in French—"aubergine" and "navet" and others—and came over. "Hello, you must be Jerome and Lacy. I'm Dakota!" she enthused, and shook hands with them both. "Hello, Moses. Nice to see you again."

"Yeah, Mrs. Fox. Nice to see you, too," said Moses.

"Your home is lovely!" said Lacy. "Simply lovely. I love this kitchen. I'd kill to have a kitchen like this. Actually, right now I'd like to have any kitchen!" She laughed at her joke.

"Oh, I know," said Dakota, sympathetically. "I feel awful about your home. If there's anything we can do to help, just ask."

"Well, you're taking in Moses, and that's a big help," she lied.

Had Moses still been in the room, his mother's gushing about the kitchen and her clumsy admission that she is now homeless would have embarrassed him. Fortunately, Moses's attention had been diverted by Sylvana, who was showing him her brother's room, which had a big "Hewitt's Room" sign on its door.

Chapter 15

We're Going to Say Grace

Todd Fox arrived home as everyone was sitting down to eat. Jerome stood up and shook hands with Todd, who was tall, athletic, and handsome, had wavy brown hair, and exuded confidence, success, and friendly charm. Jerome took an immediate dislike to him, particularly to Todd's trying-to-be-understated cologne.

Jerome was uncomfortable around men who led "perfect" lives. Many of these men were genuinely nice people, Jerome thought, but they made him uneasy nevertheless. "Everybody has secrets," he said frequently. He wondered silently, "So, what is Todd Fox's secret? Is he banging his secretary? Does he even have a secretary? Is he gay? Is he insecure? Does he secretly harbor fears that his success is fragile and that it could all be taken away in a month? Did he embezzle funds? Make a payoff? Does he like to wear women's clothing and have Dakota dominate him? Is he dyslexic? Does he snort coke whenever his family is not around? Does he have a really tiny penis, or an abnormal fear of words that start with Q?"

Jerome pondered all these questions in a matter of seconds after meeting Todd. He had no doubt that Todd was sizing him up in pretty much the same way. Then he noted that Todd seemed more interested in looking at Lacy than at him. After shaking Jerome's hand, Todd put his left hand on Lacy's right shoulder and lightly spun her towards him so he could shake her hand.

Smooth, thought Jerome. *I mean, look at his wife. She's tall and gorgeous. And so is he, when you come right down to it. He clearly has an eye for the good-looking ladies, and knows he can always get them to notice him. I hate him for that. No, I don't. I'd do the same thing if I looked like him. And why wouldn't the ladies like him? No wonder he's got it all. I'll bet he's still unhappy anyway. Something is bothering him. Otherwise, why would he be flirting with Lacy like that? Okay, not flirting exactly, but paying attention and checking her out. Why wouldn't he check her out? She's great looking. At least I think so. Look at Lacy's breasts. Okay, don't really look at them, but you know they're there. Now that's a chest to be proud of. Why am I thinking about Lacy's breasts right now?*

Despite this furious, and somewhat disturbing, silent exchange, what Jerome actually said was, "Well, I would say 'It's nice to meet you finally, Todd,' except that until this afternoon, I'd never heard of you or your lovely family."

"Is that right?" said Todd. "Why is that, Moses?" he said, turning his attention to the mortified teenager. "Are we some secret you're trying to keep?"

Moses blushed bright crimson, and Jerome thought, *Of course, Moses has secrets, too.*

But Todd jumped in to save the boy. "I'm kidding you, Moses. The truth is," he said, looking both Lacy and Jerome in the eyes at the same time, "we met Moses about three days ago ourselves. I'm not surprised you didn't hear about us, considering what you are going through."

"That's for sure," said Jerome. "Well, it's a pleasure to meet you both and Sylvana, too. And it's very nice of you to feed the homeless like this." Jerome glanced at his porcelain plate of coq au vin and resisted the temptation to put "air quotes" around the word "homeless." This house seemed too refined for air quotes.

"It's our pleasure having you here," said Dakota.

Todd said, "Yes, it is. We're going to say Grace. I'll ask Sylvana to lead us tonight in honor of her helping a special friend."

Sylvana brought her palms together and folded her fingers. Dakota, Todd, Lacy, and Moses followed suit. Jerome simply rested his palms in his lap and lowered his eyes slightly towards the table. Sylvana said, "Bless us O Lord for this food we are about to receive and for the lives of Moses and his family and for bringing them here to us tonight. Amen."

"That was very nice, Sylvana," said Lacy, smiling at the girl. Jerome smiled as best he could.

"Very nice, Sweetheart," said Dakota. Then she asked the Lights, "Where are you staying now?"

Lacy said, "We're living with my folks right now, over on Aspen Lane."

"Oh, that's right. Sylvana must have heard that from Moses, and I'd forgotten."

"Of course, 'living' there is about all we're doing," said Lacy. "We have almost nothing of our own with us, since just about everything was destroyed by the sinkhole." Suddenly, for Lacy, saying those words together, words she had never uttered before, was starting to feel natural, as if it were merely a casual comment at a tea party: "Oh, yes, my dears, back when that dreadful sinkhole demolished our home . . ."

"Is there enough room for you all at your parents'?" asked Dakota.

Lacy replied, "Yes and no. With Moses over here and his sister Miriam—she's fifteen—staying at her girlfriend's house, I think we're okay for now. But we set up an appointment for tomorrow with a real estate agent, and she's going to show us some apartments. For now, until we know where we stand with the insurance company, we think we're better off renting something."

Todd leaned back from the salad Dakota had placed in front of each of them and said to Lacy, "What do you mean 'where you stand with the insurance company'?"

Jerome picked up the beat. "It looks like they aren't going to pay for much. They say the sinkhole was an Act of God, and we're not covered for that."

"I'm sure you're not too happy about that," said Todd, matter-of-factly. "Still, from what I know of insurance, I guess I should have known that's what they'd say. What will you do now?"

Lacy could see where this might all lead, so she jumped in before Jerome could say anything that might prove awkward. "We're not sure. Our attorney is looking into our options."

"Who's your attorney, if you don't mind my asking?" said Todd.

"We met with Sumner Stoke this morning. Do you know him?" asked Lacy.

Todd looked as if he were trying hard to remember every attorney he had ever encountered, perhaps so Jerome would think he actually knows that many.

† † †

"No, I'm afraid not," said Dr. Clements to Gideon. "I doubt that Celeste will be able to return to work for several weeks, if not months. I understand she works for you, Reverend, is that right?"

"Yes. She's my executive assistant, and it will be hard to get by without her."

"We'll do our best to get her back in good health, but we are probably looking at up to six months of rehab. It would be unwise—and probably impossible—for her to sit at a desk and work multiple hours until she makes a great deal of progress. The good news is that we believe she will make an almost full recovery, without surgery. Her injuries should all heal in six to eight weeks, and then her physical therapy will kick into high gear, strengthening muscles and restoring her sense of balance. She'll probably walk with a cane for a while until she gains more confidence. The other aspect is psychological. She's likely to find the next few months difficult emotionally. I'm sure she will look to you for spiritual guidance, and we think she also needs a psychiatrist who is experienced in patients with Celeste's kind of injuries. He will manage her pain and other control medications."

"Yes, of course. That makes a good deal of sense," said Gideon.

The doctor continued, "She has spoken to me about her feelings towards you."

Gideon tensed up inside, and tried hard not to show it. "Really?"

"She said that she has been a fan of your program for many years, and that going to work for you was her dream come true. She really looks up to you, Reverend."

"That's . . . kind of you to say, Doctor, but I assure you there's nothing between us."

"Oh, that's not what I meant at all," replied the doctor. "I mean I believe your presence has a very calming effect on Celeste, and that's a good thing. Her faith is extremely important to her, and she sees you as her spiritual guide. I think you'll do her a world of good whenever you visit."

Gideon, who was rarely flustered in public, was put off his usual game. He stammered for the first time in God-knows-how-long. When he was able to speak clearly, he said, "It's my intention to visit Ms. Fallow as frequently as my duties will allow. I'm glad to know I can be some help."

"Absolutely."

"And I want to thank you for the great care you've given her. I have prayed that she would have someone like you to help heal her. I'm confident that you did a great job and that she will get better. That's a great comfort to me. Thank you, too, for telling me honestly what her situation is. I'll make plans to cover for her at the church office for several months."

"That would be best," said the doctor.

Chapter 16

And the Evening and the Morning Were the Fourth Day

The next morning, Lacy woke up and, for a moment, was not sure where she was. She had expected to wake in her own room in her own house, and it took her several seconds to remember that was not possible. She was, once again, in her parents' house, in her other "own room," the same one in which she had lived years earlier. It was still painted the same shade of lavender she had so proudly chosen at age fourteen. She remembered the room as being much bigger. The next thing she remembered was that Moses had stayed at the Foxes' house, and that added to the air of strangeness that enveloped her. She checked the clock. "My goodness, it's eight o'clock!" she called to no one, then immediately shook Jerome and repeated her revelation.

"I guess we both needed some extra sleep, eh?" said Jerome. He swung his feet out of bed and rested his elbows on his knees as he rubbed his face with both hands.

"Yeah, but we have to be at Stoke's office in thirty minutes!"

"Oh, damn, that's right!" said Jerome, suddenly wide awake and seemingly trying to move his body in two directions at the same time, which resulted in him losing his balance and sitting back down on the bed. "We can skip breakfast and get something afterwards. Let's get dressed and go."

The two flew around the room. Fortunately, they had few wardrobe choices to make. Jerome grabbed the razor he had borrowed from his father-in-law, and scratched away the most obvious whiskers. In ten minutes, they were both ready, went downstairs, told Darcy that they had to run to a meeting and that they'd be back later, and ran out the front door to their car at the end of the driveway. A light rain was falling.

At 8:30 sharp, they entered Sumner Stoke's office. He was already there and ready for them. He showed them into a small windowless conference room with six chairs around an oval table and a photo of the Eiffel Tower irrelevantly displayed on one wall.

Stoke shook hands with Jerome and Lacy and motioned for them to sit. As he took his own seat, he shoved a pile of paper in their direction. "I've prepared a contract for me to represent you against Big Rock Mountain Mutual. I will need a $1,300 retainer from you. I should be able to do everything you need and deliver our appeal to Big Rock Mountain by close of business tomorrow. After that, you have no further commitment to me. If you want to proceed against them after that time, then we'll need another contract. Right now, it's a pretty simple and straightforward appeal and, as I said, it won't be too expensive. If they turn us down, though, any appeal could get expensive in a hurry, and I doubt that it would be successful." Stoke looked rather pleased with himself. He had pulled things together quickly for the Lights, and that was not his typical method. He liked the high profile of their situation, though, and he hoped he might get some great publicity out of representing them. He knew already that they had a Popsicle's chance in summer of winning.

Jerome had an inspired idea. "Are you saying they can refuse our appeal, turn us down, and win?"

"I'm afraid so. That's exactly what I'm saying."

"Because they're allowed to exempt acts of God, and our sinkhole was an Act of God?"

"Right. That's the precedent I found."

"Okay. So, they can officially blame our loss on God, right?" asked Jerome, clearly leading somewhere.

Sumner now knew he was being pulled in some direction, but could not yet see where it was. "Right," he said, a bit more slowly.

"So, why can't we do the same thing?" asked Jerome, as if this were the most logical conclusion.

"I don't follow you," said Stoke.

"Why can't we blame God?"

"But that's exactly what Big Rock Mountain wants you to do. You blame God, they blame God, they refuse to pay, and you go away. If that's your big plan, save your thousand dollars and don't sign the contract."

"No, I want to sign it and make them officially blame God."

"Again," said Stoke, "I don't get what you mean." He sniffed up his nose.

"Don't you see?" said Jerome, with unexpected conviction. Lacy stared at him the way a dog might look at a duck for the first time. "Once they are officially allowed to blame God, then *we* blame God, and we go after God. But there is no God, so when we announce that we want to sue God, and the government officially tells us that we CAN'T sue God because they can't serve papers on God, then we can say, 'AHA! See? Even the government says there is no God!' And then we can go after the insurance company again and win."

Stoke paused and looked astonished. He had the same look as a holiday traveler who has been told that all the flights out have been cancelled and there are no hotel rooms left near the airport. Then he said, "You're nuts, you know that? That is the most bizarre idea I've ever heard."

"Thank you," said Jerome.

Even Lacy, who thought she could anticipate nearly everything Jerome might say, was in shock. A couple of times she looked as if she might say something, but failed to speak.

"On the other hand," Stoke continued, "some of the most surprising legal victories have been won on the backs of some rather unusual arguments, so who's to say it wouldn't work? As your lawyer, however, I have to advise you that this strategy is highly risky and unorthodox, and may get thrown out of court before we even go to trial."

"But you'll do it?" asked Jerome.

"I don't know. I'll have to think about it. I guess the first step is to file the appeal with Big Rock Mountain and see what happens. So, I'll need that $1,300 from you to get started."

Lacy had the new checkbook, and got it out of her purse. She wrote the check to Stoke, twice glancing over at Jerome with a slightly astonished look. Stoke, meanwhile, passed the contract for legal services to Jerome, who signed it quickly and gave it to Lacy to sign as soon as she'd torn the check from her book.

Stoke said, "All right, Mr. and Mrs. Light, I'll get back to you towards the end of the week and let you know where we stand." They all stood up, shook hands again, and Jerome and Lacy left the office.

As they walked to the car, Lacy said, "You don't really think that's going to work, do you?"

"No, I suppose not," said Jerome, "but I can't let them off the hook that easily. This 'Act of God' thing really has me going nuts, you know."

"But we can't afford to fight and lose. It could deplete our savings, and then we'll really be up the creek."

"Let's see what Stoke says after Big Rock Mountain reviews the appeal," Jerome said, as they got into the car and drove back to George and Darcy's house for a late breakfast and to get ready for their appointment with the real estate agent.

† † †

Gideon Calhoun had already arrived at his church office. Although his staff was busy in the outer offices, it felt empty to him without Celeste right outside his private office. He called his personnel director into his office.

"Stephanie, I spoke with Celeste's doctor yesterday. It's going to be quite a while before Celeste can return to work. Can you find me a temp who can be my assistant for the next few months?"

"I'm sure I can," the proper woman replied. "In fact, I was going to suggest that we pay one of our volunteers to fill Celeste's spot. I have someone in mind who's really dedicated. She wouldn't want a permanent job anyway. You know, there are literally hundreds of people who would jump at the chance to be your executive assistant, even for a day a week. This opening could be a major public-relations coup for you."

"I suppose that's all right, but I don't want to look at Ms. Fallow's suffering as an opportunity for public relations. She's in a great deal of pain."

Stephanie hastened to say, "Of . . . of course, Reverend, I understand. I'm sorry if I seemed insensitive. I'm praying every minute for her recovery."

Gideon looked directly at the personnel director, his face a tableau of sincerity. "Also, I want just one assistant. I hope you're not thinking of having two or three people split the job. The job is important; it needs a professional."

Stephanie, like everyone else on the staff—and absolutely all the volunteers—always called Gideon "Reverend" or "Reverend Calhoun." He had never been sure what to make of that. Part of him desperately wanted to say, "Call me Gideon," but another part—the professional minister trying to run a thriving religious community—knew he could not ignore the business aspects of his decisions. Good business, he knew, depended on a certain level of self-discipline that could be maintained only if some distance remained between him and the people he paid or involved in his ministry as volunteers.

And so, he let them all call him "Reverend." He could not quite remember how strange it had felt the first time a stranger called him that in earnest, and not in the teasing way his siblings had used the honorific right after he finished divinity school. Still, it was a title he had craved since he was young, perhaps eight or nine years old. He recalled how he had adored and respected the pastor at his parents' church, and how there seemed to be no finer job in the world than to be that minister. Little Gideon—Deon as his parents had called him—used to pretend for his parents that he was "Reverend Bombardier." (He didn't know anyone with that name, and had no idea what it meant, but thought it made a great name). At age nine, he would pretend the dining room table was an altar, and he would stand behind it as his parents watched from the other side. He would go through the rituals and the elements of a traditional service.

It was amusing to Gideon's parents, but also concerning, because young Gideon spent most of his church time in the Sunday School, not in the main service. He seemed to have gotten the hang of the minister's "act" from a few observations. His parents would talk, when he was asleep, about how Deon seemed to have a gift for preaching, maybe even a calling from God. Once, when he had trouble sleeping in their small, one-floor house, he heard his father remark on "Deon's gift," and it served only to enhance his conviction for his life's work.

Now he had been on his own as a minister for more than thirty years! How hard that was to comprehend. Where had that time gone? It seemed that the last few years, he was sleepwalking through the motions he had rehearsed and learned so well. Nothing new was ever demanded of him. Far from it; his "flock" of parishioners and TV audience members wanted and expected the same experience, the same rhythm, and the same words week after week. Rarely did he feel compelled to write a sermon that dealt with anything newer than two thousand years ago. He longed to break out of that mold, to say something new and topical. Yet whenever he tried, his flock complained. They wanted old-time gospel; they wanted to remember the Savior at the center of their faith; they wanted predictability and joy. They did not want hellfire and brimstone, unless it was directed at "damn liberals." Gideon had decided early in his career that he was not going to become political. Why alienate people who more than anyone needed God, who needed Jesus? He had proven that one could be theologically conservative and still be politically liberal or neutral.

"I thank you humbly for your prayers, Sister Stephanie. Soon we will have thousands of people across the country praying for Sister Celeste. I will ask for their prayers on Sunday."

Chapter 17

Fidgeting

At one time, "The Gideon Calhoun Hour" had become a daily program, but that ended after five years. It was not that it had waned in popularity; in reality, it had grown. But Gideon was worn out, and had no time to pursue the other aspects of ministry that called to him.

He knew some other televangelists got around this problem by taping all of their shows together on a single day, and then showing them days or weeks later, except on the big holidays, such as Good Friday, Easter and Christmas. Gideon wanted no part of that. He called them "God Mills," churning out God like a commodity. He had the disillusioning misfortune to have gotten to know some of his fellow evangelists rather well at National Religious Broadcasters conventions, where he had once delivered the Keynote Address. It was disillusioning because he learned that some of them were precisely what the anti-Christian Liberals thought they were: charlatans—cynical hacks simply milking a cash cow. Gideon thought they gave televangelism a bad name, and he had no wish to emulate them.

So, Gideon had voluntarily reduced his program to once a week on Sunday mornings, because he felt that was the most holy time of the week, the time that God wanted set aside for spiritual thoughts and healing. He admired any group, such as the Amish or even Muslims, who managed to keep one day of the week as holy, who did not work except in emergencies. They understood that God wanted people to take that day, as He had done, and renew both their bodies and minds. Gideon believed that people are stronger, better prepared to serve the Lord, if they take one day a week to cleanse themselves, to think of God with little interruption, to be well-rested. The Bible should have said what God did on the Eighth Day, for people would then see that the day after the Sabbath is a magnificent day, full of promise and new vigor, if you have kept the Sabbath.

Stephanie left his office to recruit people to serve as Celeste's temporary replacement. She'd reach out first to her current volunteers; she was sure that many of them could desperately use some extra income. Stephanie knew she would have far more candidates than she could ever use, so she decided to interview them and take the first three who seemed qualified. Two of them could split the duties of the week, and the other one would be "on call." The personnel director had learned that it's good to have backups when you're dealing with temps and volunteers, even when they are highly motivated.

What Stephanie did not say to Reverend Calhoun is that she doubted Celeste would ever return to work.

Gideon sat down to look over the pile of mail that was too big by far. Normally, Celeste would have intercepted the mail and weeded out a few items that needed Gideon's personal attention. Most of the mail was sorted first in the mailroom. The Church of the Forgotten Savior received well over 1,200 pieces of mail a week, much of it something like fan mail for the great Reverend Calhoun. These pieces, he rarely saw. He would receive a monthly tally of how many positive and negative comments he got, if they fit the usual pattern of such letters. That included statements like:

Dear Rev. Calhoun:

I watch your show every week, and I think you are the greatest living American.

or

Dear Reverend Calhoun,

God Bless You for healing my sister's hip. She sent you a letter last month asking you to pray for her recovery, and you answered back to say you were praying for her, and now she is able to walk around like she was 30 years old again.

or

Dear Nutcase—

You are the scum of the earth, you charlatan. I hate self-righteous people like you, and I hope you rot in Hell.

Yours Truly,

These letters were easily categorized and recorded. Then a pre-selected response letter was generated. Gideon was proud that he had written over twenty-five different types of form letters, so that the response seemed a little less impersonal, and in the last few years, his IT staff had programmed a system so that people who wrote frequently never got the same letter back twice in a row, or even two out of three times. He knew that if his parishioners—especially the TV viewers—got the same letter repeatedly, they would stop writing, and eventually stop watching. For Gideon, though, his intent was not to fool anyone; he believed they deserved to feel special, to feel that their letter had truly been read and acted upon. Of course, he did not mention that he personally did not read most of their letters, but at least he had written the reply they got with his computer-generated signature on it. That seemed honest enough for him.

Celeste would then receive the mail that seemed to the sharp and dedicated minds in the mailroom to be extraordinary in some way. No one who knew Gideon personally ever wrote or emailed him in care of the CFS, because they knew it was unlikely their letter would get through. Most of them, in the past few years, had taken to using his private email address: gccalhoun817@gmail.com. The first "c" stood for his middle name, Calvin. So far as he was aware, no one outside his family or close friends knew this address.

The other common letter received in the mailroom was a request for a prayer. A few years ago, viewers could request a "Prayer Pak" over the phone. It contained a half-dozen prepaid postcards that were addressed to the Church, located in Stonecrest, Arkansas, on one side, and had a multiple-choice table on the other side, where the viewer would indicate specifically the type of prayer they desired. The Prayer Paks were still around, but more and more prayer requests were now received at the CFS web site. This fact pleased Gideon to no end, because it meant that his audience was not comprised solely of elderly people left behind by the Computer Age. Instead, his demographics showed that he was able to attract a wide range of ages. He figured that was the key to his longevity.

Gideon fidgeted at his desk. It was an uncomfortable feeling knowing that there was no one in the outer office. Celeste had started a few days before the retirement of Carrie, his assistant for fifteen years. There had always been someone out there before.

At another desk, far away in the Foxes' house in Marshfield, Ohio, sat another fidgety fellow. Moses had only two more days of his junior year. His thoughts were already turning to summer . . . and Sylvana.

His first night at Sylvana Fox's house had been one of fragile and pleasurable disappointment. After his parents left following dinner, he and Sylvana "studied" together in the den. Todd Fox went to his home office and stayed there until nearly bedtime. Dakota Fox was busy reading in the living room, which doubled as a conservatory. It was an unusually large room, one end of which housed a grand piano and several chairs set up as if for a string quartet, complete with music stands. The other end was the sitting area, with a Louis XIV-style sofa in the center, and a half-dozen similar side chairs forming a semicircle, a kind of audience for the music. Dakota loved to sit and read in this elegant setting.

Moses had been acutely aware of his strange surroundings as he tried to study for his chemistry final. It seemed unbelievable to him that he was there. He even thought of it as "there" as opposed to "here." On the one hand, he was thrilled to be sitting alone in the same room with Sylvana, and kept stealing glances at her, most of which she caught without letting on. On the other hand, he was scared to death of what he might be called upon to do. It is harder to be a good boyfriend in private than it is in a crowd of people. The pressure is greater, the terrain less familiar. Although he wanted to kiss and hold Sylvana, he was glad for all the obvious reasons not to do so. Part of him hoped she would make the first move, but most of him was terrified that she would.

So, nothing happened. They studied for a while, then Sylvana talked about one of her girlfriends at school, and how she had completely blown her English final. She asked if Moses wanted to watch some TV to relax. They turned on a sitcom and Moses moved over and sat next to Sylvana. He was nearly paralyzed with fear the entire time, which made laughing at the TV impossible for him, leaving Sylvana to laugh for the two of them. At one point, when she was particularly amused, she leaned over and bumped his right shoulder with her left, and smiled at him. His heart dripped with honey. Luckily for him, she straightened right up again and resumed watching the show. His body slowly returned to this galaxy, and he was finally able to pay attention moments before the show ended.

"That was great, don't you think?" asked Sylvana, as Moses got up and went back to his original "study" chair. "I used to watch that show all the time when I was about twelve. I loved it then, but I hardly ever watch it anymore."

"Oh, yeah, my sister loves it, too."

Sylvana pouted slightly. "I think it's so sad that you and your sister and your parents have to split up. Do you miss her?"

Moses wondered, "Is there a right answer to this question? If I miss Miriam too much, I'll look like a weirdo, and if I don't miss her at all, Sylvana will think I'm insensitive!" He paused before he spoke.

"Hunh. I guess I hadn't thought about it. But yeah, I miss her a lot. We fight sometimes, but she's a good kid. I mean, maybe this is what it'll be like when we're grown up and married and, like, only visit each other once in a while. But we'll always be close, you know?"

Sylvana looked pleased. "My parents are always talking about how families have unconditional love, and that seems like such a cool concept: unconditional love. Like, someone loves you no matter what you do? And you know you'll always be close to them, no matter what."

"Yeah, that is cool," said Moses, in a voice that would not completely convince anyone that he meant it. Oddly, though, he did mean it. Moses did not yet realize that he was, at heart, a romantic, and would remain so the rest of his life, later learning to be more comfortable in that skin. But at that moment, in Sylvana's den, he was anything but comfortable.

Dakota Fox appeared at the doorway to the den. "Time for bed, I think. Finals tomorrow, so no horsing around."

Moses blushed. What did she mean by "horsing around?" Mrs. Fox must have noticed he was flustered, so she added, "I mean, you need to get your sleep. Moses, we serve breakfast at 6:45, okay?"

"Okay, Mrs. Fox. I figured out how to use Hewitt's alarm clock, and I'll be dressed in plenty of time." That is what he said, but what he thought was, *You* **serve** *breakfast in this house? Is this like a palace?*

"There are towels on the foot of your bed, and you can use the shower at the end of the hall. Sylvana has her own shower," said the mother.

The image of Princess Sylvana in the shower was more than Moses could bear. He had been studiously trying to avoid any such thoughts all evening, and now here was Mrs. Fox, for cryin' out loud, throwing that naughty and delicious picture right at him. He knew the words were meant innocently enough, but the more he tried to convince himself of that, the more terrified he became of noticeable stiffening in his groin. And the more he tried to suppress it, the more he thought of the reason for it.

Both women, of course, thought that his agony was adorable. Both of them more or less guessed at the source of his fidgetiness, and they were completely incapable of stifling mischievous smiles.

And now, here at the Chemistry final the next afternoon, Moses again felt fidgety. He had been a perfect gentleman after what he would later call "the erection debacle," and he had gone to bed quickly and respectfully. He neither kissed nor even touched mother or daughter on his way upstairs, though he did say a sweet "Goodnight."

"Mr. Light, would you please try to sit still!" the Chemistry teacher growled. That only sent him into a brief but even more violent flurry of fidgeting until, exactly three seconds later, he composed himself and sat unnaturally still.

Chapter 18

We're All at God's Mercy

So, you found something?" said George Day to his daughter Lacy.

"Yep. We can move in this weekend, and we only had to sign a six-month lease. It's not as quiet as Tadpole Lane, but it's in good shape, and it's got central air, although it's unfurnished."

"And it has three bedrooms?" asked Darcy.

"Of course, Mom," said Lacy, as if this question were insulting in some way.

"Okay, I'm sorry I asked!" Darcy retorted. "So, where is this apartment? Or is it a house?"

"It's back behind the Double Dee Foods store, just off Sycamore. And yes, it's an apartment. That seems like the best thing to do for now. We need to get our feet planted somewhere for a little while, while we figure out what we're doing. Moses needs a stable home during his first semester of senior year. Then we can consider buying something in November or December to move in after Christmas. Houses are usually cheaper then, so we might get a real bargain."

Darcy nodded almost imperceptibly, and then said, "Speaking of Moses, how did it go for him at that girlfriend's house? Not that I approve of that, by the way, but he's your son."

Lacy replied with a sarcastic tone, "Well, thank you for letting us make the decision, Mom!" She paused precisely one second before she said, "I'm kidding! I know you don't approve, and I'm not crazy about it either, but—"

"We're all at God's mercy," Gideon said the next day to Janet, when the receptionist informed him that Celeste had been moved to a new room. Gideon usually spent the first half of each Thursday at Mercy Hospital, visiting those patients who had specifically requested him or named him as their clergy. He would also visit anyone the hospital staff told him he might be able to help, even if the patient had not named Gideon or the Church of the Forgotten Savior directly. Many patients were treated as celebrities when they returned home, blessed by having sat and talked with the great evangelist.

Celeste Fallow was in physical therapy when he arrived to see her. He had deliberately not gone to her room first. He quickly recharted in his mind his course through the various wards to ensure that he could easily flow back to Celeste's room in an hour or so.

When at last he saw her, she was sitting up in a wheelchair in her room. A religious program was playing quietly on TV. She looked a bit forlorn, but otherwise clearly improved from his last visit. As he got closer to her, he realized she was not despondent, but merely sitting with her eyes closed, resting if not sleeping.

"Celeste?" he said quietly in his baritone voice. He gently placed a hand on her shoulder. She opened her eyes sleepily, needing a moment to calculate her surroundings, which seemed to change every time she woke up. Then she became aware of Gideon's body to her side. "Celeste?" he repeated. "It's Reverend Calhoun."

"Oh, my! So it is." Her voice showed greater enthusiasm with each word. "I can't completely turn my head to look at you, Reverend." As if to demonstrate that were true, she tried pushing the middle of her face to one side, but it kept bobbing back as if it were hitting a foam-rubber wall.

Gideon moved around to her front so she would not have to employ such acrobatics. He wanted to cheer her up and cheer her on. "But that's wonderful, my dear," he said. "Before today, you couldn't turn your head to the side at all. Look at all the improvement you're making!"

"I'm sure you're right," she said demurely. "Perhaps I just can't see it yet. And I am on some wonderful pain medicines, you know."

"Yes, I know," he smiled. It was her first lighthearted comment. "How did your physical therapy go today?"

Celeste had to think about it, to make sure it was today and not some other torture to which she had been obliged. "I think it went very well, but I guess you'd better ask the doctor or someone, because I can't remember what we did. I seem to remember standing, though. Unless that was a dream. I am on some really wonderful pain medicines, you know? I kind of like the way I feel right now."

"I can see that, Celeste," and he laughed with her for the first time. Hers was the kind of laughter that betrays its creator as failing to understand what is so damned funny. "I believe it's a good sign that you are able to feel so well, despite your injuries."

"What did I hurt, exactly?" she asked.

Her question was so unexpected, that he groped briefly for the "right" answer. Then he said, "You hurt your neck, mostly, sort of like a severe whiplash. You were quite lucky that you didn't break your neck, but you did break some ribs, unfortunately, and one bone in your left leg."

"Was I in a car accident?"

Gideon was less surprised this time. "Yes, Celeste, your car was hit. It was not your fault. It was a young man who had been drinking. He ran a red light."

"Oh, that poor young man," said Celeste, earnestly concerned for his well-being. "Was he arrested?"

"I believe he was, yes. He is quite relieved to know that you are going to be all right."

"Will I be? Is that what the doctors say?"

"Yes. Haven't they spoken to you about it?"

Celeste furrowed her brow slightly. "I suppose they have, but I can't seem to separate what I hear in dreams from what I hear from a real person. This isn't a dream now, is it?"

Gideon looked at her seriously for a moment to make sure she was not toying with him. Then he burst out laughing. "Oh, Celeste, how will you ever be sure? If I tell you it's a dream, then it probably is a dream. But if I tell you it's not, then I could be lying to you in your dream!"

Celeste, of course, could not follow this reasoning at all. "So what is it?" she asked.

"No, Celeste, it's not a dream. I am really here with you, and you are awake now."

"This nightmare keeps getting worse," said Jerome to Lacy as they entered the Days' house. "We can't afford all new furniture."

George said, "How did things go for you two today? What'd you get done?"

"Mostly we made arrangements for furniture for the apartment, Dad," answered Lacy. "We're going to rent-to-buy for now, we decided. They'll let us put some money towards buying either this stuff or something else once we know what size and style we're going to need."

"That sounds good," said George.

"Yeah, and they'll deliver it Saturday morning, so we'll have to spend the day over there, moving in, so to speak," said Jerome.

Lacy added, "We'll spend tomorrow picking up odds and ends we're going to need. The Red Cross called earlier and said they have some donated items we can look through. Pots and pans and silverware, that sort of thing."

Chapter 19

No One

Thursday night, Sylvana and Moses sat together in the Foxes' den after dinner. Todd planned to work late and then exercise at the gym. Dakota would go to a club meeting after fixing dinner and eating with the kids. Moses had been uncomfortable with only the three of them at the fancy dining room table, but he had made pleasant, if strained, conversation. Most of it revolved around plans for Friday night after the last day of school.

Moses realized that he had not even thought about his sister for a couple of days, and, much to his surprise, that he missed her. "I'm going to call Miriam, okay?" he asked Sylvana.

"Your sister?"

"Yeah, I miss her, you know. I'm used to seeing her almost every day."

"What about your parents?" asked Mrs. Fox. "Shouldn't you call them, too?"

"Oh, yeah, I forgot to tell you that they called my cell phone before. My dad's mother fell and injured her hip, but it looks like she's gonna be okay. I should've told you."

"That's okay, Moses. I think you're a little distracted." Sylvana giggled.

When dinner ended, Moses went to call Miriam while Sylvana did the dishes and Dakota got ready to go out.

"Hey, Sis, what's up?" he asked when Miriam finally came to the phone at the Polskys' house.

"I want to go home!"

"Aw, Mir."

"I want to go home now, back to our house, the way it was."

"Are things okay with you and Jessica?"

"Yeah, they're fine," said Miriam. "She's being extra nice to me, and her Mom is, like, Supermom or something. I just want *our* house again. I don't want to live in some stupid apartment."

"Me, neither, but it is what it is, you know? Some things you have to accept, like I have to accept that I'll never know who my birth parents are. I didn't want to be an abandoned baby, but maybe it turned out better for me than if my birth parents kept me. Maybe I wouldn't even be alive now. So, we have to accept what happened and move on."

"Do you believe in God, Moses?" asked Miriam.

"What?"

"I heard on the news. Channel 10 said that our house getting destroyed was an Act of God. What does that mean?"

"Yeah, Mom and Dad told me. That's what the insurance company calls it when they don't have to pay you."

"Moses, don't tell anyone else, but I don't even know what insurance companies do exactly. Why would they have to pay us anyway?"

"Well, see, it's kind of like gambling. Mom and Dad pay the insurance company money when nothing is wrong. And then, if something goes wrong, the insurance company pays it back to them."

Miriam paused, and then said, "That's stupid. Why don't Mom and Dad just keep the money in the first place?"

"It's like the insurance on the car, see? When I started driving, the insurance company charged Mom and Dad more to insure the car, because sixteen-year-olds are more likely to have an accident. So, if I do have an accident, maybe it will cost $10,000 to fix the car and pay for the doctors. But Mom and Dad maybe only paid $5,000, so then the insurance company gives them a lot more back."

"Who'd want to have a business like that? That's so stupid."

"I don't want to talk about insurance. That doesn't have anything to do with you and me, Mir, except Mom and Dad might not have enough money to buy a new house."

"Why not? They don't have to pay any money for the old house, do they?"

"Well, yeah. They, like, have to pay the mortgage on the old house."

"The organ?"

"No, the mortgage. The mortgage. That's how you buy a house. If a house costs $200,000, most people don't have that much, so they borrow money from a bank and it's called a mortgage. It just means 'loan.' And Mom and Dad had a big loan on the house that they still have to pay."

"So they have to pay for a house that doesn't exist anymore?"

"Yeah, 'cause it's not the bank's fault that the house was swallowed."

"But it's not our fault, either, is it?" Miriam was becoming more upset and more exasperated.

"No, Mir. It's an Act of God, which means it's nobody's fault. God did it, and so the only ones who get screwed are Mom and Dad."

"So, you think God is screwing Mom and Dad?"

"That's not what I said."

"Do you believe in God, Moses?"

"Yeah! Well, I don't know. Maybe. Right now, I don't know. It seems like God wouldn't do something like that, pick out one family and hurt them. Maybe 'Act of God' doesn't really mean that God did it, but just that no one did it."

"So, God is no one?"

"I don't know, Sis. Why are you asking me?"

Chapter 20

Gentlemen, Start Your Engines

Gideon was restless as he met with his TV team, including his producer, floor manager, two writers, the choir director, and the program director. They met every Thursday afternoon to go over the plans for the coming Sunday services that would be taped, edited, and distributed as *The Gideon Calhoun Hour.*

"So, what do you think, Gideon?" asked Eliat Barnard, the show's producer.

Gideon straightened up in his chair as he heard his name. "I'm sorry. What?"

"Did you hear what I was saying about the Bible reading?"

"No, I was, uh, thinking about something else. I'm sorry. What is it you want to know?"

"For one thing," said Eliat, "why are you so distracted tonight? I don't think you've said ten words so far. Is something wrong?"

"No, nothing's . . . well, yes, I guess there's one thing bothering me. It's Celeste."

"Who?"

"Celeste Fallow, my executive assistant."

"Oh, right," said Eliat, who had been with Gideon from the first broadcast. "She was in an accident, wasn't she? How's she doing?"

"Well, I'm quite worried about her, actually. She was injured very badly, and I doubt she will be able to return to work anytime soon."

"That's a shame. We should take a minute and pray for her recovery," said Eliat.

Gideon looked around the table at the faces of the team, but said nothing before bowing his head.

Later, after the meeting and after everyone else had left, Eliat approached Gideon. "What's going on, Gideon? I've never seen you so distracted. Is it Celeste, or something else?" Eliat was the only CFS employee who did not call him Reverend or Brother Gideon. Gideon did not call him Brother Eliat.

"I have a headache, that's all."

"Really? I didn't see you rubbing your head or anything. I've known you over twenty-five years, Gideon. You're not yourself tonight."

Gideon looked aside, his eyes playing back and forth as if searching the room for an answer. Finally, he looked at Eliat. "No, you're right, of course. I'm upset about Celeste. She was working out so well, and I need a good assistant."

"Why not get Carrie back until Celeste recovers?"

"Stephanie has already started interviewing people. Besides, I'm not sure Carrie wants to come back after what happened."

"But that's not really what's bothering you, is it?"

"No."

They were both silent for a moment, then Eliat asked, "So, what is it? Something serious?"

"In a manner of speaking. I don't really want Celeste to come back, at least not as my assistant."

"Why? I thought you said she was working out well."

"Too well. I can't ask her out on a date if she works for me."

☼ ☼ ☼

"What was that all about?" asked Sylvana when Moses got off the phone.

"Miriam is upset, that's all. She wants our old house back."

"What were you saying to her about acts of God?"

"I guess she heard someone on TV talking about our house. They said it was an Act of God that destroyed it, and Miriam thinks they're saying God destroyed our house."

"Well, didn't He?"

"Didn't who do what?" said Dakota, putting on an earring as she entered the room.

"Oh, it's nothing, Mom," said Sylvana as she squirmed in her peculiar way that always told Dakota she was hedging.

Dakota instinctively turned and looked at Moses, who wilted under the pressure. "It was my sister, Mrs. Fox—"

"That's Ms. Fox, Moses," she interrupted.

". . . Ms. Fox. We were talking about the insurance on our house."

"Isn't that an unusual thing for a young girl to talk about? Is this because of that 'Act of God' thing that your father mentioned at dinner?"

"Yes, Ma'am, I guess it is."

"I suppose if a sinkhole isn't an Act of God, then nothing is, but I certainly hope your insurance company helps you out."

"Thank you, Mrs. . . . Ms. Fox. We'll be all right. My sister's a worrier, that's all."

"I'm going out now, you two. I should be home about 9:30, 10:00 at the latest. Please be on your best behavior, Sylvana."

"*M o o b b . . . m*!!!"

"I'll see you later." And Dakota scurried out the door to the garage.

"Oh, thank God she's gone," said Sylvana. "Do you believe her?"

"I like your Mom," answered Moses.

"All the men like her 'cause she's gorgeous, in case you didn't notice."

"Hey, I don't look at your Mom like that."

"Do you look at me like that?"

Moses figured there was no right answer to that question. He didn't like where this was headed.

Sylvana did not let up. "Well?"

Moses might someday feel less comfortable than he did right then, but he could not imagine it. "I like the way you look. I don't know how I'm supposed to look at you 'like that'."

It was a good answer, maybe even a perfect answer, and it made Sylvana like him even more. He probably could have recited verses from the Koran or played "Dixie" on a kazoo at that point, and it would have made her like him more.

"Come on, you!" she said. She took Moses by the hand and led him to the sofa in the den, ostensibly so they could watch TV. "Let's watch something fun," she told him. "And since we don't have any homework for our last day, we can veg out!"

Moses sank into the comfortable leather sofa, and Sylvana sat to his right, her leg not quite touching his. She reached for the remote and turned everything on. Expertly, she switched the channel to an entertainment-news program. "Do you mind watching this show?" she asked.

"No, that's fine," Moses answered.

She slipped her left hand under his right wrist and intertwined her fingers with his. His pulse raced, and he stared straight ahead at the show, but he did not withdraw his hand. A minute later, Sylvana leaned her weight into him, and put her head on his shoulder, which wasn't easy, given his height. He felt like his heart had won the pole position at the Indy 500.

After a couple of minutes at most, Moses could feel his palm becoming a little sweaty. He unlaced his fingers from Sylvana's, and pulled his arm back slightly. He then realized two things: 1) he needed to wipe off his palm; and 2) if he did not immediately reciprocate her signal of affection, he could be in deep trouble. So, he deftly pulled his hand back along his right side, surreptitiously wiped his palm on his upper thigh, and then brought the now-dry hand around her shoulders. His heart took off racing.

He knew immediately he had done the right thing. She leaned into him a bit more and gave a slight but audible sigh. A moment later, she tilted her head back, still touching his shoulder, which had the highly desirable effect of bringing her chin close to his. Moses swallowed hard, wondering why, in these situations, one's hands get moist while one's mouth gets dry. He pressed his lips together, trying to wet them without making his tongue visible.

As he opened his lips to breathe, Sylvana's lips arrived. She put her right arm around him and leaned into him. He closed his eyes, and . . . there it was! The green flag is out! This race is on!

Moses had dreamed of this moment for days, and now he was flabbergasted at how accurately he had fantasized. There was his right arm following her around and pulling her into him, his head bending to get a better angle on the kiss. There was her hand rubbing his left cheek and settling on his neck, her fingers dancing around the back.

If the two lovers had exchanged words at this moment, they would have realized that he saw the entire tableau in terms of a racecar metaphor, and she saw it in terms of a pas de deux. The metaphorical difference did not deter either teenager from advancing. Moses leaned hard into the turns while Sylvana began the adagio.

Tongues began to flicker, hands began to roam, and skin began to tingle as they explored. It was absolutely thrilling! Nothing else existed for either of them at that moment but that kiss, that wonderful, checkered-flag, high-leaping kiss. Neither of them would ever be the same.

Without breaking the kiss, Sylvana muted the TV so they could hear the garage door open. When, much later, it finally did, they were both dressed and sitting in different chairs with the sound back on.

The next morning, as Sylvana and Moses entered the high school for their last day as juniors, Jerome and Lacy drove to the local Red Cross office and received three boxes of basic supplies, including a set of vintage dishes, a few mugs and assorted drinking glasses, kitchen utensils, a couple of saucepans, blankets, and a basic first-aid kit. They were allowed to drop off these boxes at the apartment building, where they met the landlord again and were told that he had managed to get two painters to come in for that entire day to fix up the place. The painters, apparently, were impressed that they were doing something to help the family whose home was demolished by a sinkhole. The younger one, who was probably about thirty-five but looked more like fifty-five, said, "Dude, I saw these guys on the TV. Their house disappeared."

The painters' deference to the "celebrity" of the Lights came at the expense of a young family whose house was supposed to have been painted that day and who now had to make inconvenient alternate arrangements to get their children out of the house another time.

None of which mattered to Lacy and Jerome, as they were delighted to be treated as special. Maybe things were looking up for them.

Next, they headed to the mall to get linens plus some basic bathroom supplies. As they parked and began walking, they ran into Angie O'Graham, the Channel 10 news reporter, who recognized them instantly. She was wearing navy blue slacks with a crease sharp enough to slice meat, and a short-sleeved floral shirt with the top two buttons open. She looked like she was ready to go on the air in a moment if necessary.

"Hello, Mr. and Mrs. Light!" she said, shaking hands. Both Jerome and Lacy glanced quickly around to make sure there were no cameras following the tall beauty.

"Hi, Angie," said Jerome, as if he'd known her his whole life. "It's nice to see you again. Do you live around here?"

"Not too far," she said. "How are things going now? I'd like to do a follow-up piece on you soon. What's new?"

"We're moving into an apartment tomorrow," Lacy answered. "Do you know the complex over on Sycamore near the Double Dee Foods?"

"Yes, I did a story over there a couple of weeks ago."

"I hope it wasn't a homicide or burglary or anything," said Jerome, laughing at the thought.

"No, nothing like that. Actually, I live pretty close by there myself. Do you think I could come by with a cameraman on Monday?"

"We probably have to be getting back to work by Monday," said Jerome. "We've been out this whole week."

"How about I meet you tomorrow as you're moving in? I think our viewers would like to know what's happening to you; we've been getting lots of emails and phone calls about the 'Sinkhole People.'"

"I have to tell you, Angie, there won't be much to see. We don't have a moving van or anything. We'll just be sitting around waiting for a furniture delivery," said Lacy.

Angie asked, "Do you know what time?"

"Not yet. The delivery guys'll call us in the morning."

"Could you call me when you know?" She handed him her card. "I'd like to come over with a camera and show how different your life has become as a result of the disaster. You know, we're struggling at the station with what to call the sinkhole. 'The Light Sinkhole' is kind of confusing. Someone suggested 'The Marshfield Sinkhole,' and that's probably what we'll go with."

"The Marshfield Sinkhole," repeated Jerome. "Sounds like a wrestler." All three of them laughed. Jerome felt good laughing again, and especially being able to laugh about the house. He caught a glimpse of Angie laughing, and for the briefest instant, desired her.

Chapter 21

Coming Out

Sylvana spotted Moses at his locker before lunch. She was happy to see him, but was afraid to display too much emotion, since it seemed that every student and teacher knew he was staying at her house. The Light family attracted a great deal of attention in every corner of Marshfield, as Angie O'Graham had correctly attested. Sylvana snuck up behind Moses and briefly considered nibbling his ear, but settled instead at simply startling him.

"Hey, Moses!"

He jumped slightly and turned towards her. He thought immediately of the previous evening alone with her, and blushed. Sylvana couldn't help but notice. "Whoa! What are you thinking?" she asked.

"I think you know," he said.

She looked down coyly and smiled. "I'm going to a party tonight with some friends. Will you come?"

"Joe and Marty asked me to go out with them tonight."

Sylvana was surprised. After their evening together, she had not expected any competition for Moses's attention. "Oh, well, uh . . ." she stammered, trying not to appear upset.

"But hey, Syl, I mean, I'd really rather be with you. I didn't know what to tell them, or if you'd want to go out with me."

"Not go out with you?" Sylvana reported.

"I was afraid that maybe you just wanted me when we're alone, and not with your other friends."

"WHAT?" She stepped back and let her voice rise a bit too much. "What are you talking about? I thought you were my boyfriend!"

"Am I? I mean, I am. I want to be. But you know, other than that movie, we've never been out. I don't mean 'out' like, you know, 'out of the closet,' I mean 'out on a date.'" He paused, then added ". . . you know?"

Sylvana could no longer restrain herself. She lunged at the helpless, pathetic boy, and kissed him on the mouth. It lasted about one second (she counted "One Mississippi" in her mind), and then she pulled back. "I guess we're 'out' now, aren't we?" She smiled and laughed, and Moses fell in love.

"Maybe Joe and Marty can come with us?" he said at last.

"Sure, if they want to. But tonight, you're mine."

It did not matter to either of them that other people were standing in the hallway gawking at them. A few smiled. Most had no idea what had happened or why anyone should look at Moses and Sylvana. Sylvana's friend Rebecca was among the clueless. As Sylvana turned to leave a paralyzed Moses at the locker, Rebecca approached her and guided her friend away from the crowd.

"What's going on, Syl? What was that all about?"

"Oh, nothing. I just gave my boyfriend a little kiss." She almost sang the words.

"You're kidding! What happened?" asked Rebecca, as the two girls left Moses standing at his locker watching them walk away.

Six days after her accident, Celeste Fallow was indistinguishable from the other Mercy Hospital patients in Physical Therapy as Gideon entered the large room full of stairs that went nowhere, and other forms of sublime torture. The room was full of frail people, most of them in hospital gowns with pastel bathrobes. Gideon spotted Celeste sitting in a corner using a weight machine under the guidance of a young therapist. He could see the concentration and pain in her face, and he decided to wait before revealing his presence to her. He imagined her healed and whole and happily his. It was most unministerial, he thought.

Celeste squinted her eyes nearly shut as she tried to move the weights by leaning her torso forward in a move designed to strengthen her back muscles. As she leaned back and relaxed her muscles, she also opened her eyes fully, and on her third such move, she noticed Gideon across the room. She nearly cried out to him, but thought better of it given the number of people between them. Nevertheless, the fact that the world-famous minister was there to see her gave Celeste a tremendous lift. Few, if any, of the other patients noticed him, or, if they did, failed to recognize him in his plain blue suit.

Gideon could see Celeste saying something to the young man working with her, and saw Celeste nod in his direction. The young man looked across the room, found Gideon, and smiled. Gideon waved back, barely moving his hand across his torso. He did not want to call undue attention to himself. A few minutes later, the young man pushed Celeste's wheelchair to where Gideon waited.

"Celeste, you seem to be doing very well," said the Reverend.

"I do? It's so hard," she said, but she smiled as broadly as she could. "Reverend Calhoun, this is Gregory."

"Hi, Gregory. Thank you for taking such good care of Celeste." He shook the young man's hand.

"I've heard of you. You're on TV, aren't you?" said Gregory.

Gideon had long ago abandoned any pretense of humility when confronted with this kind of attention. He knew it was pointless to do an "aw, shucks" routine, and he also knew that people meant no harm, and would be disappointed if he did not acknowledge his celebrity in an appropriate fashion. He considered it a privilege and a responsibility to talk with people in his "Reverend Calhoun" manner, instead of as the quieter person he felt inside.

He answered, "Yes, I am. I hope you've had occasion to view my program, but I know it's not for everyone." Gideon had decided on that "scripted" response many years ago, after first fumbling around with words that tended to confuse or pressure people. He hated to see people flustered, and so he crafted a remark that he thought would a) welcome them to his faith, and b) give them a gracious way out. It seemed to work well in most situations, though some people had no idea how to act around a famous person, and it made little difference what he said to them.

"Well, sir, I, uh, haven't had the pleasure of your show . . . yet," said Gregory, "but I've sure seen your face a lot."

"Thank you for your courage in speaking up," answered Gideon, who believed it took courage for most people to approach him and admit they know who he is. Of course, there were some for whom "courage" was too kind a word, but Gideon gave everyone the benefit of the doubt.

Gregory gave Celeste a few words of encouragement, and left to work with other patients. It was clear he felt that Gideon would take care of getting Celeste back to her room, a task Gideon was more than happy to accept. He began pushing her wheelchair towards the hallway and the elevator to her floor.

"He seems like a nice young man," he said to Celeste. She did not respond in any way, so he repeated the remark. When he got no reply the second time, he tapped Celeste on the shoulder. She turned her head as much as she could, and he moved his face in front of hers. "He seems like a nice young man."

"Oh, he is, he is," said Celeste, and turned back to face forward.

Gideon then rested his left hand on her shoulder, and without turning, she raised her left hand and left it on his fingers. He paused a moment, then resumed pushing the wheelchair.

That weekend, Gideon would come back to see Celeste twice, including after *The Gideon Calhoun Hour* on Sunday morning. Sylvana and Moses went to the party Friday night, although Joe and Marty did not show up, and on Saturday Moses packed his stuff up at the Foxes' house, picked up Miriam at the Polskys' house, and drove to the new apartment to help Jerome and Lacy move in.

Chapter 22

A Buddhist Was a Gigolo?

On Monday, June 17, eight days after the sinkhole swallowed the Lights' house, Jerome and Lacy both returned to work. For both, the past week had been an ordeal. They were glad for a return to something that felt "normal," but their coworkers were not about to leave them alone.

Jerome's boss, Hiram Crawley, great-grandson of the dictionary's founder, asked to see Jerome. "Jerome, don't worry about a thing," he said. "You've been with us a long time, and everyone at Crawley's is like family."

Though Jerome knew it was a cliché, he appreciated the support.

"If you need extra time off to get your family settled, take all the time you need," Crawley told Jerome. "We can't have our most famous editor out on the street!"

Moses and Miriam slept in, well past their parents' departure that morning, a luxury they'd not enjoyed on a weekday in a long time. Moses woke up first, surprised to find himself in the apartment, in a bed that belonged to strangers. In the kitchen, he hadn't a clue where to find anything, so it took him some time to fix a simple breakfast. It was nearly 10:00. He decided to call Sylvana before Miriam got up. He took his phone into his bedroom, shut the door, and dialed her cell. No point talking to Mrs. Fox first.

"Hello?" she answered.

"Hey, Syl, did I wake you?"

"Um, yeah, a little. I was kind of waking up."

"Can you talk now?"

"Sure, Mo. Is something wrong?"

"No. It's cool. It's just, like, weird you know, being in this place that doesn't feel at all like home, not like anyone's home."

"Yeah, I guess that would suck. I'd like to come see your room, you know? Maybe I can help you decorate it."

"Um, sure."

"Oh, yeah!" she said, not even waiting for his response. "That would be such fun. Can we go out today and get you something for your room?

I want to give you a housewarming gift. But I have to see your place first, or I won't know what to get."

Moses swallowed, then gave a brief laugh. "I'll get a say in this, won't I?"

"I don't know. We'll see," she teased. "What time will you pick me up?"

"Well, my sister is here, and she's still asleep, so I have to find out where she's going today, 'cause I promised Mom and Dad that I'd be her driver this summer. Next summer she'll be old enough to drive herself, so I want to have my own car by then. I can't afford one now."

"Can't your parents buy it for you?"

"Oh, man, no way! The sinkhole really fucked us up."

"Don't use that word, please."

"Sorry. The sinkhole messed us up real bad. We have to keep paying the house mortgage and now we have to pay rent on top of it, until the insurance company comes around."

"What if they don't?"

"Don't come around? I don't know. My mom and dad are real worried about that. We could be wiped out, pretty much."

"Oh, Mo!"

"Well, my parents are trying to be cool about it, not to let me know how worried they are. But I can tell, and they keep talking to me about not spending any extra money this summer except what I earn at the camp."

Sylvana wanted to reach right through the phone. "Let me take you shopping, okay? We can go to the mall and I can buy you some things. I've got some money saved."

"I'd feel kind of weird about that, Syl. One gift would be really nice, but I can't let you spend all your money on me."

"Why not?"

"Because. And what would the guys think? I'm some kind of gigolo?"

"Oh, yeah, right! You're a regular Richard Gere."

"Who?"

"Richard Gere, that Buddhist guy in the movies. He was in *American Gigolo*."

"A Buddhist was a gigolo?"

"Well, something like that. I don't know. Anyway, let's go to the mall today, okay? Come pick me up soon?"

"Why don't you bring your car and we can use that?"

Sylvana paused. Why that had not occurred to her was a mystery. Why did she assume her boyfriend would pick her up? "I tell you what, that's a good idea! I'll get dressed and come right over."

"Well, wait a minute. How about you come over at eleven? That way I can get Miriam up and figure out what's going on before you come over."

"Okay. See you at eleven. I better run so I can get ready."

"Okay. Bye."

"Bye. I . . . Bye." And she clicked off a moment before he could.

There was a knock on Moses's door, and he got up like a shot to open it.

"Who were you talking to?" Miriam asked Moses. She was already dressed.

"No one."

"It was Sylvana, wasn't it?"

"Yeah. She's coming over in a little while."

"Is that all right with Mom and Dad?"

"I'm sure. Besides, she's not coming to stay here. She wants to see the place, and then we're going to the mall. What are you up to?"

Miriam smiled, and then frowned. "I don't think I like this apartment, do you?"

"I don't know. It's different, that's for sure."

"I hope we get a new house soon. I don't want to live in this dump. My friends think we're, like, poor."

Moses lamented, "Yeah, well, we *are* poor right now. That's why you should get a summer job. You're old enough."

"But when you're away at camp, who'll drive me to work?"

"I don't know. Why don't you find a job first and then worry about it. Tell me what you're doing today. Do you need me to drive you someplace when I go out?"

"Maybe I'll come to the mall with you guys."

"You can if you want. Nothing's goin' on," Moses lied.

"You love her, don't you?"

"We like each other. I think she's gonna be my girlfriend now."

"Did you kiss her already?"

"That's none of your business. But . . . yeah. But don't tell Mom and Dad. I'll tell them when I'm ready."

"Could we pick up Jessica on the way to the mall?"

"If it means you'll have a playmate so you stay away from me, yeah."

"Cool! I'll call her and tell her. What time?"

Moses checked his watch. "If Syl gets here on time, then we can be at Jessica's about 11:15."

"Okay." Miriam pranced off to use the phone that had been installed on Friday. The phone company had said normally it would take four or five business days when you ordered new service, but considering the sinkhole and everything, they sent somebody right over.

Chapter 23

Monday, Monday. Can't Trust That Day.

Sylvana arrived on time. She had on an expensive pair of jeans that adored her body. Miriam had a fleeting thought that her brother had good taste. At least she had nothing against Sylvana; in fact, she wanted to go to the mall with them in order to check out Sylvana. Miriam felt protective towards her older brother, and always had since she'd learned he was adopted. She would not tell anyone that she hoped Moses's first romance would be a good experience for him. Sylvana was not to find out that she was Moses's first girlfriend.

Miriam acted as if all she wanted was to be a bratty little sister. She was pretty sure that once they got to the mall, she and Jessica could kind of "tail" Moses and Sylvana. Maybe they could all meet for lunch. If their Mom were along, she'd have told them, "Let's pick a time and place to meet . . . and you all better be there!" And most of the time, they were.

"I want to see your room before we go," Sylvana said as she gave Moses a hug and a kiss on the cheek.

"Oh, right. I forgot. We don't have a lot of time, 'cause we have to go pick up Miriam's friend."

"Okay. It won't take long. Will you show me?"

Sylvana grabbed Moses's hand as he headed past her and down the hall. She followed him excitedly into his room.

"Is this a lot smaller than your old room?" she asked.

"For sure. I had, like, twice as much room before."

"But it's nice! I like it. It's a nice color, and the bed looks all right, too. I want to get something to go on the wall right over the bed!" Even though Sylvana meant nothing by it, the fact that the girl he adored was in his bedroom and talking about his bed almost destroyed the last of Moses's composure. It took all his strength not to act as he felt.

She pushed farther into the room so that Miriam could not see her from the hallway, and motioned Moses to come closer. He, too, stepped out of Miriam's sight. Sylvana leaned forward and up on her toes to kiss Moses sweetly on the mouth. She put both hands around the back of his neck and pulled his face down closer to her level. The sudden quiet was evidence enough for Moses's sister, who headed out into the living room to wait.

Jessica was already outside when they pulled up in Sylvana's car, and she jumped in the back seat with Miriam. They hugged each other and made appropriate noises until they got to the Raw Spark Mall, which was basically the only thing in the "township" of Raw Spark, Ohio.

Miriam "channeled" her mother, and extracted Moses's promise to meet. Then the two couples went their deliberately separate ways. Moses had no interest at all in choosing where he and Sylvana went. His feet never touched the shiny marbleized floor of the mall as Sylvana grabbed his elbow.

"Where are you taking me?" he laughingly protested as she literally dragged him away.

"No place special. We're going to get you some much-needed clothing. I can't be seen with you in some of the stuff you have!"

"What's wrong with the stuff I have? I just bought most of it last week."

"No offense, Big Guy, but your taste is not exactly cool. It's not bad, but we can cool you up sooo easily."

"I thought we were going to decorate my walls."

"We will, but first let's hit American Beagle."

When they got to the store, Sylvana began picking out things she wanted Moses to try on. Moses started checking the price tags. "I can't afford all this stuff now, Syl."

"Let me buy it for you."

"No way. I couldn't do that. My parents would kill me."

"Why? Think of it as charity, like when my Mom donates clothes to the Red Cross."

"I don't need charity, Syl!" Moses barked.

She was taken aback. "I'm sorry. You're right." Her eyes began to tear.

"Oh, geez, I'm sorry, Syl. I know you're trying to be nice."

"I'm so excited to be going with you. I know if you had money, you'd spend it on me."

"Yeah. I would. And I think it's sweet you want to get me something," he told her. "Look, get me just one thing here, okay? And then you can pick something out for my room, okay?" His attempts to console her were pathetic, but he'd had no experience dealing with a crying girlfriend before. So, Sylvana picked out a shirt instead of pants. She reasoned that the right shirt would be more noticeable than the right pants. Moses tried it on, and had to admit it looked good.

Then they went to a store that carried various artworks, posters, and other decorative things. Sylvana had her mother's taste in décor, and zeroed in on a poster of "Le Mal du Pays (Homesickness)" by Magritte, in which a lion lies down on a bridge behind a man with a black suit and black wings. She reasoned that it was more masculine than "Le Blanc-Seing," another favorite, which she almost bought. She figured Moses did not want a surreal picture of a woman on a horse. They took the picture and the shirt out to her car and put them in the trunk. She told Moses to climb in the front seat a minute, and she ran around to the driver's door. As soon as she was inside, she grabbed Moses and gave him the most passionate kiss of his young life. The temperature in the car, already warm when they got in, soared.

Chapter 24

You Do Have a Gift

I'll have to make lots of changes in my life," Celeste told Gideon sitting in a lounge on the hospital floor to which she had been moved. "I'll need a house or apartment that is fully accessible. I won't be able to carry groceries up any steps, and I'll need grab bars in the bathroom."

"The Lord is sorely testing you, Celeste. But you don't have to leave it all in His hands. You can ask for help, you know."

As a blind person pays greater attention to auditory cues than a sighted person, Celeste had gained clarity about her life in inverse proportion to the mobility and convenience she'd lost. "I've been praying every day for God to send something or someone to help me, Reverend."

"So many prayers are coming your way, Celeste, from so many people. I asked the congregation to pray for your recovery yesterday."

"Yes, I saw the show. Thank you, Reverend; I was very touched."

"Please call me Gideon."

"Oh, yes. You told me that once before, didn't you?"

"Yes, I did. See? Your memory is coming back."

"You've been so kind, visiting me every day. I can hardly believe it. Even my own sister doesn't come that often."

Gideon blushed slightly at the realization that he had seen Celeste more than her own family. Had others noticed? What did Celeste make of it? But he replied calmly, "It's nothing really. I come by here almost every day anyway, and it's my pleasure to visit you."

Now it was Celeste's turn to blush. "May I ask you a question?"

"Of course."

"Have you ever been married?"

It was not a question Gideon had expected. "Yes, I was married once. She died about eight years ago."

"What was her name?"

"Julie. Julie McElwain when I first met her. We were too young. I was only twenty-three when we got married."

"How old was she?"

"Let me see. She was twenty-one. I was barely out of seminary. It was a mistake. She wasn't prepared to be a minister's wife. She had no idea."

"I guess I can see where that would be a shock to a young girl." Celeste paused. "Was she pretty?"

"I thought she was the most . . . pleasant-looking person I'd ever seen. I know that sounds like faint praise, but I mean it as the highest compliment. Lots of women are beautiful; they have the right jawbone or nose or hair. But when I looked at Julie, I saw something more than beauty, something far richer and deeper. I saw a woman I wanted to be around all the time, a woman who fascinated me, who pleased my senses in every way. Well, um, not quite every way until we were married."

Celeste laughed, and it would have been impossible for anyone to be offended by her laugh. Gideon laughed, too, and it helped him relax a little. Celeste asked, "Do you still miss her?"

He looked down at his hands clasped in front of his belly as if they held a note with the right answer. "Not any more. She had so many issues, mostly depression. I was unable to help her. She wanted me to give up my ministry, but that wouldn't have saved her. I had only one choice. God called me to ministry when I was young, and I couldn't allow anyone to prevent me from that calling. Maybe the Devil put her in my path to distract me, to lead me down another path. If so, then the Devil never made a more perfect temptation. Or maybe God was testing me, to make sure I was worthy of His calling."

"Oh, Reverend, what a sacrifice . . . giving up your wife. I can't believe God forced you to choose such a fate."

"I can't either, Celeste, and that's why I'm not bitter. I serve Him proudly through His Son, Lord Jesus."

"Amen, Reverend."

"Julie and I never had children. We both wanted them, but . . . well, she couldn't." He paused, not really looking at anything, then lifted his face and spoke directly to Celeste. "What about you? How long were you married?"

"Me? Oh, I guess it was about 14 years when Andrew left me, and young Matthew went with him. Now, I spend time with my sister's kids."

"Have they been in to see you?"

Celeste suddenly flinched from some invisible pain, then calmed again without complaint. "Yes, you've just missed them a couple of times. They're good kids."

"What're their names?"

"Maria is the oldest; she's fifteen. Then Christina is thirteen, and Danny's ten. It's a shame they don't get to see Matthew much. He and his Dad moved to Colorado. Did I tell you Matthew's going to come visit me next week? He'll stay at my sister's."

"That's wonderful. I'm sure it will be good to see him again."

"I'm not so sure he'll want to see me, at least not looking like this!"

"When's the last time you saw him?"

"The weekend after I started working for you."

"You mean with me. I could sense right away, Celeste, that we would make a good team."

A tear appeared in Celeste's eyes, and she didn't have the emotional or physical strength to wipe it away.

Gideon hastened to ask, "I'm sorry. Did I say something wrong? I shouldn't be asking you about your son."

"Oh, no, Gideon! That's not it at all. I mean, yes, it makes me sad Matthew's not living with me all the time, but I'm perfectly all right talking with you about it. You do have a gift for saying the right thing to calm someone down."

"I'm truly sorry for all the sorrows you've been put through. It's more than one person should have to bear, but sometimes our will is tested. You're doing fine, Celeste."

Chapter 25

I Have an Idea

Sumner Stoke let his shoulders sag. The attorney had arrived at his office Wednesday morning, after a brief appearance with a client in court, to discover a message from Big Rock Mountain Mutual. Their attorneys had responded much too fast to the appeal he'd filed five days earlier. He took the envelope they had sent by overnight courier into his private office. A short time later, he asked his secretary to get Jerome Light on the phone. She found him at his desk at Wexford Press.

"Mr. Light," Stoke said, keeping it formal. "I'm afraid I have bad news from the insurance company. Their Legal Department dismissed our appeal summarily. They wrote that there can be no appeal of an Act of God claim denial involving sinkholes or other geological incidents. They cited the same precedents I had found. I'm afraid we've reached a dead end with them, and your only option is to quit now or sue them."

Jerome was terse. "I know what you're going to recommend."

"Well, as I told you before, the likelihood of winning a suit is almost nil, and it will be very expensive very quickly. I'd need a $20,000 retainer just to get started. Your only hope, frankly, is that because of the high profile of your case, they might want to settle out of court, but if I were their attorney, I would not recommend a settlement. It would set a bad precedent and they know they're going to win if you take it to court."

"Okay, Mr. Stoke. Would you do me a favor and send me a copy of their statement?"

"Have you thought about your comment when you were here, about wanting to sue God? I hope you were kidding."

"I was not kidding, Mr. Stoke. Couldn't we do that?"

"You might find an attorney willing to take that case, but I doubt it. I'd be the laughingstock of Marshfield, if not all of Ohio. I can't represent you if that's what you want to do."

"I see. Well, please mail me a copy of the letter from Big Rock, and let me weigh my options."

"Will you get back to me and let me know what you plan to do?" the attorney asked.

Jerome snapped, "What do you suggest I do? Go away?" He was becoming impatient. The more helpless he felt, the more he lashed out.

"I understand your frustration, Mr. Light, but it may be time to get on with your life. Big Rock won't pay, and the courts have refused to make them pay in the past. I'd hate to see you throw good money after bad trying to win a case you can't win."

Jerome was steaming as he hung up the phone. Hiram Crawley, his boss, came by and saw Jerome barely able to contain himself, his fists clenched. In his deep, gravelly voice, Crawley said, "What's wrong, Jerome? You look like you're ready to pounce on someone."

"Look, I'm sorry, Hiram, but I don't know what to do next," Jerome told him, and related the story from the attorney.

"I feel for you. That's a tough situation. Let me know if there's something I can do to help."

"Could you give me $180,000 so I can pay off my mortgage?"

Crawley didn't answer. He waved his hand at Jerome and moved on down the hall. Jerome went back to his desk and called Lacy.

That night at dinner, it took every ounce of Lacy's love and patience to keep Jerome from punching something. He was alternately depressed and angry. His head slumped forward on his shoulders as the fight in him ebbed, then snapped to attention as his resolve flowed in again. "Dammit. We didn't work so hard to lose it all like this. It would be one thing if we hadn't spent a fortune on home insurance, but we did, and that makes it so fucking infuriating!"

"I know. I know," answered Lacy, words that never quite reached Jerome's consciousness.

"How the hell can they treat us like this? How can it be okay to say, 'Oh, well, God did it, so you're the big fucking loser here!'? We can't get money; we can't sue the insurance company; we can't sue the government. If God did it to us, why can't we sue God? Oh *that's* right; because there *is* no fucking God!!!" He slammed his fist on the counter.

"Keep your voice down, Jerome!"

"Why? The kids aren't here."

"But the other apartments might hear you."

He spoke calmly at first, "Yeah, Lace. Good time to remind me that we're in a fucking APARTMENT, instead of the house we bought and saved for and paid for, and now doesn't even fucking EXIST!"

"Well, what do you want me to do about it? Why are you screaming and cursing at *me*? Why don't you go outside and scream at the sky or the moon or God or something? Because you're not the only one affected by this, you know? It sucks! So what? We can't do anything about it! And that sucks, too, but for crying out loud, can't you do anything but complain?"

Jerome still seethed, but somewhere inside, he knew Lacy was right and that he had pushed her as far as he could before they'd both start to say things they didn't want to say. He got up from the table, went into the living room, sat on his rented recliner, and grabbed the rented remote to the rented TV. He tried to pick a show and stay with it, but had no patience. NBA playoffs? No. Reality show? A couple of cute young women, but . . . no. News headlines? Good for a few minutes. A rush of rulings from the Supreme Court as they wrap up their session? Who fucking cares? MTV? Definitely no. A cooking show? Bor-ing. Animal documentary? Puh-lease! Eternal Word Network? Too Catholic. Hey, there's that evangelist again. What's his name? Oh, yeah, Gideon Calhoun. What a quack!

He got up from his chair, the rage having dissipated almost entirely. Lacy was still in the kitchen, more or less hiding out until the storm passed. "I'm sorry, Honey. I'm having a hard time dealing with this."

"So am I, Buster! But, thank you. Apology accepted." She went to him, and he hugged her.

With his arms still around her, and his chin near the top of her head, he said, "I have an idea."

Chapter 26

You're Jerome, Aren't You?

Gideon smiled at Celeste. "It's been just over a week, and look at all the progress you've made!"

"I suppose I don't see it as clearly as you do, Gideon."

"Oh, but you should. You can feed yourself now and turn your head without pain. And you're smiling again!"

As if to prove his point, Celeste smiled.

"The doctors tell me you'll be going to a rehab facility soon."

Celeste said, "That's what they've told me, too."

"I'm sure you're going to like that better than here. I know several facilities, and I'd like to suggest one. It happens to be near my home. It's particularly good—clean and bright, and top-notch everything."

"That sounds good. Goodness knows I have no idea which place is best. I'd just be taking potluck. What's the name of your place?"

"It's called Better Days Care Center. I'm a member of their board, and we donated money to help them get started several years ago."

"Then it must be good."

"The point is that you will have better days after you get out of here."

"I don't know how I'm going to pay for all this. It must be costing a fortune."

"The auto insurance will take care of all of it, including some aides when you finally go home."

"Home," mused Celeste. "I have no idea when I'll be able to go home again."

"Keep making strides like you have this past week, and you'll be home before you know it."

"I hate to ask this, Gideon, but . . . well, what about my job? You can't go months without some help."

Gideon knew the day was coming when he'd have to face this question, but he was unprepared to face it so soon. "Celeste, I will make sure there is a place for you."

"I want to stay with you!" Sylvana whined.

Moses kicked some dirt in front of him. "Syl, we . . . Geez. We can't be together the whole summer!" She pouted; he took the bait. "Of course I want to see you. You have no idea how much. But I've got to earn some money for college. And . . . I promised I'd do the camp job. You know?"

"I know."

"I can't let the camp down. Hey, maybe you could get a job there!"

Sylvana looked up, surprised she'd never thought of that.

"Seriously!" Moses was getting excited at his own brilliance. "I can call the director of the camp; she's always telling me how hard it is to find new counselors."

"Call her right now!"

Moses quickly dialed the camp office, and within moments he had made an appointment for Sylvana to be interviewed. "I can't believe it.

One of the counselors for the younger girls quit. You'd be perfect for that job, and then we can be together."

"Can we really? Aren't there rules?"

"Yeah, well, counselors aren't allowed to date counselors-in-training, but since you and I are both CIT's, it'll be all right."

"Ohmygod, I'm gonna be so nervous at that interview!"

"Relax, Syl. You're perfect for it. Just be cool."

Chapter 27

Onward, Christian Soldiers

At noon the next day, Jerome's mobile phone played "Onward, Christian Soldiers" sung by the Mormon Tabernacle Choir. Jerome had downloaded it from the Internet as a joke. He made a mental note that it was time to get a different ringtone, and then wondered who would be calling his cell phone when he's at his desk. "Hello?" he said into the phone.

"Is this Mr. Jerome Light?" answered a deep, mellifluous voice.

"Yes, speaking."

"Mr. Light, my name is Thaddeus MacConnell. I'm an attorney in Columbus. I was talking with my friend Sumner Stoke . . ."

"Oh, yes."

". . . and he told me some intriguing legal actions you were considering. He said he was not interested in pursuing that case, but I am, Mr. Light."

"You are?"

"I'd like to meet with you and talk about it. Is there any chance you could come to Columbus on Friday?"

Jerome had to gather his wits, which were scattered all over the office floor, judging from the way his head and eyes pivoted. "Um, sure. I could do that, I guess."

"Could you meet me for lunch at 12:30 near the State House?"

Jerome's mind caught up with itself. "Maybe, but, tell me, why can't we discuss it now? If I come to your office, are you going to charge me?

Because I can't afford that right now."

MacConnell gave what appeared to be a short laugh and said, "No, there's no charge. I'm inviting you, remember? I'll even buy you lunch."

"I'll have to take the day off from work."

"Is that a problem? If not, we can make it another time. Dinner perhaps."

"That would be better. Tell me where to meet you."

They quickly dispatched those details, and then the attorney said, "So, do you still want to talk about it now?"

"Yeah, I guess so. I mean, you kind of caught me by surprise, Mr. MacConnell."

"Call me Mac."

"Well, Mac, I wonder what you heard from Sumner that you found so intriguing."

"He said that you were upset by an Act of God ruling against you by your insurer, and that you said something about wanting to sue God. Is that right so far?"

"Yes, and I'm glad you called, because I have an idea that I'd like to run past you on Friday."

"Good. Frankly, I haven't given this much thought yet, but I've come up with some ideas of my own."

"Should I bring my wife?"

"You can if you like, but it might be easier for you to talk openly if she's not here, unless she's a hundred percent behind you on this."

"I wouldn't say a hundred. It's, uh … I'm not sure what she's thinking, except that she probably thinks I'm nuts."

"She may be correct, Mr. Light. And I may be 'nuts' too. I'll see you on Friday."

Jerome said goodbye and slapped his phone on his desk with a self-satisfied smile.

On Friday, Jerome left the office slightly early for the drive to Columbus. Lacy was not with him. As he did on most car trips of more than thirty minutes, he threw a Mark Knopfler CD in the player, and tapped along on the steering wheel to every great guitar lick. "BOOM, like thaaat!" he sang, out of key, each time the phrase came around.

Mac MacConnell had told Jerome to meet him at the Plaza Restaurant in the Hyatt, not far from Mac's office. Jerome parked in the hotel garage and took the elevator to the restaurant, arriving a few minutes ahead of the six-o'clock reservation. A man with smoky gray hair, at least 6'3" tall, and wearing a deep-blue pinstriped suit came over. "You must be Jerome. I'm Thaddeus MacConnell."

Jerome shook Mac's hand, or, more accurately, had his own hand vigorously shaken by the lawyer. "Pleased to meet you," he said, "but—"

"How did I know it was you? Your picture was in the papers a lot recently, and I saw you on TV right after your house was destroyed."

They were led to a table by the window in a corner. It was clear that Mac had made the arrangements with the restaurant. The maitre d' called him "Mr. MacConnell" in a way that oozed familiarity. MacConnell was 56 years old with a build that was nearly as athletic as when he had played basketball and baseball at Princeton. He had no trace of a beard; his skin was smooth-shaven, but not without its points of interest, such as a small curved scar near his left ear, and the weather-beaten cheeks of a man who likes to sail. His smile was tight even when he was relaxed, which gave him an air of anger that he rarely felt. Aware of this trait, he rarely smiled.

As they ordered drinks, Mac made small talk, trying to relax Jerome, but also trying to elicit information he might find useful. "Tell me about your family." "Where did you and Lacy meet?" "How long had you lived in the house that was destroyed?"

Jerome found himself speaking with increasing ease, and by the time dinner came—tenderloin medallions medium rare for Jerome, Asian salmon for Mac—he was as relaxed as if he had known the lawyer for years. It struck him how easily this complete stranger had taken Jerome into his confidence, and Jerome thought, *Wow, he's good!*

"So, let me hear this idea you mentioned, Mr. Light," said MacConnell, leaning in just enough to show sincere interest and not so much that he put Jerome on the defensive.

Jerome sat back slightly in his chair and looked out the window at the downtown Columbus streets. He knew that he was about to say something that could change his life forever, and he needed a moment to both clarify and savor his thoughts. Once spoken, it would no longer be his fantasy, but something more tangible.

"There's an evangelist on television named Gideon Calhoun. Have you ever heard of him?"

"Yes, I know the name. I've never watched his show; have you?"

"Not really, but I've come across it a couple of times when channel surfing. Something he said on one of his shows really struck me. He said, 'I am God's agent here on Earth.' I don't know if he believes it or not, but that's what he said. 'God has sent me here to bring hope and good news into your life.' I guess it's pretty standard fare for a televangelist, but I don't know how many of them say they are 'God's agent.'"

"I have no idea," said Mac. "But why bring this up? Sumner told me you don't believe in God."

"I don't. And I suppose I should ask you if you do, before we go any further."

"I don't think my religious beliefs are relevant here, Mr. Light. I'm an attorney. When we talk about a 'higher power,' we usually mean an appellate court."

Jerome stared.

"That was a joke, Mr. Light."

Jerome's laugh got stuck in his throat as it began to emerge. "Okay. I guess I didn't see that coming, because we've been so serious up to now." He tried to smile.

"That's my fault. I should've kept it a little lighter on this first meeting. We'll have plenty of time for 'serious' later."

"So . . . do you believe in God?" Jerome repeated.

"Hey, if we're going to keep this conversation light, you've got to hold up your end, too." Mac smiled a let's-lighten-up-now smile, but Jerome clearly expected an answer. "I'll tell you what Mr. Light; I will answer that question for you, but not today. Let's hear what you've got before we completely bare our souls to each other."

Jerome nodded. "Okay, it's a deal. So, you also asked why I'm bringing up Gideon Calhoun, who has nothing to do with Big Rock Mountain Insurance or my house. At least, I guess that's the intention of your question. Am I right?"

"That says it pretty well. Sumner told me you wanted to sue God. How is a televangelist going to help you get money? I assume you've already got an answer for me."

"Of course. I had an idea two days ago, and realized that my whole thing about suing God was going nowhere. I imagine it would get thrown out of court, although it shouldn't, but that would blow any chance of using it against Big Rock Mountain."

"I'm glad you figured that out."

"That's what Stoke was trying to tell me, but I needed a few days to get it."

Mac put his left thumb and index finger together right in front of his mouth, a gesture Jerome was to see a good deal more of later. "Did it occur to you that the reason I'm here is because I was considering handling your suit against God, or at least trying to figure out how we could make that work?"

"Really?" said Jerome incredulously. "Do you think we should?"

"Let's not rule anything out yet. What's your idea, then, if it's not to sue God?"

"That's where Gideon Calhoun comes in. Let's sue 'God's agent here on Earth'."

Chapter 28

That's Where Gideon Calhoun Comes In

Gideon entered Celeste's "pod" at the Better Days rehab center, and spotted her watching TV.

"Celeste! It's good to see you sitting up, getting out of bed."

"Hello, Gideon. What a nice surprise."

"Well, I've tried to come every day, but I guess I've missed a few."

"Every day? There's no need for you to come every day. You're a busy man, an important man. I praise God each morning and night that you come to see me at all."

"You must be kidding, Celeste. Of course, I would come."

"But why?"

"What do you mean, why?" asked Gideon.

"I mean, I'm not your wife or your family. You didn't cause my accident. I just . . . work with you. But you're such a good man, you take on too many burdens. Surely the Lord needs you to do more things than visit me."

"Maybe the Lord does, but I don't."

Celeste's eyes looked away from Gideon for a second, as if searching for a cue card to tell her what to say next. She wasn't sure what Gideon meant by that. "Are you saying you need to visit me?"

"Yes, Celeste, I guess that's exactly what I'm saying." Gideon lost the majesty of a world-renowned minister and took on the appearance of a boy asking a girl to a dance for the first time. "I . . . like being with you."

Celeste appeared flustered, and Gideon thought he had said all the wrong things. She looked around the TV room to see who else might have heard Reverend Calhoun's admission, but there was no one. No witness. No one who could later tell her that she heard him right.

"Oh, I'm sorry, Celeste. I've upset you!"

"No, not at all," she stammered. "I'm, uh . . . I'm . . . flattered." She was afraid to make too much out of it, afraid that this great man was promising friendship, nothing more.

He could see his forwardness had not worked out. "I like you very much, Celeste. I'd like to see you socially even when you are well again."

Now her heart began to pound. She had never guessed. Of course! Now his visits made sense. How could she have missed the signs? Certainly she had done nothing since the accident to encourage him or tempt him, unless he went for women who were invalids and cut and bruised. *Ohmylord, what if that's it,* she thought for a second, but then dismissed that absurd idea. She spoke out loud after what seemed like an hour to Gideon. "I'd . . . I'd like that, too."

"I'm intrigued" said Mac MacConnell to Jerome as they finished dinner at the Plaza. "Tell me more."

"If we can't sue God, then let's sue God's agent! Gideon Calhoun is making millions of dollars from claiming he is God's agent on Earth, doing God's bidding, representing God. He's God's proxy, is how I look at it. Can't we sue a proxy if the main defendant is not available?"

"Where did you get your law degree?"

"I'm asking you."

Mac sighed. "Anybody can sue anybody over anything, but the judge does not have to allow the suit to go forward. It's what you were talking about before."

"Except I don't want to sue a non-existent Supreme Being. I want to sue a very real human being who has no business claiming he represents God."

"You're out of your damned mind, you know that? But I'll take your case."

Jerome didn't hear that last part. He was too busy saying, "Look, if you don't want to be invol . . . Wait a minute. What did you say?"

Mac leaned back in his chair. "I said I'll take your case. I'd like to represent you."

They spent the next half hour dawdling over coffee and working out the details of the arrangement. MacConnell wanted a retainer of only $5,000, a figure much lower than Jerome was expecting. "But," said Mac, "I want 40 percent of whatever we collect, plus reimbursement of costs such as travel, postage, filing fees, photocopying, and so on. I'm afraid if we get past the initial phase, our costs are going to skyrocket."

Jerome was floored. Obviously, MacConnell thought this case might recover some funds. His euphoria was quickly overwhelmed by the fear that the low fee meant MacConnell didn't plan to put much time into the case. "So, what happens if we collect nothing? What do I owe you?"

"You will have paid the $5,000. I will bill you for court filing fees, and that's all. The rest of the case comes out of my pocket."

"Why would you do that?"

"I guess that's another question I'll have to answer at another time. I have my reasons. Anyway, I believe in this case. I think you've been done a terrible wrong by a system that hides behind God as an excuse to save money, the same God that others exploit to make money. I believe we are going to win, Mr. Light. I believe we are going to win a lot of money."

Chapter 29

We Have a Court Date

A few days later, when he got home after work, Lacy had already eaten dinner with Miriam, who was getting ready to go out with her friends for the evening. Jerome grabbed a plate and began reheating his dinner as Miriam came into the kitchen looking like Daisy Mae Scragg in "Li'l Abner." Lacy took one look at Miriam and said, "That's not clothing; it's a Kleenex."

"Mo-ohhmm!"

"I don't know where you got that outfit, but you're not wearing it anywhere except the swimming pool."

"But Mom, it's gonna be hot out. I can't get all sweaty."

"A few more inches of fabric aren't going to ruin the way you smell. Besides, your pockets are hanging out from under the hem."

"Well, I didn't mean to cut them that short, but I can't fix it now and these were my best jeans."

"And yet you took a pair of scissors to 'em? What were you thinking? Do you think we'll go out and get you another pair?"

Miriam got angry. She stormed out of the kitchen and back to her bedroom. "Okay, FINE! I'll wear something that makes me look shitty, and you won't care!"

"Hey, young lady. You watch your tongue when you speak to us!" Lacy called after her. Jerome was mostly amused by this entire episode.

Lacy glanced at Jerome. A look of total exasperation danced on her face. She shook her head, and Jerome came over and gave her a hug. She put the side of her head on his shoulder.

"Somebody loves you," he told her.

"Aww," Lacy cooed.

"And as soon as we figure out who it is, we're inviting them over."

Lacy stepped back and gave him a pretend slap on the face. She feigned anger, but she was not-so-secretly happy that Jerome was able to start kidding around again.

Jerome smiled back at her, biting his lower lip in the way he always did when feeling particularly proud of himself. He laughed.

"What's got you in such a good mood, Mr. Smarty Pants?"

"For one thing, I love you very much . . ."

"And I love you very much, too."

". . . and for another thing, I got a call today from Mac MacConnell."

"Oh?"

"He says we have a court date! Can you believe it?"

"Oh my gosh! When is it?"

Jerome's enthusiasm waned the tiniest bit. "Not until September 14. I guess courts slow down over the summer, like everyone else."

"That's after the kids are back in school. It might be a good thing," she mused. "So, what'll happen that day?"

"I think it's basically a procedural thing. The papers we approved last week—"

Lacy interrupted, "You mean the papers you approved last week. I signed off, but I'm still concerned about some of the language Mr. MacConnell inserted."

"Well, the papers we signed last week . . . have been served to the Reverend Calhoun, and already Calhoun's attorneys have been in touch with Mac, and together they got a court date for the preliminary argument. We'll tell our case to the judge, and they'll tell their side of it, and the judge will decide whether to accept their petition for a dismissal."

"But that could be the end of it, right? I mean, if the judge dismisses the case right then and there?"

"Well, yeah, it could be. But Mac thinks the judge is going to let the case proceed. Apparently Calhoun's lawyers are treating it as a minor nuisance. I guess big shots like Calhoun get sued all the time."

"Maybe they'll settle before you get to court. Do you think?"

Jerome paused, having forgotten to consider that possibility, and amazed at himself for such an oversight. "I suppose . . . well, I'd be . . . I think it'd be good if they did, as long as it's enough money. It has to pay MacConnell's fees and still leave enough for us to get on our feet."

"I wonder if Gideon Calhoun is even aware he's being sued by us."

† † †

"I'm well aware of what could happen if this heathen gets us into court!" said Gideon to Dabria Curara, his lead attorney. "Dab" was a feisty ball of explosive energy. "Why don't we settle this thing out of court as usual?" he continued. "Tell them that if they fail to keep the exact nature of the settlement a secret, they will forfeit everything."

Dab had the throttle on her fighting spirit wide open. "Gideon, this suit is different. It's very disturbing. Do you know what could happen if we let Mr. Light and his attorney succeed? Every lunatic who's ever lost anything will be knocking down our door and the door of every other God-fearing minister and priest in this country."

Gideon was exasperated. "I can't defend the entire religious community in America!"

"You don't have to, but you have to fight this case and you have to win."

"But if we settle—"

"If we settle, and word gets out, as it will, then we will face suits like this every day."

Gideon sat back in his desk chair and rubbed his palms together, lost in thought. "I need to pray for guidance, Sister Dabria, before I agree to anything. I need to ask the Lord how He wants me to proceed."

"Of course you do, Brother Gideon, and I will pray alongside you."

They fell into silence for a minute. Gideon closed his eyes. When his intercom buzzed, he told his new executive assistant to hold his calls, and went back to his meditation. Finally, he opened his eyes and waited for Dab to open hers, then said, "I believe I know what to do for the time being. God has not revealed His entire plan to me, but He has told me to listen to you, to allow you to proceed. So what's first?"

"First, we file a brief with the court seeking dismissal of the suit on the grounds that it is without merit. Mr. MacConnell is claiming that, as God's agent, you can be held financially liable for those events judged to be 'Acts of God.' Our first problem is that the case has been filed in Ohio, and we will have to defend ourselves there. Our second problem is that courts have upheld the Acts of God claim in the past, which puts them on the side of blaming God for certain disasters. Our third problem is that we must separate your agency for God from those Acts."

"I don't tell God what to do," Gideon insisted. "I am God's servant, not His master or advisor. God's behavior is totally beyond my control."

"And that's exactly what we will file in our brief. I think we'll get an outright dismissal, but I can't promise that."

"And if we don't?"

"Then we have a new set of problems. But let's cross that bridge later."

Chapter 30

Humpty Dumpty

At Camp Cormorant, Sylvana and Moses had seen little of each other since the two hundred campers had arrived. They'd talk to each other in passing in the "mess tent," which was not a tent at all, and they would wave as she led her campers one way while he led his another. Their free time almost never coincided. Only two evenings had they been able to sit and talk as other counselors relieved them.

Moses was the closest thing to a celebrity at the camp, having been spotted by several campers one month earlier on the TV news and in the local papers. His principal job was to help with the 10- to 11-year-old boys, a particularly impressionable group. It hadn't taken long after the kids arrived for a boy named Theo to say, "Is it true your house was destroyed by monsters under the ground?"

"Not by monsters. It was a sinkhole. You know what that is, right?"

"Of course. It's like when your sink has a hole in it."

"No. It's not a sink like in your kitchen. It means the house sank into a big hole in the ground."

"How did the hole get there?"

"I don't know, Theo. Maybe there was an underground river."

"Wow!" Theo had seen the Ohio River, and now he imagined it rushing under Moses's house. He ran to tell the other boys about it, and soon Moses was inundated with questions: "What did it look like?" "How come you weren't hurt?" "Why didn't other houses sink, too?" "Do you think monsters live under houses?"

The girls soon learned of Moses's fame, and had their own questions: "Did you cry?" "Are you famous?" "Is Angie O'Graham as pretty as she looks?" Boys and girls both wanted his autograph to show their parents. The other counselors, especially Sylvana, were amused by this celebrity worship, and wasted no time kidding Moses about it when the campers were not around. Moses rather enjoyed it for the first couple of days, but after that, he wished it would all go away. Bebe, the camp director, couldn't help but notice his anguish. She told him that all the attention would soon pass, and she was right.

It was an ideal summer night. The temperature had cooled as the sun set over the lake next to the camp. Frogs sang in a chorus as a light breeze rippled the water and rustled the oak and hickory leaves overhead. The air smelled of algae and yellow buckeyes. Moses was thrilled to be here in this country place, where so many more stars revealed themselves, with his beautiful girlfriend, both of them off duty until their midnight curfew. The perfect weather was the whipped cream on the chocolate milkshake of his life at camp.

He and Sylvana met at the camp office, and walked down to the dock on the lake. A nearly full moon crept up to watch as they took off their shoes and sat on the edge of the dock. The water beneath them barely flinched now that the boats had gone home to sleep, but it was restless enough to lap at the pylons at the end of the dock, sounding like a dog taking a lazy drink of water.

Moses put his arm around Sylvana's shoulders, and she leaned into him, the top of her head resting near his collarbone. She said, "I can feel your heart beat."

Moses thought that it might be a cliché, but no girl had ever said it to him before, and he liked hearing it.

"What are you thinking about, Mo?"

"Oh, nothing, you know . . . stuff."

"Are you thinking about me?" she asked, her voice soft and high-pitched.

"No, I'm thinking about Humpty Dumpty. Of course I'm thinking about you; you're all I ever think about."

She smiled contentedly, but her face was directly below his and he could not see her expression. She squeezed his upper arm and leaned into him slightly harder. He was pleased with himself. He was so pleased that he wanted to share his pleasure with Sylvana; he drew his body back a little and bent his head and kissed her lips. Their passion lacked the desperate flailing that had occurred the first time, back in Sylvana's house. He leaned her back against the dock and kissed her throat gently, and then her neck, and then her mouth again. The last rays of sun had disappeared, and the moon tenderly bathed them in its soft light, helping them find each other in what would otherwise be total darkness.

Moses pulled his t-shirt over his head and spread it out next to Sylvana. Then he lifted her shirt over her head and placed it beside his own. "I don't want you to get splinters or anything," he said. To Sylvana, it was the sweetest love incantation she'd ever heard. She lay back on the t-shirts, now smelling his summery body both above and below her.

He leaned into her again, trying to force his too-big frame to navigate the body before him. He bent at the waist and twisted slightly sideways, and managed to kiss the tops of her breasts, an inch above her brassiere. He noticed then that she had changed into a frilly number instead of the sports bra he had detected under her shirt earlier. *Very cool*, he thought.

Sylvana moaned and put her fingers in the hair at the back of his head. He was quickly developing an erection, and he knew that soon he was going to be beyond the point of stopping. "Can I make love with you?" he asked, unsure of the proper protocol in situations like this.

"Mmm. Yes. I want you to."

A toad made its way across the dock and plopped into the shallow water with a kerplunk that momentarily distracted Moses, who then returned to one of the nicest moments he was ever to know in his life. Later, the two young lovers lay side by side on the dock, looking up at the moon and the stars, not speaking. She took his hand and intertwined her fingers with his, and for Moses, the Earth stood perfectly still and time stopped. He was convinced that if he moved, he would wake up from a dream in which he and Sylvana were lying naked in the moonlight on the dock. He sat up; she was still there. A tiny cloud slid quickly across the face of the moon, making it seem as if the moon had winked at him. The toad, now shiny-wet, made his way back onto the dock and looked at Moses without blinking.

♥ ♥ ♥

"I never looked at you this way before," Celeste told Gideon. "You have always been my idol, and I thought God had surely blessed me when I came to work for you. It's not going to be so easy for me to think of you as just a man, and not a holy man."

"Celeste, I am not holy. I am the Lord's Servant. I don't know why God chose me to spread His word, but I am humbled in His Presence, and I am reverent, but not holy."

The Rev. Calhoun was helping his former executive assistant move back home from the Better Days Care Center after her three weeks in rehab. Unbeknown to Celeste, he had worked with her sister Elysia and her friend Louise to make some adjustments to her house so that it would be easier for her to get around. Celeste was still unable to walk without assistance. She had practiced with a walker at Better Days, where they felt she was healing well.

Celeste was a nice-looking woman. Her hairstyle was a bit old-fashioned, but she had a nice figure, a pretty face, and an especially engaging smile. Following the accident, those features had been compromised, but she was beginning to look as she had, and her smile had returned.

Gideon knew logically that it was premature, but he could not convince himself that it was too early to fall in love with Celeste, and he believed that he was ready for a deeper relationship with her. He was terribly lonely. He could feel it even when he stood in front of 1,500 people in the Church of the Forgotten Savior, and he marveled that he could feel alone in such an environment. That Celeste was not at his level of commitment was hardly a deterrent; he knew he would have to work harder. He had her respect; now he needed her trust, her comfort in his presence. Then she could fall in love.

He rode in the Access van with Celeste as it took her home. They chatted about the weather (she was SO happy she could return home in warm weather) and politics (did he have a favorite candidate in the upcoming election) and food (she was DYING for a good cheesecake).

As the van driver helped Celeste into her house, Elysia and Louise both called "Surprise!" and rushed to greet her.

Celeste was beaming. "Oh, my goodness! It's so nice to see you. And so good to be home."

Elysia gave her sister a big hug and kiss on the cheek. "Welcome home, Cellie." Celeste reached out her left hand and took Louise's right hand, holding it firmly as she gave it a little shake. Louise's eyes started to tear up, and she laughed weakly at herself for being so emotional.

"What have you been doing here? Everything looks so different."

Elysia was the only one who could speak. "We rearranged some furniture and other stuff so you could get around the house easier. We moved the dishes down lower so you don't have to try to reach up to get a bowl or a cup or a plate. We even installed a couple of extra telephones so you can answer the phone wherever you are without having to rush into the other room. That was the Reverend's idea."

Spurred by Louise, who was still unable to collect herself, Celeste began to cry, too. "That is so sweet," she said, taking each of them in with her eyes, her voice trembling.

Normally, Gideon would have watched such a scene—he'd been witness to many emotional events—with an appropriate level of detachment, but now he maintained no such distance. He helped Celeste to a chair on which a high cushion had been placed, and he gently lowered her until he saw her face relax, the fear of the unknown dissipate. Gideon understood that almost everyone who has dealt with badly broken bones remains afraid of falling for a long, long time. "Easy does it, Celeste. You'll be able to do this on your own soon. Nothing to be afraid of."

He no longer called her "Sister," preferring the more familiar protocol of her given name. Celeste, on the other hand, still occasionally lapsed and called him "Reverend" and, once, even "Brother." But she had noticed his change of names for her, and was secretly pleased. *In time,* she thought, *I will be able to call him Gideon and not feel awkward about it. In time; perhaps soon.*

Chapter 31

Agents

The week before the initial appearance with the judge, Sylvana and Moses and Miriam were all back in high school, Gideon had begun to spend all of Sunday and Monday nights at Celeste's house by sleeping on her sofa, Lacy was completely enmeshed in writing a complex instruction manual, and Jerome was unable to concentrate on almost anything except the court date for the preliminary arguments and Gideon Calhoun's petition to dismiss.

"Mr. MacConnell," he said into the telephone for the second time that day, "should Lacy be there at the table with me, or in the audience, and what should she wear?"

Mac could imagine that he might someday wish to strangle Jerome, or at least get him to calm down and let him do his job, but for now he patiently explained, "As I said before, Mr. Light, I will go over all those details with you a couple of days before."

"But Lacy needs to know if she has to take time off from work. I mean, she wants to, and she kind of supports me, but—"

"What do you mean she 'kind of' supports you? Well, wait a minute, first of all, we're not going to be meeting in a courtroom. Judge Schuster wants to keep this phase of the process as private as possible, so we're going to meet in her chambers. There won't be a table. We'll sit in chairs on one side, and they'll sit in chairs on the other side. There won't be an audience, other than a court reporter."

"I see."

"Doesn't Lacy support you a hundred percent?"

"She's worried about the kids. She's worried this case is going to stir up a lot of animosity towards us, and the kids will bear the brunt of it. She wants to win the case, of course, but she doesn't want people burning crosses on our lawn or something. Not that we have a lawn. . . . And she's kind of embarrassed, too, that some people think she's married to a crackpot."

"It would help if Lacy were in the judge's chambers with us. You can't both look like crackpots."

"Wait! Are you saying I'm a crackpot?"

"Heavens, no! You're as sharp as I am. But the judge may think of this as a nuisance suit, and if she thinks that and sees you without your wife, she may draw her own conclusions. With Lacy there, too—who, I might add is a good-looking woman—she'll see you as an ordinary couple united in this suit. Remember, we don't have to win our case next week; we just have to keep it going forward."

Judge Vera Schuster was not at all pleased that this case had ended up on her docket. Raised in an A.M.E. church, she considered herself a devout Christian, but she also believed in the separation of church and state. She had once told a colleague, "I don't understand why people are worried about keeping prayer in school. There will always be prayer in school as long as there are tests and strict teachers."

The judge was still a handsome woman at sixty. Her short almost-white hair atop her slender five-eight frame gave her a distinguished appearance that was enhanced when she wore her judicial robe. She was still married to her first husband, had three healthy adult children, and generally considered herself to be blessed by good fortune. Until now.

"Are you ready for me to bring everyone in?" asked her clerk.

"As ready as I'll ever be, I suppose," she said. "Go ahead and show them in." She straightened a few items on her desk that were already perfectly neat, and ran both hands from her temples to the back of her neck, smoothing her hair that was already perfectly in place.

When Jerome, Lacy, and Mac had entered the waiting room outside Judge Schuster's chambers, Gideon and Dab were already there having a quiet conversation. Gideon stood the instant the plaintiffs arrived, and he introduced himself cordially minus his usual flair. Jerome had not realized how tall Gideon was until that moment, but recognized his face immediately. Lacy shook hands first with Dabria and then with Gideon. Mac introduced himself a bit too effusively, thought Jerome.

The five of them sat quietly waiting for the judge. Gideon was the first to break the uncomfortable silence. "I understand your home was destroyed a few months ago. I'm sorry for your loss."

Dab placed a hand on Gideon's forearm, a subtle hint not to go further with this "sorry" business, lest it be misinterpreted.

"Thanks," said Jerome, seemingly ready to say more, but unable to think of what else to say. He leaned forward in his unpadded arm charm, his elbows on his knees, and looked at his feet, his hands clasped as if in prayer. Finally, he asked, "How was your trip to Columbus?"

"Our flight was fine. It ran a few minutes late, but that gave me more time to read my book."

"What are you reading?"

"It's called *Timing God.* I don't agree with its conclusions, but it presents some unique perspectives on God. You might want to read it."

"I think I've heard of it," said Jerome, and lapsed back into silence, afraid to pursue this line of conversation further. After all, the lawsuit identified Jerome as an atheist, or at least it said he was a "person without a belief in any traditional form or concept of deity."

That was when the clerk appeared and asked them all to enter Judge Schuster's chambers. Everyone gratefully accepted the invitation.

Dab Curara entered first, Gideon right behind her. She crossed the room purposefully to Judge Schuster's desk, where the judge was now standing. "I'm Dabria Curara, counsel for Reverend Calhoun, Your Honor, and this is Reverend Gideon Calhoun."

"How do you do?" said Vera, shaking first Curara's and then Calhoun's hand.

"Fine, thank you, Your Honor," said Gideon.

The Reverend Gideon Calvin Calhoun seemed entirely appropriate next to his tall, stunning lawyer. He wore a perfectly ironed robin's-egg-blue suit that seemed to love being worn by such an important figure. Gideon was poised and debonair. Under his abundant angel-white hair, he had a movie-star face that was both kind and fiercely wise. He was six-feet-two, with wide shoulders and long arms that the judge could easily imagine embracing several people at once. She detected a faint scent of gardenia, but wasn't sure if it came from the minister or the lawyer.

Dab had moved in front of a chair facing the desk on the far side of the room, and Gideon stood beside her as Thaddeus MacConnell followed the Lights into the chambers.

"Judge Schuster," said Mac. "It's a pleasure as always. How are your children?"

Vera had experienced MacConnell's charming and well-practiced demeanor before, and took his familiarity in stride. "They're doing very well, thank you. I trust your family is well."

"They're all extremely well, thank you. Please allow me to introduce Jerome Light and his wife, Lacy."

Jerome was wearing a navy-blue Geoffrey Beene with a pale gold pinstripe, a suit he had to purchase for the occasion since his clothes had been destroyed in the "old house," a phrase which he was still having trouble accepting more than three months after the sinkhole had destroyed his home. Lacy had gone with him to the mall and chosen a chic dark-burgundy business suit with a pleated skirt that reached an inch below the knee. She wore a classy Vera Wang scarf knotted once at the neck with one end draped over her left shoulder.

The judge began, "Mr. MacConnell, I have read your complaint against the Reverend Calhoun and the Church of the Forgotten Savior Ministries, Inc. It is an unusual complaint, to say the least, and it relies on some rather shaky legal interpretations, I'm afraid."

Jerome shifted uneasily in his seat, glad, at any rate, that this chair was padded, but wondering if he was going to be sitting in it long enough to care.

Judge Schuster continued, "However, in your favor, there is no direct precedent for such a suit, and so we may have no settled law upon which to rely."

"That is our position as well, Your Honor," said Mac.

"I am disturbed by your statement that Mr. Light has no belief in a deity, and yet you claim that the defendant is an agent of that very deity which the Lights say does not exist."

"Your Honor, please allow me a small correction. Mrs. Light makes no such statement of belief."

"Do you believe in God, then, Mrs. Light?" asked the judge looking directly at Lacy.

"I believe in some sort of God, Your Honor," she answered, "but I don't claim to know the whole truth."

"That's wise of you, Mrs. Light. I'm afraid I don't know the whole truth, either." The judge smiled at Lacy, then turned her gaze back to Mac. "So, Mr. MacConnell, how do you intend to prove that Mr. Calhoun—I'm sorry, Reverend Calhoun—is an agent of God if your clients do not agree that there is such a God."

Mac had anticipated this question, and was ready. "We don't see that our beliefs are relevant, Your Honor. It is enough that the Reverend publicly represents himself as 'God's agent on Earth,' uses that representation to appeal for donations, and receives money from thousands of people in all fifty states based on that representation. These people believe he is God's agent, and many of them believe he is God's only agent."

For the past two months, Mac had investigated the judge and found that she is a devout Christian. He worried about this strategy, focusing on the role of Calhoun's audience, and he worried that she might be biased against their suit. In the end, he calculated that she would feel compelled to bend over backwards to be fair.

The judge now looked to her left. "Ms. Curara, in your petition for dismissal you argue that the Lights do not have standing to bring this suit . . ."

"Correct, Your Honor."

". . . and that in any event the Reverend Calhoun is only a 'servant of the Lord' and servants cannot be held liable for actions taken independently by their master over which they have no control."

"Exactly, Your Honor. Reverend Calhoun did not direct God to destroy the Lights' house, nor was he even aware of its destruction until this suit was filed."

"He did not see reports on the national news?"

"No, Your Honor. The Reverend is a busy man; thousands of people depend on him for support and guidance, and he has no time for gossip and sensationalism." Dab looked defiant. She had wondered how she might work this notion into her argument, and was pleased she'd been able to do so seamlessly.

Mac spoke up. "Your Honor, the destruction of a family's home and all their possessions is hardly the stuff of the tabloids alone. Every national news program, as well as Reuters and the Associated Press covered this story. It is hardly appropriate for counsel to suggest that what the Lights suffered was merely 'sensationalism.'"

Judge Schuster moved quickly to regain control before the two attorneys could get more deeply into these irrelevant side issues. "I agree with you, Mr. MacConnell. The losses that the Lights suffered are neither trivial nor manufactured for the press. I caution you both, however, not to engage in these sideshow issues. News coverage of this story will not impact my decision on the petition to dismiss."

"Your Honor," continued Dab, mentally kicking herself and trying to regain the momentum she had so quickly surrendered, "agency is the key to this issue. As cited in our petition, in *Lambourne v. Topnotch Talent Associates*, the agent representing Rachel Miller, an exotic dancer, was found not to be liable for financial losses suffered by the plaintiff when Ms. Miller could not fulfill her contractual obligations due to a sudden illness. The court found that the Talent Associates had no control over the health and vitality of their client and had not caused her illness, and therefore had no liability to compensate Lambourne."

The judge was having none of this argument. "With all due respect, Ms. Curara, this court does not find this citation to be compelling or relevant in this situation. When Ms. Miller could not perform, she was not paid, and Talent Associates received no compensation for its services. Reverend Calhoun's ability to collect revenues has been unimpeded by those events deemed to be 'Acts of God,' and so his agency in this regard is an entirely different relationship. There was also a written contract involved that indemnified the talent agency. I assume there is no written contract between God and Reverend Calhoun in this case, is there Ms. Curara?"

It was at that moment that Dab Curara knew what was going to happen. Her best argument for dismissal had just been tossed aside. Nevertheless, she persisted. "It is a contract based on faith, on the word of God as revealed in all Holy Scriptures. But that is not the point we wish to make, Your Honor."

"I should hope not," said Judge Schuster, tossing her head back over her shoulder. This case was complicated enough, she felt, without having counsel arguing in open court about the role of the Bible.

Dab Curara leaned over and exchanged a few whispered words with

Gideon, then said, "The defendant is prepared to stipulate that he has no contract with God."

The judge looked at Calhoun directly for the first time. "Reverend Calhoun, it is well known that you have claimed more than once on your television program and in your ministry that you are God's agent. So, are you His agent?"

Gideon had not expected this question, and so was, for one of the rare times in his life, nonplussed. He whispered to his attorney, and waited for her to nod before he spoke. "Your Honor, I am a humble servant of the Lord. I believe the Lord has called me to this work, and I am powerless to refuse Him. The Lord expects certain things from me, and I am bound to carry out His wishes. If that makes me His Agent, then the Lord has many Agents, and not just Gideon Calhoun."

Judge Schuster leaned forward. "So, if I understand you correctly, Reverend, you are saying that you *are* God's agent, but not in the usual sense of that word. But how are you different? Doesn't a talent agent promote his client's abilities as you do? Doesn't a real-estate agent try to get the most money for her clients as you do? Doesn't an insurance agent seek to bridge the gap between the insurance company and the average person? And don't all of these agents make money for their efforts? So, how is your agency for God different?"

Dab was not about to let Gideon get any deeper into this quagmire. She put her hand on his upper arm and pushed gently backwards to keep him silent. "Your Honor, there are other kinds of agents as well. There are government agents and FBI agents and ..."

"Are you seriously comparing Reverend Calhoun to an FBI agent?"

"No, Your Honor, we are simply saying that the relationship that a minister has with God is a unique form of agency and should shield the defendant, or any other clergyman or woman from direct responsibility for Acts of God. Gideon Calhoun is a man, not a God, and we believe you have no choice in this matter but to dismiss this frivolous and dangerous suit."

"Exactly how is it 'dangerous,' Ms. Curara?" asked the judge.

"If the plaintiff's claim prevails, then any minister or rabbi or priest anywhere can be held liable by anybody who loses anything. It will be an unconstitutional infringement by the law on the freedom of religious institutions in this country."

The judge hesitated and looked at both parties before she spoke. Jerome sat as if his entire body had been injected with Novocain. Mac showed no inclination to interrupt his opponent's self-destruction. And Lacy felt like falling through the floor. Judge Schuster said, "You may well be right, Ms. Curara. But the possibility of dire results based on one of the possible outcomes of the case does not abridge the plaintiff's right to sue. The plaintiff claims only that Gideon Calhoun is God's agent, and Reverend Calhoun does not disagree. The question is one then of what level of responsibility the defendant has while accepting the bounty of that agency. So, it seems to me that the plaintiff's issue deserves its day in court. This suit is certainly unique, perhaps even far-fetched, but it hardly seems to me to be frivolous. Petition to dismiss is denied. We will schedule the trial in open court as soon as possible, given that the Lights' losses are mounting every day."

Judge Schuster stepped into the next room to confer with her clerk. Jerome and Lacy looked at Gideon and Dab in amazement. No one spoke. The judge came back in and said, "The earliest we can try this case is April twenty-fourth of next year. Jury selection will begin on the twenty-second. Is that acceptable to both parties?"

Both attorneys indicated approval, shook hands with the judge, and ushered their clients out of the chambers. As they stepped into the hallway outside the judge's chambers, Gideon looked back over his shoulder at Lacy and Jerome. He seemed about to say something to them when Dab put an arm around his waist and hustled him away. Mac deliberately slowed his clients down to let the minister get far ahead and avoid any sort of confrontation. When they were out of sight, Mac gave a small smile and shook both their hands. "Congratulations," he said. Jerome turned to Lacy and gave her a high five.

They took the elevator down to the street level, and as they left the building, they saw a billboard across the street facing the courthouse. It said, "Don't make me come down there—God."

Chapter 32

Hungry Wolves

Back in Marshfield, Moses and Sylvana were alone together for the first time since they began their senior year. His parents planned to stay over in Columbus for the night after the meeting with the judge. Miriam was at her friend Jessica's house. Moses felt guilty as he drove Sylvana to his apartment. He figured he could have told his parents that Sylvana would be over after school, but he had said nothing, and he was reasonably sure that Sylvana had not told her parents that the Lights were out.

"We really need to study, you know," he told Sylvana.

She replied, "Not right away, we don't. We have the whole weekend." Sylvana then did quick little jabs of her fists at Moses's stomach, like a toy mechanical boxer, as she smiled and said in a deep voice, "Come on. Lighten up, Dude!" She had never used this term before, and used it now to sound like Moses's friends Joe and Marty. "We can study when your family is home. But there's some other stuff we can't do then."

Moses gave in as easily as he knew he would. "Oh? Like what?"

"Like I think you know like what," she said, and then continued in a talk-to-the-five-year-old voice, "Or are you just too scared to be bad in Mommy and Daddy's house?"

Moses threw his books down on the faux-wood coffee table someone had donated, and grabbed Sylvana's wrist like a swashbuckling pirate abducting the fair maiden. "I'll tell you who ought to be scared!" he bellowed, and she laughed nervously as he pulled them together. He stifled any possibility of protest by sealing her mouth with his lips. Without parting, they slid down together until they were both on the sofa. Had Moses not been eight inches taller than she, the little gymnastics routine they did might have seemed graceful. Instead, they landed awkwardly and were bounced apart.

They had never made love in a real bed before, and they both felt like doing so would be crossing some sort of line, from playful sex to something more "adult," something more committed. It was not lost on either teenager that their parents were, by reason of their long first marriages and no divorces, different from most of their friends' parents. The seriousness with which the Lights and the Foxes treated their mates added a level of sobriety to each kiss that Sylvana and Moses shared.

Thus, when their lips were forced apart by the bounce on the couch, they looked at each other's eyes cautiously, trying to see if the other wanted to back down and, in a way, hoping they would.

Sylvana was the first to speak. "Hey, Mo, shouldn't we get some dinner or something, or check on your sister?"

"Oh, Miriam's fine. She texted me from Jessica's house. But, um, I didn't tell my Mom that you might be here for dinner. I kind of hinted I'd probably be at your place for dinner, or maybe we'd go out to a movie. So, I don't think my Mom prepared anything for me. Let me look." He stood quickly and went to the refrigerator, then leaned into the hallway and shouted back, "Hey Syl . . . there's not much here. Whattaya want to do?"

"Can we order a pizza? Then we don't have to go out!" She pursed her lips and made a Little-Miss-Innocent face.

✝ ✝ ✝

"I certainly did not expect that," said Gideon Calhoun to his attorney as their car-service limo left the courthouse and headed to the airport. A light drizzle coated the car.

"I wish I could say I was surprised," Dab Curara replied.

"You're not surprised? You said you thought we'd get a dismissal."

"I really thought we would, but I never considered it a sure thing. Unfortunately, it's going to get expensive now to defend."

"We can afford it."

"Yes, I know we can, Brother Gideon, but I also know that the publicity will hurt us. This one's bound to get national attention. Mrs. Light has already been interviewed on national television. Wait till your enemies get hold of this one."

"I have no enemies, Sister Dabria. The Lord walks beside me. I fear no evil."

Dab shifted uneasily in the back seat of the limo as it neared the terminal. "The Lord is surely testing you this time, Brother. The Lord is surely testing you."

"I expect you're right," he said, looking out the window as thunderclouds moved in from the west as they so often do late in the day in Columbus. "The Lord has even made me sympathetic to the Lights. They are not bad people bent on destroying us. They lost everything. They are desperate."

"I hate to disagree, but they did not lose 'everything.' They still have jobs and good health and a roof over their heads. You may not see it, Brother Gideon, but they are hungry wolves in sheep's clothing. They mean to destroy not just you but all religious people with their war on Christianity."

Gideon never turned to look at the attorney again, but stared out the limo window and was silent, even as they pulled up to the terminal and got out. He forgot to grab his valise from the driver, who handed it to Dab Curara instead. She chased the minister, who was already inside. He was trying to read the monitors and find their flight when he realized he had no idea where they were going. He scanned the lists of cities back and forth, and then finally looked at Dab in utter confusion.

"Come on. Gate C-55. Don't worry."

The next day, Gideon went to see Celeste, who had graduated to walking with a cane. She still was drawing a disability check, still not working. It was his Saturday routine to see Celeste from before lunch until dinner was over, and she had grown to depend on his visits. There was no doubt in her mind that she and Gideon were "an item." She felt that nothing in her life had been so perfect. She wondered, sometimes at night, if she might have been called to be Gideon's companion and confidante and, perhaps someday, helpmeet.

Their routine was becoming well established. He would show up with a small gift: flowers or sweets or even some of his own small pamphlets containing the pearls of wisdom he sold on *The Gideon Calhoun Hour* for $7.95 each, including third-class postage. He would prepare lunch using ingredients he had brought with him. As a cook, Gideon was a fine minister. His concoctions tended towards oatmeal, fried eggs, and pancakes made from a mix. A ham sandwich was not necessarily beyond his capability, though he felt stretched in its making. Dinner, on the other hand, was always take-out or deliver-in. He did not want Celeste lifting a finger to help.

Today, he accomplished the rare feat of making the pancake batter too doughy and burning it. As he set a plate of pathetic looking pancakes at her place, he told her how he wanted today to be different. "I'd like us to try going out to dinner tonight."

He made this surprise announcement as a statement of fact. He did not turn it into a query, nor did he solicit her opinion. He wasn't demanding it, but nevertheless, Celeste was left to wonder momentarily if she was expected to respond. She determined it would be best if she did, and she said, "Where would we go?" She was, after all, trying to act as though it were a perfectly normal thing for them to discuss. She quickly discarded the thought that perhaps she should have said, "Are you crazy?"

Gideon pondered the question, realizing that although he had been sincere a moment ago, he had not anticipated the logical next step of selecting a restaurant. He had done most of his mental preparation in the logical expectation that Celeste might be skittish about a number of things. First, she had not gone out in a car since returning home from the Better Days Care Center. Second, she was certain to have noticed that they had never been seen together in public. Third, what if she fell down?

"How about a nice Italian restaurant? Or a good steakhouse?"

"Oh, Gideon, I haven't had a steak in ages, since before the accident! I'd love that, if it wouldn't be too expensive for you."

He thought it quaint that she assumed he might not be wealthy. He was, in fact, reasonably wealthy, but not nearly as rich as some of his NRB brethren, who blatantly pushed over-priced merchandise. He knew it was costly to have a large ministry, but he did not feel that gave him license to bilk gullible people out of their meager savings. Gullible. Yes, he knew that many of his audience members were naïve in their outlook, and that it would be so easy to hoodwink them as some others did, or to overcharge them, as many did. He believed he was justified in making a decent wage for his efforts, but nothing extraordinary. If he lived a flashy life, his parishioners would have a right to question his prices. His ministerial talent was a gift from God, not given so he could fleece the believers. The Meek shall inherit the Earth. Gideon had always assumed it would be acceptable to save a small amount each year for his retirement or to support a family should he ever have one. That prospect was appearing dimmer all the time, and he began to look at his burgeoning bank account as a moral liability.

"Then it's settled. We'll go to Morgenroth's. They have the best steaks in town, plus an extraordinary collection of teapots and paintings of cows."

The chink in her armor finally showed. Instead of remarking on the notion of dining in a place that exhibits cow portraits, Celeste asked, "Do you really think I'm ready to go out?"

"Absolutely. I don't think it's even worth discussing. You are recovering splendidly, and your doctor said you should be getting outside more. Anyway, I have a surprise outside for you. Come see."

"Let me finish my, uh, pancakes first. Oh, tell me what it is."

"Not until you're outside."

She managed to eat the crispy-outside-gooey-inside pancake much faster than she might have imagined, and was quickly ready to step outside for the surprise. She took Gideon's arm with one hand and held her cane in the other, her bad leg next to him, so that as she walked, her limp brought her closer to his side. They stepped together out the front door where she could see a bright powder-blue new van in the driveway and a ramp leading into an empty area behind the driver and front-passenger seats. She hugged his arm close as she saw it and realized what he had done. This van was not a church vehicle; it was his own.

That same Saturday at the Lights' apartment was anything but routine. Jerome was two sizes too big for his skin, and fidgeted more than usual. He could not help remembering Thaddeus MacConnell's final words as they had parted the evening before: "Get ready for the wildest ride of your life." Suddenly, it struck Jerome that this exercise was no longer theoretical, no longer "what if . . ." It was real now. He wasn't sure he'd ever thought it would be.

On Tuesday, MacConnell phoned Jerome in his office to explain the next steps. Mac said he planned to subpoena and depose several witnesses. "I expect some of them are going to be mighty reluctant to help us in any way. They won't want their testimony to help you beat the Reverend Calhoun, but they won't have any choice."

Mac intended to use their testimony to prove that Calhoun had repeatedly and consistently over many years referred to himself as "God's agent." The enigmatic lawyer felt that in order for them to win the case, it was critical to establish that Calhoun received money from people who believed him to be God's literal agent, not merely someone who spoke about God. Mac had already lined up ten CFS congregants or former congregants whom he would compel to say exactly that.

Jerome looked at the wall and noticed a small mark he had not seen before. Still holding the phone to his left ear, he licked his right index finger and began rubbing at the spot.

"But there's one other thing, Mr. Light. There's one other thing we must do to win."

Jerome now licked his thumb and continued to work on the tiny stain. "What's that?" he asked.

"We must prove that there is a God."

"What?" exclaimed Jerome. He lifted his thumb off the wall but still held it up.

"We don't have to prove that Gideon Calhoun talks to God, but we must prove that Gideon believes in this God. They may engage in what I call a 'Santa Claus' defense. Children can't sue a department store if they don't get what the store's Santa promised them. Believe it or not, I talked with a father a few years ago who felt the department store should have to pay for the toys that Santa talked about with his kid, because it was an 'implied contract.' I threw him out of my office."

"Good God!"

"Exactly! That's what we need to prove!" Mac laughed at his own joke, but Jerome did not see the humor in it. "They can claim that belief in God and a general obedience to what Calhoun believes God wants him to do is not a form of agency. That's the argument I'd make if I were them, so we need to be ready to counter it. We don't want Calhoun to control the whole belief thing. We want to concentrate on the money he collects from others who believe."

"This is surreal," Jerome said. "You really expect me to pay you to prove in court that there *is* a God? What the . . . How did I . . . Oh, man!"

MacConnell let the silence take hold for a few seconds, then said,

"Not only do I expect us to prove there is a God, but I expect them to prove there isn't, or at least that Gideon Calvin Calhoun has nothing to do with this God of his, except to believe."

"Amazing!"

"This case is far bigger than you can imagine, Mr. Light. The implications are huge."

Chapter 33

The Fall

That next weekend, Jerome and Lacy went to watch Moses's tennis match for a fall league he had joined at Sylvana's family's country club. Todd Fox had pulled a few strings. Moses was seeded #2 in this, his first match of the season. Sylvana was already in the stands when they arrived. She was wearing an amazing sundress that appeared to have been designed especially for her, which, in fact, it had been, as a gift from her mother on her seventeenth birthday. As they climbed into the bleachers near her, Jerome was stunned by his son's taste. Sylvana looked radiant.

"Hi, Mr. and Mrs. Light," she beamed. "Moses's match is next."

Lacy and Jerome sat on the bench behind and above Sylvana, each one looking over a different shoulder. They did not intend to make the girl nervous, but it had that effect. She wondered if they knew about her and Moses. *No*, she thought, *how could they?*

As they waited for Moses to appear from a small preparation area below the stands, Lacy managed to startle Sylvana with the simplest of questions. "How are you, Sylvana?" They made small talk for a few minutes, and then Jerome spotted Moses heading to the court. The racket he carried was borrowed from Marty Karlovits's father, who used to play a lot, but had to quit after he developed "tennis elbow." It was a good racket, but not as good as Moses deserved. Its greatest distinction was that it was better than they could afford right now. Moses's superior graphite racket from last spring had been lost to the sinkhole.

Moses looked more handsome this year, Jerome realized. Forced to buy all new clothes, shoes, and equipment, and having grown taller and leaner than he was last April, Moses had been transformed from a boy to a man. It seemed to have happened overnight. Jerome watched him move with a grace he had not possessed before, a more muscular lad than he had ever seen. It was one of the rare times that Jerome thought consciously about the fact that no one knew anything about Moses's biological father or mother. Had they been tall? Were they kids like Moses and Sylvana? Are Moses and Sylvana lovers now? Could they have a baby? Jerome looked down at the pretty girl at his knees and wondered if she could be pregnant right now. Somehow he doubted it, but he had no doubt of another reason for Moses's instant maturity.

Moses won his match in two straight sets, and came over briefly afterwards, sweating profusely but with a huge smile on his face.

"Great job, Moses!" called Lacy, and Sylvana kissed his cheek.

"Oh, well, you know, he's just sixteen," said Moses. "He's pretty good, but he's not ready for top seed yet. Anyway, I better go see the guys, and shower. I'll see you at home in an hour."

"Okay, Son. Congratulations! Great job!" called Jerome, who felt the weight of his own years more heavily than ever before. How could this man be his son?

"Bye, Baby!" waved Sylvana. It was clear that she was smitten.

Moses won that tournament, and the next one. By the end of the tennis season in the fall, he was undefeated and starting to get some notice from colleges.

Early on the Saturday before Thanksgiving, Gideon went to see Celeste.

"I thought we could go for a drive today," he told her. "Get out and enjoy this beautiful fall weather."

"That would be wonderful, Gideon. I'm tired of being stuck in the house." It was more than a figure of speech. It had been over five months since her accident, and she had not returned to work. She was grateful that the insurance company still considered her "disabled," but she didn't feel that way. Celeste was reasonably sure she could hold down a desk job now. But Gideon hadn't brought it up, and she was terrified to say anything about getting her old job back. So, she stayed home mostly, except when Gideon came by with the van.

He already had a picnic lunch he'd picked up at Crysta's Catering in Stonecrest, and planned to drive them to a scenic spot by the Eleven Point River, less than a two-hour drive. He had arranged for a friend to stake out a prime location there for the rendezvous. The friend and his wife were to stay in that spot until Gideon arrived, and then pack up and go. Celeste wouldn't know the couple, and it would seem like good fortune that they found such a nice place to picnic. It had the added benefit that it did not require Celeste to do any appreciable hiking.

They wound their way from Stonecrest through the Arkansas countryside and a little way over the Missouri line. The temperature was a perfect 70 degrees, and the mid-morning sun made the landscape look unrealistically bright. Gideon put on his favorite country music station—seemed like no one called it "Country and Western" anymore—and the drive flew by.

Shortly past noon, Gideon pulled the van up beside the road, a brief distance from the river. "Look," he said. "There's a couple just packing up! What a perfect place for our picnic." Celeste merely nodded, barely paying attention. The long drive—her longest by far in over a year—had left her groggy and more relaxed than she could remember. She hoped her muscles would respond now that she needed them to carry her from the van. She no longer needed the ramp to climb down, but simply opened her door, swung her feet around, and let gravity slide her down. She always winced when her feet first met the ground and her body got the slight jolt that came from the abrupt stop.

Celeste could not yet lower herself to sit on the ground, and if she did, she'd have a terrible time trying to get up again, so the first thing Gideon did was to set up a couple of folding tailgate chairs that said "CFS" on the back and had the Church logo, which was a stylized cross appearing off-centered from behind a small hill, all inside concentric circles. The cooler of food that Crysta's Catering had prepared served as a perfect side table. Gideon spread out a large Scots plaid blanket beneath a grove of chestnut oaks, anchored it with the chairs, and placed the cooler between them. Celeste sat down and looked out over the river as Gideon dug in the cooler and produced two glasses of sweet tea.

She was content to sit quietly, contemplatively, and listen to the sounds of the river. Gideon did nothing to disturb her mood, aware of all the sensations the place was stimulating for her. She sipped her tea and occasionally asked simple questions of Gideon. "How is your tea? Wasn't it lucky to find this spot? What time do we have to head back?" His answers were brief and pleasant. "Very refreshing. Amazing good luck. We'll go when it's time for dinner."

After a while, he stood and took her hand, helping her rise. "Come on. Let's walk a little ways up river."

"Okay," she said, "but I can't go far."

Once she was on her feet, he continued to hold her hand. To this point, he had never done more than kiss her, and then, only once and briefly, an impetuous move he had quickly regretted. Now, by the river, she was radiantly aware that he was touching her. She walked carefully on the uneven ground, and he did not hurry her along.

The waters of the Eleven Point ran as clear as polished diamonds, and the fresh smell of the river was invigorating. He had always liked this place, far from everyone and everywhere. He was glad it had not been overrun with motels and tourist traps. Everything he liked about the Ozarks was present in this almost sacred wilderness, dotted with few homes. It was a place that cries, "Leave me as I am." Gideon pointed out some fish fighting against the steady current and then giving in to its push. Celeste felt nearly intoxicated by the combination of the cool fall air and the inviting water. She dared not say a word lest she appear drugged.

Gideon sensed that Celeste was reaching the limit of her endurance, and gently guided her back to the picnic blanket and chairs. As she gratefully sank into the chair, Gideon poked around in the cooler and brought out two sandwiches and a small translucent sandwich bag. "Hey, what's this?" he asked. "I didn't pack it." He handed Celeste a sandwich still in its wrapper and put one on his lap.

"I don't know, Gideon. It's not mine."

"We'd better see what it is," he intoned seriously, and reached inside the small bag. A tiny jewelry box emerged in his hand, and he wasted no time flipping it open and presenting a stunning diamond-and-amethyst ring to Celeste, as he knelt on one knee before her. Her hand flew to her mouth, and the sandwich bag fell to the blanket.

Chapter 34

2,418

Right after Thanksgiving, Jerome had his first pre-trial meeting with Thaddeus MacConnell. MacConnell had been busy doing discovery for the case, and had deposed a large number of people already. Jerome could only imagine the bill that was coming.

Mac had so far taken the depositions of Magnus Schopenhauer, Jack Glisson, Dr. Sapna and another geologist, Mike Engelhardt, as well as the EPA's Valerie LePine, and even Angie O'Graham, who, after all, was the first person on the scene with a camera. Mac had subpoenaed the original videotapes from the night of the sinkhole. Even though he'd found nothing that might help the case, he knew that having a local "celebrity" like Angie on the stand would go over well with jurors, and he had every intention of calling her. He was confident she would welcome the exposure. He'd already contacted MSNBC, and felt reasonably certain they would cover the case.

He need not have worried. When the media learned that an atheist was suing famed televangelist Gideon Calvin Calhoun (the media loved to use his full name, though he never did), the hype machine was in full gear. Angie O'Graham was filing regular reports on Action 10 News, trying to ensure that no one else would get to the Lights and scoop her story.

Predictably, that was when Jerome began to get hate mail and, despite having an unlisted phone number, the occasional nasty call or stony silence. He also stopped reading the paper after he saw an editorial condemning his "ill-advised tantrum." A few co-workers at Crawley's made their displeasure clear, and only one or two friends wished him good luck. No one, not even his siblings, voiced support for what everyone saw as his lawsuit, although Lacy also got the cold shoulder at her office and in temple. One woman told her she should not have sex with her husband until he dropped the suit.

It saved money for Jerome and Lacy to go to Mac's office rather than for him to visit Marshfield, so that is where Jerome found himself one early December morning, about four months before the trial.

"Do you want to know an amazing statistic?" asked Mac as soon as Jerome entered the room.

"Sure."

"We subpoenaed five years' worth of tapes of 'The Gideon Calhoun Hour,' and we got a bunch of students at Capital University to watch them and record how many times Gideon Calhoun made certain statements, and do you know what we found?"

"I have no idea."

Mac looked extremely proud of himself. "We counted 2,418 times that he said he is 'God's agent here on Earth.' Over twenty-four hundred times! Can you imagine? And that's just in five years."

MacConnell then explained that the huge number was significant because it was what distinguished Gideon from other clergy or representatives of God. "It's that word, 'agent,' that will win this case."

Back in Stonecrest, Arkansas, a giddy Gideon began to make preparations for his wedding to Celeste, who seemed to be walking much better since she accepted his proposal on the banks of the Eleven Point. They had decided to be married before Christmas so they could spend that holy time together as husband and wife. Gideon had never been comfortable with what he called "snaking around," a term which left everyone wondering if he meant "snaking" or was saying "sneaking" with a Southern accent. Despite his delusion that no one at CFS knew of his courting Celeste, it had not been a well-kept secret, and no one considered it "snaking."

He was always in the pulpit during Advent, and this year would be no exception, no matter what else he had going on. The second Sunday of December, he had the choir sing "Rudolph the Red-Nosed Reindeer." The congregation at first was shocked that he would choose such a "secular" song instead of something more traditionally Christian. But Gideon said, "'Rudolph the Red-Nosed Reindeer' is actually the most brilliant Christmas carol of all. In a very brief poem, it tells a story of alienation and redemption. It *is* the Christ story, but with a happy ending. Rudolph is an outcast, ridiculed by his peers, yet he brings light into the darkness and is ultimately recognized as a savior. 'Then how the reindeer loved him!' What would have happened to world history if all the people of Christ's time had loved him? What if Christ had not perished on the cross, had not died for our sins, but merely had died a natural death as an old man? Would we still be saved? Yes, I think we would be. I don't believe that God sent his Son to Earth preordained to die a violent and premature death. People did that to Christ; God did not decree it. Christ was Rudolph."

This sermon proved to be his most popular ever, his audience swelled by the notoriety of Jerome's lawsuit against him. More and more Americans had begun tuning in to see who this Gideon Calvin Calhoun was. When they saw him preach that Rudolph the reindeer represented Jesus Christ, the last obstacle to general acceptance fell away. Suddenly, Americans were in love with Gideon the way they had been in love with Billy Graham. Even people who did not share Gideon's brand of Christianity thought he was a good, respectable guy.

Celeste thought so, too. On the following Saturday, the minister and the single mother were married by an assistant pastor in a quiet, private, unannounced ceremony held in a small chapel of the Church of the Forgotten Savior. Only Gideon's office staff knew, and he had told them only an hour before so that there was no chance of any media coverage. The only people on Celeste's side were her sister, Elysia, and her friend, Louise Baldwin.

Jerome had been cast in the media as the bad guy, and he lost all the sympathy he and Lacy had enjoyed right after the sinkhole. Todd and Dakota Fox, Sylvana's parents, were becoming more and more agitated as the story gained prominence. When they first learned about the case, they had been somewhat sympathetic, but as the full impact of the impending trial grew, their sympathy waned. Already, one local station had done an interview with Moses that led them to do a separate one with Sylvana. Fortunately, the station did not use a soundbite from their daughter, but they knew it was only a matter of time.

"Thanks a lot, Dad!" said Moses in great frustration. "Thanks a fucking lot!"

Jerome was taken by surprise at the front door as he arrived home from the office. "Whoa, calm down, Mo. What's your problem?"

"Your stupid lawsuit is my problem! What the hell are you trying to prove, anyway? That you can be the biggest asshole in America?"

"Hey, Moses, you criticize me all you want, but you leave the curse words behind or I'm leaving the room! You got it?" He slammed the door harder than he intended.

"Fine, but I still want to know what the . . . what you're trying to prove. We got screwed by God or by fate or by nature, and you won't accept it and move on, man. Shit happens—sorry. What about all those people in Asheville in Hurricane Helene? You think they're all going to get to sue God or God's agent? They're a whole lot worse off than you are."

"Than *we* are."

"No! Not *we*, Dad. YOU! You never asked me or Miriam or probably even Mom if this was something we wanted. 'Cause it's not! None of us wanted this. None of us. So, why don't you call up Mr. Calhoun or something and apologize and just stop?"

Jerome was stunned. Why hadn't he called it off? Why was it so important to sue . . . and win? He didn't speak at first, but put down his papers by the door and found the nearest chair.

"Dad, the Foxes—"

"I don't know, Mo. I have to do it. I don't think I can explain. I can't stop. It . . . means something. It's a statement I have to make." Outside, a dog began to bark loudly.

"But Dad, you're killing us! Now the Foxes say they don't want me going out with Sylvana. I can see her at school, but not outside, because they don't want their family linked with you in the press."

Jerome's shoulders stooped deeper. He took an audible breath. "Mickey Mantle, Roy Rogers, Jimmy Stewart. They're why I have to do this."

"What? Maybe you *are* crazy."

"I'm fifty-two years old. All the heroes of my youth are dead. I have almost no heroes older than me. There are no heroes today at all. Europeans came here so no one could tell them what to think about God. It's time for atheists to have that right."

"Dad," said Moses, "no one is telling you what to think."

"Are you kidding? This country is moving towards a theocracy, and somebody has to stand up in court and stop it. The Christian Right is trying to say it's a Christian country and anyone who doesn't respect that should get out. I have to prove that in America, nobody can say that they alone speak for God. What do you think it means when Mr. Calhoun says he's 'God's agent?' It means he's got a direct pipeline to God. If people believe that, then they believe anything he tells them to do, and that includes hating people like me. I have to make people understand that we're *all* at risk."

"I get it, Dad. But that's not what anybody thinks you're doing. Everybody thinks you're in it for the money."

"I was, but I don't care about the money now. If I win, I'll give most of it to charity. I just want to . . . Oh, crap, Moses. I just have to do it, okay? I'm sorry it's hurting you, but it will hurt us all more if I stop. I can't wait for another hero; I have to do it myself."

"I understand why you're upset, Sylvana, but we can't take a chance this year," said Todd Fox to his daughter, who was as distraught as Moses. "Do you think colleges won't know that you're mixed up with this crazy lawsuit that Moses's father has cooked up?"

"I don't care. If a college won't accept me because of my boyfriend's father, then I don't want to go to that stuffy old college anyway!"

"You can still see Moses at school. It's just for a little while. When the trial is over and the Lights lose, it'll all blow over and you can go out with Moses if you want."

"What if the Lights *don't* lose? Am I supposed to give up my boyfriend? Am I supposed to be the loser instead of them?" Sylvana had always possessed the power to break her father's heart.

Todd put his hand on Sylvana's shoulder. "They're not going to win. They can't win. We'll all lose our religious freedom if they win. But if that happens, you can see Moses again if you want to after it all dies down."

Chapter 35

The World's Rarest Flower

The Christmas-to-New-Year's break was one of the busiest times at the Church of the Forgotten Savior. Gideon always insisted on being available all that week to his congregants, including many people who live far away and came only once a year, . He walked with one lucky family from Oklahoma, who were thrilled to run into the Reverend Calhoun in the fabulous Kingdom Gardens attached to the six thousand-seat Savior Hall. Their daughter, about eight years old and as blond as the Oklahoma brush in August, saw a beautiful flower and asked if she could have it.

Gideon gently cautioned her. "Oh, no, my dear, you cannot. It's the only one like it, and if you pick it, it will not return. It was a gift to me from a group of Vietnamese pilgrims; it's an orchid that grows nowhere else in the world."

Later that day, he worked a line into his next sermon, and it was to become another piece of his legacy. "The world's rarest flower. Do you know what it is? It blossoms just once, sending up one frail flower. That flower may last a few seconds or many years. And even though it's quite rare, it grows everywhere on Earth. Do you know it now? It is YOU." He then read from Matthew, chapter 6, and talked about giving to the needy in this season of giving.

Celeste was beaming as she greeted Gideon after the service and after he had spent over an hour meeting and chatting with worshippers, trying to make his way back to his dressing room. "Gideon, that was wonderful, what you said. 'The world's rarest flower.'" She still walked with a cane and a limp that she now knew she would have the rest of her days, yet she had never been happier in her life.

Her son Matthew was with her for the holidays. His last name was

Lacking, like his father. It was his first time attending a service at CFS, and even he, jaded at fifteen, was impressed by the grandeur of the place and his new stepfather.

"What did you think, Matthew?" asked Gideon.

"That's the biggest choir I ever seen!" replied the boy.

"The biggest choir I ever saw," corrected Celeste.

Matthew was surprised. "You, too? I thought you'd seen 'em before."

Gideon laughed. "Your mother has seen the choir before. She says you like to sing, Matthew, is that right?"

"Aw, nothing like that. I like, you know, popular stuff."

"Really? What groups do you like?" Gideon asked the boy.

"Oh, Cold Smoke, the Furballs, Scratcheye, Inbred . . ."

Again, Gideon laughed. "I don't think I know all of them. But Cold Smoke is pretty good. I was listening to 'Up the Rainforest' the other day."

"You were? Yeah, that's one of my favorites, too." Matthew was impressed. When his mother had called to tell him she was getting married again, he had groaned, but then he had to admit, at least secretly, that it was pretty cool having a celebrity in the family, even if it was a minister.

"What about Spatial? Do you like them?" asked Gideon.

"I never heard of them. Are they country?"

"No, they're a Christian band, but I think you'd like them. I'll give you my CD at the house later. You can keep it. Do you like Hall and Oates?"

"Haulin' oats? I've never been on a farm."

Gideon laughed again. "No, Hall—H-a-l-l—and Oates. They were my favorite band when I was a lot younger. 'Sara Smile?' No, I guess I'm showing my age."

"You sure do have a lot of people who work for you," said Matthew.

"Not for me. For Jesus."

Matthew was, of course, staying with his mother and Gideon. The house was small, not what he expected for a famous guy. But he had his own room, at least, and he got to spend time with his Aunt Elysia, Uncle Bobby, and his cousins, Maria and Christina. Maria was his age, and, he had to admit, a lot better looking than he had remembered. *Too bad she's my cousin*, he thought. That didn't stop him conjuring up her image in his bed at night, but it did make him feel guilty later.

Chapter 36

The Floodgates of Hell

Right after the first of the year, Thaddeus MacConnell called and asked Jerome to meet him in Columbus. "There's a lot we have to do in the next three months," he said.

When Jerome took the afternoon off and drove down to Mac's office, the lawyer explained that he had been taking depositions since October. Some of Gideon's supporters had already been deposed, and it was clear that they believed God had spoken to the good Reverend.

"Calhoun's team wants to take your deposition soon. I want you to be prepared."

"Okay," said Jerome.

It'll all be happening before you know it."

Sure enough, Jerome looked out Mac's window for an instant, and suddenly . . . it was spring outside, a beautiful early March day, with the trial six weeks away. When Jerome turned back to face Mac, it was to a different, fancier office than the one he'd visited in January. Lacy was there too, extraordinarily attractive in a muted red suit and a scarf that made her look oh-so-chic.

"I guess we're ready," he said.

"Good," said Mac. "They're ready for us in the conference room." Dab Curara had made an arrangement with Rosenblum & Vroom, the biggest firm in Marshfield, to use their offices to take depositions.

"Who's in there?" asked Lacy.

Mac replied, "The lead attorney is the woman you met last fall in Judge Schuster's chambers, Dabria Curara. She's tough . . . and good. Watch out for her, and don't give out any new information without checking with me first. Then you'll also meet her second chair, a young woman named Lindsay Meier. I doubt she'll do any questioning. And of course the court reporter is also there. Her name is Kathy. She won't say anything unless she can't hear you."

Mac opened the door to the hall, and led the Lights to the pristine conference room. Dab and Lindsay stood and shook hands with each of them as they entered.

The session was long, the questioning tedious, and Jerome found it hard to remain civil at times. He was confronted time and again with slight variations of the same questions about his attitude towards religion. At one point, Ms. Curara seemed to indicate that CFS might countersue him for religious discrimination, but when Mac asked her to clarify if that was her intention, she backed off. At another point, she asked Lacy questions that were definitely aimed at finding any lack of support she might feel for the trial. Lacy was shaken a couple of times, but did not crack. When Gideon's attorneys left, Jerome swiveled his chair around to look out the window.

Jerome turned his chair to face Mac. It was now Wednesday, April 16, and Mac was in his own office again, doing his final preparation of the Lights for the trial. Lacy was at her office in Marshfield, where it seemed she tried to spend as much time as possible. Moses and Sylvana continued to sneak around to see each other. Miriam's grades had suffered slightly at school. George and Darcy Day worried constantly about their daughter, but tried not to let her see. Gideon and Celeste were getting used to living with another person, and finding themselves more deeply in love as Celeste's healing continued at a gallop. Mac was saying to Jerome, "And of course, there might be several appeals."

"Not by us, there won't."

"What do you mean?"

"I mean that it's gone far enough. Win or lose, we accept the decision of the court. If we win and they appeal, then we say 'Help us cover our expenses, and we're done. Oh, and tell the world we're not evil.' But if they win, we walk away. We can't throw more money at this thing, and I can't throw more trouble at my family. I'm a pariah."

"That's the last time I want to hear that from you, Mr. Light. You're the victim here. You can only be a pariah if you're the bad guy here, and you're not. If the jury finds out that you believe you're the bad guy, then they'll believe it, too. We want them to believe you have been screwed by the system. Besides, there's something I need to tell you."

Jerome snapped to attention. "What?"

"I've been approached by other interests. There may be others jumping in to this case."

"*What?*"

"Don't worry; I'm still your lawyer. But we're going to need a lot of help for the appeals, especially if we win. If you think this case is tough now, wait'll you see what the wrath of God's agent looks like if he loses."

"I don't get it."

"Several organizations have offered to file amicus briefs in support of our case. And we're going to need their support. I mean, ultimately, this thing could go to the U.S. Supreme Court."

"Holy shit! This is outta hand. I didn't ask for their help. Did you go to—"

"I believe your brother, the Unitarian one . . ."

"Carl?"

"Yes, Carl. I believe he called some people about helping your cause."

"Well, I didn't ask him to do that! Who did he call?"

"We've had discussions with the American Humanist Association and the Unitarian Universalist Association, and expressions of interest from the Freedom from Religion Foundation and the American Ethical Union."

"Who's 'we'?"

"My secretary and me, and my intern, Reg Lundin. You see, Mr. Light, neither of us can lose."

"How's that?"

"Well, if we win the case, I expect we will get a substantial financial award. You'll get your money, I'll get paid very well, and we expose the charlatans like Gideon Calhoun and keep at least one of them from bilking old people out of their meager savings. Calhoun's got the money; he'll still retire a very rich man after we—"

"You're not exposing anything! People hate me, and they may not have liked Calhoun before, but now he's getting their sympathy. Imagine what will happen if he loses? He'll be a martyr. They'll make me some kind of demon. In the future, instead of saying, 'Your name is Mudd,' they'll say 'Your name is Light.' You're wrong, Mac. If he loses, Gideon will be even bigger than he is now."

"Not when I get him to admit on the stand that he's never spoken to God, that he is not God's agent, that he has no personal relationship with God," Mac said.

"He's not going to admit that. His belief is sincere. He believes God talks to him."

"No he doesn't. It's all an act. He's a showman, for Christ's sake. Sure, he's a Christian, but he's a showman first."

"He's never been more popular, thanks to me."

"Look at it this way, then," said the calm and stalwart attorney, "maybe he'll win!"

"Oh great."

"That's not what I mean. I intend for him to lose, but maybe he'll win. In that case, we're both still okay. You'll be no worse off, and I'll be at the forefront of a new breed of litigation. The secular associations out there have a lot of money, and I'll get some excellent work out of it. You'll get out of everyone hating you … eventually, anyway. And the religious world will stay the way it's always been, at least until we get to the Supreme Court. Maybe those old ladies who send Calhoun their savings really are buying themselves a little salvation, or a little peace of mind."

✝ ✝ ✝

"There is no peace of mind that can come without Jesus!" said Gideon Calhoun to Dab Curara as they sat in the living room of Gideon and Celeste's home on a plushy, dark-green sofa.

"Amen!" said Curara. She had been in Gideon's house many times, but had never seen so many lights on. As a bachelor, he had kept the rooms dark, both to save electricity and to preserve his privacy. Thanks to the many evergreens surrounding the house, even open drapes would have let little sunlight into the room filled with dark-wood shelves, darkly bound books, and paintings of the Virgin Mary and Jesus and Old Testament tableaux covering the walls. Celeste's influence was felt immediately in every room of the house, and Dab realized that she was seeing some of the artwork for the first time.

"No matter what happens, I shall have peace of mind, Sister Dabria. I know that Jesus walks with me and sits in the courtroom with me, not in judgment of me or anyone else there, but in support of the righteous. 'Do not be afraid of any man, for judgment belongs to God.'—Deuteronomy 1:17."

"Jesus shall prevail, Brother Gideon. Jesus shall prevail."

Gideon paused in the midst of this exchange, and then said, "But Jesus needs our help. Jesus needs us to represent him well and truly in the public arena. What do we need to do, Sister?"

"We need to distance ourselves from some of your public pronouncements," she told the evangelist.

"What do you mean?"

At that moment, Celeste entered the living room carrying a silver tray. "I've brought you both some sweet tea, and some cinnamon rolls."

Gideon smiled at his wife. "Thank you, Celeste."

Celeste had caught the end of the lawyer's comment as she entered the room and could not help asking, "What public pronouncements do you mean?"

Curara filled her lungs with a deep breath and said, "I mean that if we insist that you are literally God's agent, we could lose."

"But that's just an expression," protested Gideon. "I am here to do God's work. I am called to the ministry."

"I know what you mean, Brother Gideon, but there is a great deal of cynicism in the country towards evangelists, especially your brethren who choose to share the Word on television."

"As Jesus himself would do if he were alive today. Not that I am comparing myself to Jesus in any way."

The attorney chose to ignore Gideon's clumsy disclaimer, and continued telling him what she knew he did not yet understand. "Those of us who know you, know that you are a good man, a sincere man, called by God to praise the name of Jesus Christ the Lord as our personal savior, but . . . those who do not know you fear you are another righteous sinner, another humbug like Marjoe or a huckster like Bakker or Swaggart."

"Those men have strewn pebbles on our path."

"They have strewn boulders, Brother Gideon. They have created outright hostility towards people like you. You don't see it because you have so many followers, and because your staff withholds the hate mail from you, but it is there. We must assume that they will try to fill the jury with such people, people who have not accepted Jesus Christ into their lives."

"Do not worry about the jury, Sister Dabria. Jesus will turn their hearts. They will see me with clear eyes and know what is in my heart."

"That may be, but they must not see you as claiming to be God's agent, or you will lose and the floodgates of Hell will open upon you." She tapped the knuckles of each hand together and then flung her open hands outwards, as if throwing open the doors that separated them from that demon world.

Chapter 37

Christians and Jews

On Tuesday, April 22, 2025—Earth Day—Thaddeus MacConnell met with Jerome and Lacy at 7:30 a.m. at a café near the courthouse where Judge Vera Schuster was soon to open the trial of *Light v. Calhoun et al.*, or, as the newspapers were calling it, "Sinkhole Man v. God." Sitting quietly with the trio was Reg Lundin, a young, curly-haired attorney that MacConnell had brought on as his assistant.

"You both look great," said Mac, the eldest attorney of the bunch. "Very classy. That's important. Mrs. Light, I need you to wear a different outfit every day. We need to convey that you are not suing just for the money, that you are elegant and intelligent, and you still have your dignity. Ultimately, your words on the stand will matter, but first impressions come from what you wear. I know you don't have a full wardrobe, but even a simple change such as a scarf or change of earrings will make you appear fresh each day."

"Okay," said Lacy, wondering how quickly she could get to a store to add some accessories. With money tight for the past seven months, she had skimped on fashion. She thought wistfully about all the things she had lost to the sinkhole, including some nice jewelry left to her by her maternal grandmother. She realized that she had no idea where to shop in Columbus. Marshfield was too far for them to drive home each night and back the next day, so she and Jerome had taken a room at the Holiday Inn, not too far from the courthouse. They planned to go home every other night to check on the kids, but after a long and agonizing discussion, they had decided to let Moses and Miriam go from school to home daily to do homework and get their stuff together for the next day. Then they were to go to Lacy's parents' house for dinner each night, and sleep there. Lacy did not trust them to cook a full meal and not burn the apartment down.

Mac ordered his eggs Benedict while Jerome, after checking the menu prices, ordered toast and tea. MacConnell said, "Jury selection is going to take a couple of days most likely. We need to be ultra-careful about whom we seat. This case will be won or lost in the next two days. I've been on the phone with Jo Wormwood." With a cloth napkin, he wiped a bit of egg off the corner of his mouth.

"Who's that?" asked Lacy.

"She's our jury consultant. She's the woman who—"

Jerome jumped in. "Who's on TV sometimes. I've seen her. She's a knockout!"

"She owed me a favor."

"Really? What kind of favor?" Jerome took extra time spreading jam on his toast.

"I did her a huge favor years ago: I broke up with her."

"No kidding? Wow!"

"I'm pretty sure we'd have killed each other. She's as competitive as I am, and that was before she made it big. You should hear her now. She made a bet with me that if I follow her advice, we'll win this thing."

"What's the bet?" asked Jerome.

"If she picks the jury and we win, she wins, and I have to take her to Fiji for a week."

"And if you win?"

"Well you see, that's the problem. There's no way *I* can win. If I pick the jury her way and we lose, I still take her to Fiji for a week." He peered at Jerome over his cup as he sipped his coffee.

Jerome looked confused. "And what if you pick the jury your way instead of her way?"

"Why would I do that? I'm not crazy! She's the best there is. She knows exactly what we're looking for in a jury."

Jerome flinched at that prospect. "What are you looking for? They'll never let you seat a jury of all atheists."

Mac laughed lightly and said, "No, that's for sure, and that's not who we want, anyway. You're not going to convince atheists that Calhoun should be liable, even if they are completely sympathetic to your point of view. I mean, they will certainly agree that the sinkhole was not an act of God, but then what? Their blame will be fixed on the insurance company, as yours initially was, but that doesn't help us. Big Rock Mountain is not a litigant in this case."

"So we're going to pin our hopes on Christians? That doesn't give me a lot of confidence," said Jerome, nursing his tea.

"And maybe even a couple of conservative Jews," interjected Reg, who had ordered nothing but black coffee. "We want people who are firm believers in God, but who don't trust fundamentalists like Calhoun. Remember, your beliefs are not on trial here. At best, what you believe is completely irrelevant; at worst, it's detrimental. The law has settled the question of whether there are 'acts of God.' Our job is to prove that God has agents on Earth who receive financial bounty for their work and therefore are responsible for God's debts, as it were. And finally, we will prove that Gideon Calhoun is one of those agents."

"I'm in shock," was all Jerome could say.

Mac paid for the food; Lacy, like Jerome, had eaten almost nothing. Then the four immaculately dressed people crossed the street to the courthouse. Several journalists were waiting outside the old brick building, and Lacy spotted Angie O'Graham, trapped behind several beefy men wielding video cameras. A man—someone neither Jerome nor Lacy recognized—was the first to spot the plaintiffs, and shoved a microphone in front of Jerome.

"Are you an atheist?" the man screamed at Jerome, who continued walking, trying his best to look straight ahead but also to look relaxed and happy . . . but not too happy. "C'mon. Are you an atheist?" the man with the mic repeated. Getting no answer, he tried a different approach, "What do you expect to get if you win?"

"Lacy! Jerome!" called Angie over the shoulders of several other reporters who were trying to track the Lights as they walked without surrendering an inch to the crush of reporters behind them. It was a skill they had honed over years of covering public figures who had no desire to talk with them. "Lacy, it's Angie O'Graham. How are you feeling today?"

Lacy was thrilled at a question about her feelings, instead of about "the case," as it had come to be called among her family and friends. She kept walking with Mac and Reg and her husband, but turned her face towards the personable reporter who had, after all, been the first one to cover their story. "Hi, Angie! I'm feeling great, thank you!" she called, and smiled her most appealing smile.

Angie felt empowered, enjoying the surprised glances from the networks' reporters who wondered how this unknown lightweight had succeeded where they could not. "Are you optimistic?"

Lacy glanced quickly at Mac, who gave an almost imperceptible shrug of his shoulders and a slight nod of his head, tacitly allowing Lacy to respond. Then she looked again at Angie, who was now falling farther behind the quartet as they neared the front doors. She called over her shoulder, "We feel glad that we're finally getting our day in court. It's in God's hands now!" She waved at Angie, then looked back straight ahead and saw, from the corner of her eye, Mac's mouth barely curling up, as broad a smile as he was likely to allow himself.

There were more reporters and photographers gathered directly outside Judge Schuster's courtroom, but Mac, taking the lead, guided the group through them and into the sanctuary of the court. Jerome realized that he had never been in an actual courtroom before, and he was surprised at its relative smallness. In the movies and on TV, the rooms always appeared larger. He had imagined it would be something like the stately courtroom in *To Kill a Mockingbird*, with a balcony along both sides and across the back, a gallery of hushed but captivated onlookers leaning on the wooden railing as Atticus Finch, this time played by Thaddeus MacConnell, used his mellifluous baritone to awaken the assembled throng to the great injustices visited upon Jerome and Lacy Light.

Instead, the room was inelegant, almost mockingly so. There were chairs for spectators rather than the pew-like benches Jerome had expected. There was only a ten-foot ceiling—nice, but hardly the impressive palace of justice he had envisioned. The room was basically a square, and the judge's bench looked nothing as imposing as, say, the Old Bailey. The walls were tan; there was no other word that would describe them. There was an American flag and an Ohio flag on floorstands at the front, but otherwise, the room was devoid of decoration. The significance of this blandness was not lost on Jerome; this room was about the disputes that came into it, not about the place itself. Because the room was so understated, it made Jerome feel more strongly the importance of what would take place here.

That was when Dabria Curara led Gideon Calhoun and two others to the defendants' table. There was a man, slightly shorter than Jerome, trim and refined looking, with a full head of hair that was either an extraordinarily bad toupee or the most amazing natural wave ever created. He had full eyebrows, and appeared to be about sixty-five.

Mac looked at Jerome and nodded his head towards the defendants. "That fellow is the chairman of the Board of Trustees of CFS Ministries, Inc. I purposely didn't depose him, because I want him somewhat less prepared when I call him as a witness. His name is Terre Béliveau. I guess he's a Frenchman who became born again when he moved here."

Gideon Calhoun said something to Celeste as she took a seat in the audience behind the defense table, and then strode over to Jerome. "Mr. Light. Normally I would say it's a pleasure to see you again, but I'm afraid that there's very little pleasurable about being here, so I simply want to say 'hello' and hope that you and Mrs. Light are in good health."

Lacy, who had stood the moment Gideon came over, reached past Jerome's suddenly paralyzed arm and shook hands with the famed evangelist. "Thank you, Reverend Calhoun. We wish we were meeting you under less, well . . . under other circumstances."

Jerome shook Calhoun's hand as well and said, "Hello, Mr. Calhoun. Thank you for coming over. It's no pleasure for us, either, I assure you."

Reg, who was closest to the defense team, felt compelled to jump in before either of the Lights could say anything that might come back to haunt them later. "Right! We appreciate your reaching out to us, Reverend.

I'm afraid I need a few minutes with my clients before the judge appears." He made this last part more like a question.

"Of course, Mr. Lundin. Of course. I merely wanted to be polite." Jerome was impressed that Gideon knew Reg by name.

As soon as she had gotten the list of "veniremen" (which Jerome had learned meant the pool of prospective jurors), Dab Curara had turned it over to Barbara Collyer, a jury consultant CFS had engaged. Collyer's staff immediately got to work learning all they could about each person. More than that, Barbara had pre-tested arguments to see which kind of person would be most sympathetic to Gideon and least sympathetic to Jerome. She reported to Dabria that they, too, wanted deeply religious jurors, people of great faith who felt that Christianity was too much under siege. Dab knew that if she asked directly about such fears (justified or not), the plaintiffs would use a peremptory challenge. Her questioning had to be subtler, had to find some other clue that would tell her a juror's inclinations.

Judge Schuster's deputy clerk asked for order, and the room fell quickly silent. The veniremen and women were brought into the courtroom and the arduous process of selection began.

Chapter 38

We'd Rather Trust a Lawyer

Halfway through the morning, the deputy clerk called a fifteen-minute recess in the jury selection process. Jerome and Lacy stepped into the hall outside the courtroom as MacConnell huddled with Reg Lundin. A moment later, Gideon and Celeste came through the doors into the hall, along with Terre Béliveau, who headed immediately towards the restroom. Jerome looked at the other couple, and Lacy whispered, "Don't say anything." But it was too late.

"Is this your wife?" Jerome asked, walking over to the Calhouns.

The Reverend looked surprised at the sudden casualness of his legal and spiritual nemesis, but regained his composure rapidly, drawing on his frequent experience with parishioners who would suddenly confess all manner of odd behavior to him. "Yes. Celeste, this is Mr. Light. Mr. Light, my wife Celeste. We were married just before last Christmas." He turned to Celeste, who did not move at all except to hold up her hand.

"How do you do, Mr. Light?" inquired Celeste a bit more formally than Jerome had anticipated. She did not smile or betray any other emotion. Jerome thought her stiff demeanor matched her very prim and proper dark-blue suit and pleated skirt that fell about an inch below her knees.

"Please, call me Jerome. I'm not used to the formality of the courtroom. Mazel tov on your wedding. I read something about it in the paper." Jerome waved Lacy over to join them, which she did with the greatest reluctance. "Honey, this is Celeste Calhoun. This is my wife, Lacy."

The women shook hands politely, with a healthy wariness of each other, born of their shared involuntary attendance at an event that had none of the daily reality they each respected and craved.

"You both have been through a lot," said Gideon, lapsing into his role as a minister, disregarding for the moment the antagonistic role in which they'd all been cast. "It must have been very difficult for you these past few months."

Lacy, more accomplished as a diplomat than her husband, responded quickly, before Jerome could possibly say anything they might regret. "We had some bad luck, but we've made the best of it."

"Where are you living now?" asked Celeste.

"We've rented an apartment not too far from our old house so the children can stay in the same school."

"How many children do you have?"

"Our son Moses is a senior in high school, and Miriam is fifteen. What about you?"

"Well, Gideon and I were just married, but I have a son from my first marriage. His name is Matthew. He lives with his father in Colorado. He's the same age as your daughter. Is she a freshman, too?"

"Yes. Would you like to see her picture?" Lacy asked, opening her purse. It was an oversized model, forced to carry too much stuff. She had lost her collection of different style purses when the sinkhole hit, and could not afford to replace them. Now she was afraid to leave her most precious possessions in the apartment, so she made do with this one basic-black shoulder bag, from which she produced her new smartphone displaying a recent photo—the only kind she now had—of Miriam.

"Oh, yes. Let me show you Matthew's picture as well." Celeste searched her small, dark-blue clutch.

Gideon and Jerome looked at each other as if they had accidentally bumped together in the shower at the local exercise spa. Gideon said, "I guess it's a good thing our lawyers aren't here right now."

Jerome smiled. "You know 'Family Feud' on the TV? Well, they asked people to name a profession most people don't trust much."

"I know of the show, but I'm afraid it's not something I have time to watch," said Gideon.

"Well, guess what came out on top as the least trustworthy profession?"

"Lawyers?"

"Right. And guess who else was up there?"

"Umm . . . car salesmen? Police?"

"Right. Politicians, and DMV clerks, et cetera. And do you know who was not on the list? Insurance agents. Insurance adjusters. Anyone to do with insurance."

"Hunhh."

"So people trust insurance companies more than they trust lawyers."

"I guess so," Gideon said, unsure where Jerome was taking this point.

"Except I don't think that's really true. Ask anyone who had a bad car accident if they think they might need a lawyer to keep the insurance company honest, and just about everyone is gonna say yes. Most of us don't think the insurance company is on our side when you come right down to it. We'd rather trust a lawyer when it's our own money on the line."

The courtroom door opened again, and Mac stuck his face out. He noticed Gideon and Jerome talking, but instead of glaring as he was inclined to do, he said, "We're starting again," and everyone poured back into the court.

Moses met Miriam in the parking lot after school. Dozens of cars were coming to life and lining up to pull away, like a column of chariots racing to freedom. "Hey, Mir, c'mon let's go!"

"All right! What's the hurry?"

"Sylvana told her parents she had a meeting after school. She's driving over to our place right now."

"A meeting?" said Miriam, climbing in the passenger seat of Moses's car. "What kind of meeting would she have?"

"I don't know. Like a stamp club or something."

"A stamp club?" Miriam started to laugh. "That better be all she's licking today."

Moses started to grab Miriam's wrist, but then realized that was a really bad idea, especially as he wanted to get on the road home instead of fighting with his little sister. "That's not funny, Miriam. You shouldn't say stuff like that."

"Like what, Big Brother? You mean about s-e-x?"

"Knock it off, wouldja?"

Miriam figured she had pushed her sensitive brother far enough, and she stared straight ahead, her hands tucked under her armpits as if she were really pissed off, although inside she still thought her comment had been funny.

Moses drove a bit too fast. Miriam found herself holding the grip over her head to keep from sliding around the front seat with each turn. About a block before they got to the Double Dee Food store near their home, he spotted Sylvana's car pulling into Sycamore. He gunned it through a yellow light and caught her in the parking lot outside their apartment.

"Hey, Syl. Sorry I'm a little late," he said, as he jumped out of his car. "I had to pick up Miriam."

"No problem, Mo. I just got here."

"Yeah, we saw you pulling in." Moses did not want the neighbors to see him with Sylvana, in case any of them might say something to the Foxes, so he scooted past her without a kiss and went inside to unlock the door.

Miriam, who no longer had her own cell phone—a cost-cutting measure—said, "I'm going to call Jessica, okay?"

"Yeah, sure. Call from your room, okay, so we can be in the living room."

Miriam disappeared down the hall, and Moses settled his long body into the sofa that was the same one they had rented last summer. It was hardly ideal, and Lacy could barely hide her contempt for its pattern, but Moses had quickly adapted to it, especially when he had the chance to share it with Sylvana. As the pretty teenager cuddled up to him, Moses said, "I can't hang out here too long. My grandparents are expecting Mir and me around 5:30. We're supposed to get our homework done before we go there for dinner."

"Am I part of your homework?" Sylvana asked impishly.

"Yeah, you're my biology project. I might have to dissect you or something."

"Mmm. That sounds kinda naughty. I don't know if I'd like that."

Moses kissed her passionately, but then withdrew. "We can't do anything. Not with my sister here."

"But she's in the other room. She knows better than to come out." Sylvana took Moses's head in both hands and pressed her lips on his. As she kissed him, Moses reached down and uselessly tried to suppress the growth in his trousers, thereby making matters worse. In a moment, Sylvana's hand brushed Moses's aside and continued the already discredited suppression technique.

Moses extracted his lips from hers, and leaned back against the sofa. His head faced straight forward for all of two seconds before he tilted it back and moaned. "Ohmygod, what are you doing to me?" Recognizing that no words were called for in response, Sylvana's head and torso followed Moses as if drawn by a huge magnet implanted in his chest, and she hoisted herself up high enough to be able to descend on the helpless boy as if her lips were the lunar landing module gently but inexorably moving towards a landing on the barren surface of the moon. Her upper body slunk against his, as if it had turned into a dirigible from which all the air had been slowly drawn. If passion could be measured in calories, this was one fattening kiss.

"Let's go to my room, but you can't scream or anything," said Moses.

"Me? Scream? Whatever do you have planned that would make me scream?" she said with all the innocence of a screen siren.

Moses forced himself off the sofa cushions and, minus his shoes, took Sylvana's hand and led her down the hall past Miriam's room to his own messy chamber. He locked the door and tore off his own shirt, revealing in the half-light from the window that tennis was, indeed, good for upper-body strength. Sensing that a bodybuilding contest was about to ensue, Sylvana removed her own top and, in the spirit of fairness, her brassiere. Sadly, her soft body was no match for his firm one, but in a grand conciliatory gesture, Moses hugged the curvy girl to his chest and tried to comfort her. Judging by her whimpers and moans, it appeared she was still agitated by his superior musculature.

Miriam heard her brother shut the door to his room, and heard Sylvana's tiny expressions of distress. She liked Sylvana, and thought it was pretty cool that it was her brother who had won the heart of this great smart, rich, sexy senior. She turned up her radio and dove with renewed vigor into her English homework.

Chapter 39

Sleepless in Ohio

Gideon awoke with a start Tuesday morning at 5:00 a.m. His stomach hurt like the devil, and he lurched to the bathroom of the Westin Columbus suite he had reserved, a few blocks from the courthouse.

Celeste, who was still not used to sharing a bed with anyone, woke up when the bathroom light went on. She could hear Gideon moaning gently, and went to the bathroom door. "Are you all right, Gideon?"

"Not quite. I . . . I'll be okay."

"Are you sure? You don't sound too good."

"I have trouble like this sometimes. I'll be okay. Thank you."

"All right," said Celeste, warily returning to the bed. She lay there for several minutes, listening for any hint that Gideon might be in distress. It was quiet, but he did not return. After fifteen minutes, she got up again and returned to the hallway by the bathroom. The light, she could see, was still on. She whispered, "Gideon?" No reply. She whispered more loudly. Again, no reply. She rapped lightly on the door, and spoke softly, "Gideon? Are you okay?" Her heart was in her throat.

She might have had a panic attack any moment had he not finally answered. "I'm okay, Celeste. I was just praying," he said gently, patiently.

His tone was so serene, she relaxed immediately. "Oh, thank you, Jesus. I was beginning to get worried about you."

The bathroom door opened. He looked a bit haggard, and his pajamas were badly rumpled, but he had a weak smile for her. "Let's go back to bed. Maybe we can get a few more minutes' rest before we go back to this cir . . . to the court."

A few blocks away at the Holiday Inn, Jerome and Lacy were playing out a similar scene. This night was their first away from home for the trial. Both had taken leaves of absence from their jobs, creating instability and uncertainty that neither wanted to acknowledge. They were perturbed about the kids, about their financial situation, and about the case. Jerome had told his wife of MacConnell's plans for an appeal, and how the case was becoming so much bigger than they'd ever intended or foreseen.

Lacy had been exhausted after the day's events, and she had fallen asleep soon after they'd settled into the room and called Lacy's parents to check on Miriam and Moses. She was heartened to hear Miriam's voice, and to know that the plans they'd made for the children were working out. When Lacy asked her mother to put one of the kids on the phone, Moses had pointed to Miriam. He was not anxious to talk with his parents.

Jerome had been the one who could not sleep. He left the TV on when Lacy turned off her bed lamp and dozed off. He muted the set and read the closed captions at the end of a cop drama. When that was over, he watched local news. He considered waking Lacy when Angie O'Graham's report on their trial came on. Instead, he watched transfixed as he read, rather than listened to, Angie and then MacConnell, and a few words from Lacy. The sounds of the day were still so familiar to him that he didn't realize there was no sound. There was little substance to Angie's report; what was there to say yet?

Still, the reporter managed to find an angle that made Jerome all the more aware of how important the case had become. That realization did nothing to help him feel sleepy. He got up and went to the bathroom during each of the next two commercial breaks, and he tried to find some bit of good that might blossom from this out-of-control plant he had nourished from a seed, a seed he now feared might have been bad from the start. He turned off the TV and wandered into a restless sleep at 1 a.m., two hours before Lacy began fretting and waking.

At 5:30, she could stand it no longer. She said to Jerome, "Are you asleep?"

"Mm-hmm," came the reply.

"I can't sleep."

"Okay."

"What?"

"Okay."

"Okay? It's okay that I can't sleep? That's how you feel?"

"Go back to sleep."

"I can't sleep. That's the problem! How come you can sleep through . . . this?"

"Huh?"

"I said, how come?"

"Huh?"

"I said, how come *you* can sleep through this? You'll sleep through anything!"

Jerome finally began to parse his surroundings and who this insane woman was and what her words meant. "I couldn't sleep. I was up forever. I just fell asleep."

"Oh, Baby, I'm sorry!" said a suddenly remorseful Lacy.

"What am I going to do?" said Moses to no one. He was alone in his bed at his maternal grandparents' house. Now that both he and Miriam were in the high school, it no longer mattered if they woke up far from the school bus stop; Moses would simply drive his little sister to school.

"I can't believe I did that." The boy did not normally talk out loud to himself, but was astonished that he had made love with Sylvana there in his own bedroom with his sister in the next room. He knew it was wrong on so many levels, not the least of which was both he and Sylvana lying to their respective parents. More than anything, though, he was surprised at his own weakness, his own inability to do the right thing when it came to sex. It was amazing to him how easily he was swayed from exercising some restraint. It was not enough to see Sylvana in school each day and snatch a brief conversation with her during lunch. She had begged him to let her come over, and he had no resistance. Worse, he had involved his sister. Two people is a plot; three makes it a conspiracy.

He wondered how he was going to last until the trial ended. His parents had said it might take four weeks, given the witness lists prepared by each side. Four weeks! Maybe when the trial was over, and his dad had lost— he did not think of the trial as his parents', but as his father's alone—as certainly he would lose (wouldn't he?), then maybe the Foxes would take some pity on him. Surely they'd at least take pity on their own daughter, right? They'd have to allow her to go out with Moses again, wouldn't they?

Moses wanted the trial over *now*. It wasn't just Sylvana; other kids at Marshfield Senior High were shunning him or giving him a hard time. Even one of the teachers said something nasty, and the vice principal had asked him if his parents were going to sue them for the words "under God" in the Pledge of Allegiance. He had answered, "No!" with great annoyance in his voice. Unable to sleep further, Moses put on a bathrobe that was his grandfather's and went down to the kitchen, where his grandparents sat drinking coffee.

Chapter 40

Jerome v. God

At 5:30 that Tuesday morning, almost everyone was awake. Miriam slept soundly until her alarm went off at 6:10. Her first thoughts were of Moses and his girlfriend. Sylvana woke up minutes before her mother came and knocked on her door. She awoke with a huge smile on her face and a burning desire to get to school early. Mac MacConnell snored right through the alarm for an extra fifteen minutes. He decided to skip his shower and hurry to the hotel coffee shop to meet the Lights who, he was not surprised to see, looked like hell.

"I hope you two plan to fix yourselves up," he said with all the tact of an interior decorator whose clients insist on hanging their black velvet picture of dogs playing poker. "We can't have the jury see you looking like that." They stared at him without speaking. "Tough night, eh? Well, don't worry; that's pretty standard for the opening of a trial. You'll be sleeping like babies once things get rolling."

Reg Lundin joined the trio, and the four of them ate quickly and silently, until Mac decided it was time for the day's instructions. "We'll finish jury selection today. It went pretty well yesterday; I'm pleased with the jurors we sat. I don't think any of them are hostile to atheists, but they are all good church-going people, and not one fundamentalist. That's better than I had thought we might do."

Jerome and Lacy returned to their room to get ready. As Jerome showered, Lacy called her mother. "Hey, Mom, how's it going? Did the kids get off to school all right?"

Darcy was surprisingly upbeat. "Of course. Dad and I got up early and fixed them a good breakfast so they won't be too hungry. Oh, but Moses seemed to have some trouble sleeping. He came down to the kitchen right after we did."

"Did he say what was bothering him?"

"Just that he had a lot on his mind." Darcy realized as she said it that Lacy also had a lot to preoccupy her, and she didn't want to worry her daughter. "Don't worry, dear. He's fine. He went off to school just fine. I'm sure he just misses you and Jerome."

"We miss him, too. And Miriam. Is she okay?"

"She's fine. In fact, she seemed especially in a good mood. She hugged Moses when she came down for breakfast."

"She did? How unusual! I guess . . . well, I don't know. Anyway, thanks for watching the kids, Mom. We'll drive home tonight after court."

"How's it going? Oh . . . I saw you on the news last night, but they really didn't say much about the trial."

"There's not much to tell, Mom. Jury selection's almost done. The trial itself will start tomorrow. We'll tell you about it when we come over this evening."

The morning dragged by as the deputy clerk repeated the same list of questions for each of the prospective jurors, with lawyers for both sides occasionally asking questions, and frequently rejecting a surprised prospect. By mid-morning, six of the eight jurors and alternates had been picked, including two African American women, an Asian man, and three Caucasians, two of whom were clearly over sixty-five.

During a break, Jerome stepped into the narrow hall of dark wood outside the courtroom. A police officer waited in the hallway, apparently prepared to testify in another case in another courtroom. He had smallish feet crammed into black shoes that shined unnaturally, and he appeared top heavy, the result of too much time spent sitting in a squad car eating too many fat-laden lunches prepared by his wife, who felt that the more out of shape he became, the less he was at risk to be chasing gun-toting criminals down muddy alleys. His feet had to move constantly underneath his too-short legs to keep him from toppling over. This ballet reminded Jerome of a circus performer moving nimbly about to keep several plates twirling atop tiny spindles.

By 3:30, the full jury was chosen and asked to return the following day for a four-week trial, based on the witnesses each side had listed. Dab and Barbara were surprised—and a bit concerned—to find the process had been less contentious than expected. Jerome swallowed hard as court was adjourned for the day, and he shook Mac's hand. "I guess we're into it now," was the deepest sentiment he could manage.

Mac put an arm around Lacy's shoulder and pulled her to him, then released Jerome's hand and maneuvered himself and Lacy into a group hug with Jerome, who was none too comfortable at this sudden physicality. "Now is when it starts to get really exciting," Mac whispered, trying to pump up his clients' spirits. "I don't see how we can lose."

"You don't?" said Jerome, with the sort of surprise usually reserved for a bride's abrupt change of mind at the altar. "Because I sure do."

"Well, let me rephrase that. I'm confident we will win the case, but even if we don't, we are going to make life very uncomfortable for Mr. Calhoun and his ilk."

Lacy had not seen this side of MacConnell before. She recoiled from Mac's casually placed arm around her shoulder. "What exactly do you mean by 'his ilk,' Mr. MacConnell? Is this some kind of crusade for you?"

MacConnell dropped his arm and was taken aback by Lacy's reaction, having misjudged her state of mind. "No, not at all."

"Because I have to tell you that I am not at all comfortable with what we're doing here, Mr. MacConnell. I'm not at all sure we're doing the right thing. The Reverend Calhoun seems like a genuinely decent man, and I don't think he had anything whatsoever to do with us losing our house. I don't understand why he should have to pay us one thin dime. I don't understand why our family got into this mess in the first place or why I allowed it to get this far. I don't understand why our son has to stop seeing his girlfriend so we can play God and decide who has to pay for a goddamn sinkhole."

"Please, Mrs. Light, lower your voice."

"Why? So you won't lose this precious case? I think you should lose it."

"Can we have this conversation in private, Mrs. Light? I will do whatever you and Mr. Light want to do as long as we discuss it in private."

Lacy stopped talking and looked both defiant and exasperated. She inhaled and exhaled quickly through her nose. She looked Mac right in the eyes and then jerked the top of her head towards the exit from the courtroom that had been, thankfully, almost entirely emptied before her outburst. Only one old woman was still making her way out of the court, slowly heading towards the door. She gave no outward appearance that she had heard any of Lacy's words.

Thaddeus MacConnell gathered his papers and headed for a small conference room he knew was nearby. Finding it empty, he ushered the Lights in and shut the door. Sensing a crisis, Reg Lundin hung up his cell phone and rushed to follow the others. By this time, Mac was no longer startled, but angry. "Why did you have to pick THIS minute to tell me what you think? Were you waiting for the worst possible moment to spring it on me?"

Now it was Lacy's turn to be taken aback. "I'm sorry. You're right. I should have said something sooner, but I'm not sure I knew how I felt until just this minute."

"Lacy!" Jerome scolded.

"Don't you start, Jerome. Don't you start. You got us into this . . . stupid f . . . freaking mess. I'm so mad at you right now. And I'm mad at God, too! I'm mad at the EPA and the government and the TV and the Foxes and the entire damned legal system, but I'm NOT mad at Gideon Calhoun! He may be the only true gentleman I know right now!"

Mac said, "That 'gentleman' is making millions of dollars a year from selling snake oil and calling it religion!" Reg leaned against the closed door and folded his arms.

Lacy hissed, "I don't give a damn how much he is making, Mr. MacConnell. He didn't get any of it from me, and he doesn't owe me a damn thing! If he's breaking the law, then let the law deal with it. We lost our house, not our freedom. We didn't suddenly move to a new country where religious freedom is banned. No one forces anyone to send their money to his church or any other church or synagogue, or to no place."

"I won't argue with you, Mrs. Light. I think you are wrong about the damage that people like Calhoun cause to society. I think you are wrong that he can claim to speak for God and not bear responsibility for doing so." Mac looked to the side of the room, then quickly back to facing Lacy. "But it doesn't matter what you or I think. It only matters what you want to do about it."

"What can we do now, Mr. MacConnell? It has gone so far. Tell us," and for the first time, she seemed inclined to include Jerome in what was going to happen, "what are our options?"

MacConnell landed heavily in one of the conference room chairs and swung his hands onto the table where he folded his right hand over his left. "Well, you can tell me that you want to end the case right now and withdraw your lawsuit. In that case, all my hours of work will have been in vain, and I will feel compelled to bill you for my time and expenses, which, under our contract, I am allowed to do." Mac's left hand made a Victory sign; then he flipped his left hand palm up, as if Victory had again lost her head, and tapped his right index finger to his left middle finger. "Second, you can direct me to try again to reach an out-of-court settlement with Calhoun, perhaps for as little as one dollar and court costs, in which case I will announce that you and Rev. Calhoun have settled for an undisclosed amount, and the world will think we won, and I will be flooded with clients who will pay me handsomely as the expert for suing for 'acts of God.' Again, I would need to bill you for time and expenses. Or . . ." and he spread both hands out as if he'd released a dove, ". . . or we can leave here and not say another word about it and let the jury decide what is right. Who knows, Mrs. Light? They may see it the same way you do."

"And what about me?" asked Jerome. "Don't I have any say in what we do?" Lacy and Mac looked at him expectantly. "Maybe I shouldn't have insisted on this case, Lace, but I'm not ready to stop it now. I'm convinced that what we are doing is important, even if we lose. Mac is right: Calhoun and all the others like him are getting away with too much. It has to stop. But even if nothing changes, how can we stop now? What do you suppose happens to us, to our kids, if we pull the plug now and say 'we're sorry, we didn't mean it,' and try to pretend like it never happened? We've already lost so much to the sinkhole. We can't afford to pay Mac for his fees and costs. And a settlement? That's a joke. It's not even honest. I want to come back here tomorrow and get our day in court."

"Well, I don't!" said Lacy with conviction. "Leave me out of it."

"How can I do that?" Jerome asked Lacy. "You're not just part of this case; you're part of me. I can't be here if you're not here, too."

"I'll come, but I don't want to testify. I don't want to be forced to say things I don't believe."

"Fine," said MacConnell. "I won't call you. It won't hurt our case. Know, however, that the defense might call you." He turned and looked at Jerome. "I guess it's just '*Jerome v. God*' now, eh?"

Chapter 41

Fair Is Not a Consideration

Lacy was still upset, but less so, when she and Jerome pulled up to her parents' house that evening. "So, what are we going to tell Mom and Dad?" she asked Jerome as he parked.

"I guess we'll tell them what we agreed . . . that you're not going to testify and that Mr. MacConnell thinks that jury selection went our way."

"What if they want to know why I'm not testifying?"

"Tell them . . . Mr. MacConnell's strategy is to keep you away from the defense attorneys. That's the truth, you know."

She got out of the car and looked across the hood at Jerome, then lowered her face to look at her own feet scuffing the ground like a nervous colt. "It's not the whole truth. But I don't want my parents to know how I feel. They would . . . well, I think it would upset them. And what if Angie O'Graham comes snooping around again and interviews them? I don't want them to have to lie for us."

"I don't, either," said Jerome. "But I thought you were a big fan of Angie. She put us on the map, you know."

"I think she's great, but if she's doing her job right, she's going to smell something wrong here, and I don't want my parents involved."

Jerome's face got a look of understanding, and he realized there was nothing more to say. He nodded a couple of times to let Lacy know he got it, then shut the door and locked the car, leaving their bags in the trunk.

"Oh, Lacy, how good to see you," said Darcy as her daughter entered the house. "Come on in. Let me get you both something to drink." As quickly as she had rushed to greet Lacy, she disappeared towards the kitchen. A moment later she reappeared in the doorway. "Um, what would you like to drink?"

Jerome knew they should both follow Darcy to the kitchen. "I'll just have water, Mom," said Jerome.

"Do you have any wine open?" asked Lacy.

Miriam and Moses arrived to join their parents and grandparents for dinner. Moses was not in a good mood, having been forced to say goodbye to Sylvana at lunch, knowing they would not be able to meet the rest of the day. Before yesterday, he'd been getting used to seeing her only at school. Now that they'd spent extra time together on Monday, it felt like being torn apart all over again. Miriam knew what was bothering him, and wisely said nothing.

"Hi, kids," said Jerome as the siblings entered the kitchen. "It's good to see you."

Miriam went right to her dad and hugged him. "It's good to see you too, Daddy. When's the trial going to be over?"

"Wow, right to the point, eh, Miriam? Well, it really is just getting started. They've picked the jury, so the actual trial itself begins in the morning."

"Oh," said Miriam, quietly. She had thought her parents wouldn't come home until it was over. She was not pleased to hear they'd be leaving again. "How long will it take?"

"They're still telling us four weeks. Of course, that could change. Mom's not going to testify now, so maybe that will shorten it up a little." Jerome did a double take as he caught Lacy looking surprised at him.

"How long did you think I was going to be up there?" Lacy demanded to know. "I assumed it would be maybe ten minutes or something. I don't have that much to say, really."

"Are you kidding?" asked Jerome. "You were gonna be up there at least half a day. The defense was going to want a lot of time with you."

"So maybe it's a good thing I won't be testifying."

Jerome looked down at his shoes for a count of two, then back up at Lacy.

♥ ♥ ♥

"Yeah, probably," said Gideon Calhoun, answering Celeste's musing that the Lights had the option of going home each night, a benefit denied to the Arkansas travelers. He sat at the desk in the suite they had taken in the same Holiday Inn where Jerome and Lacy stayed, having decided that being in the fancier Westin sent the wrong message. He was busy writing emails to his staff.

"It hardly seems fair," Celeste said.

"Fair is not a consideration, my dear. God does not attempt to make life 'fair' for His children. We are here in Columbus for some reason that God understands and we do not. It was hardly 'fair' for Mr. and Mrs. Light to lose their home and not be compensated after years of paying for insurance. That sinkhole was part of God's plan, too. Make no mistake, it *was* an act of God, and it was part of God's plan that we must help the Lights."

"Do you really think so? Oh, of course you're right, Gideon. You amaze me more every day! You are such a good man." Celeste walked up behind him and, leaning her chest into the back of his head, crossed her arms over his chest. She kissed the top of his head, and he clasped her hands, as if to pin her there. He smiled as she said, "I'm feeling so much stronger these days, my love. I think I could . . . if we were to . . ."

Gideon spun and looked at her. She smiled, and all he said was, "I'd like that."

Chapter 42

Opening Arguments

The next morning, Jerome and Lacy left Marshfield in the fog at 5 a.m. so they could drop their bags at the hotel and still get to the courthouse nice and early. They were to call Mac as soon as they arrived at the hotel, and he would gather the rest of the staff.

Mac had returned to his usual ebullient self, but Jerome seemed more somber than ever, and Lacy said barely a word. Consequently, Mac and Reg did most of the talking at breakfast, going over last-minute details of the opening statement and the witness list. Two interns from OSU joined them at the table, furiously making notes of everything Mac said.

By the time they arrived at the courthouse, the media contingent had grown larger than the previous day. They were all immediately beset. Jerome realized it was going to be this way every day from now on. He tried his best to smile, but heeded Mac's admonition to say only "Not right now," when asked any question. "Let me throw the occasional breadcrumb to the press. You two have to remain stoical so we don't have to do any damage control later. You'll be amazed at how easily anything you say will be twisted. If you say 'Have a nice day,' they'll print that you're a control freak."

Jerome laughed, but it was more perfunctory than sincere. Behind him, Lacy spotted Angie O'Graham in the throng of reporters, but this time ignored her and stayed with Mac.

Inside, the security was tighter than ever. To enter the building, they had to pass through the usual metal detectors and X-ray machine, but outside Judge Schuster's court armed guards hand-checked the contents of purses and briefcases, including Mac's. Jerome looked at Lacy and they knew that their little escapade had become momentous, indeed. Lacy said later that was the instant she knew how the trial would end.

Mac led the team to the plaintiffs' table, where he and Reg began to set up shop. Mac arranged the chairs as he wished everyone to appear, putting Lacy closest to the jury box, then Jerome, then himself, with Reg seated slightly behind and between Jerome and Mac. He told Jerome, "No offense, Mr. Light, but Mrs. Light makes a much more appealing and sympathetic plaintiff than you do, and I want the jury to feel close to her. I'm glad we're closer to the jury box than Calhoun's team."

"Hey, I'm not offended. I agree with you. I seem to be a lightning rod for hatred. If I could be in another room, or even another state right now, I'd be happy."

Reg and Mac were methodical and organized as they began to lay out the materials they'd need. Jerome studied the jury, which had already been seated.

Once the courtroom had been filled, the doors were closed. The videographers took their places. The buzz in the room was like a chorus of singers who had learned only to mumble. The deputy clerk stood and tapped his staff, then declared, "All rise," and Judge Vera Schuster entered the room from a doorway off to one side near the front. With her dark skin and black floor-length robe, she looked like a shadow crossing the room until she took her place at the bench and faced the assemblage.

"Hear ye, hear ye. The United States District Court for the Middle District of Ohio is now in session, Judge Vera Olivette Schuster presiding. God save the United States and this honorable court." Jerome bristled at this final sentence.

The judge had clearly had her hair done for the trial. She looked more intensely immaculate than was her habit. Certainly, the court reporter noticed, even if the deputy clerk was as oblivious as his wife always accused him of being. Judge Schuster took her seat quickly and was ready to go. "Good morning," she said. "Please be seated." Everyone sat . . . and waited. The judge seemed momentarily lost in thought.

Finally, she read from her notes. "We are here in the matter of Jerome and Lacy Light versus Gideon Calvin Calhoun and CFS Ministries, Inc."

"This case is uniquely unusual. I have found no precedent for it. The interest in this case is unusual, too, and it is not often that my courtroom is full of spectators, with many others gathered outside wishing to attend. Justice is pleased. Justice requires that people attend, which is from the same root as 'attention.' Justice cannot be served if no one is paying attention. I am delighted that so many people want to pay attention to this case. They will not be able to do so if those of you who are privileged to be inside this courtroom do not allow them to pay attention, but instead draw attention to yourself. I will not tolerate even the slightest interference from anyone in this courtroom, including counsel. I demand respect for the law, for each other, for this court, and for the people inside and outside this room who are paying attention to what we decide here."

She looked at the jury box. "Ladies and gentlemen of the jury, I thank you in advance for your service. You have a challenging job ahead of you. I am sure you are up to the challenge. To be responsible and respectful, you, too, must pay attention. Whatever you decide in the end, let it be based on your best evaluation of the arguments, and not on some mental flip of the coin because you were inattentive.

"Just as you must pay attention in this courtroom, you may attend to what you say outside this room. You are not to discuss this case with anyone, including each other. You are to avoid watching television news coverage or any other media discussion of this case. If even one of you should speak to a reporter or any other person regarding this case, I will sequester you all for the duration of the trial, and if any of you has been privileged to see the kinds of hotel rooms this court can afford on your behalf, you would do well to avoid that fate." Soft laughter rippled through the room.

"Counsel, I warn you that I will not tolerate a circus atmosphere from you or your clients. I am ordering you *not* to speak to representatives of the media during this trial. We will not have this case tried in the media before it is tried in this room. The public can make up their own minds based on the record that is available thanks to the television cameras. You will do your speaking about your case here, where I can ensure that the debate is a fair one that follows the rules of evidence, not of demagoguery. Together, we will do our best to reach a fair conclusion that no future review will be able to impugn. I have no doubt that one of you will be left unhappy and considering an appeal of the jury's decision. Nothing we do or say in this trial will likely deter that result. Therefore, it is safe to say that the best thing you can do to be ready for that eventuality is to conduct yourself flawlessly. This court will have zero tolerance for anything that resembles a circus."

The jury of six, with two alternates, sat transfixed and ready. Judge Schuster reminded them to follow the information in the handbook they had each been given and to keep an open mind. She said they could take notes, but only for their own usage, and that they could not ask questions prior to their deliberations after closing arguments. For the next half-hour, she explained other minutiae important to the jurors. Jerome wondered if the whole day would be gone before anything happened.

Without fanfare, or even a pregnant pause to warn Jerome out of his deepening stupor, Judge Schuster said, "If the plaintiffs are ready to proceed, you may present your opening argument, Mr. MacConnell." And the trial began.

Thaddeus MacConnell, in his navy-blue pinstriped suit, pale-blue button-down shirt, and yellow patterned tie, rose to his full height and stood by his desk, facing Judge Schuster. "Thank you, Your Honor." He walked toward the jury box. "Ladies and gentlemen, it is an honor to be with you here today. In the brief moments I shared with each of you during the jury selection process, I quickly gained respect for you, respect for your integrity and for your personal beliefs. If I did not think you were able to understand difficult concepts of law, and if I did not think you were able to listen fairly and without bias, I would have asked that you be dismissed. Indeed, I used my privilege to excuse several members of the jury pool from which you were drawn." Mac stood tall and dashing halfway between Jerome and the jury. Only his forearms and hands, held in front of his chest, moved as he spoke. He commanded attention by his stature.

"Each of you was carefully searched as you entered this building and this courtroom. The court has an interest in making sure that you brought nothing dangerous with you. Well, you know the saying, 'The pen is mightier than the sword?' It means that words and ideals have more power than weapons and anger. The guards did not confiscate your personal beliefs as you entered this room. You have those beliefs, and everyone in America can breathe easier because you do, because in your heart you are good people, with a useful blend of moral outrage and ethical behavior. You have values. Those values are the center of your lives. Your values helped you choose your friends and your spouses or partners. You've taught your values to your children and even grandchildren for a select few of you." He smiled at the older jurors. "Your values help you earn a living every day. Your values led you to this jury and this case. Your values are not on trial here. *You* are not on trial here.

"This case is not about values. It is not about whose religion is right or wrong. It can't be about that, because in America we agree that no single religion is more right than others in the eyes of the law."

MacConnell turned and walked slowly, his legs extending fully and carefully with each step, toward one end of the jury box, where he reversed course and strode to the other end. His speaking pace was as deliberate as his stride. His eyes were always on different jurors.

"In America, we all agree on core values, and one of those is respect for the law. America is the greatest country on Earth in part because it is a country of laws. Every religious belief has equal protection under the law. That is the only way possible in a democracy. Our Founding Fathers knew that. The very first thing they declared when they were done creating the foundation of our democratic republic was that we would make no laws establishing religion. That principle is not on trial here. We are not seeking to change that. We are here to uphold that bedrock of our Constitution.

"You will be asked a simple question. Can an American repeatedly make a statement in public, on television, in church, and not be held accountable for what they have said? Can a man charge money to teach people his beliefs, and then say he didn't really mean it?" He pursed his lips and took a deep breath through his nose.

"The plaintiffs, Jerome and Lacy Light, and their two children, are decent, hard-working Americans like you. They pay their taxes, mow their lawn, give to charity, teach their children good values, spend money carefully, and obey all the laws. They're the kind of people who make America great. And last June, a sinkhole destroyed their house. That's not something you get to say every day. A sinkhole destroyed their house. It destroyed their roof, their walls, their furniture, their bathtub, their clothes, their TV, their dishes, their photographs, and their shelter. They accepted this tragedy better than I would have, better, perhaps, than most of you would have. They said, 'We've got to move on with our lives. We still have each other.' And they picked themselves up even though the house represented most of their savings."

Jerome successfully stifled any expression on his face as he heard himself portrayed so nicely. Lacy's eyes moved from Mac to one of the juror's faces and back, but no one else noticed her move at all.

"Jerome and Lacy could do that because they knew they had insurance. They figured they'd be all right, but they didn't figure correctly. Their insurance company said the sinkhole was an Act of God, and there's no help for the Lights. They're supposed to accept the loss and get over it. Now, a lot of people might want to blame the insurance company for being kind of cold, but they were simply following the law. They really couldn't do anything else. The insurance company is not on trial here.

"An 'Act of God.' What an interesting term. I'm no preacher, so I can't really tell you what that means in theological terms. I can tell you what it means in legal terms. There's actually a lot of case law defining it, and you don't want me to bore you with all of that. What it boils down to is that some things that happen are nobody's fault. There's no person who was negligent or vicious, who caused something to happen. We say God made it happen. Well, God is not on trial here today, either."

It seemed every spectator in the courtroom shifted as one in his or her seat, as MacConnell paused in his delivery and slowly changed the direction in which he had been walking as he spoke.

Mac continued. "So there's a lot that is *not* on trial here, right? We're not trying values, or morals, or religions, or insurance companies, or God. So, what *are* we trying? We're trying a man who makes tens of millions of dollars a year by saying that he is God's 'agent' here on Earth, who profits by claiming to know what God plans. He brings in a fortune by intervening with God on behalf of people who come to him to help them pray to God. He's kind of like a spiritual arbitrator, a paid negotiator who says, 'If you keep my ministry afloat, I'll talk with God and see what I can do to make your lives better.' But, you know . . . that's not entirely a fair remark I just made about the defendant. Because he's a better man than that. He will pray to God on behalf of all people on Earth. He will talk with God about helping anyone. You don't have to pay him to ask him to intercede with God. He prays for the sick and the weak and the hungry, and he means it. He asks God to heal the sick and strengthen the weak and feed the hungry, and, as he will tell you on his TV program, he gets results! He can make things happen because he talks with God. He is God's agent among you. Wow! I can't talk with God. I can talk *to* God, but I don't have the power to get a lot of things changed. Aren't we lucky to have Gideon Calvin Calhoun here in America so he can talk *with* God and help make our country great? I mean that sincerely. I'd gladly pay someone a lot of money if they could get me in good with God." A few spectators tittered, which brought smiles to the faces of half the jurors, all of whom took the occasion to shift in their seats.

Mac continued without waiting for the laughter to subside, "That ability *is* worth money. I don't think Gideon Calvin Calhoun should owe any apologies for taking your money to pay for his services.

"Now, on the other hand, he seems to feel that being God's agent is a one-way ticket. He can *get* money for the job. He can *get* paid when those Acts of God turn out right, but he has no responsibility when they turn out wrong? That's what he wants you to believe. We will demonstrate that he not only *says* he is God's agent here on Earth, but that he also *believes* it, and profits from it. If *he* believes he is God's agent, and millions of other people believe it, and he is paid as God's agent, then he *is* de facto God's agent, and he gains all the benefits and liabilities that go with that job."

Sitting at the plaintiffs' table, Jerome was fascinated by Mac's take on the case. Jerome had never heard it put this way, so succinctly. He thought if he were on the jury, he might be persuaded. He began to feel better about suing Gideon.

"What does it mean to be an 'agent?'" said MacConnell, turning on the balls of his feet. "It means you are someone's legal representative. I am Jerome and Lacy Light's agent in this courtroom. I represent them. They talk with me, tell me what they need. I advise them. I am responsible to them if I don't do my job. Most of you have agents, too. Maybe you're working with a real estate agent or a travel agent or an insurance agent. Every one of those people had to pass a licensing test, just as Gideon Calvin Calhoun had to be ordained.

"We are going to prove that it was an Act of God that took away Jerome and Lacy Light's home and memories, and that while God's agent did not cause that destruction, he is just as responsible as the being he represents. Thank you."

As Mac took his seat beside Lacy, who was sitting between Mac and Jerome, the courtroom stirred, and the jury members looked as if they'd witnessed an execution.

Dabria Curara was up next. Jerome had to admit that she looked fabulous. He had thought, the few times he'd seen her, that she was a striking woman, but now that the trial had begun, she was radiant. She had mastered the knack of looking stunning without looking sexy, or at least, not overtly so. Her hair was down, removing the more severe look she had when it was pulled back. Jerome realized it was ironic that she had calculated how to look less calculating. He had expected her hair to be longer, but it barely brushed her shoulders.

"Ladies and gentlemen of the jury," she began.

Under the guise of paying attention to her statement, which he forced himself to do, Jerome found it was his first chance to study the high-powered Ms. Curara. She had moved into the center of the court, her legs no longer hidden by the brutish desk assigned the defendants. He tried to will himself to watch only her mouth and face as she spoke, but he frequently found himself studying her body, how it moved, and how her dark burgundy knee-length skirt and matching jacket perfectly followed her every gesture. He realized that Dab Curara must work out to have such toned legs, nicely showcased by her modestly high heels. As Mac had done, she slowly marched back and forth several feet in front of the jury box, often barely an arm's length from where Jerome sat. He managed to turn his attention back to her words.

". . . no responsibility whatsoever. The plaintiffs will demonstrate for you that the Reverend Calhoun has said that he is God's agent here on Earth 2,418 times in the past fifteen years. Truthfully, the number should be much higher than that. We openly admit that the Reverend Calhoun has called himself God's agent, but it is just a phrase, almost meaningless in the total ministry of the very Reverend Gideon Calhoun during his long, distinguished career. He has never asked for contributions because he is

God's agent. He could as easily have said he is 'God's helper' on Earth. Aren't we all God's helpers? Don't we all serve God in our own way?

"Imagine if someone tried to hold you financially liable every time you talk about yourself. See if you've ever said any of these phrases. 'I practically live at the Mall.' 'I must be the luckiest person alive.' 'I'm Santa's helper.' Do any of those sound familiar? Suppose someone fell down and got hurt at the Mall. Should they be able to sue you because, since you 'practically live' there, it must be your home and your fault? What if you could be held responsible because your good luck must have come at the expense of someone who had bad luck? What if a child gets a toy that's defective and believes that toy came from Santa? Is it you who has to pay that child's parents because, as Santa's helper, you are somehow involved?" With both hands, Dab pulled the bottom of the back of her jacket to straighten it as she scanned the jury.

"We will convince you that these ridiculous scenarios are equivalent to what is going on in this case. The Reverend Calhoun did not cause anything bad to happen to the plaintiffs. The Church of the Forgotten Savior, for which Revered Calhoun works, did not cause anything bad to happen to the plaintiffs."

Jerome noticed that she never referred to him or Lacy by name, apparently not wishing to make them any more real to the jury. He glanced at the defendants' table and got the impression that Gideon was not even listening to his attorney, but trying to meditate with his eyes open.

Dab Curara swiveled her head, right to left, looking into the eyes of every juror. She said, "And how do we know that the Reverend Calhoun was not involved? Because he suffers no delusion that he can actually talk to God, or hear from God, or know the mind of God. God is too great to speak to a humble man like Gideon Calhoun. We mere mortals can only praise the glory of God. If we could talk with God and convince God what to do, then we ourselves would be gods. The Reverend Calhoun has never said he is a God; indeed, he would never say such an outrageous thing. Yet the plaintiffs want you to believe that this good man wields some godlike power and that, in wielding it, he hypnotizes over two million people around the world to give him their money. How cynical a view is that? How preposterous. Gideon Calhoun does not talk with God. Gideon Calhoun does not control God. Gideon Calhoun is no more God's agent than any of you. Gideon Calhoun does not owe the plaintiffs one thin dime. The Church of the Forgotten Savior does not owe the plaintiffs one thin dime. Not . . . one . . . thin . . . dime."

Jerome could not believe his ears. Had Gideon Calhoun admitted that he did not talk with God? When Dab ended her speech, Jerome quickly glanced to MacConnell for a clue, but Mac sat calmly, betraying no emotion. As a young litigator, he had learned the hard way that juries can misinterpret the tiniest gestures and facial expressions, and he now could sit passively without looking imperious or cold. Mac knew that to look at his client at a time like this would be the kind of thing that someone on the jury would notice and be influenced by.

Judge Schuster waited for Dab Curara to take her seat, relieving Jerome of any further need to watch her. "We will take a fifteen-minute break and then be ready for our first witness. Court is recessed."

Immediately, the buzz among the spectators became louder than at any point in the past three days. Once the jury had left the room, Mac simply stood up and walked away. Jerome gave a confused look at Lacy. Reg said, "Mr. MacConnell wants to meet you in the conference room." Jerome wondered how Lundin knew, since Jerome had not seen the men exchange a word, but he and Lacy followed Reg out.

In the conference room, Mac was curt. "Have a seat," he told the Lights.

"What just happened there?" asked Jerome.

"Gideon Calhoun fell on his sword. And our case got a lot more difficult."

"How difficult?"

"Well, they figured out our strategy, so now we'll have to counter. We'll stay with our witness list for now, and prove all the things she said we'd prove, but the impact is gone. Now we have to prove not only that Calhoun says those things on TV, but that he says them privately as well."

Lacy said, "Won't that be easy to prove?"

Mac replied, "It shouldn't be too hard. In fact, we've already got witnesses who'll testify to it. But I was counting more heavily on his televised statements, and they're ready to say that's nothing but an act.

The jury may buy that argument."

"So what do we do?" asked Jerome.

"We're going to have to ratchet up the other side of our case."

Jerome furrowed his brow. "The other side?"

"The side where we prove there is a God, and that God has chosen Gideon Calhoun as his agent."

"But that's impossible!" said Moses to Sydney Lee, the high school principal into whose office he had been called. "She can't be dead! She's in class, right now." Three times, he jabbed his index finger towards the classrooms.

"No, son, I'm afraid she's not. The police called here about a half hour ago, and one of her teachers told us that you are—have been Sylvana's boyfriend. We thought you should be told as soon as possible and not find out by accident, but we could not reach your parents."

"Oh my God!" wailed Moses, and grasped his temples with all ten fingers. He was stunned, and then, as if a wall holding back the floodgates of facial emotion had broken far upstream, he began to realize the impact of this most horrible news. He had no idea how to cry from such grief, and so he cried haphazardly. "But . . . what happened? Was she alone?"

The principal herself could barely deal with Moses's pain. Tears welled in her eyes. "As far as we know, dear. We don't have much information yet, I'm afraid."

"I . . . I . . . oh, God . . ."

"Do you want me to leave you alone for a little while, Moses? Take all the time you need."

"Do her parents know?"

"I believe so. The police said they were on their way to the hospital."

"The hospital? So maybe she'll be all right?"

"No, Moses, I'm so sorry. She died on the way there. Her parents have to identify her body."

"Oh, Christ. This can't be happening."

"You don't have to return to class today. Mr. Lundquist, the school counselor, is going to drive you home. You have a car here, don't you?"

Moses had to think for a second to understand the question. "Yes. It's . . . I have to tell my sister. I'm supposed to drive her home."

"Do you want us to bring her here? That would be better than going to her classroom."

"No, I'll . . . I mean, yes. I want to see her, my sister. Can you get her?"

Ms. Lee asked an aide to call for Miriam Light to come to the office, and then draped an arm over Moses's shoulder. He suddenly buried his face in her chest and began to cry profusely. A few minutes later, the aide led Miriam into the office. She was stunned to see Moses there, and even more shocked to see him crying. "What is it? What's the matter, Moses? Did something happen to Mom and Dad?" Panic leapt into her voice.

Moses looked at her. His lips trembled and he couldn't quite get the words out. Principal Lee looked at Miriam and answered her question. "No, dear, your parents are fine. But I'm sorry to tell you that Sylvana Fox has been killed in a car accident this morning."

"WHAT!?" screamed Miriam. Her tears came instantly, and she hugged her brother, both of them weeping at precisely the same time that Todd and Dakota Fox sobbed over their beautiful daughter's broken body at the hospital.

Chapter 43

Solar Eclipse

At 11:15, the deputy clerk again commanded silence in the courtroom and Judge Schuster returned to the bench. "Mr. MacConnell, are you ready to present your case?"

"Yes, your Honor. Thank you. We would like to call Michael Engelhardt to the stand."

Jerome had not seen his former next-door neighbor but once since the sinkhole had hit so many months ago. Mike, of course, had been the only person other than Jerome to see the Lights' house disappear under Tadpole Lane. He answered half a dozen questions from MacConnell and was released when the defendants had no questions of him. Borgin

Mindling, the other neighbor who had been first at the scene, was next, and treated in a similar fashion.

Next, Mac called Angie O'Graham to the witness stand. He wanted her up now for several reasons. First, he wanted a "star" witness up early to keep both the jury and the media attentive. Second, he wanted to get her station's videotapes on the record for review by subsequent witnesses. And third, he thought she was beautiful, and he hoped that down the road, after the trial, he might call her.

"Ms. O'Graham, you and your camera crew from WQMO-TV were the first professional news team to arrive on the scene at Tadpole Lane, is that correct?"

"Yes, although it was just me and my cameraman, Richard Mahler, who were there."

"And how soon after the incident did you and Mr. Mahler arrive?"

"I believe we were on the scene in under thirty minutes. The sinkhole struck at 8:48 . . ."

"And how do you know that?"

"I'm sorry, I was told later by someone at the U.S. Geological Survey that it struck at 8:48, and we pulled our van onto the scene at approximately 9:17."

"Tell me what you observed when you first arrived, and how long it took you to begin videotaping the section we are about to see."

Angie gave a very professional rendering of the facts, as though she were delivering the news. She told Mac how it had taken no more than three minutes from the time Richard—"everyone calls him Rick"—parked the van until he was outside the van with the camera on his shoulder. Mac thought about the fact that he might have called Rick as a witness, and would have if Rick were not a dog-faced stiff. Far better to keep Ms. O'Graham on the stand a little longer.

"Could we roll the videotape now?" he asked Reg Lundin. As the scenes from that night appeared on the TV monitors, including one in front of the jury box, Mac asked Angie to describe the images. The tape was raw footage from which only a few seconds had been culled for previous on-air use. The next tape, provided by the station, was Angie's original live broadcast from the scene. Combined, the tapes created a perfect tableau of chaos and confusion, precisely what Mac wanted to demonstrate.

Dabria Curara had a few questions of Angie when Mac had finished introducing the tapes as Exhibit A. Then, as the judge was dismissing the fetching Ms. O'Graham, a police officer approached the plaintiffs' table and handed a note to Jerome. He read the brief note and showed it to Mac, who immediately raised his hand, stood, and said, "Your Honor, may I approach? I'd like counsel for the defendants to join me for a confidential word if I may?"

Judge Schuster looked perplexed, and mildly annoyed, but waved MacConnell forward. "All right, Mr. MacConnell. Ms. Curara, would you join us, please?"

The two attorneys approached and stood no more than three feet from the judge, who covered her microphone with her hand. "What is it, Mr. MacConnell?"

"Your Honor, the officer has just handed Mr. Light a note indicating that there has been a death at the home of the Lights, and they are requested to telephone immediately. Could you please give us a few minutes to assess the situation?" He showed the note to the judge.

"Ms. Curara, any objection?" asked Judge Schuster.

"No, Your Honor," said Dab, looking Mac straight in the eye, as if to say, "You'd better not be yanking my chain, Buster."

Jerome and Lacy were already bolting from their seats and making their way to the door. The note had not specified who had died, but said there was someone from the kids' high school who wanted them to call. Lacy was in a panic as she ran from the courtroom, following the police officer who had delivered the note.

The officer led them to a security office on the same floor and gave them the number of the school in Marshfield. "You have to dial 9 to get an outside line," he told them.

Lacy and Jerome had, like everyone else in the courtroom, been obliged to surrender their mobile phones before entering, and they did not take the time to retrieve them now. So she grabbed a desk phone in the security office and dialed rapidly. On her first try, she hit a wrong key and, with a whimper, had to start over. She got it right the second time, and said to Jerome, "It's ringing."

"Hello, this is Lacy Light. You tried calling me and my husband." Jerome held his breath as Lacy listened. "Oh, God, no!" she said, desperation in her voice. Jerome was near tears, fearing the worst. Lacy said, "Where is Moses now?"

"What happened? Is Moses all right?" Jerome interrupted.

"Wait a minute! Wait a minute!" Lacy said into the phone. "I have to tell my husband." Then she looked at Jerome. "Moses is fine, but Sylvana has been killed. In a car accident."

Jerome felt the blood drain from his head, and he reeled backwards, reaching for a chair. Sylvana was dead? "Holy . . . shit!" was all he said.

Lacy resumed talking to the person in Marshfield. "Can you find Moses and bring him to the phone? Thank you. I'll hold." She covered the microphone with her palm. She and Jerome shared a pitiful stare, their hearts breaking simultaneously. Tears flowed down both their faces.

"Moses, it's Mom . . . Oh, honey, I know . . . I can't believe it either . . . Oh, baby, you won't . . . No, you won't; you'll see . . . Dad and I are going to come right home . . . Go to Grandma and Grandpa's; we'll meet you there . . . Where's your sister? . . . Okay, good. Tell her to go with you . . . Yes, I think you should call Mr. and Mrs. Fox. You'll probably have to leave a message . . . Okay, Moses. We'll get through it . . . I love you too, sweetie. We'll see you in a couple of hours."

Lacy hung up and turned to Jerome. Mac had entered the room and was standing beside Jerome. She looked at them both and answered the question Mac hesitated to ask. "That was our son, Moses. He is at school with Miriam. He was told at school that his girlfriend . . . died this morning . . . in a car accident. The counselor is going to give them both a ride to my parents' house. That's all I know."

"I'll go inform the judge," said Mac. "I'm sure we can get a brief delay, but probably just the rest of today and all of tomorrow. The judge is not going to want to keep some of the witnesses waiting over the weekend. But you go ahead. I'll have Reg show you out a back door so you don't have to face the press. He can drive you to the hotel. If you go back in the courtroom, you're going to be mobbed, I'm afraid. So just go, right now. Your son needs you. Call me tonight on my cell. Go, go, go."

Mac returned alone to Judge Schuster's court and asked Dab to join him. He led her over to the deputy clerk and told them both, quietly, what had occurred. Dab nodded, "We can agree to a recess until Friday morning. I'm sorry for their loss."

The deputy said, "I'll alert Judge Schuster. She'll go along." He disappeared to her chambers, and a moment later she followed him back into the courtroom.

"I have been informed," she told the spectators, immediately hushing them up, "that there has been a tragic death of a person close to the plaintiffs. I am ordering this trial recessed until nine a.m. Friday morning. Court is adjourned."

By that time, Jerome and Lacy had recovered their cell phones and were in Reg Lundin's car pulling out of the garage. Reg said, "I could drive you home to Marshfield if you're not up to driving."

"No, that's okay," said Jerome. "We'll need our car. Thanks."

They decided not to check out of the hotel because they'd be back the following night anyway, and they didn't want to take time to pack. Jerome leapt out of Reg's car and into his own. Lacy ran up to the room to grab her make-up bag and Jerome's shaver. Five minutes later, they were on the road. Lacy's cell phone rang. It was Mac, telling them the judge had granted the recess.

They drove in silence for the first five minutes, both of them unsure what to say. Finally, Jerome broke the quiet. "I can't believe it. I just can't believe it. That poor girl."

"And her parents! I can't imagine what they are feeling right now. We have to see them, Jerome. We can't leave things like this."

"We owe it to Moses."

"Oh my God, Jerome. Poor Moses."

Jerome's eyes began to fill with tears, and he had to wipe them away as he drove. They both stared out the front windshield and rode in silence most of the way. They got to Marshfield right at 2 p.m. and went straight to Darcy and George's house.

Miriam's eyes were red and puffy. She'd been sitting in the family room next to her grandmother on the couch, mostly being held by Darcy. George, feeling uncomfortable and not knowing how to help, had gone into his little workshop in the basement and was busily running his router over the same wooden spindle. When Lacy entered the house, Miriam jumped up and ran to her, a renewed outburst of tears flooding her mother's jacket shoulder. Lacy put her palm on the back of Miriam's head and stroked the girl's hair without a word exchanged between them.

Jerome helped Lacy out of her jacket and hung it up with his own, then approached his calm but somber mother-in-law. "Where's Moses, Darcy?" he asked.

"He's in the guest room. He hasn't come out since he got here."

Jerome looked at Lacy, still holding and comforting Miriam. Lacy nodded her head upwards once to tell Jerome to go to him. He glided quietly up the stairs and knocked on the closed door. There was no answer. "Moses, it's Dad. Let me come in, please."

The door opened about halfway before Jerome could see Moses pulling it open for him. The blinds were down and the room was as dark as the midday sun would allow. Jerome walked in; Moses closed the door behind him. The two men stood a few feet apart. Moses shrugged his shoulders a couple of times, and Jerome bit the corner of his mouth, unsure what to say first, afraid to touch his son. Finally, he said, "How you doin'?"

Moses opened his mouth as if to speak, tilted his head side to side as he breathed in heavily, no words coming even when his lips began to move. He struggled like that for a second or two before he said, "Why, Dad? Why'd it have to be Sylvana?"

Jerome could see his son's heart breaking, and it left him nearly speechless. "Oh, Mo, there's no answer to that question."

"She was a good person, Dad. She never hurt anyone. She believed in God. She . . . oh, hell . . ." and he rocked slightly back and forth as he groped for the words to make sense of it all. "She didn't deserve . . . I mean, she was never . . . Oh, God, Dad. I loved her so much! I want her back. I just want her back." The giant boy lurched forward and threw himself into his father's arms.

Chapter 44

News Crews Blues

Angie O'Graham was on the phone to her senior producer at WQMO. Judge Schuster had delayed the trial until Monday, deciding there was no point pulling everyone back to Columbus for a Friday session. The producer wanted Angie back in Marshfield as soon as possible, and she was happy to oblige.

"C'mon," she said to Rick, her cameraman. "I got the story on why the Lights rushed out of here. My friend at the coroner's office said that Sylvana Fox was killed. That's the girlfriend of the Lights' boy. We can still make the 6 o'clock news if we hurry." The rest of the news crews were packing up and grumbling about the postponement, and didn't notice Angie's hasty departure.

Two hours later, Angie and Rick used their GPS to pull into the Foxes' driveway. As Rick got the camera out, Angie went and rang the doorbell. Todd Fox opened the door and, recognizing Angie, said, "Please leave us alone," as he closed it again without waiting for her to respond. Rick saw the door shut and Angie turn and shrug her shoulders, her palms turned upward as if she were explaining that the dog, indeed, ate her homework. As she walked to the van, Jerome and Lacy drove up the street from the opposite direction. Miriam was in the back seat, but Moses, unable to face the Foxes' house without Sylvana there, had stayed in the apartment. They were surprised to see the Action 10 News van, and Jerome might have kept driving if Angie had not spotted them and signaled for them to stop.

Jerome rolled down his window. "Uh, hi, Angie. You heard about Sylv . . . about the Foxes' daughter?"

"Yes, of course. We just drove up from Columbus to interview the family."

"What did they say?"

"They . . . said I needed to talk with you."

"They did? What did you ask them?"

"One minute, Mr. Light. Rick, are you ready to roll?" She held one index finger up and slightly shook her hand at Jerome.

"Um, yeah. No problem. Just one second . . . there!" said Rick as he hoisted the camera to his shoulder.

Angie stepped back and moved toward Jerome's car. She didn't want to take a chance on asking him to get out of the car, afraid he would drive away. She went into on-air-reporter mode. "Mr. Light, we want to know why Sylvana Fox was not allowed to see your son Moses?"

"What? Where did you hear that?" called Lacy, shouting across Jerome's body.

"Believe it or not, that was reported in your son's school newspaper. We've known about it since last Friday, but it didn't seem important until now."

"In the newspaper? At the high school? Here in Marshfield?" sputtered Jerome.

"I take it you knew nothing about it?" asked Angie, with Rick zooming in on Jerome, one arm leaning on the doorframe of the car.

"The newspaper story or Sylvana?"

"Let's start with Sylvana. You did know that Sylvana Fox was not allowed to visit your son, didn't you?"

"Yes, of course."

"What did you think of that?"

"Todd Fox told you to ask me that question?"

"No, Mr. Light. But it's an important question."

"Why is it important?" he demanded, and from behind him Angie could hear Lacy saying, "C'mon, let's go, Jerome."

"Wait a minute, please, Mr. and Mrs. Light." She knew that if she did not shift gears quickly, he would—literally. "Our viewers are very interested in your trial in Columbus. We've already reported that your trial has been postponed until Monday . . ."

"Till Monday? Are you sure?"

"Yes, I was still in the courthouse when the Judge ordered it. She's already scheduled a different trial to fill the last two days this week."

"Wow. We . . . didn't know that yet."

"And we've reported that you left the trial abruptly because of the death of Miss Fox, is that right?"

"Yes."

"Our viewers want to know why the Foxes would not allow their daughter to date your son. We've been told that it was because of the trial, because the Foxes disagreed with your lawsuit against Reverend Calhoun."

"That's not true! It's . . . well, it is true. But we don't think it's important."

"People here in Marshfield are shunning you and your family, and you don't think it's important?" A car drove by and honked as the driver recognized Angie.

"That's not what I said, Angie. It's damned important, but it's none of their business, your viewers."

"Where is Moses now? Is he in seclusion?"

"Seclusion? What are you talking about? He's home, that's all."

"When was the last time he saw Sylvana Fox?"

"It was . . . probably in school."

"No, I mean socially outside of school."

"It's been ages. He wanted to see her but she wasn't allowed to—"

"No, Daddy," said Miriam, opening her window. "They were in love. He saw her almost every day after school. She came to our house."

"What?" said Lacy to Miriam. She turned to the camera. "Would you please turn that off?" But before she could be sure Rick had stopped shooting, she swung her shoulders again towards Miriam. "Sylvana was in our house? When?"

Rick widened the shot to include Miriam, and then zoomed in on the exasperated girl. Miriam started to cry. "I shouldn't have told you! Moses is going to kill me. But he loved Sylvana, and she loved him. And they made love when you were in Columbus, and now I'm glad they did, so that she had somebody to love her before she died."

"Could you shut that thing off?" shouted Jerome, motioning at the camera.

"Just one more question, Mr. Light," Angie said, her mind racing to keep the interview going. "Do you think you'll cancel your lawsuit against Reverend Calhoun now that this tragedy has occurred?"

"No! I . . . wha . . . why would I . . . cancel the lawsuit?"

"That's my question, Mr. Light."

"This lawsuit isn't about my family. It's about whether organized religions are allowed to sell virtual snake oil and get paid for blatantly misrepresenting their power. It's about . . . " Lacy frantically pounded the palm of her left hand against Jerome's right shoulder. "Ms. O'Graham, I can't say anything more about the trial. We're forbidden to talk with the press."

"Thank you, Mr. Light. Is there anything you'd like to add, Mrs. Light?" Angie was proud of herself for resisting the temptation to ask the Lights' daughter any questions, at least for now.

Lacy said, "No. Please just . . . leave us alone. Please." Angie turned towards Rick, who immediately stopped recording and lowered the camera. *At least*, thought Lacy, *they listened to me.*

Jerome rolled his window back up, and told Miriam to do the same. Then he said, "We came here to pay our respects to Sylvana's family. We'll park and wait here until Ang—. Until the news crew is gone."

Two minutes later, Angie and Rick, since they had never set up the uplink to the station, had packed up and pulled away. Jerome opened his door, and his wife and daughter quickly followed suit. The three of them crossed the street and went up the sidewalk to the Foxes' front door.

Chapter 45

What About Tomorrow?

Dakota Fox embraced Lacy tightly, and they both cried. "I'm so sorry," said Lacy, between sobs.

"Me, too," Dakota told her. "I wish I hadn't kept them apart."

Todd Fox shook Jerome's hand perfunctorily and then crossed to an oversized easy chair and sat on the forward edge of the cushion, his elbows on his knees. Jerome unsurely followed him into the living room with its high cathedral ceiling and a second-floor landing overlooking the room. Miriam came in behind her dad. A handsome young man—tall, slender, and clean-shaven, wearing True Religion jeans and a black polo shirt—came forward. "Hi, I'm Hewitt. Sylvana's brother."

Jerome was initially surprised; he'd forgotten they had another child. "Hi, I'm Jerome Light," he said, shaking Hewitt's hand, "and this is my daughter, Miriam."

"You're the people in the God case, right?" asked Hewitt.

"Uh, right. That's me . . . us."

"My parents told me about it. I, uh . . . well, I know about it."

Todd could stand it no longer. "You're going to stop all this nonsense now, I hope, Mr. Light. I hope you'll honor Sylvana by ending this charade. Everyone's been hurt enough."

Jerome was astonished. As his brain fumbled for an appropriate response to someone whose daughter had been dead less than twelve hours, Lacy entered the room arm in arm with Dakota. Lacy said, "No, Todd. We loved Sylvana, and we want to honor her memory, but that's not the way to do it."

Todd swiveled his head and glared at Lacy. He had not expected this response, and was even more surprised when Dakota took Lacy's side. "Todd, we can't ask that. That's not . . . it's not fair to anyone. We have to respect Sylvana's choice, and she . . ." Dakota lost her voice again and turned away from the others as she tried to regain her composure. "She liked the Lights and she didn't think we should refuse to see them because of religious differences."

"She loved Moses," said Miriam, wanting them to know. "She really did. She told me."

Dakota looked pityingly at the young girl, so similar in many ways to Sylvana at that age, and she said, "I know, honey. She told me, too. And I kept them apart." Her voice broke again.

Miriam looked at her parents, who returned her gaze with some concern at what their daughter might say. Miriam said, "It's okay. Moses will be okay. And Sylvana will watch over him."

Jerome started at this comment, amazed to know Miriam felt that way. He wondered what else she believed that she might not be saying.

Todd was not ready to give up. His anger at and resentment of Jerome had found new purpose now that his only daughter was gone. "Do you understand, Mr. Light, how you are hurting this country? How you are hurting this family, and your family, and everyone in Marshfield?"

"Todd!" cried Dakota.

"It's true, dammit," shouted Todd, standing again. "If they win this case, ministers will go the way of doctors. They won't be able to get insurance. They'll be afraid to talk about God for fear that some—" he motioned his arm angrily in Jerome's direction "—some atheist will sue their pants off. You damn liberals complain that there's no doctors to do abortions, but you're not worried that pretty soon there won't be any doctors at all! Or priests. Or ministers! You're destroying America!"

"Todd!" said Dakota, "that's enough! I won't have you insulting Sylvana's . . . these people this way! Not in my house! Not today!"

"What about tomorrow?" asked Dabria Curara as she briefed Gideon and Celeste on the postponement.

"I thought maybe we'd fly down to Stonecrest for a couple of days," said Gideon. "We could use a little break."

"That's a good idea, Brother Gideon. I'm going to stay here in Columbus. I have a friend from college I can visit, and it will give me a chance to work with Lindsay and the team to get ready for Monday."

"We'll . . . see if we can get a flight out in the morning. Maybe just rest up tonight, Sister Dabria."

But when they went to their hotel, Gideon went straight to the front desk. "Where can I rent a car?" he asked.

That night, Moses refused to come to the table to eat dinner with the family. In truth, it wasn't much of a dinner, since Jerome and Lacy had expected to be in Columbus for the next two days. No one, however, wanted to go out to eat, so Lacy made scrambled eggs and cooked some frozen vegetables. She tried to get Moses to join them, but he said he wasn't hungry and stayed in his room. Lacy brought him a glass of water.

Jerome, Lacy, and Miriam ate in silence most of the meal. Lacy wanted to ask Miriam how she knew that Moses and Sylvana had made love, but she thought better of it.

After dinner, Miriam, having changed into her customary jeans, went to Moses's room and sat at the foot of his bed where he was lying on his back, staring at the ceiling. "I told Mom and Dad that you and Sylvana were in love. I told them you made love."

Moses shot up and said, "You told them that? How could you? Geez, Miriam. That's none of your business."

"I know. I'm sorry. I didn't mean to. It slipped out." She started to cry, not heavily, but sincerely.

"Okay, okay, Mir. Listen, don't cry, okay? There's been enough tears today. I mean, it's not like you told the whole world."

"Wellll . . . I told Angie O'Graham."

"What? Oh my God! Are you crazy? You told a reporter?"

Miriam couldn't look at her brother, but hung her head and continued sobbing. "I'm so stupid!"

"No, you're not stupid. But you sure weren't thinking. At least it wasn't on camera."

"Welllllll . . . "

"WHAT? Oh come on, you're kidding right? Tell me you're kidding."

"No. Angie was trying to interview Mom and Dad, and the cameraman was with her."

By now, Moses was sitting up in bed, his elbows wrapped around his knees, staring at his little sister who looked totally pathetic. Suddenly, he started laughing. "I can't believe it. I have to be the only guy ever who lost his virginity and it's all over the news! Holy shit!" He fell over backwards and couldn't stop laughing.

Miriam turned and watched him, an incredulous look on her face. She knew only that he was hysterical. "I'm really sorry, Mo. I'm sorry I told on you. Please don't be mad. I . . . Are you laughing or crying?"

That sent Moses into even greater fits of laughter. "That's the craziest thing I ever heard!"

"It's not funny!" she said. "I didn't do it to be funny."

"You should see the look on your face!" He kicked his feet in the air.

Miriam began to relax. She began to smile. Then she punched her brother in the arm, or tried to, but missed as he rocked back and forth, and her momentum caused her to fall over and land on his side.

"You are such a loser!" he laughed.

"I am not!" she exclaimed, and she began to laugh as well. Moses tickled her sides. In seconds, they were both laughing too hard to speak, or even to breathe.

The apartment was small enough that it was impossible for Jerome and Lacy not to hear the strange noises coming from Moses's room, even with his door shut. Lacy went to check. She knocked on the door, but heard only . . . laughter? She entered the room to the strangest sight: both her children on the floor next to Moses's bed, pushing each other feebly, and laughing as if they hadn't a care in the world. She stood watching them, unable to imagine what they found so funny.

Jerome appeared in the doorway behind her. "What's going on?" The question seemed to ignite the two teenagers into greater peals of laughter.

"I'm not sure," said Lacy. "I found them like . . . well, like this." More guffaws. Lacy could not stifle a small laugh herself, and soon the four of them were in hysterics.

Jerome awoke early the next morning. He had not been sleeping well since the sinkhole, and had had particular trouble the past week. He thought about the fact that before the incident, he could sleep through anything, and now would give anything if he could sleep. The rest of the house was quiet. He dressed silently and went out into the apartment building hallway as someone plopped a half-dozen copies of the Marshfield Daily Messenger on the stoop outside. It reminded Jerome of their lives back on Tadpole Lane, when he'd go out and pick the paper off their driveway each morning. It wasn't a great expense, but it was a luxury they had decided not to afford since they'd moved into the apartment. He waited till the delivery person disappeared, then opened the front door and brought the stack of papers inside.

A large color photo of sunrise over Lake Talley near Marshfield filled about half the front page, but what caught Jerome's eye was a photo in the lower left corner, a black-and-white shot of Sylvana Fox, and the headline "Local Girl Killed, Sinkhole Man Trial Postponed."

Oh my God, thought Jerome. *They make it sound as if I killed her!* He decided to "borrow" one of the papers, and took it back into the apartment to read. The article gave some new details about the accident that killed Sylvana, and it mentioned that Moses had been her "friend." It also said that the trial was in its early stages and was drawing national attention. *Great*, thought Jerome, unhappily.

Lacy had heard the front door shut, and came out in the pre-dawn light to see who was up. She shuffled over to where Jerome sat, and picked up the newspaper section that Jerome was not reading. "Where did you get this?" she asked.

"I borrowed it from a neighbor. Well, they don't know yet, but I'll put it back. Did you know that Sylvana was hit by an ambulance? Apparently, she didn't hear its siren and entered an intersection right as the ambulance raced through. The ambulance driver is in critical condition, and the aide is in the hospital. Strangely enough, the only person not hurt was the heart patient in the back. It says Sylvana died at the scene, probably instantly."

"I had no idea. I deliberately didn't watch the TV news last night. I can't believe that Angie tried to use us that way, and I don't know what Miriam was thinking."

"Miriam was thinking she was protecting me, believe it or not," said Moses sleepily, as he entered the living room. "I'd be really pissed off except that she honestly thought she was standing up for me and for Sylvana."

"And what she said is true?" asked Jerome.

"Yeah, Dad. I had Sylvana over here when you were in Columbus. I was still seeing her even though her parents forbade it. I'm sorry."

"No, don't . . . it's . . . I don't know what I think. I think you were wrong to involve your sister. She didn't see you . . . ?"

"Oh, God, NO, Dad! What do you think, I'm a pervert or something? She must have heard us in my room. I was trying to be quiet."

Lacy piped in. "Moses, what you did was wrong. And Sylvana, too. She knew her parents were against it, against us. I think they were wrong, but she is their child, and I have to respect their wishes. We did not forbid you to see her, but we did expect you to use some common sense and not sneak around."

"Sneak around? Oh, gimme a break! I wasn't going to stop seeing her unless she told me to stop, which she didn't. She wanted to see me, too. Was I supposed to tell you that?"

Jerome spoke up. "Actually, yes, Moses. In our house, you're going to tell us whom you're bringing here. We have a right to know. Do you think we would have refused to let Sylvana in our house? We liked her, Moses.

We really thought she was special. We were glad you liked her. But to bring her here to make love when we're out of town is just—"

"That's not why she came here. She . . . well, maybe it was for her, but I let her in because I love her, not so I could . . . you know. We were going to do our homework together."

Jerome stifled a laugh. "Moses, I was a teenager too, you know. I understand what you wanted to do, but, well, did you consider that you might get her pregnant?"

"I don't even want to think about that now, Dad. That's so weird that you'd think about her getting pregnant when she's never gonna be pregnant or have babies or anything now. Shit, Dad! It sucks that she's dead and that she didn't get to grow up. I'll miss her a lot, probably forever, but I'll get to meet another girl someday and fall in love and get married. At least Sylvana got to have someone love her before she died. That's what Miriam was saying. So, I'm never gonna apologize that I loved her, and she knew it and she loved me back. And . . . I thought I'd kill Miriam if she ever told, but now I'm proud of her that she did."

In his passion, Moses had not noticed Miriam come into the room and stand by her mother. "I'm proud of you, too, Moses," his sister said, and she ran to his side and hugged her face to his chest.

Jerome and Lacy decided to leave it up to the kids whether to skip classes that day. Moses said he wanted to stay home Thursday and Friday. Miriam decided to go to school, where her friend Jessica said to her, "It sucks about your brother's girlfriend," and Miriam said, "Did I ever tell you that she asked me once if I knew anyone who'd had an abortion?"

Chapter 46

Brother Jerome

The three Lights were finishing a quiet and solemn breakfast when Lacy's mobile phone rang. Jerome and Lacy looked at each other, afraid that someone in the press had gotten this new, unlisted number, or that something had happened with Miriam. Caller ID said, "Uknown Caller," so Lacy answered hesitantly, "Hello? Yes, this is she . . . Oh, how are you? . . . Good . . . I'm fine, thanks. What can I . . . Oh, really? . . . Um, no, I think, I mean, yes, we'll be here." She covered the mouthpiece and whispered to Jerome, "It's Gideon Calhoun!"

She returned to the conversation. "Between 10:00 and 11:00? Okay, that should work . . . No, of course not. Do you need directions? . . . Right, the interstate to exit . . . uh huh. That's right . . . Yeah, we use our Garmin all the time . . . Okay, we'll see you then. Oh, our apartment is number 704. That's in building 700 . . . Okay, Mr. Calhoun, uh, Reverend Calhoun . . . Thank you . . . Goodbye."

She hung up and returned to the table almost in a trance. Jerome spoke first. "Calhoun is coming here?"

"Yes, he . . . he said he heard about what happened to Moses's girlfriend, and he wants to talk with us. He's bringing his wife, what's her name?"

"Celeste, I think."

"Yes, that's it. Celeste. They're both coming. They're going to leave Columbus in a few minutes and drive here. He said he doesn't want the press to know."

"I should think not. I wonder what the hell he wants from us."

"He didn't say, but he was, well, he was very friendly. Serious, but friendly."

Moses said, "Maybe I should leave. I mean, what would I say to him?"

"No," said Jerome, "you're not being forced out of here by anyone. You can . . . well, I guess if you want to go, you can, but you don't have to, you know."

Lacy said softly, "Why don't you wait here and see, Moses. You can always leave later."

They scrambled to clear the dishes and clean the apartment before the unexpected guests arrived. Lacy and Moses made the beds while Jerome took care of the kitchen. Then, as Lacy cleaned the bathroom, Jerome brought out the small vacuum cleaner they'd picked up at Goodwill. Periodically, he looked out at the parking lot to make sure there were no reporters out there. At 10:30, the doorbell buzzed.

Jerome said, "I'll get it." Instead of buzzing them in, he opened the front door and went out into the building foyer where he opened the main door for Gideon and Celeste. They were both wearing clothes that surprised Jerome with their casualness. Gideon was in jeans with a polo shirt, while Celeste wore black slacks and a dark green top. Jerome supposed the Reverend did not want to stand out. "Welcome to our home. I hope you didn't have any trouble finding us."

"None at all," said Gideon, heartily shaking the hand offered by Jerome, who was distractedly thinking how surreal this scene was.

Jerome also shook Celeste's hand. "My wife and son are inside. Please join us."

"Thank you."

"I'm afraid you won't get to meet our daughter. She went to school."

"Good for her!" said the minister, not insincerely. He noticed the smell of fresh coffee.

"Come in, please. Let me take your jackets. I guess it's a little colder up here than you're used to in Arkansas this time of year."

Gideon said, "That's true. But it's a nice change. It's the same weather we had about a month ago, and I love it. Oh, here's Lacy. Hello, my dear." Lacy thought for a moment he might embrace her, but instead he simply took her right hand in both of his.

Celeste stepped forward, a bit awkwardly compared to Gideon's practiced stride, but in a way she hoped would convey empathy, if not grace. "Oh, Mrs. Light, I'm so sorry for your loss." Celeste hugged Lacy warmly. Lacy, at first, was inclined to stiffen, but almost instantly gave in, even welcomingly, to the embrace. "Where is your son?"

"Um, he's in his room. Would you like to meet him?"

"Yes, I would, if he's willing. He shouldn't feel he must come out."

"I'll ask him. Excuse me," said Lacy, and she wiped her palms on the sides of her stomach as she went down the hallway to Moses's room.

"Can I get you something to drink, some coffee or tea, perhaps?" asked Jerome.

"We're both avid tea drinkers," said Gideon. "That would be terrific if it's not too much trouble. Any tea at all will do."

"Please, have a seat. It's not our permanent furniture. We rented it after, uh, well . . . you don't care about that. Anyway, have a seat. Make yourselves comfortable, and I'll bring out the tea. We already boiled the water just in case."

"Excellent," called Gideon as Jerome scurried from the room. He and Celeste sat side by side on the sofa with its too-soft cushions. They had to separate a bit to make sure they didn't fall into each other, a hazard they learned the hard way.

Lacy reappeared with Moses behind her. "This is Moses. He's a senior in high school this year. He'll be graduating soon. Moses, this is Reverend and Mrs. Calhoun."

"How do you do?" said Moses, bowing slightly.

"How do you do, son?" said Gideon, rising to shake his hand. "Please, you don't have to bow to me. Although I appreciate that you felt like it." He laughed lightly, and it helped put Moses at ease.

Jerome came in with a tray holding four cups of hot water, a box of teabags, the sugar bowl, some milk in a pitcher, and four spoons. "Oh, Moses, can I bring you a cup, too?"

"No, thanks, Dad. I'm fine."

They proceeded to distribute the cups and share the tea, making small talk about the weather, the traffic in Columbus, and a pair of cardinals Celeste had spotted in the trees outside.

Finally, Gideon said, "I expect, Brother Jerome, you are surprised we are here. I'm a bit surprised myself, to be honest."

"Of course," said Jerome, fidgeting slightly. "I was wondering."

"I want to put your mind at rest. I did not come to ask you anything about the trial. I am not here to negotiate or to ask you to drop your case. You are doing what you feel you must do, and so am I. That's the way of the world. We can't change it."

"I agree."

"Good. My lawyer doesn't know we're here. I expect she'd be pretty angry with me if she knew. Can I assume you did not tell your attorney after I phoned you?"

"Oh, right, no. I mean, yes, you can assume that. No, we, we didn't tell him. It never even occurred to me, frankly. I guess that doesn't make me a very good client." He laughed. Moses, sitting on the arm of his mother's easy chair, covered his mouth with his fist and coughed.

"Either of us, really. That's a good thing, Brother Jerome. You never want to be someone who is well practiced in suing or being sued. Believe me."

"That's for sure, but . . . well, could you please not call me 'Brother' Jerome, sir? I know you're being polite, but it feels, well, it doesn't feel right."

"Oh, of course, Jerome. I'm sorry. It's an old habit of mine. I forget sometimes not to be so . . . well, it's both formal and familiar, I guess."

Celeste said, "The Reverend once said 'Brother' to the Dalai Lama. Isn't that what you told me, dear?"

Gideon laughed at his own folly. "Yes, that was probably a mistake, but he took it really well. I liked him, you know? It was special meeting him. There really is a holy aura about him."

"Anyway," said Jerome, sitting up straighter, "we haven't told anyone that you're here. I even checked the parking lot to make sure no reporters were hanging around."

"That's good. I should have thought of that. I guess you are getting the media treatment a bit, aren't you?"

"We're never going to get used to it," said Lacy. "They can be so rude."

"I've learned to deal with reporters and cameramen, but it took me years. They used to really get my goat when I was younger."

"So . . . why are you here, Reverend?" asked Jerome.

Gideon cleared his throat and looked down momentarily at his legs. "I'm not exactly sure. I think God asked me to come."

"Oh?" is all Jerome said.

"Maybe that's the wrong way to start. I felt in my heart that I had to come. You call yourself an atheist, right?"

"Yes?" Jerome replied, as if asking a question. "You're not here to convert me, I hope."

Gideon chuckled, "No. It's . . . not what I do. Although I'd be pleased if you decided on your own to come to Jesus."

"Are you going to tell me you're worried about my immortal soul?"

"Actually, I wasn't going to tell you that, but the truth is, I am. You seem like a good person, but unless you accept Jesus Christ as your lord and savior, you cannot enter the Kingdom of Heaven. I don't expect you believe that or even care, so I'm just going to leave it at that."

"That's a good idea. We have to agree to disagree."

"Oh, we don't 'disagree,' Mr. Light," said Gideon, making air quotes with his fingers. "I'm quite certain of what I believe, which, I understand, may not be—"

Lacy had tried to remain respectful, but couldn't. "Excuse me, Reverend, but I am Jewish, and I'd prefer that you not come into my house and tell me that I'm going to Hell when I die."

Gideon was taken aback. "Mrs. Light, I'm . . . I'm terribly sorry. I've offended you, and that was not my intention at all. I . . . You're quite right. It was rude of me to say anything in your own home. I didn't come here to talk about God at all. I came because, well, because you have suffered a terrible loss, and I am genuinely sorry. I came to help, not to upset you. I do apologize."

Lacy was gracious, but a little cold. "Apology accepted, Reverend. I know these are stressful times for all of us."

Celeste stood up and said to Lacy, "Perhaps it would be best if you and I took a walk, Mrs. Light. I need to get some exercise. I'm still recovering from a car accident last year. It's so nice out; would you be willing to walk me around your neighborhood?"

"I guess . . . uh, certainly. Is that all right with you, Jerome? I'll take Mrs. Calhoun out for a little walk."

"Call me Celeste."

"All right, Celeste, if you'll call me Lacy," she responded, and then led her to the front door. "Moses, did you want to come with us?"

"Uh, no thanks, Mom. I'll stay here. Okay, Dad? Yeah, I'll stay."

Jerome looked perplexed. "Nice of you both to wait for my answers. Go ahead, honey. Moses will stay here with us guys." He held up both thumbs and wiggled them side to side, then wondered why he'd used that gesture.

Lacy nearly said something to Jerome, but decided against it. *Us guys?* she thought. *Since when does Jerome use that expression? Is Gideon Calhoun one of the 'guys'?* She and Celeste stepped out of the apartment.

Jerome asked Moses to bring some Girl Scout cookies from the kitchen—a box he'd been obliged to buy from a co-worker—and offered the Reverend more tea, which he declined. Moses needed a few extra seconds to locate the cookies, then fumbled around for a plate to put them on, knowing that his mother would be mortified if he served the cookies from the box. While he was gone, Jerome and Gideon fumbled awkwardly to find a point of conversation, and they both welcomed the boy's return.

"Moses," said Gideon, "I'm told that the young woman who died was your girlfriend. You must be terribly upset."

"Yes, sir, I am. I loved her, a lot."

"Her death leaves a great hole in your heart, then. How will you fill that hole?"

"Sir?"

"Are you religious, Moses? Or do you go along with what your father believes? I'm just asking; I'm not telling you what to believe."

"Well, sir, I'm not sure. I want to believe that Sylvana is up in heaven and that I'll see her again someday, just like I want to see my Granpa again if I could. But I kinda doubt that'll happen. I'm sorry. I know you believe it, Mr. Calhoun, and I hope you're right, but I have my doubts."

"Actually, Moses," said Gideon, "you might be surprised to learn that most people have some doubts, at least sometimes. There're not a lot of people who know what their eyes cannot behold and who never question it. My own faith is sometimes tested. I've had doubts from time to time; I've wondered why God would take a newborn baby or a young mother giving birth. I'll confess that I don't always understand God's methods, and I get angry at God. But I never get angry at Jesus. I never doubt that Jesus died for me and for all of us, and that He is the way and the truth and the light."

Jerome replied, "I've got to say I'm surprised that you sometimes have doubts about God. Is that something you ever tell your congregation?"

"I don't hide it if someone asks, but, no, I don't trumpet it, either. I don't doubt there is a God, though. I only have doubts sometimes that we don't fully understand the nature of God. We are but humble animals who can see the glory of the Lord, but not make sense of all we see."

"I cannot disagree with you, Mr. Calhoun, except that the glory of life is not about this God you worship. It's about nature and love and . . . and miracles. The miracle of evolution, the way things change and grow and get better without any intelligent designer," said Jerome.

"'Evolution.' It's a word I hear too much."

"Do you deny evolution?"

"I don't deny that things change, that God has not yet fulfilled all His plans. But I don't believe we are descended from the apes, Mr. Light. I don't accept that!"

"Is that what God told you, Mr. Calhoun?"

"Not directly. God does not speak to me in your language."

"God does not speak to you at all. That's what your lawyer said in court yesterday."

"She . . ."

"So your ideas don't come from God, do they? They come from faith. From what you want to . . . no, what you need to believe. It's what makes sense to you."

"Precisely. My faith is my life. You cannot take either from me, for I shall have eternal life in Christ Jesus our Lord." He carefully picked cookie crumbs from his shirt.

"I cannot believe we are having this conversation," said Jerome.

"Would you like me to pray for Sylvana with you, Moses?"

"That's not—" began Jerome.

"Wait a minute, Dad. He didn't ask you."

"Would you ever dare to pray, Mr. Light?"

"Would you ever dare not to?" Jerome snapped back.

The thought hit Gideon like a lightning bolt! It had never occurred to him that *not* praying might be anything more than foolhardy, like knocking down a bee's nest. Not pray? Rely on God to help without having asked for His help? Believe so deeply in the Lord that you'd have the bravery not to pray? It wasn't a thought he'd ever entertained; yet now Gideon wondered, "Why not?" Did he not trust God? "Does God really require an entreaty?" No, impossible. Gideon's God was a loving God. But wouldn't it show more faith in God not to pray? No. No. He must praise God! But why?

"I . . . I talk with God. It's important to me. God hears my prayers."

"He does," said Jerome, making it not quite a question.

"Yes, He does. Like the shepherd hears the lambs bleating and the mother hears the babies cry. The Lord knows who I am, because I tell Him. God calls me to His service, and I answer."

"You're his agent here on Earth."

"I am God's faithful servant. I do not wish to play semantic games. Your lawyer will twist my words; you know he will."

Jerome, becoming agitated, said, "And your lawyer will twist my words and try to make me look like the bad guy here."

"What you are doing is wrong, Jerome," said Calhoun, trying to remain calm, but not entirely succeeding. "I understand why you're doing it, but it's wrong. To most people, it looks like you're just trying to make money."

Jerome's face looked pained. He gazed hard at Gideon. "You have made a fortune off the misery of others, selling snake oil for millions of dollars a year!"

"You must know that . . ." and Gideon stopped. He leaned back slightly. "We can't have this conversation. It's wrong. And it's wrong because your son is grieving a loss much greater than any we might suffer in that Columbus courtroom. I came here because your family is under attack, and you need my help. These are all Acts of God."

Jerome sat back and placed the side of his thumb against his upper lip. "I'm sorry."

"You're what?"

"I'm sorry," repeated Jerome. "You're right . . . we can't . . . I should never have gotten mad at you and started talking about the trial. It's . . ."

"You're afraid I'll tell the judge and she'll have to declare a mistrial. Well, you have my word I won't do that," said Gideon.

"No, you don't get it. It has never been about the money for me. I don't care if you . . . no, never mind. I . . . never mind. The trial has to go ahead, but I'll tell you that I'm sorry I ever started it. My family has suffered. We've all suffered. Maybe Sylvana would still be alive."

"Dad!"

"It's true. We don't know." Tears formed in Jerome's eyes.

Gideon felt he had to relieve Jerome's anguish. "It's not your fault. You are following God's will." He stood and placed a hand on Jerome's shoulder.

Jerome snapped back, "Can't you talk about anything besides God for five minutes? What is it with you and God? I'm an atheist, remember?"

"Yet you must prove God exists. You, the non-believer, go to court to prove God exists, to say to the world that God has hurt you . . . and you don't see God's hand in that?"

"No, I don't, but I'm sure you do."

"The sinkhole was an act of God, Mr. Light. That is not what I have said; it's what the insurance company and the law have said. You must accept that fact."

"Your God, Mr. Calhoun, is not my God. You sell God's favors like candy and make a fortune. Do you know how dishonest it all is?"

"There is nothing dishonest in what I do, Mr. Light. God is as real to me as this chair, and as close to me. I know in my heart that God is awesome, and that God wants to take care of his flock."

"And that's why He destroys houses and kills innocent young girls!"

"I do not question God's plans for me or for any of us."

"Perhaps it's time you did question it. Perhaps if you really did talk to that God of yours, you'd find out why He's such a jack … Ohhhh! I don't know why I'm even talking to you about this. You can't talk to God because He doesn't exist. I know you believe, but believing doesn't make Santa Claus real, either!"

"You think I'm a fake?"

"I think you're convinced that you're sincere."

"What do you think, Moses?" asked Gideon of the astonished boy.

"Leave my son out of this!" Jerome scolded.

Moses grimaced. "No, Dad. Stop leaving me out of everything, okay?" He turned to face Gideon. "I . . . I don't have any thoughts. I think you're both so fixed on your own ideas that you can't see how ridiculous you both look. You . . . I . . . I'm going back to my room."

Jerome waited for the boy's door to slam shut, and had his heart broken when Moses closed it instead with a quiet click.

Gideon and Jerome looked at each other, and a look of shame crossed both their faces. Gideon spoke first. "I'm sorry, Mr. Light. I've … made a mess of this visit. I wanted to reach out to you, to your family. I didn't come here to fight about my beliefs or your beliefs. I wanted to help. I'm a fool."

"No, it's my fault, Reverend. I can't help . . . I . . . I appreciate your coming. It was very decent of you. I'm not sure I could be so . . . kind."

"You've lost so much. I can't imagine what it must be like. Tell me about the sinkhole."

"What?"

"The sinkhole. Your neighbor said yesterday that you were with him when it hit. What happened that night?" Gideon refilled his tea cup and sat down again.

"What do you mean? We were standing outside and suddenly my house disappeared and then blew up."

"Nothing else? No warning? No noise?"

"The sky. I remember the sky was a really strange yellow color. That's why I stepped outside. I don't know what it was. A coincidence, I guess."

"I suspect . . . oh, never mind."

"What? You think it was God?"

"No. It was . . . maybe. I don't know. A yellow glow. It's odd, that's all."

"Yes, it was odd."

"I wish we could know for sure," said Gideon. "I wish there were a way I could prove God's existence and glory to you."

Jerome said, "You're very different than I imagined you."

"I get that a lot."

"I thought you would be more theatrical."

Gideon smiled, "Like I am in the pulpit? There's nothing about religion that isn't theater. But that's not the real me up there. I'm an actor, and I make no apology about that. It's like Lenny Bruce said about the grandeur of Catholic churches, 'I live in a shithouse. What would I want to go in one for?' You can't preach goodness to people if they don't come to hear you."

Celeste and Lacy returned from their walk, their cheeks aglow and smiles on both their faces. Lacy was laughing as if she'd been talking with her best friend. "Hello," she said, "how's it going here? Where's Moses?"

Gideon replied, "He decided to go back to his room. I think we were a little too serious for him."

"Oh. I hope he's okay."

"He'll be fine, Lacy," said Jerome, still reeling slightly from Gideon's use of salty language. "He'll be fine."

"We should probably go," Gideon announced. "We need to catch a plane back to Arkansas before our lawyers find out what we've done, and I'm sure you have lots of things you need to do."

"We didn't expect to be in Marshfield today, so, yeah, I guess we need to take advantage of the time. We'll be going to the funeral home tomorrow, and the funeral is on Saturday."

"It's terribly sad, isn't it?" asked Gideon. "I'll be praying for her family, and for your son."

"Thank you," said Jerome. "I know you mean well. It was good of you to come." He shook Gideon's hand.

"Yes, it was," added Lacy. "I enjoyed meeting you, Celeste. Thank you." She gave Celeste a heartfelt hug, then hugged the minister as Jerome shook Celeste's hand. The Calhouns quickly grabbed their things and made their exit to "goodbyes" all around.

<h1 style="text-align:center">Chapter 47</h1>

<h2 style="text-align:center">Flying Off into Space</h2>

Miriam missed the escapades at the apartment, but had her own unexpected encounter at the high school.

As she turned a corner in the hall while heading for the girls room, she nearly crashed into Dakota Fox, who had retrieved some things from Sylvana's locker.

"Ms. Fox! Oh my gosh, I'm so sorry."

"Everyone is sorry, dear," Dakota said dismissively.

"No, I meant, you know, excuse me. for almost knocking you over. But, I mean . . . I'm sorry about Sylvana, too." She paused. "I really liked her, you know? I wanted to be like her."

Surprised, Dakota said, "You are . . . you remind me a little of her. You're about her height, and you have her same skin. You could be her—" She caught herself. "What a thing to say to you, of all people."

Miriam saw the look of horror on the woman's face. "Thanks. I'm flattered."

Dakota didn't know whether to stay or go. She hesitated, as Miriam continued.

"Everyone loved your daughter. I mean, everyone."

"Your parents, included?"

Miriam gave a slight giggle. "My parents especially. My dad told Moses how lucky he was to have such a great girlfriend."

"Your father." Dakota shook her head.

"I know why you're mad at him, but you're wrong. My dad's a really good man. He has to do what he's doing. He has strong principles."

"That's not what I see. I'm afraid your father is just in it for the money. Where's the principle in that?"

"You're wrong about him, Ms. Fox. The money doesn't matter so much to him. Look, Sylvana liked him before things got . . . complicated. She had some good talks with him. They respected each other."

Dakota sighed and looked defeated. "My daughter was a special person. I wanted her to be happy, to be with a good man for the rest of her life, to live well."

Miriam smiled at the distraught mother. "Sylvana was happy. She was with a good man. My brother is the best."

Jerome knocked on Moses's door. "Come in," said Moses, with little enthusiasm.

"I wanted to see how you're doing," said Jerome. Moses's room smelled of dirty socks, which was most unusual.

"I'm okay."

"You left kind of suddenly. Not that I blame you. That was kind of . . . absurd out there."

"Yeah."

"You mind if I sit with you a little bit?"

"No, it's okay."

"Would you rather be alone?"

"No! It's okay."

Moses's room was, surprisingly, neater than usual. The Magritte poster Sylvana had bought for Moses was displayed prominently on the wall beside the bed. Sylvana had signed it "Love ya forever." The boy slumped against his pillow, his head against the wall, since there was no headboard on the bed.

Jerome sat on the foot of the bed as if he were afraid the mattress might give way. He looked right at Moses, whose gaze was held fast by a spot on his rug beside his bed. "It sucks, Mo. It really sucks. Your mother and I want to shelter you and your sister from everything bad, but we can't."

"I know."

"I kind of feel like we let you down."

"Forget it, Dad."

"When I was a kid, I used to put a record on the record player and then place little things—dimes, small toys—on the record, and turn the player on at 33-1/3." Jerome mimicked placing tiny objects on the turntable. "That was the kind of slow speed of the big records. The things I put on never moved when it was just starting to spin, and even when it reached 33-1/3, they stayed put. Then I would change it to 45 and watch the toys go flying off into the room. And that's how my life feels, like one of those thin dimes or cheap toys. Each year comes round and round faster and faster until I'm ready to go flying off into space. Only, it's not me who controls the speed. And whoever, or whatever it is that makes each year go faster, I want it to stop."

"What do you mean?" Moses finally turned his face to look at his father.

"I mean, life seems to speed up the older you get. I can't believe you're ready to go off to college already. It seems like we brought you home a couple of weeks ago. And now look at you."

"Yeah."

"You're a good kid, Mo. I mean it. I'm proud of you."

"Why?"

"Well, you're smart, and you have a good heart, and you work hard at school. I've seen some of those kids at your school. Do you still call them Goths?"

"Yeah, Goths. They're not so bad once you get to know 'em."

"I guess most people are like that."

Moses swung his legs over the side of the bed. "They want everyone to think they're weird. You know, Dad, it seems like all most of us ever think about is wanting people to like us. Like Marty and Joe, all they talk about sometimes is how they're falling in love with this girl or that girl. Kids will try one personality on, and if it works for them, that's where they stay. If not, they move on to something different, like something wilder. And as soon as somebody likes them that way, then they don't need to change anymore. I mean, if they like somebody and that person likes them back, why change? That's what I think the Goths are all about. They don't hassle me, and I don't hassle them."

Jerome looked with surprise and admiration at his son. "That's good, Mo. That's good. You can do great things. You have greatness inside you. So, you have to *be* great. If you don't do the great things that the world needs, who will?"

"I don't want to do great things, Dad. I just want . . . I just wish I could rewrite the last few months."

Jerome leaned forward, his elbows on his knees. "We don't get to write the script of our own life. We only get to decide how each chapter starts, but then life takes over and writes the rest of it in ways we may not have intended. You know, pretty soon you'll go off to college, and I really don't want you to go. And I don't want Miriam to leave, either, when her turn comes. I love you both with all my heart. You both make me really happy. I wish we could all stay like this forever, but, well, we can't."

"Not like this, Dad. Not without Sylvana."

"I know. It sucks."

"Dad, did you ever pray? I mean, when you were younger?"

"Yeah, I used to, when I was a kid. I said prayers every night. My friends told me about how you had to thank God for your parents or God would take them away. I didn't know I was an atheist yet."

"I used to pray, too, even though you told me there was no God listening."

Moses ran his hand through his hair, and Jerome unconsciously did the same thing as he said, "Your Mom told me. I guess it's hard not to pray. But you know, it's very important to have a certain toughness, an ability to fight through the tough times that life hands all of us. There are times when we feel we can't do it all, all alone . . . all the time. If you had a bacterial infection, you'd get help and take medicine, but 'emotional infections' are a lot harder to deal with. There's no medicine to make the hurt go away. It takes time, Mo. It just takes time."

"I think Mr. Calhoun would have a different answer."

Jerome let out a brief laugh. "Heh. Yeah, I'm sure you're right about that. He's an interesting man. He's kind of a surprise. I'm not sure I've judged him fairly."

"What do you mean?"

"I mean he seems pretty genuine. I figured all of those evangelists are nothing but phonies, but Calhoun is actually a pretty nice guy. There don't seem to be any skeletons in his closet."

"Like what?"

"You're too young to remember some of 'em. Jim Bakker and Jimmy Swaggart and some other evangelists pulled all kinds of scams. Bakker even went to prison."

"Dad? You don't think Sylvana's in heaven now, do you?"

"I don't, no. But you have to make up your own mind what you believe, son."

Moses put his feet back onto his bed and lay back. "Yeah. I guess so."

Jerome stood hesitantly, paused a moment by the bed, then left the room and closed the door behind him.

The next day was Friday, and Miriam again returned to school without Moses. The viewing at the funeral home was scheduled for 2 to 4 p.m., and again that evening from 7 to 9. Moses wanted to go early so that he would not have to face too many other students, most of whom planned to go in the evening, although he knew that Sylvana's best friend, Rebecca Crane, would be there. At 1:30, Jerome, Lacy, and Moses set out for the Hurwitz-Johnson Funeral Home, all of them in black, including Moses, who found his suit at a thrift shop.

Moses was grim-faced as he entered the funeral home. He was trying to be resolute and strong, but in keeping the tears at bay, he took on an unnaturally serious look, unsure he should be there. Sylvana's brother Hewitt greeted the Lights at the entrance to the parlor in which Sylvana lay.

The room tried too hard to be serene and sympathetic. The walls were covered in honey-oak panels. The windows allowed in light, but afforded no view of the street. The curtains were burgundy velvet with gold-braid tiebacks. A luxurious faux-Oriental carpet covered most of the floor. Sylvana's casket was against one wall, surrounded by hundreds of large, fragrant flowers, mostly lilies, carnations, and forget-me-nots. Some were arranged on the floor under the casket, while the rest were in tall vases on pedestals around the casket, the top half of which was propped open, but Moses was relieved that Sylvana was not visible from the doorway.

Hewitt Fox introduced the Lights to a few family members who had arrived early: his mother's parents, his father's father, and his mother's sister and her husband. Sylvana's best friend, Rebecca, wearing a plain black dress, crossed the room and clung to Moses, hugging him for several seconds until she felt she could look at him without crying. She told him that she planned to stay the entire day, and that her parents would be there that evening after work.

Jerome noticed that Hewitt appeared to be staying near the hallway, about as far from his sister's body as possible, and Moses was tempted to stay there as well. But slowly, like a far distant comet gradually hauled closer by the sun's powerful gravity, Moses entered the room and drifted towards the coffin holding the young woman who would always be his first lover. No one spoke to him as he reached Sylvana's side for the last time. Jerome and Lacy let him linger there alone until Lacy could stand the pain no longer and went to her son's side. She gazed at the girl whose vibrancy had so recently blessed her house, and put an arm around Moses's waist. That was his cue to cry.

Jerome, meanwhile, sought out Todd and Dakota Fox, both of whom were doing their best to remain calm, almost sociable. Jerome gave Dakota a hug and shook Todd's hand. Todd told him, "I'm sorry about the other day. I had no right . . ."

"It's okay," said Jerome. "No apology necessary. I'm sorry, too."

"Yeah."

"I can't tell you how much we liked Sylvana. She was a wonderful girl."

Todd said, "And she adores . . . adored your son. We do, too. He's a good kid. We shouldn't have kept them apart."

"That's . . . in the past."

"You have a daughter. Miriam, right?"

"Right. She's a sophomore."

"Can you understand what it would mean to you if your daughter suddenly disappeared from your sight?"

"It's too horrible to imagine, Todd. Our kids mean the world to us. We're not supposed to outlive them."

"Sylvana meant everything to me," Todd intoned. "In my memory, she's as alive as when she was in school or out with friends or anywhere out of my power to protect her. I'm proud of who she became. She wasn't perfect, but she came awfully close. Sylvana had such goodness in her heart, and it's a source of pride to me that I helped to put it there."

"It's nice you can say that. A lot of kids today, well … I feel the same way about Miriam."

"Is she here with you?" Todd glanced around the room.

"No, she went to school. Moses took the day off."

Todd lowered his voice. "Have you thought any more about what I said, about the lawsuit?"

"I thought you just said . . . oh, never mind. Uh, no. I can't … it's … complicated."

"I won't tell you what to do, but I wish you'd change your mind."

Dakota came over and took Todd's arm. "You're not talking about that again, are you?"

"No, dear," said Todd. "I just asked Jerome a question."

"Gideon Calhoun sends his condolences about Sylvana," Jerome said quietly.

Dakota and Todd both said, "What?" at the same time. Todd said, "He said that?"

"Yeah, he, uh … our attorney told us. Gideon, um, Reverend Calhoun, heard about Sylvana."

"Wow!" said Dakota. "That's . . . amazing!"

Another family arrived then to pay their respects, and Todd and Dakota turned to greet them and receive condolences. Jerome was about to join Lacy and Moses when they turned and came towards him. "I've gotta go, Dad," said Moses, and the three of them left without saying another word.

Chapter 48

Gideon, You Are Wicked

Gideon and Celeste were frantically taking advantage of the unexpected opportunity to be in Stonecrest. Gideon made a not-entirely-surprising visit to the Church of the Forgotten Savior offices, heralded by Dab Curara having called there looking for him, and leaving a message for him to call her. He was able to arrange a short meeting with his assistants and go over plans for the Sunday service, the first of three or four in a row that would have to use a guest speaker. Unlike some of the other television evangelists, he did not have his own airplane, so commuting from Columbus to Stonecrest each weekend was out of the question.

It struck Gideon that he was probably looking at the future of CFS. He had always considered himself an indispensable part of the Church, but now he saw it functioning without him. It left him feeling as if he'd entered a room where familiar furniture had been hastily rearranged. He took a few minutes to reach Dab and confirm his return to Columbus on Sunday. He answered a small amount of personal correspondence, then fled home to Celeste as quickly as possible. She was doing laundry when he arrived, and he was delighted to realize he might never have to do his own laundry again.

"I picked up a few things to eat while we're home," she told Gideon when he offered to fold his own underwear. "And when I got back, I found a bird's head on the front steps. Just the head. I'm sure it's that cat we've seen around. You know, I put some food out for her a week ago, so now I'm sure she was thinking, 'Who wouldn't like a bird's head on their porch? They're going to love me and feed me forever.'"

Gideon laughed and pulled Celeste to him in a kind of clumsy hug. "Well, that's certainly an extra special gift. I should cherish it forever."

"I threw it out in the woods."

"Good," he said, and laughed again.

On Sunday, they headed to the airport in Memphis. As an in-demand speaker, Gideon traveled frequently, and long ago decided to join the Delta Sky Club so he could relax away from the crowds around the gates. He did not like to afford himself too many luxuries, but he learned quickly that sitting in the main concourse was an open invitation to people to talk with him, and they often did. Sitting in the Club, appointed with contemporary furniture, did not make him immune to fans' visits, but it was less common. He was far more likely to be approached when he traveled in the South, and he often wondered if it was because he had more viewers there, or because Yankees were more reserved and Californians took celebrities for granted.

He grabbed a copy of the Memphis Commercial Appeal when he checked in, and sat next to Celeste, who was doing embroidery. She had been unable to embroider for months after the accident, and went at it now with a peculiar abandon. Without looking up from the paper, Gideon said, "Here's a man in Massachusetts who was convicted of starving his infant son to death on purpose because he thought God ordered it. He even admitted it."

"That's terrible!" said Celeste.

"That's so sad. And stupid. No wonder people like Mr. Light have such a bad impression of religion. Can you imagine thinking God would order you to kill your son?"

"But God told Abraham to kill his only son Isaac, right?"

"Yes, my love, but that was different. Remember that God stopped the sacrifice and would not let Abraham kill Isaac. And anyway, I'm not so sure that ever really happened. There were only three witnesses: Abraham, Isaac, and the ram, and the ram didn't last long. I believe the story of Abraham is a parable, not an historic fact."

"My word," said Celeste. "You surprise me every day, Gideon."

"You can't kill someone in the name of God, and that's only the most obvious thing you can't do. It's lunacy."

Celeste stopped working and looked up at Gideon. "I can't believe you're getting so worked up over this story, Gideon. It's a terrible thing, but it's not like you to say such things."

"The Lord is merciful, Celeste. We both know that, and our friends and family know that. But Jerome Light does not understand, and there are millions of others like him. How can we make them understand and praise God when there are stories like this?" he said, slapping the middle of the page with the back of his fingers.

A family entering the airline club heard that famous voice and looked over. They instantly recognized Gideon, and, following the lead of the fortyish big-haired brunette, the mother in the family, they came to the sofa where Gideon was sitting. The woman said, "Oh, Reverend Calhoun, I am so thrilled to meet you! We watch your show every week. We think you are just the greatest American!"

Gideon did not stand up, knowing that if he did, he would not be allowed to sit down again for a long time. Instead, he put his newspaper on his lap and reached up to shake the woman's hand. "Thank you very much, Sister," he said.

"Oh, it's Elaine. My name is Elaine Griffin, and this is my family: that's my husband, Robert, and my sons, Josh and Jesse." Gideon wondered why she didn't call them "our" sons.

Each of them stepped forward to shake Gideon's hand, while Elaine said, "I think it's terrible what you are going through, but you know how those bug-eyes are."

"Bug-eyes?" asked Gideon, perplexed.

"Yeah, them people what lives in Ohio. Bug-eyes. Why do they call 'em that?"

"It's not 'bug-eyes;' it's 'buckeyes.'"

"Okay, why they call 'em that?"

"I'm not at liberty to say," said Gideon, as he got up and excused himself to the men's room. When he got back, the Griffins had settled a respectable distance away, and he forced himself to give a little wave and a smile as he sat back down next to Celeste.

"So, you're not 'at liberty to say,' eh, Gideon?" said Celeste, giving him a teasing smile. "I'll have to remember that line next time you're 'in the mood.'"

"Hush!" said Gideon, but laughed to himself as he pulled the newspaper up to shield himself from any further interruptions.

On the plane, the Griffins, as luck would have it, were seated behind the Calhouns. Celeste asked the flight attendant for a bottle of water, and then proceeded to knock it over, spilling half its contents directly onto Gideon's lap. She grabbed the bottle before the rest could spill, and then handed the bottle to Gideon.

"Why did you hand me the bottle, dear? Did you want me to drink the rest, or do you expect me to finish pouring it on myself? Or are you trying to make it look like I did it?"

"Oh, you stop!" she said, flummoxed. "Just hold it while I try to get some paper towels to dry you off!"

"Sit still, my love. I'll ring for the stewardess and we'll let her bring something."

"I'm so sorry."

"It's just water. Forget it."

The flight attendant brought a handful of paper towels. As he mopped himself up as best he could, Mrs. Griffin asked the flight attendant a question. "What time is it in Columbus?"

"Well, Ohio is in the Eastern time zone, so you have to add an hour."

"So, what time *is* it?"

Gideon leaned over and whispered to Celeste, "Clearly, this woman should not be let out of the house, much less on an airplane."

"Gideon, you are wicked," she said, and slapped his arm playfully.

Chapter 49

Who Is in Charge?

Dab Curara began every court day at a disadvantage. She had to dress for the jury, and her appearance had to be different every day, unlike a male attorney's. She had to appear the same height each day, so her heels always had to match in size, but not in style or color. She knew that some female jurors would be judging her shoes more than anything else. The same with her make-up, a part of her morning regime, but not of MacConnell's. When she traveled to Columbus, she brought two large suitcases, including one exclusively for her ten pairs of shoes. Dab had already put in an hour's work before leaving her hotel room, which is why she got breakfast by room service each morning.

The next few days passed much more quickly, as Thaddeus MacConnell called a long list of people to the witness stand, starting with Valerie LePine from the EPA, followed by Dr. Sapna, the geologist from Purloyne University, and a phalanx of technical experts. Dabria Curara strategized—correctly, as it turned out—that the jury would be quickly bored by these witnesses whose sole function was to prove what was never in doubt: that the Lights' house had been destroyed by a sinkhole that had been undetectable and, therefore, unpredictable. She did minimal cross-examination: enough, she felt, to show the jury that she was engaged and attentive.

Mac, on the other hand, believed he was scoring points with the jury by calling witness after witness whose testimony was unassailable, if not exciting. He wanted to establish in the jury's mind a sense that his case was based on accurate information and his witnesses were all reliable analysts.

He called Magnus Schopenhauer, the insurance adjuster, to describe his investigation of the "claim scene" and what he had told the Lights at that time. Once again, Magnus peppered his speech with "I mean" before nearly every sentence. Then Mac called Jack Glisson, the insurance agent, to recount his conversations with the Lights, particularly the discussions in which Glisson confirmed that Big Rock Mountain Mutual Insurance Company considered the sinkhole to be an "Act of God" not covered under the Lights' home insurance policy.

Mac did not ask Glisson about Jerome's reaction, but on cross-examination, Dab went straight to that point. "Mr. Glisson, what did Mr. Light say when you told him he was not covered by insurance?"

"He said something like, 'There is no God. It was an accident. Maybe God decided to show us who is in charge.' Something along those lines."

"Mr. Light said there is no God?"

"Something like that."

"And how did you respond?"

"I told him that I believe in God and that anyway it doesn't matter what he believes or I believe because the law says that certain things can be called an 'Act of God,' and there was nothing I could do about it."

Mac felt he had to question Glisson again when Dab sat down. "Mr. Glisson, excuse me. I'd like to ask the court reporter to read back your testimony about what Mr. Light said to you."

After a brief pause, the court reporter found her notes and read, "He said something like, 'There is no God. It was an accident. Maybe God decided to show us who is in charge.' Something along those lines."

"Thank you," said Mac to the court reporter, and then turned back to the insurance agent. "You concluded that Mr. Light personally did not believe in God, is that correct?"

"Yes, sir. He said as much."

"And yet he suggested to you that God decided to 'show us who is in charge.' Now, you testified that you believe in God. Do you believe that God could show us who is in charge if He wanted to?"

"Yes."

"Do you believe God does that from time to time?"

"Yes, I suppose so."

"How might that occur?"

"Well, in floods and hurricanes. Things like that. You know, natural disasters."

"And sinkholes."

"I suppose so."

"So, if I said to you that God sent a sinkhole to destroy my house to show me who's in charge, you'd say that was consistent with me believing in God?"

"I'm sorry, sir, I don't get . . ."

"Let me try again. Do you believe that God can punish people for whatever reason?"

"Yes, sir, I most certainly do."

"So, it's justifiable for an insurance company like Big Rock Mountain to say that God was responsible for certain disasters?"

"Absolutely."

"Even with no evidence that God caused the sinkhole that destroyed the Lights' house?"

"Well, no one knows God's plan."

"So, God could have been aiming at the house next door and just missed?"

"I didn't say that."

"No, I know you didn't, Mr. Glisson. You mean that no one knows

God's reason for what He does, is that right?"

"Yes, that's right." Glisson rearranged his position in the chair.

"So, it's part of our faith. We believe, without evidence, that God must have been punishing Jerome Light, or maybe someone else in his family, for something. Is that fair to say?"

"Objection!" said Dab Curara. "What is the point of this questioning? It seems to be badgering the witness based on his personal beliefs."

"Mr. MacConnell?" said Judge Schuster.

Mac replied, "Not at all, Your Honor. I believe my next question will clarify my intention."

"Very well. Objection overruled . . . for the moment."

"Mr. Glisson, is it fair to say God may have been punishing the Lights?"

"Yes, I think so. We'll never know."

"No, we won't. And isn't that exactly the point of Mr. Light's question to you? You said he wanted to know if God was trying to show him who is in charge. Would a person who does not believe in God ask such a question?"

"Uh, no, I don't suppose so."

"You said you might ask that question and that you believe in God."

"Yes."

"So, you seem to have jumped to a conclusion about the beliefs of my client based on a single statement that he almost immediately refuted. Do you still say that Jerome Light does not believe in God?"

"I . . . it's not my place to say what he believes. I may have made a mistake."

"I'm sure Mr. Light will accept your apology later, but let me ask you finally if you personally believe that the sinkhole that hit the Lights' house was an Act of God."

"Objection! The witness's religious beliefs are irrelevant in this case."

"I withdraw the question, Your Honor. I have no further questions for Mr. Glisson."

The next witness, Dr. Susan Patrick from the Insurance Institute of America, gave the legal definition of "Act of God" and explained the legal precedents on which that designation was based. And the trial for that day came to an end.

Chapter 50

Are You Insane, Mr. Light?

Finally, on the morning of the fourth day back—Thursday—Mac informed Judge Schuster that he was calling Jerome S. Light to the stand. Jerome had always felt that the description about electricity crackling through a courtroom was nothing more than journalistic cliché, yet on hearing his own name called, as anticipated as it had been, he felt a jolt, something like lightning, and sensed that the jury and the spectators suddenly sat more upright.

Mac had spent two hours with Reg and Jerome in a pre-testimony conference at which they outlined what questions Mac would be asking with Jerome on the stand.

Mac began in his usual calm manner. "Good morning, Mr. Light."

"Good morning."

"You and your family have been through quite an ordeal this past year, have you not?"

"I guess you could call it that, yes."

"For the past few days, we've heard the experts testify that a sinkhole swallowed your house on the evening of June 6 last year. Where were you at that time?"

"I had stepped outside my house and was across the street talking with one of my neighbors."

"Mr. Engelhardt, I believe."

"Yes, sir."

"And what did you observe then?"

Jerome proceeded to describe the loud boom, the hissing sound, and sight of his roof caving in. Then he talked of watching the house collapse as if a giant invisible foot had squashed it, the explosion that followed, and of the panic in the neighborhood.

"Did you know at that time what had caused your house to disintegrate?"

"No, I had no idea. I thought maybe it was a bomb or God knows what."

"God, indeed, Mr. Light." A few titters flitted about the courtroom.

Mac then led Jerome through a lengthy examination of his meetings with the insurance agency and his conversations with attorney Sumner Stoke. "So, each time you spoke to someone about the loss of your home, the place you and your family had lived, you were told that it was an Act of God that destroyed it, that took away all your possessions, and left you homeless. Is that correct?"

"Yes, that's what I was told."

"Did anyone tell you differently? Did anyone say your loss was caused by any other means?"

"No, sir. Not one person. Everyone agreed it was an Act of God."

"So, if everyone agrees, then why couldn't you accept that and move on?"

"I lost almost everything I had, even though I didn't do anything wrong. It's pretty hard to accept someone telling you to move on, especially when we paid our insurance premiums on time year after year."

"But the insurance company refused to pay."

"That's right."

"And do you think they should pay you?"

"I thought so at first, but there's this 'Act of God' thing, and all the experts told me they don't have to pay, so …." Jerome couldn't think of a way to finish the sentence, but Mac jumped right in anyway.

"So, you accept now that it was an Act of God that destroyed your home?"

"Yes."

"Then why would you sue Reverend Calhoun? He's not God, is he?" Mac turned slightly and looked directly at Gideon briefly before again facing Jerome.

"No, I'm pretty sure he's not God." There was a smattering of laughter from the spectators. One or two laughed out loud, but most giggled and were quickly silent.

Mac waited for the courtroom to calm down, and said again, "Then why sue Reverend Calhoun?"

"Because he claims he is God's agent here on Earth."

"And you have heard him make this claim?"

"Yes, several times."

"And you believed him each time?"

"It doesn't matter whether I believed him; others believed him. Millions of others believe him still. They send him their money because they believe him."

"Millions of children write letters to Santa Claus. Does that make him real?"

A few spectators coughed. Judge Schuster watched Jerome carefully. Jerome glanced at Lacy, and let his eyes wander quickly around the room before fixing his gaze on MacConnell. "In a sense, it does. Walk anyplace around Christmas and you'll see lots of Santa Clauses. They may not be able to do all the things in Clement Moore's book, but that doesn't make them any less real. To all those children, they are real. Even grown-ups bring their children to see him and tell them that it's really Santa Claus. And the people in the Santa suits act like Santa and say all the right things to the children. It's a carefully crafted charade, and everybody has a part to play. The stores that pay the Santas expect them to do certain things that Santa would do, and say certain things that Santa would say."

"Do you think Gideon Calhoun is playing a part?"

"No, I think he believes he is God's agent and that he is entitled to money because of it."

"And that makes him responsible for your house?"

"That makes him responsible for … well, yes, for my house."

"In what way?"

Jerome realized his next words would be his big pitch, the moment he had contemplated for months, and he held back long enough to collect his thoughts and catch his breath. Then he looked right at Mac and said, "Look, when things go wrong, people want to be able to say, 'Okay, we know why.' It's human nature to want to blame somebody else, to find a reason that your life is not as good as you want it to be. And so that reason is 'God.' In most people's minds, God is the reason that things go poorly. That's what God is. You've heard people say it hundreds of times, something like 'My brother died last week; God called him home,' or 'How come our team lost last night? It was God's will.'"

A siren went by on the street outside, and Jerome paused a few seconds to let the whine fade. A shaft of light filled the courtroom as the sun rose quickly above the buildings of downtown Columbus.

Jerome continued, "God is not this Creator or ethical judge or everything else that the Bible portrays God to be. In most people's minds, on a daily basis, God is culpability. God is responsible. When something is called an Act of God, it simply means that you can't find a person to blame, or to pay you, or to hold responsible, or to seek vengeance against. We humans like reasons; we like to be able to explain things like where we came from and what happens when we die. If we cannot find a person behind something, like a sinkhole, then we look for some other reason, 'cause when we lose things through no fault of our own, we're mad. Well, to be mad at something, to be angry at something, you have to ascribe to it certain human characteristics. You blame that thing. You hold it as having human qualities."

He took a short breath while he gathered the forces of his thoughts for a final assault. "And if it has human qualities, then it has *choice*. God had the choice whether to make people have a bad day or have something bad happen, or to treat people really well and make something *good* happen. Isn't that what most people hope? We hope that when times are tough, God might take pity on us and make things better, especially if we ask for help in prayer. And that's what everyone is hoping for. When they pray, they are trying to restore some balance or find some good."

Jerome looked from Mac to Lacy and back again, then said, "Well, to think that prayer is going to make a difference is to think that there is some intellect out there that chooses what happens. That's a comforting thought to most people. And because most people accept that as being logical or legitimate, we say most people believe in God. Okay, so most people believe in God, and think God is capable and culpable. When the sinkhole ate my house, and Big Rock Mountain said it was an Act of God, then people like Gideon Calhoun believe that's true. They believe God destroyed my house, and they tell everyone else that."

Mac interrupted, "How do you know they tell other people that God destroyed your house?"

"I saw Reverend Calhoun say so on a video of *The Gideon Calhoun Hour*."

"Your Honor," said Mac to the judge, "plaintiffs wish to introduce Exhibit F, a videotape of the television program to which Mr. Light is referring, and we ask permission to play this tape for the jury."

"I will have to see the tape first, Mr. MacConnell, before I can permit you to introduce and exhibit this videotape. Can you continue your examination of the witness without showing the tape at this time?" asked Judge Schuster.

"Yes, Your Honor."

Dab objected. "Excuse me, Your Honor, but the defense is not prepared to stipulate the reliability of any statements by the witness referring to matters that have not yet been entered into evidence. We believe that this line of questioning should be suspended until you have ruled that the evidence is admissible."

"Have you seen the videotape in question, Ms. Curara?" the judge asked her. "Do you have it on your list of exhibits?"

"I've seen a videotape, but I don't know if this is the tape I was shown."

The judge looked at Mac. "Mr. MacConnell?"

"It is the same videotape, Your Honor. There will be no surprise exhibits from plaintiffs."

"All right, then. Can you tell me, Ms. Curara, in the video you saw, did Reverend Calhoun in any way mention the sinkhole that hit Marshfield, Ohio, last year?"

"Yes, he did, Your Honor."

Though she lost the objection, Dab had still accomplished her goal, which was the disruption of Jerome's obviously impassioned speech. She hoped she had successfully muted any emotional build-up, as Judge Schuster instructed Mac to continue his interrogation of Jerome.

"So, Mr. Light, you were saying that you had seen Reverend Calhoun state that your house was destroyed by a sinkhole that was created as an Act of God. Is that correct?"

"Yes, sir."

"Please continue."

"Well, my point is that when something like the sinkhole happens, Gideon Calhoun and most people believe that God was responsible. In order for God to be responsible, God must be real, because unreal things could not make a house disappear. Gideon Calhoun believes the sinkhole that hit my house was a deliberate act of an intelligent being for whom Reverend Calhoun acts as self-proclaimed agent, and on whose behalf he collects money." Gideon grimaced slightly at this version of his statement, and he involuntarily hitched his shoulders back. Jerome did not notice Calhoun's reaction, as he focused on Mac in an effort to maintain his train of thought. He said, "It seems to me that someone's agent who collects money on his behalf ought to be responsible for that someone's debts. God owes me a new house, and I believe I am entitled to that from the money that Reverend Calhoun collected on God's behalf."

As soon as Jerome stopped speaking, he noticed that the courtroom buzzed as it always buzzes on TV or in a movie when a bombshell is dropped. It gave him great satisfaction, and he thought for a moment how eerie it would have been to have the room completely silent.

"It's an interesting perspective you have, Mr. Light. But why Reverend Calhoun? Why not another minister, or an imam, or a rabbi?"

"Belief in God does not make someone responsible. Not even getting paid to talk about God makes you responsible. But Reverend Calhoun is paid by people specifically because he claims he talks with God and knows what God wants and will do." He blinked several times.

Mac said, "Let me see if I have this straight. You are not saying that Reverend Calhoun directly or even indirectly caused your house to be destroyed?"

"Correct."

"Yet you say that he is nevertheless liable for the damage to your house because he represents the entity that caused its destruction?"

"Precisely."

"Are you insane, Mr. Light?"

"Pardon me?"

Mac came quite close to Jerome and glared at him. "It's not a rhetorical question, sir. I want to know if you are now insane or have been recently treated for insanity."

"No. I resent the implication."

"There is no implication. Some people have publicly questioned your sanity. I want to know if you have ever been treated for any mental disorder."

"I have not. I saw a psychiatrist briefly after a particularly hard semester in college. Uh, that was quite a few years ago, as you can see," he said, and pointed to his thinning hair. A few spectators laughed, and Judge Schuster banged her gavel once. Jerome said, "But I was not diagnosed with any disorder."

"Weren't you depressed when your home was destroyed? Didn't you need to see a psychiatrist then?"

"It … it never occurred to me. No, I wasn't depressed. I was too busy taking care of my family."

"Would you call yourself a good family man, then?"

"Yes. Of course, I would."

"You're looking out for them?"

"Yes."

"Do they agree with you that Reverend Calhoun is responsible?"

"Objection, Your Honor. The question calls for hearsay evidence," said Dab.

"Sustained."

Mac wheeled so the jury would not see him smile at the ploy he had so cleverly pulled off. He knew the defense would have to object to the question, and he would have been in deep trouble if they had been any less competent. He had managed to show that Jerome was close to his family, and the sticky question of their support had been raised and swept off the table by the other team.

Over the course of the next hour, Mac probed Jerome for information about the family's finances and how much the sinkhole had cost them. Jerome produced a letter from the company holding the mortgage on their Tadpole Lane property, which could not possibly support a new structure. The mortgage company said they would not foreclose on the property as long as it was not habitable, but they could no longer waive the monthly payments. The Lights, in short, were being forced to pay for a house that no longer existed on a lot that could not be sold.

Just before noon, Mac announced, "I have no further questions at this time, Your Honor."

"We'll recess for lunch, then, and resume at 1:00 p.m. sharp," said Judge Schuster.

Chapter 51

I Did Not Believe Him at First

Moses took his lunch break in the school cafeteria, as he did every day when his mother was not around to prepare a meal for him and Miriam. Joe Block, who had the same lunch period, had to look for Moses, who was near the interior wall instead of at their usual table by the window.

"Hey, Mo. Good to see you back."

"Yeah."

"Man, that was sad at the funeral. I feel so bad, Bro."

"Let's not talk about it, okay?"

"Right, yeah. I understand." He leaned forward, his elbows on the table and his right fist in his left palm, and looked at Moses, who failed to look up from his food. "What's the latest with your dad and mom? Is that trial thing still going on?"

"Oh, it's on all right," Mac said to Jerome and Lacy over lunch in Kenosian's, a crowded deli downtown, a place so packed with young business and government people that their media-famous faces were barely noticed and rarely bothered. "Curara is going to beat you like an old rug this afternoon. I hope you're ready for it. You can't let her upset you."

"I think I'm ready," said Jerome. "I've had months to think about it."

"And I hope you'll remember the things we went over," added Mac. "Above all, nothing about being an atheist. If she gets into your personal beliefs—and she will—you can be agnostic, or humanist, or questioning, or confused, but you can't be an atheist or you'll lose the jury. Her list of defense witnesses already indicate she's going to go after you on the atheism."

"The thing is, I'm not so sure anymore. Maybe it was an act of God that the sinkhole hit our house."

"Thataboy!" said Mac.

"No, I'm not practicing here. I mean it."

Lacy shot forward in her seat. "You can't be serious."

"Oh, but I'm totally serious," said her husband, calmly.

"My God, I think you are," said Lacy.

"You'd better not be kidding around, Mr. Light," said Mac. "I don't need any surprises up there this afternoon."

"Maybe it is a kind of God that's behind it all. Not the God of Gideon Calhoun, but a different, I don't know, thing. Fate. Luck. Whatever you want to call it. I'm not saying it was a plan to take out our house and punish our family. Was it? Did we lose our house for no reason? Did Sylvana die for no reason? Is there some master blueprint that says our fate is determined for us by our DNA? That once we're created, we can change our fate only in minor ways?"

"It sounds like you're questioning whether or not we have free will," said Gideon, who had walked up at that moment to wish Jerome good luck.

"Oh, Gideon!" said Jerome with great surprise—and a bit of embarrassment. "I didn't see you coming over."

"I guess there are a lot of things you didn't see coming," Gideon quipped.

"Reverend Calhoun," said Mac, reaching out to shake Gideon's hand. "I'm afraid I have to insist that you and my client talk no further at this point. I'd be in deep trouble with the court if I allowed this."

"I understand, Mr. MacConnell," said Gideon. "I came over only to wish you all good day, nothing more." He gave a smile and a slight wave of his hand as he hustled away towards Celeste and his legal team, drawing a glare from Dabria Curara for having detoured to the Lights' table in the first place.

"Jerome," continued Mac in a hushed voice, "are you saying you now believe that God deliberately destroyed your house?"

"No, that's not what I'm saying, but I guess I'm more ready to accept that possibility."

"I'm stunned," said Lacy.

"I'm a little stunned myself," said Jerome, "but I'm a whole lot less sure of myself about everything these days. A lot of things I took for granted just . . . I think . . . well, Gideon's a pretty amazing guy. I mean, look at him. I wish I had faith like he does. He knows what he believes, and he lives it every day."

"Please don't get into any of that this afternoon," Mac told Jerome.

"No, don't worry. But you once told me that if we're going to win this thing, I need to prove there's a God. I think maybe I can."

Mac got a worried look on his face, but said nothing except that they had to get back to court.

At 1 o'clock, Judge Schuster reentered her courtroom and took her seat. "I took advantage of the break to review the videotape submitted by plaintiffs. I am going to permit it to be entered as Exhibit F, and ask that it be played now for the jury."

The lights were lowered, and the deputy clerk played the video on a large projection screen placed a few feet from the jury box. It showed Gideon Calhoun in his robes leading a Sunday service, with the date from last June imprinted on the bottom, a date before Jerome had filed his suit against Calhoun and CFS.

"This week, we witnessed again the extraordinary power of God. (Hallelujah!) Perhaps you saw it on the news. A sinkhole struck a house in Ohio. Just one house. With all the land and houses that it could have hit, this extraordinary event found the very center of someone's house. The house was instantly destroyed, yet not a single window of any other house was broken! And amazingly, it took place seconds after the owner stepped out of the house. Can you doubt that God was sending a powerful message to that family?" The videotape went black after those words, and the lights were brought back up.

The judge spoke, "Mr. Light, will you please return to the witness stand. I remind you that you are still under oath. Ms. Curara, you may proceed."

"Good afternoon, Mr. Light. How are you this afternoon?"

"I'm fine, thanks, and you?"

"I'm very well. Thank you for asking. Let me first say that I am sorry for the losses your family has suffered these past few months."

"Thank you."

"The first thing I want to know, Mr. Light, has to do with the videotape we just watched. You testified earlier that you had seen this episode of the program. Are you a regular viewer of *The Gideon Calhoun Hour*?"

"No, I'm not."

"Did you just happen to catch this particular episode on one of the rare occasions when you watch Reverend Calhoun preach?"

"No."

"How did you come to see this episode?" asked Dab.

"Mr. MacConnell showed it to me in his office a month or so ago."

"How very thoughtful of him." A few spectators laughed, but quieted quickly. "So let me get this straight. You saw this statement by Reverend Calhoun after you had already decided to initiate legal action against the Reverend, is that correct?"

"Yes. I don't recall the exact date."

"Had you heard about this videotaped statement before you saw the tape in Mr. MacConnell's office?"

"Uh, like a few days before, when Mr. MacConnell called to ask me to come to his office."

"But at no time prior to hiring Mr. MacConnell to sue Reverend Calhoun did you learn of this statement in any way and from any person or report?"

"That's correct. I did not know about the statement."

"Then I am having trouble understanding your earlier testimony about why you have chosen to bring this suit against the defendant instead of against other members of the clergy. Did you pick Reverend Calhoun at random?"

"No, I didn't. I saw—"

"No, you didn't. You decided that out of all the ministers and priests and rabbis and mullahs in this country, that Reverend Calhoun alone was responsible for your loss. This morning, you pointed to his statement about the sinkhole as proof that he was telling people that God deliberately destroyed your house. You gave the impression that you resented his remark. So, I ask you, Mr. Light, did you resent what the Reverend said about your house? Since you didn't see that statement until months after you began litigation, resentment cannot be the reason you singled him out, so what is the reason?"

"I did resent it at the time I saw it. I don't resent it now."

Dab decided not to pursue that remark immediately, but to continue to focus on Jerome's rationale for the suit. "Did you have any resentment towards Reverend Calhoun when you decided to sue him? Millions of people think he's an excellent minister, but there's nothing so different about him from other Christian ministers. So why pick on him to pay for your losses?"

"I'm not picking on him—"

"Objection, Your Honor," Mac jumped in. "Ms. Curara knows better than to editorialize about Mr. Light's state of mind or motivation."

Dab did not wait for Judge Schuster to speak. She said, "I'll rephrase the question, Your Honor. Why did you choose Reverend Calhoun to pay for your losses?"

Jerome could feel his adrenaline starting to pump, and he knew he needed to sit back and try to calm his nerves. He adjusted his bottom in the chair and took a deep breath. "I have no personal animosity towards Reverend Calhoun. I think he's an honorable man, a good man. I did resent his remarks about my house on national television, but not until after I'd decided to seek legal action against him. I used to resent his claims to be God's agent and the millions of dollars people pay him because of it."

Curara turned away from Jerome and faced the jury as she asked her next question. Several of the jurors, unaccustomed to her glare, forced themselves to sit more upright.

"You are a dictionary editor, is that right, Mr. Light? That's your regular job?"

"Yes."

"So you know the meanings of words and you choose your words carefully, don't you?"

"Yes, I suppose I'm more aware of words than most people."

"So this word 'resent' is not just a figure of speech to you, is it? Let me read you the definition of the word 'resent' from the same dictionary you edit, *Crawley's Abridged English Dictionary, 7th Edition*." She went to her desk, picked up the book and read from it. "It says that as a verb, 'resent' means 'to feel ill will, indignation, or annoyance about or towards something,' and it comes from the Old French word *'ressentir,'* which means 'to be angry' or 'to feel strongly.'" With both hands, she threw the book back on the desk, where it landed with a loud thud. "Are you angry, Mr. Light? Are we here because you got angry and needed to take it out on someone?"

"No, I'm not angry. I … The word 'resent' was first used in English to mean feeling gratitude as well as indignation."

"But you don't mean to suggest we are here because you felt gratitude towards Reverend Calhoun?"

There was a murmur of laughter in the courtroom, but not enough to warrant the judge's gavel.

"No, I—"

Dab was not through, and cut Jerome off. "Are we here because you are angry at the Reverend?"

"No, it's not … it's not anger. It's … I do resent that he makes his living off a lie."

"So now he's a liar? This man you just said is a good, honorable man, is a liar? This man that millions of people believe and look up to? You are telling this court that your judgment about religion is better than millions of other people? That you know the truth and they are all deluded by this honorable man?"

Mac stood and said, "Your Honor, would you please instruct counsel to ask one question at a time and to stop making speeches instead of allowing Mr. Light to answer her questions?"

"Ms. Curara, please consider this your first warning. I will not tolerate badgering of the witness."

"I'm sorry, Your Honor. I will wait for Mr. Light to answer the question."

"I don't think Reverend Calhoun is a liar, because he clearly believes he is telling the truth. He says he is God's agent here on Earth. He believes that."

"And you do not believe him?" asked Dab Curara.

"I did not believe him at first. Now … I think I do."

Dab appeared shaken. She said, "You … You believe he is God's agent?"

"He believes it. Millions of people believe it. Who am I to question it?"

This response caught both Dab and Mac completely by surprise. The plaintiffs, after all, needed to prove that Gideon is God's agent and is therefore financially liable. But if the Reverend really were God's agent and Jerome believed that, it would justify the belief of Gideon's followers and justify, or even sanctify, the money they sent Gideon. Mac became instantly and acutely aware of the paradox they now faced.

The situation was no less changed for Dab, but she had no time to sit with her staff and prepare a revised game plan. She had been certain she could prove that Jerome was an atheist . . . but now? Now she had to worry about a new attack. She had planned to prove that Gideon was not God's "agent," and she thought the one witness she could be sure would agree with that statement was Jerome S. Light. Yet here he was, saying that he believes Gideon. If he's telling the truth, a major foundation of her defense was destroyed. Dab decided to stall until she could formulate a new strategy.

"You are saying that you now believe Reverend Calhoun is God's agent?"

"He says he is, and I cannot prove otherwise."

Outside the courthouse, everything seemed quiet and normal. A man in a suit stooped over to pick up a toy thrown to the ground by a baby in a stroller. The young mother pushing the stroller smiled and thanked the man as he went on his way to an interview for a job he desperately needed. A driver trying to make a left turn was waved forward by another driver going the opposite way, who used his car to block traffic for a moment; yet no one honked or cursed. The sun shone brightly everywhere, but a slight breeze made it a perfect day to be out and about in Columbus, Ohio. Inside the courtroom, Celeste Calhoun stared proudly at Jerome. For reasons she could not explain, she was not surprised at his testimony. She wished she had her embroidery with her, but she had not been allowed to bring the needles inside the courthouse.

The defense attorney continued, "So, forgive me, Mr. Light, but your testimony seems inconsistent. You said you used to resent the Reverend's statements about God and the money people sent him. But now you agree with those people who support him? Please help me understand you."

"I don't agree with his followers. It's possible to have a different opinion from someone without thinking they are wrong."

"Really, Mr. Light?" said Dab, incredulously. "Because when I think I'm right, and someone doesn't agree with me, that pretty much makes me think they're wrong."

"That may be true in matters of fact, but not in matters of faith. Faith means believing something without any scientific evidence to support you. I have faith that I'll still be alive tomorrow, but there's no way to prove whether I'm right or wrong until tomorrow. You may believe I'm going to die tonight. One of us has to be wrong, but we can't prove it right now, so we have to take it on faith."

"That seems like a strange statement coming from a man who is an atheist, a man with no faith."

"Objection, Your Honor. That is a conclusion not supported by any evidence. It is not a question."

"Sustained. The jury will ignore the last remark by Ms. Curara."

"Are you an atheist, Mr. Light? Do you believe in God?"

"I believe in something greater than myself."

"Would you call that 'something' God?"

"Some people might. I don't know what to call it."

"Please help me out here, Mr. Light, because it seems rather important that if you wish to collect money from Reverend Calhoun for being God's agent, you ought to believe that God has an agent or—"

Mac popped up again. "I must object again, Your Honor. Once again, counsel is making speeches instead of asking questions, and once again her 'facts' are not supported by any evidence presented so far. Mr. and Mrs. Light are not concerned with whether or not Reverend Calhoun is God's agent. We contend that the Reverend says he is God's agent and receives money based on that claim."

Judge Schuster looked scoldingly first at Mac, and then at Dab and said, "Sustained. I hope I will not have to warn you again, Ms. Curara, to limit yourself to questions and save your interpretations for later. And Mr. MacConnell, if you have any further objections, you will avoid turning those into speeches. You will state you have an objection and you will allow me to recognize you before you launch into your own version of the 'facts.' Am I clear?"

"Yes, Your Honor," said Mac.

"Thank you, Your Honor," said Dab, and she turned again to Jerome on the witness stand.

While the judge chided the two attorneys, Jerome had tuned out as he recognized Mac's clever new tactic. In one unrehearsed moment, he had switched the game from proving Gideon's agency for God to simply proving that the perception of that agency by Gideon's followers was enough. It was brilliant! No longer did it matter whether Jerome himself believed in God or believed that Gideon is God's agent.

"Mr. Light, I can bring many people to this witness stand, and I will, who will say that you are an atheist. Would you please tell us what you believe in terms of religion, in terms of what you say is your faith?"

Mac brought his entire long body up in what seemed an instant, as if he had managed to bypass any steps between sitting and standing. "Your Honor, we object. The question is irrelevant."

Judge Schuster looked surprised. "Is it, Mr. MacConnell? I'm inclined to believe plaintiff's attitude towards religion is highly relevant." Dab Curara looked annoyed and disgusted.

"Mr. Light's beliefs are not on trial here. It makes no difference whether he believes in God or not, or even whether Gideon Calhoun believes in God . . ."

Dab Curara had heard enough. "We resent any implication that Reverend Calhoun does not believe in God."

"That's not what I said, Ms. Curara. I said his beliefs don't matter. What is on trial here is whether he makes a claim to represent God and whether he collects tax-free money based on that claim."

"You made your point, Mr. MacConnell. Objection sustained. You may no longer inquire into plaintiff's religious beliefs, Ms. Curara."

"But Your Honor," cried Dab, "a great deal of our case depends on showing that the plaintiffs do not believe in God and therefore cannot believe that the Reverend Calhoun is the agent of God, the precise claim they have made in filing this litigation."

Judge Schuster was impatient. "It is not any concern of this Court as to what your case depends upon. If you have no defense other than the plaintiff's religion, I wish to tell you that your client is in serious trouble!"

Dab knew she was quickly losing points in front of the jury, and she decided to cut her losses to get the focus back on the case and off of her. "Your Honor, we have no further questions of this witness at this time, but we reserve the right to recall Mr. Light to the stand at a later time."

Now it was Jerome's turn to be shocked. He had no idea what had just happened. Had his side won a point? Or had they been cleverly outplayed by the unpredictable Dabria Curara?

"You may step down, Mr. Light," said Judge Schuster. "Call your next witness, please, Mr. MacConnell."

"Your Honor, we had not anticipated that this witness would conclude his testimony today. Our next witness is not in the courtroom today."

"Very well, we will adjourn for today. I expect you will be ready to proceed tomorrow morning, Mr. MacConnell."

"Yes, Your Honor," said Mac, as the spectators all rose while Judge Schuster retired to chambers.

Chapter 52

Suddenly a Christian

The weather was perfect, so Mac, Reg, Jerome, and Lacy walked to the hotel. Lacy was anxious to get up to their room and call the children. Mac and Reg ushered Jerome to a corner of the lobby lounge to talk.

"That was a close call today," said Mac. "We had to take that atheism card away from her."

"You were amazing!" said Jerome. "I saw the way you shifted the strategy."

"She's not through with you yet, I suspect, but her strongest attack has been blunted. She may still call her witnesses who will tell everyone you're an atheist, but she won't get far, and the jury has already seen that tactic backfire. Now she'll have trouble getting the jury to line up against you personally."

"I think we're home free," said Mac's eager assistant.

"Not so fast, Reg. The jury still heard her call Mr. Light an atheist, so she may have scored some points anyway. Although that was quick thinking on your part, Mr. Light, to say you believe in a higher power. You had me worried at lunchtime."

"But I do," said Jerome. "I can't explain it exactly. I don't think that God is an old guy with a white beard, but . . . something is out there. Look at what's happened to me in the past ten months. And you heard what she said about my house. My place just disappeared, and not a single window broken at my neighbors'. That's just weird."

The three men continued to talk and drink for about a half hour. Then Mac and Reg got up to leave and Jerome headed for the elevator to go back to the room. When the elevator door opened, there was Lacy coming to find him. She had fixed her hair and makeup, and Jerome looked at her as if he had not really seen her for a long time. Instantly, he was filled with the love that only decades-old familiarity can bestow. As she stepped into the lobby and took his arm, he said to her, "You know, there are times when my love for you is so palpable, I think it will step outside my body and become some kind of friendly and appealing creature that will attach itself to you even as I stand here."

"What a sweet thing to say!" she replied. "Buy me a drink, sailor?"

"Uh, sure. I already had one with the guys, but I could have another. Maybe we could have an early dinner and then go upstairs and . . . you know . . ."

"Oh? Feeling a little frisky, are you?"

"Let's just say it was a good day, and I'm feelin' lucky."

They went back into the lounge that Jerome had just left, and sat on a sofa off to the side. Lacy took Jerome's hand and intertwined her fingers with his. They had not made love in weeks, and it was now on both their minds.

A well-dressed man, about Jerome's age, was sitting alone at a nearby table, cradling his scotch and soda and staring at Jerome who, upon noticing the fellow for the third time, finally asked, "Is there a special reason you're looking at me?"

The guy looked embarrassed at being caught staring. "I was wondering. You're not him, but you look like a guy I knew in high school."

"Did you like him?" asked Jerome.

"Huh?"

"Did you like this guy in high school? Or are you sitting there thinking, 'Here's my chance to beat the crap out of that guy I used to hate?'"

"Huh? Oh, I see. No, he was a buddy. You're not him, but you know, in this light. I was trying to tell. Sorry."

Jerome could have let it drop, and knew he should, but instead he said, "Do you know who I am?"

"You're that guy from the . . . You're *Jerome v. God*, right?"

"Yeah, except that's not my name. It's Jerome Light. I'm from Marshfield."

"Oh, yeah. I'm Lance Doubleday," he said, getting up and leaning way over to shake Jerome's hand. "Pleased to know you."

"Where you from, Lance?"

"I'm in town from Ontario. Here one night. This your wife?"

"Yeah, this is Lacy."

"Hi," is all she said as Lance shook her hand. She did not want to encourage him to stay, no matter how nice he seemed. In fact, she did not want to get to know him at all.

"I don't know much about the trial," Lance continued. "I read a little about it in the paper. It says you're an atheist, and you're suing Gideon Calhoun."

"Yeah, well, I'm not an atheist exactly."

"No, you seem like a nice guy."

"Wait a minute," said Jerome. "You mean that I couldn't be a nice guy if I were an atheist?"

"No, listen . . . No. I'm sorry. That came out wrong. I . . . it doesn't matter."

Jerome said, "You know the saying 'Nice guys finish last?' That was Leo Durocher of the Chicago Cubs said it. Well, which way did he mean it? Did he mean, 'We're in last place because we're nice guys?' Or did he mean, 'We don't want to be in last place, and that explains why we can't be nice guys?' Because I wonder if it's true," Jerome said, "that you can't come out ahead just by being nice. When people want to know how I can be an atheist and still be a nice person, it makes me want to tell them, 'I'm nice because it's more fun to be nice, not because I'm afraid of being punished after I die.' So, can I be nice and not have to explain it?"

Lance was embarrassed again. "Sure. Sure."

"Besides, I'm not an atheist."

"I'm sorry. I should've minded my own business. I'll slither back over here and leave you two . . . alone." Lance backed up towards his seat, eager to make a getaway.

"It's okay," said Jerome. "I, uh, I know you didn't mean anything. It's the trial, you know?"

"Yeah. Sure. Good luck with that." With that, Lance grabbed his drink and went to sit at the bar.

Lacy took a sip of her wine. "Okay, if you're not an atheist, what are you?" she asked her husband.

"That's hard to say." Jerome held his drink in both hands and stared into it. "Can't I believe in some kind of God without having to be Christian or Jewish or something?"

"You can do whatever you want, sweetheart," Lacy answered, trying to lighten up the mood before whatever romantic notions Jerome had disappeared completely. She leaned forward and kissed him on the lips. "Whatever you want," she repeated.

"Finish your drink," he replied with a smile, and he sat back on the sofa.

♥ ♥ ♥

"I'm finished," said Gideon, lying next to Celeste in bed.

"What do you mean?" she asked.

"I mean, no matter how this trial turns out, my ministry is finished."

"I don't understand. Why?"

"If we lose, there'll be no end to the lawsuits; we'll be bankrupt. And if we win, it will be because I have told the nation that I don't talk with God, that I've never talked with God. My congregation will never forgive me."

Celeste was sympathetic, as usual. More than anyone else in the world, she alone had grasped in a few short months the essence of Gideon Calvin Calhoun, his fears, the chinks in his veneer of confidence and calm. "Of course they will. Most of them, anyway. They let Jimmy Swaggart get away with terrible sinfulness. He still had a ministry. You're no sinner, Gideon."

"Oh, but I am, Celeste. We all are. But I'm not so sure that matters anymore. I say those words, but they're automatic. I don't feel the passion of ministry I once did. Are we all sinners? What if we're all simply human, trying our best to get through this difficult world? What if sin doesn't matter?"

"It has to matter," said Celeste. "If nothing is sinful, I pity mankind."

Gideon put the back of his forearm across his forehead and sighed. "You're right, my dear. There is sin in the world. There is a right way and a wrong way to behave. But what if Jerome Light is right? What if there is no punishment for our sins? What if God doesn't care what we did?"

"Gideon, I don't even want to think that's possible. It isn't possible!"

"People will think worse of me for renouncing God than they thought of Swaggart or Bakker, who only gave in to temptation. Denial of God is the greatest sin."

"But you're not denying God. You are still a man of God."

"I have been prideful, Celeste. I am guilty of pride. I let myself think that I have talked with God, that I know exactly what God wants. Well, I don't know, sweetheart. I don't know. God never told me in words. I felt God's desire in my heart. It is prideful for me to think that I know how to interpret that desire any more than others can. I know that life is good and worth living, and that we must live by our principles or die. But I don't know what God wants me to do, or what will happen to any of us when we die."

Celeste was in shock. She wanted to hate Jerome and Lacy, but she couldn't. Gideon had made her get to know them, and she recognized them as decent people. She'd always thought someone like Jerome, someone who truly denied God, had to be a bad person, an evil person, and maybe a communist. Gideon, bless his soul, had opened her eyes, had demonstrated the truth of God's love. Hate the sin, love the sinner. She was so ashamed that she could not be as good as her husband.

"You can be a very sexy man. Did you know that?" said Lacy as she curled her naked body next to Jerome's.

Jerome cried, "Help! I've fallen in love and I can't get up!"

Lacy, who looked better naked than many women look all dolled up, turned towards Jerome, and pushed her breasts against his side as he slid an arm under her. She started to bend her leg up and over Jerome's, sliding her smooth skin against his hairy shin and thigh. Suddenly, she pulled her leg back and grabbed for it, falling back from Jerome's embrace. "Dammit, I have a leg cramp!"

"I'll massage it for you."

"Would you? Thanks, sweetie. That'd be great."

Jerome said, "I just have one question."

"Yeah?"

"How come you never have a breast cramp?" Jerome cracked himself up with that one, and it helped Lacy forget that her leg hurt. She stood up and walked it off for a minute, giving Jerome a chance to ogle his wife in the half-light of the hotel room.

"You look terrific," he said.

"Thanks. You're not so bad yourself." She climbed back in bed and pulled the covers up to her waist, then rested her head in the crook of Jerome's arm, her ear against his body below the shoulder. "It's nice to hear your heart beat," she said quietly.

Speaking as quietly, Jerome responded, "If you lean over a little farther, you can hear my stomach growl."

They both began to giggle and then to laugh, and it was several minutes before they regained their composure. They lay together silently for a while, until Lacy asked, "What are you thinking?"

"Hmm? Oh, nothing much. In fact, I was thinking about how I used to have long hair. What do you think most of us boys took away from the story of Samson and Delilah in the Bible? 'Don't cut your hair short! Long hair equals virility!' I mean, there's Victor Mature looking all virile and manly and strong, until his long hair disappears. We also learned that you could only trust a girl so far. Never around your hair, and never around your privates."

"You are such a pig," she said, and they laughed again. As the laughter subsided, Lacy turned serious. "I can't believe you're quoting stories from the Bible."

"Yeah, I know. I guess it's kind of on my mind."

"What do you think is going to happen?" she asked Jerome.

"At the trial?"

"At the trial . . . and to us. Are we going to be okay?"

Jerome lay back and breathed as he stared at the ceiling. "We as a couple, we'll be just fine. We as a family, with two kids going to college and no savings and no house . . . it's gonna be hard. But we'll make it."

"You sound like you expect to lose the trial."

"Hmmm. Maybe I do. Maybe I do expect to lose. I haven't thought much about it, except that every day it seems to be more of a mistake. Why the hell did I do this to us? It's as if we've always been on a collision course with God, except that no matter what we do, God wins. God punches a sinkhole below our house and now we punch back, except that if we win . . . If we win, it'll be because we went to court to prove there is a God. God wins! And if we lose, God gets away with punishing us for . . . for what?"

"What are you saying, Jerome? Are you saying you believe God is punishing us, or using us? Are you suddenly a Christian or something?"

"Jesus Christ, Lacy, I'm not a Christian . . . am I? I've always made fun of those people whose lives get all messed up—on drugs or fighting in a war or gambling—and they suddenly find Jesus. At the worst moment of their lives, Jesus shows up and gives them redemption. Damn it, we lost everything, and I don't want to find God in that."

"Oh, honey, that's not God. I don't believe God would deliberately destroy our house."

"Why not? Gideon's God is a vengeful God. Maybe he's right. I've been an atheist. Maybe God hates that. Every day something new screws up our life. But killing Sylvana—that was the lowest blow."

"You can't mean that. You can't believe God is like that. You don't even believe in God."

"I know, but . . . but what if . . . Wouldn't it explain our run of bad luck? Wouldn't it explain why I was so stupid as to start this trial? If we win, I lose. If we lose, I . . . lose."

Chapter 53

The Plaintiffs Rest

Claire Light, Jerome's mother, could not sleep easily, even after years of being alone. She was confident she would never get used to the sickening realization, each time she woke up, that her husband would not be there.

It bothered her that she trusted almost everything in life less than she used to. She had always considered herself a trusting person, trying to find the good in everything and everybody, but now that was more difficult. She had seen enough sorrow; she had seen enough greed. Claire's I-like-everybody attitude that had carried her through her teens and right through middle age had taken a beating, and now she was a widow, forced, for the first time, to make do with the crumbs of attention her family and friends would randomly drop.

On the one hand, she could understand it. When she was young, her parents had been there, taking responsibility for her welfare. She'd married right after high school, and he had always been in charge, making sure the bills were paid and that everything in the house was working. She had not done much to help her parents when they got older, and she realized now what a selfish mistake that had been. In fairness, she thought, both parents had not lived past age sixty-two, and had never needed the kind of help that Claire now needed. How could she expect her children to care for her?

It was 3:20 in the morning when she got up, finally accepting that she would not be falling back to sleep anytime soon. In her green and yellow cotton nightie that had seen better days, she went downstairs and turned on the TV. It was what Miriam used to call "an argument show." Talking heads. She would have changed the channel except that she heard one of the men say something about Jerome! She forced herself to focus.

"I hope they don't have the jury sequestered, and I hope they can hear me now because I want to tell that jury not to let the inmates run the asylum!" said a handsome man in a three-piece suit with perfect brown hair and a jaw that appeared to have been designed by a committee of women's-magazine editors. "If that lunatic wins this case, you're going to see people leaving the clergy faster than Bill Clinton can unzip his pants."

Another handsome white man, this one in a colorful sports coat and slight graying at the temples of his own perfect coif, said, "Gary, when are you going to stop with the Clinton jokes? He's been out of office since you were in your teens!"

"Oh, come on," said perfect-hair Gary, feigning insult.

"Well, now seriously, we all know it won't be the end of the clergy if Gideon Calhoun loses this case. It's just like you to exaggerate everything! What's really going to happen if Calhoun loses? We're—"

Gary interrupted, which, as it turned out, was the one thing he was best at doing. "If any jury could convict a respected evangel—"

"It's not a conviction, Gary! He's not going to jail!"

"You know what I mean, if they find against him and award money to this Light-in-the-Loafers guy—"

"Are you saying Light is a homosexual?"

"No, that's not what I'm saying, but you can draw any conclusion you want about the guy because he's the kind of crackpot who is—"

"Wait a minute! Wait a minute!" said sports-coat guy. "What's really going to happen if Calhoun loses is absolutely nothing. It's a very narrowly defined case. Calhoun says he is God's agent. How many others are saying that? They all choose their words carefully. They're a very clever bunch—"

Gary interrupted, "They have to be clever, because the cards are stacked against them in this secular society we've created—"

". . . and nobody's going to be lining up to sue them—"

". . . where we write laws to protect the atheists and pagans and witches, and we don't allow prayer in the schools but we do allow gay clubs—"

"What in the world are you talking about? What do gay clubs in our schools have to do—"

"I'll tell you what I'm talking about, which is that Gideon Calhoun is a great man, a great American, whom millions of people respect and admire, and yet if he loses, you know very well that every nut with a toothache or a bumpy sidewalk is going to be taking him to court to—"

Claire was completely confused by this chaotic exchange. She was pretty sure that the one fellow was calling her son something bad, but she wasn't sure why it mattered so much to him or what the other fellow's name was, much less what point he was trying to make. She reached for the remote.

Gary said, ". . . and are you ready to admit—"

"Yes, we're ready, Your Honor," said Mac as the trial resumed Tuesday morning. He quickly sat as Reg Lundin rose from his seat—the two of them presenting a stark contrast in height as they bobbed past each other—and called to the stand the chief financial officer for the Church of the Forgotten Savior, a man named Ebenezer Biggs.

For the rest of the day, Reg laboriously took Biggs through the church's books for the past few years, noting certain spikes in donations. He explored in great detail the method of contributions and fund-raising used by CFS, and the fact that contributors could take a tax deduction for almost any amount of money donated to Gideon Calhoun via the Church.

"Doesn't that mean that taxpayers like you and me and Jerome and Lacy Light are helping to pay the Reverend Gideon Calhoun? We pay him in part because he claims to be God's agent, and therefore has a large, loyal, and generous following."

Biggs replied, "No, you're not paying him. The Church gets to keep and spend more of what it brings in because it is tax-exempt. The IRS is not losing money from taxpayers; it's just that we get to keep more of what is ours by being generous and charitable. It's a great incentive for religious freedom, Mr. Lundin."

"I appreciate how wonderful that sounds, Mr. Biggs, but I did not ask you about religious freedom. I asked you about how much money Reverend Calhoun takes from the Church, and how much less he would take in personally if you did not get such big charitable contributions from viewers?"

"I cannot speculate on the Reverend's compensation. If the tax laws were different, perhaps Brother Gideon would accept less, or perhaps not."

"Would you say that he is probably paid a higher salary and benefits when the Church takes in more money?"

"Yes, I would assume it is as true for the Reverend as it is in every business, including yours and Mr. MacConnell's."

"And wasn't it your testimony a few seconds ago that people give more to the Church because they get a tax break—that the tax break is, in fact, designed to encourage people to donate more to charities and churches?"

"Yes, I believe it's well established that the charitable-giving deductions promote greater charity. I see nothing wrong with that."

"Neither do I, Mr. Biggs. Neither do I. In fact, I personally send more money to my favorite charities, and I'm pleased that the government is, in effect, chipping in. It's great to see the government willing to accept less revenue if taxpayers are sending that money directly to the charities of their choice. Some people say that keeps the government from basically endorsing or blessing certain charities. Is that how you feel, Mr. Biggs?"

"I . . . I don't follow you."

"Please allow me to rephrase it. Do you think the government should be able to tell you how to spend your own money?"

"No, sir, I don't," said Biggs.

"Fine. Do you think, then, that the government should decide which are the best charities? Shouldn't you be deciding what charities you like?"

"Well, you can do both. I decide my favorite charities, and the government is always deciding where to put its money. I get to elect the people who will decide what to do with my money, the money we Americans are willing to give."

"How very patriotic of you, Mr. Biggs, but again, off the point. You don't want the government telling you how to spend your money, yet you give it money to spend any way it wants to."

"Not just any way, sir."

"That's correct. Not just any way. We like to control our government, don't we? We call it 'government of the people, by the people.' So, if the government is giving out money, it's the way we want it spent, right?"

The spectators in the courtroom began to fidget. Lundin's recitation was hard to follow, even for the most attentive jurors.

"Yes, we should control the government, not the other way around. Unfortunately, it doesn't always work like that."

"You're right again, Mr. Biggs. Yet you agree that the government should be supporting faith-based initiatives, don't you?"

"Yes, I do."

"Through tax breaks and direct grants?"

"Yes."

"You said churches should be tax exempt and not send money to the government. But that's not enough support for you, is it? You think the government should also be sending you money?"

The people in the courtroom finally began to see where Reg was going, and a quiet "ohh" filled the room.

"I . . ." Biggs paused. "I guess so. Yes."

"Do you believe separation of church and state has gone too far?"

"Yes."

Reg paused, dramatically he hoped, from this rapid exchange. He hoped to drive home to the jury this next point. "So it is your testimony that the government of all us Americans is properly helping support the mission of various churches?"

"Yes."

"Including the Church of the Forgotten Savior."

"Yes."

"And you have said that the extra money coming in to the Church helps you to compensate Reverend Calhoun to a greater extent."

"Yes."

"Thank you, Mr. Biggs, for helping me prove that our nation's tax laws are helping to compensate the good Reverend. I have no further questions."

Reg finished this statement rapidly so the defense would not have time to object, but Dab rose anyway. "Your Honor, please ask counsel to stop making speeches to the witnesses."

Before Judge Schuster could speak, Reg said, "I apologize, Your Honor, and will attempt to do better."

Looking annoyed, Judge Schuster said, "The jury will ignore Mr. Lundin's conclusion."

After lunch, Dab had her chance to cross-examine Biggs, one of the friendlier witnesses she expected to encounter. It was essential to cast the CFS finances in a different light, and she spent four hours grilling him that Tuesday afternoon. She took him through the great expense of maintaining the CFS ministry in an effort to prove that its pockets were not as deep as implied by the plaintiffs. She asked Biggs to comment on the money paid directly to Gideon Calhoun. She asked if CFS had ever set up any other accounts in Calhoun's name or on Calhoun's behalf into which money was diverted, and Biggs said, "No, as far as I know, there is no such account. Well, that is unless you count his 401(k), into which both he and CFS pay. That is his money under his control, and is part of the compensation package I referred to earlier."

The rest of the day saw Mac interrogate a handful of other CFS staffers, though none as dramatic as Biggs.

The next day, Mac called to the stand his researcher, Monette Mausner, whom he had hired to go through hundreds of hours of videotape of Calhoun's TV programs. Ms. Mausner showed that many of the spikes in donations to CFS correlated perfectly with increased use of the term "God's agent."

Dab Curara had no interest in keeping the video researcher—an attractive Israeli student at Capital University Law School—on the stand, since the data the girl had presented could not easily be refuted, and Dab felt she'd lose points with the jury if she tried.

The rest of that day and through the next two days, Mac brought up a succession of analysts of charitable giving patterns, of government policy analysts who spoke about faith-based giving, and of a few major individual donors to CFS.

Just past noon on Friday, Mac said, "The plaintiffs rest, Your Honor."

In fact, the plaintiffs did anything but rest, at least that weekend. Jerome and Lacy returned to Marshfield and spent the weekend avoiding reporters' phone calls. Mac had a date with Valerie LePine, the EPA official, who now found herself stationed in Columbus. Of course, he told no one about it. Reg Lundin, meanwhile, spent all of Saturday with Monette Mausner at the Columbus Zoo. By the time they hit the primates, they had made dinner plans together.

The defense was busy, too. Dab sequestered herself in the offices of a downtown law firm with which she had some connections, and spent the entire time in their law library and online preparing for Monday. Gideon and Celeste flew back to Arkansas.

Chapter 54

Belief

Lacy and Jerome had promised to return to Columbus Sunday afternoon to meet with Mac and prepare for Monday's start of the defendants' case. Saturday night around 11:30, Jerome went to Miriam's room to say goodnight and found her lying in bed, under her rain-forest duvet, listening to one of his favorite songs, the now-classic Enya piece "Watermark," and reading *Perpetuonics.*

Miriam, in her Tweety PJ's, did not look happy. "Daddy, a lot of my friends say you're going to Hell."

"You don't mean 'cause I'm putting on weight, right?" He laughed, hoping to lighten Miriam's mood.

"Dad! No, I mean like when you die."

Jerome folded his arms and sat on the edge of her bed. "I can't do anything about what your friends believe, Pumpkin. What's important is what you believe."

"You don't believe in Heaven and Hell, do you, Daddy?"

"We've talked about this before, Mir. You know I don't."

"One of the kids from ninth grade told me you said you believe in God now."

"Yeah, I figured that would get around. I'm sorry I didn't say anything to you about my testimony. It's really hard to drag you and Moses into it."

"Drag us into it? Dad, we're like in it every day. Everybody knows that Moses and I have like this famous Daddy, except you're famous for the wrong stuff."

"It must be hard on you, eh? I know it's been hard on Moses, too. How come you haven't said anything to me before?"

"It's . . . I don't know."

"You're like your mother, you know. She holds stuff in, too; doesn't like to complain. Me, I complain all the time about everything, don't I?" he said teasingly.

Miriam gave a slight laugh. "You're not bad, Daddy . . . but you do complain a lot."

"I'm very proud of you, you know that?"

"Why?" she asked.

"Umm," he said as he gathered his thoughts, the backs of his fingers brushing the hair beside his daughter's face, "Because you're so nice to everybody, and you're honest, and you're smart, and you get good grades, and you don't complain about every little thing. And because I can trust you to be a good girl. That's part of it."

Miriam put her arm around his back and pressed the side of her face against his chest. "I don't want you to go to Hell, Daddy." She began to cry lightly. He wasn't sure at first that she was crying.

He swallowed hard, trying to remove the lump in his throat. "Oh, Baby, please don't worry about it. I think maybe there is something called God, something that kind of randomly controls the universe, something that made that sinkhole hit our house. But I don't believe in Heaven or Hell. I don't think we get to live forever, or that God would punish me forever. I'm not really a bad guy, you know."

"I know you're not," she sobbed. "You're the best Daddy in the world."

"Only 'cause I've got the best daughter, and you shouldn't worry about it. I'm not going anywhere for a long time. You'll be stuck with me when you have a boyfriend and you want to marry him. And you'll be stuck with me when you have babies."

"You mean *if* I have babies," she corrected.

"Yeah, *if* you have babies. And that's a long time from now, and I'll still be here."

"Promise?"

"Yeah."

He kissed her cheek and stood up, wishing her a good night and pleasant dreams. "Give me some good dreams, Daddy, like you used to."

"Okay," he said, leaning the side of his head against hers. "Here's a good dream about flying on your own, like Superman. And here's a good dream about Jessica, and another good dream about Mommy and me."

"And what about Sylvana?"

He paused a moment at the shock of realizing that Sylvana would never leave their lives completely. "Here's a good dream about Sylvana. Now, goodnight, Pumpkin."

He closed the door as he left her too-small room in this too-tiny apartment. He listened as she turned Enya back on. Jerome felt that in a small way, he touched his daughter through his music. They didn't like much of the same anything: different movies, different actors, different books, different clothes, different TV shows. But many nights, she went to sleep listening to Enya. It was a quiet and bittersweet instrumental piece, and it had the ability to make them both relax, to touch them both in the same way. During the day, Miriam's music drove him insane. But at night, she gravitated towards the totally different sound that was her father's music, and that pleased him no end.

The next day, as Jerome and Lacy drove the now-familiar road down to Columbus, he told her of his conversation with Miriam the night before, and he told her of his own evolving religious beliefs.

"Did you know that all the billions of cells in your body change every few years? Millions of old cells die every day, and new ones are born. In terms of your chemistry, you're a completely different person now than you were, like three or four years ago!"

"Don't you mean my biology?"

"Well, whatever, I don't know. No part of you is the same, yet somehow you *are* the same. You have the same thoughts and memories and feelings. So, isn't that evidence that you have a soul?"

Lacy stared straight ahead at the road, dumbfounded to hear these thoughts coming from her husband. She was afraid to say anything in reply, afraid of what he might say next.

Soon enough, they reached the hotel, found their usual parking spot, and made their way back to the lobby. They had learned that reserving a small suite was saving them money by giving them a place to prepare food so they didn't have to eat out every meal. The trial, including travel and hotel and food, was quickly eating away at their meager savings, along with paying rent on the apartment plus the mortgage on the former house on Tadpole Lane. They could not get the suite they had occupied before the weekend, but the desk clerk, whom they now knew on a first-name basis, said he'd given them an upgrade for the same money. He said he did that for all the celebrities, but they both assumed he was kidding.

They had not dropped their bags in the suite for a few seconds before

Mac called. "I'll meet you in your suite. You haven't had time to mess it up yet." Fifteen minutes later, he knocked on their door.

"Can I come in?" Gideon asked Celeste.

"Of course. I was reading, not sleeping," she answered. Even now, more than ten months after the accident, she was not fully recovered. She found she wore out easily and needed at least one good nap per day to restore her energy. Fortunately, the Church had gotten them a double-suite—basically a suite that connected through a door that locked on both sides to a regular single room. Celeste had gotten in the habit of taking the single for her naps so that Gideon could have the run of the kitchen and sitting room.

"What are you reading?"

"Oh, nothing," said Celeste. "A bit of the Bible, actually. I thought of you as I read it a minute ago."

"Really? What book?"

"Acts. Here it is, chapter 4, verse 18: '18-Then they called them in again and commanded them not to speak or teach at all in the name of Jesus. 19-But Peter and John replied, "Judge for yourselves whether it is right in God's sight to obey you rather than God. 20 For we cannot help speaking about what we have seen and heard."'"

"Amen," said Gideon. "That's a most interesting story, and one not often discussed. It tells of the courage that Peter and John showed when the authorities ordered them to stop speaking about Jesus. Indeed, the politicians could not explain how Peter healed the crippled beggar at the temple, so they decided that it was better simply to keep the apostles from talking. But Peter and John said they would obey God, not the Council. We can find parallels in that story today."

"Yes, that's what I'm saying, Gideon."

"I hope you don't think I'm like Peter. It's not the government trying to shut me up."

"Can you imagine what it must have been like for him?" asked Celeste.

"For Peter?"

"Yes. Here he had seen Jesus perform miracles, and then he found that just uttering Jesus' name could produce the same miracles. How could he possibly not share that news?"

"You're right. How can I stop proclaiming the glory of God and Jesus, even if the authorities tell me to stop?"

"You can't, Gideon. You can't."

"I may have no choice."

"No," said Celeste. "The Word of God and the blood of our Savior, Jesus Christ, will protect us. We cannot be silent."

"We can if we no longer believe."

Celeste charged ahead with her thought, failing to comprehend Gideon's words. She was in what Gideon called "preacher mode." She said, "But we *do* believe. You of all people . . ."

"I, of all people, am just a man. I have no special ability, except to separate people from their life savings."

"That's not what you do at all," said Celeste, astonished. "You're a good man, the *best* man."

"Yes, I try to be a good man, which is why I can't keep doing it."

"Doing it?"

"Selling myself as something I'm not. God has never talked to me. I've never had a real sign from God. I feel God in my heart, but I don't hear Him in my head or see Him with my eyes. Jerome Light is right. I repeat and repeat and repeat that I am God's agent, and people write me a check."

"They love you, Gideon. You give them hope. They feel good sending you money."

"You know that many of them can't afford it, Celeste. It's one thing for some millionaire to send us a million dollars. They sacrifice nothing they need so they can buy salvation. But how many millionaires do we know? We are getting hundreds and thousands from people who sacrifice so much for the same belief."

"Yes, they believe, Gideon! They believe in you. I believe in you."

"I used to. I used to believe in what I am doing. I can't anymore. I've been saying that I'm God's agent so long that I truly started believing it, but how can it be true? Celeste . . . I am beginning to doubt my faith."

He might as well have said he was pulling wings off butterflies or stealing candy from children. She was utterly shocked. This could not be happening! Not to her rock, her very own preacher, the godly man who saved her body and then her soul. She felt as if some entirely new and frightening landscape had suddenly surrounded her, as if she'd been sucked out of the apartment and deposited in a hostile environment. Then she caught herself, without saying a word, and realized that her shock had not changed the fact that she loved Gideon with all her heart, and could not find disappointment there. "You're . . . I want to understand . . . You no longer believe in God?"

"I don't know yet. It's a new feeling, but I can't go back to what I was before."

"What do you mean?"

"I don't think I can ever preach again."

"Oh, Gideon, you can't quit. You can't! It's this horrible trial. It'll be over soon, and you'll feel better. You'll see."

"Maybe. We'll see."

Chapter 55

I Can't Make Sense of God

Dabria Curara was anxious to begin her case. She felt confident. She felt prepared. More than anything, she felt she could not take another day of the plaintiff's witnesses. She ached to get her own people up on the stand.

The first witness on the list was Morgan Cheney, the head of congregational services for CFS. Ms. Cheney, a pretty blonde with a celestial nose and piercing blue eyes, testified about the manner in which previous donors to CFS were approached to provide further financial support. Dab introduced exhibits showing materials sent to contributors that did not contain any statements about Gideon's being God's agent, and Ms. Cheney identified those letters and brochures as being the typical media that were mailed.

On cross-examination, Mac got Ms. Cheney to admit that some

materials made reference to God's agent, though she continued to insist that had not been the case recently. Mac asked, "Did this practice end when Mr. Light filed suit against the Church?"

"No, sir. It'd stopped at least a few months before that." She had a charming Southern accent, sounding like the debutante at the Camellia Ball in Mobile she had once been.

"Do you think it might have been resumed if not for this lawsuit?"

"I can't say, sir. We never discussed whether we'd want to use it again."

Dab Curara then called a succession of witnesses, including contributors who swore that their support of Gideon's ministry and CFS had nothing to do with the notion of Reverend Calhoun being God's agent. Mac got all of them to admit that they had heard him make that claim. Monday dragged into Tuesday and into Wednesday, and still the defense was trying to debunk the notion that Gideon's success was based on his famous slogan of being "God's agent here on Earth."

That same Wednesday afternoon, Dabria surprised the room by announcing, "We call Lacy Light to the stand." Dab had noticed—as had everyone paying the least bit of attention—that Thaddeus MacConnell had called only one of his two clients to testify, and she wanted to know why.

She began by asking Lacy about her family, including her parents and siblings and children. They might have had the same conversation at a neighborhood party or some hideous event selling home products; it all seemed quite "womanly" until Dab said, "Are you an atheist, Mrs. Light?"

"No, I'm not."

"What religion are you, may I ask?" Mac was poised to rise and object, but held his seat.

"I'm Jewish."

Mac again was about to object when Dab asked, "How do you feel about Christian evangelists?" Mac sat down again, knowing it was too late to avoid this line of questions.

"How do I feel? I don't feel anything about them."

"You must have some opinion."

"I don't think about them much. I don't attend Christian services in person or watch them on TV."

"I'd be surprised if you did, Mrs. Light. I myself am a Christian, and I don't believe I've ever been to a Jewish service or seen one on TV."

"There's not a lot of Jewish services on TV," said Lacy. "In fact, I've never seen any." The spectators laughed lightly.

"Does that bother you? Do you believe there's too much Christian broadcasting?"

"No, I . . . well, I don't think I've ever thought about it before. There seems to be a lot, but it's no bother to me."

"So you never saw *The Gideon Calhoun Hour*?"

"Not until Jerome and I were shown some video a few months ago."

"Tell me about the night of the sinkhole," Dab said, and they launched into a twenty-minute discussion of the events that had brought them to this courtroom. Jerome, seated next to Reg, let his thoughts drift during this familiar recitation. He watched a fly stagger along the table in front of him. He wondered if the judge would admonish him if he swatted it.

Then Dab returned to the topic of *The Gideon Calhoun Hour*. She asked Lacy, "So now you are living in a tiny apartment because you've lost your house and most of your belongings, this house you still owe money on, and you see a video of Reverend Calhoun talking about your house on national TV. What ran through your mind as you watched that video?"

"I was angry . . . and upset. I thought, 'He shouldn't be talking about us like we're something awful that deserved to lose our house.' He said God was sending us a powerful message. That really hurt."

"I'm sure it did. Has the Reverend ever apologized to you for those words?"

"No, not in so many words. He's been very nice, though, when he came over to our . . . I mean, over to our table, and said . . . well, he was nice . . . and friendly. So, I forgive him."

"You forgive him? That's kind of you, Mrs. Light, but not the response I usually get from someone who is suing a client of mine." A few members of the audience tittered, and Judge Schuster banged her gavel once. Lacy laughed nervously, unsure whether Dab was intentionally making a joke. "But your forgiveness did not move you to stop these resentful proceedings, did it?"

"You mean, I—"

"I mean," continued Dab, "that you are pursuing this lawsuit in a vindictive manner because you were 'angry and upset,' I believe were your words, that Reverend Calhoun insulted you. Do you honestly believe that Gideon Calhoun personally owes you money for the loss of your house, or do you just want to punish him for hurting your family's honor?"

"I . . . we . . . we didn't see the videotape until after we'd filed the lawsuit. We did not start this lawsuit to be vindictive."

"Perhaps at the beginning, you felt you were owed something for your loss. That would have been understandable, since it had happened so recently. But later, didn't you begin to feel that Gideon Calhoun was your husband's whipping boy? Didn't you feel like stopping this charade?"

Mac could wait no more. "Your Honor, I must object to counsel's trivializing the serious nature of the matter before this court. It insults our judicial system and it insults Your Honor."

"I appreciate your concern for my honor," said the judge, "but I warn you to limit your own editorializing when you object, Mr. MacConnell. Objection sustained. Please rephrase your last question, Ms. Curara."

"Thank you, Your Honor. Mrs. Light, did you at any point want to end this lawsuit because you did not agree with it?"

"I . . . I may have harbored some doubts, but I support my . . . hus . . . but doesn't everyone have doubts in a courtroom? Isn't that what brings us here? If everyone knew the right answer, there'd be no courts. We need to . . . talk. I support my husband. We lost everything except our lives. Maybe Mr. Calhoun got it right; maybe God did punish us. Maybe we ought to figure out why, what we might have done. But the money he gets because people believe he talks for God, well . . . maybe he ought to figure out what God is telling him."

A few spectators murmured, "Ooo."

"So you have had doubts that this lawsuit is fair, but yet you refuse to stop it?"

"I never said 'fair.' And no, I don't refuse to stop it. Just because I might see things differently from my husband doesn't mean I wanted to stop this trial."

Jerome sat up a little straighter in his chair, and smiled subtly at Lacy.

Dab Curara turned away from the witness for a few seconds. She walked deliberately back to where Gideon and Terre Béliveau, the chairman of CFS, sat. The pause in the proceedings and the tension in the room caused a number of spectators to cough, as though they'd all been waiting for such a break. Dab shuffled some papers meaninglessly on her desk, buying herself time to take a few breaths and prepare herself for the next assault on Mount Lacy.

Finally, she turned and walked back to where Lacy sat, her anxiety rising with each second she had been forced to wait, the focus of so many eyes. Dab began, "You said you believe in God, and you attend religious services. Do you have a rabbi at your synagogue?"

"Yes, Rabbi Altschul."

"Do you go to him for advice sometimes? Do you trust Rabbi Altschul?" Dab asked Lacy.

"Do I go to her? Yes, of course. Sometimes."

"I apologize. Do you think the rabbi was 'called' to the clergy?"

"I don't know. She never discussed her reasons with me for becoming a rabbi."

"But she might have felt a calling, like other clergy?"

"I suppose so."

"Objection. Calls for speculation by the witness."

"Sustained."

"Do you believe some rabbis and priests and ministers are called to the clergy?"

"I'm sure some feel they were called. I can't say what motivates each one."

"But you treat your rabbi as a special person, someone you can go to for advice when other people might not be approachable?"

"I trust her. She's a smart woman, and sympathetic."

"Good. Would you say she's a godly woman?"

"I guess so."

"And you pay dues at your synagogue then?"

"Yes."

"Part of which pays Rabbi Altschul's salary, right?"

"Of course."

"Did you ever consider suing Rabbi Altschul for your losses? You've said she is a godly woman, and that she gets money from you and the other members of your synagogue for performing the same kinds of spiritual services that Reverend Calhoun provides. Why didn't you sue your rabbi?"

"That's ridiculous!"

"Is it? Any more ridiculous than suing a Christian minister you'd never met and never seen whose church is over six hundred miles from your house."

"I don't have a house anymore, remember?"

"I'm sorry, Mrs. Light . . . over six hundred miles from where you live."

"Rabbi Altschul never said she's God's 'agent,'" Lacy said drily. Holding her anger in check, she added "And I don't pay dues so I can get a line to Heaven."

"No, you don't, and neither do others. Thank you, Mrs. Light. I have no further questions."

Mac stood briefly and said, "No questions at this time, Your Honor."

Lacy walked steadily and calmly from the witness chair back to her seat next to Jerome, but inside, her stomach was churning, and she wanted more than anything to run screaming from the courtroom, jump in the car, and race home to her kids. Instead, she let herself have a good cry in the hotel room that night.

On Thursday morning, Dr. Keaton Mueller was the first defense witness. Dr. Mueller was from Harvard University. A psychologist at Stonecrest College, a four-year school closely associated with CFS, had volunteered to testify, but Dab preferred a witness whose impartiality could not be easily questioned, and so she had found Dr. Mueller. He provided a detailed psychological profile of a typical atheist, and concluded that Jerome was one—based on an analysis of answers Jerome had given in court and in his deposition. He also concluded, on cross examination, that Lacy was a more traditional "theist," a person who believes in God the Creator.

"Atheism," Dr. Mueller said, "is generally associated with a pessimistic and anti-social personality. I would not say that atheism itself is a personality disorder, but it is often found to be present in men who are suffering a rather robust Oedipal Complex. The boy has strong negative feelings about his real father, feelings about which he can do nothing. He cannot make his father no longer exist, but he can make the specter of a heavenly father disappear. As noted psychologist Dr. Paul Vitz has said, 'To act as if God does not exist is an obvious, not so subtle disguise for a wish to kill Him.' That wish grows out of the Oedipal desire."

"Thank you, Dr. Mueller. Your witness," Dab nodded at Mac.

Mac was seething inside, but hid it well. Defense counsel had boxed him in by having Dr. Mueller quote Paul Vitz's damaging opinion about atheists, an opinion Mac could not refute without bringing in other psychologists. He tried to assail Dr. Mueller's testimony in other ways. He wanted to get Mueller to present the opposing viewpoint.

Dr. Mueller told Mac, "No, I would not say being an atheist contributes to making someone depressed or negative. I would say that it's a symptom, not a cause. We often find out that people who exhibit certain disorders frequently profess no belief in God."

Mac attacked. "Are you aware of any peer-reviewed studies that show that belief or non-belief is a predictor of who might have a particular disorder? In other words, can you tell who is going to have problems simply by asking them whether they believe in God?"

"No. No correlation has been documented."

"Because there is no correlation. No cause and effect, am I right?"

"Yes, sir."

Mac said, "Pessimism is not considered a personality disorder, I hope, or about half my friends and colleagues are in trouble."

Dab stood up. "Objection. Counsel is editorializing again."

Judge Schuster said, "Do you have a question for the witness, Mr. MacConnell?"

Mac smiled. "No, Your Honor. No further questions for this man."

As the psychologist stepped down, Dab called Charlie Mackles, Jerome's co-worker from Wexford Press, to the stand, followed by other of Jerome's friends and acquaintances to testify that Jerome had always called himself an atheist and frequently expressed sympathy with atheist activists and philosophy. Each such witness was mortified to be hurting Jerome's case. Each of them had been located by private investigators looking into Jerome's personal life. Dab Curara was leaving nothing to chance, precisely as Mac MacConnell had predicted. But none of these witnesses was as mortified as Carl Light, Jerome's Unitarian brother.

"You grew up with Mr. Light, did you not?" Dab asked Carl.

"Yes, of course."

"In the same home with the same parents?"

"Yes," said Carl, who had been coached indirectly by Mac.

Mac had once said to Jerome, as if musing, "I sure hope your brother knows to stick to answering questions and saying nothing extra." He did not need to tell Jerome what to do next.

Dab began to ask Carl about the beliefs of their parents, but Mac successfully objected to that line of questioning—as he did when she tried to get Carl to disclose his own religious beliefs. Finally, she asked him to talk about religious statements made directly by Jerome to Carl. "What were his exact words, as best you can recall?"

Carl testified, "He said, 'I can't make sense of God. That idea doesn't make sense to me.'"

"What did you conclude from your conversation about your brother's beliefs?"

"I concluded that we think a lot alike."

"In what way, Mr. Light?" asked Dab.

"We don't rely on a supernatural being."

"Would you call your brother an atheist, then?"

"I don't put labels on people, Ms. Curara. I'll call my brother whatever he wants to be called."

"Did he ever say to call him an 'atheist'?"

"He may have used that word, but not frequently."

And so it went. April Fulesday, a former college girlfriend of Jerome, was next to the stand. Dab said, "The defense calls April Foolsday to testify."

The vivacious brunette, whom Jerome had not seen in over thirty years, came forward, but before she was sworn in, she said, "Excuse me. My name is pronounced 'Fuh-LEZ-day'."

Once April was sworn in and took her seat, Dab said, "Please forgive me, Ms. Fulesday. One of my associates took your deposition and I failed to consult him on how to pronounce your name." She then proceeded to question the woman—now a widow with two children—on Jerome's beliefs during their "courtship" in college. April said little of consequence, other than recalling that they had attended a Humanist organization on campus together. "Neither of us was into God at that time in our lives. Most of our friends weren't, either."

Lacy watched and listened to April with a certain detachment, but not so Jerome. As he watched April enter and sit and testify, he remembered how beautiful she was when he met her at a party, and how she had sneaked into his dorm room wearing a rain hat and his winter jacket. He closed his eyes and once again saw her naked silhouette against his window. He thought about how it had felt to kiss her. He was jolted back to the present and to Judge Schuster's courtroom when he realized he was starting to purse his lips. He glanced sheepishly around to make sure no one had seen him.

The week ended with another of the Lights' former neighbors—an Asian man whom they barely knew—talking about Jerome's beliefs. He had gained a certain perspective based on signs the Lights had placed in their windows ("Good without God") and car bumper stickers ("Atheists Don't Start Wars"), and from seeing a copy of the *Freethought Trumpet* that Jerome had, in the process of throwing out, offered to Mr. Obigoshi— whom Miriam at age four had called "Oh My Gosh-ee"—as he passed by on his daily walk.

Lacy and Jerome returned to Marshfield for the weekend, and managed to get some decent rest despite the steady barrage of family members and press inquiries, all of which they directed to Mr. MacConnell's office. None of their friends and neighbors who had testified in ways that might hurt the Lights' case reached out.

Celeste and Gideon headed to Stonecrest for the weekend. Gideon's ministry always suffered when he was away, and these past few weeks had been especially trying. He spent most of the weekend huddled with CFS staff, while Celeste tried to make something out of their neglected garden.

On Monday, they all returned to Columbus and Judge Vera Schuster's now all-too-familiar courtroom. "Hear ye, hear ye. The United States District Court for the Middle District of Ohio is now in session, Judge Vera Olivette Schuster presiding. God save the United States and this honorable court." Jerome thought it unlikely he'd ever get used to hearing those final words, but he no longer shuddered upon hearing them.

The time had come for Gideon himself to testify, but first the defense wanted to put Judge Judith O'Neill, a retired federal magistrate, on the stand to describe the legal concept of "agency." It was dry stuff, so Dab went through it as quickly as possible, having delayed this witness until right before Gideon. She knew that on this day, the jury would be alert and not miss the importance of this legal point, a point she knew would be especially relevant when Gideon testified.

Dabria and her team had done a good job of alerting the media that Reverend Calhoun would be taking the stand; the cameras and reporters had turned out en masse to get seats in the courtroom. Judge Schuster was determined to keep order, and she let that fact be known.

There was one lawyer on Dab's team whom the CFS Board had insisted be privy to the proceedings. CFS and Gideon Calhoun were being sued separately, but both sides had agreed to have Dab Curara serve as lead attorney and handle all the courtroom goings-on. Now, for the first time, Lindsay Meier spoke. "The Church of the Forgotten Savior, Inc., calls the Reverend Gideon Calvin Calhoun to testify."

The courtroom seemed to give off sparks as Gideon rose beside the defense table and made his way with great grace and purpose towards the witness stand. He knew how to enter a room, and he especially knew how to command one. He thought that if he had ever needed that skill at any time in his life, he surely needed it now.

Chapter 56

The Beginning of the End

After Gideon was sworn in, Dab made a point of being obsequious as she first approached him. She knew she had established herself in the jurors' minds as a bit aloof, even a bit cold, perhaps with a slightly arrogant and imperious air. That was deliberate, because now she wanted them to see her in awe of a witness. She wanted them to see even a cold, businesslike woman consider this holy man to be special. She hoped it would create sympathy for Gideon and also show her to be a person who can be warm and compassionate with the "right" kind of people.

"Good morning, Reverend."

"Good morning, Ms. Curara."

"How are you, today, sir?"

"I'm well, thank you, and you?"

Dab had, of course, expected this mundane exchange, and she said, "I'm fine, sir, but I did not inquire about your health merely to be polite. In fact, I want to know how healthy you are, physically and mentally."

Gideon thought it strange that she had not forewarned him about this question. She had deliberately not prepped him for this opening because she wanted him to get in the habit of talking naturally and easily about something. What better topic than his own health? She'd have asked him about the weather if she believed she could get away with it. Gideon had been a witness before, but never had seemed this nervous. She wanted him confident and calm. Had he been trying to give a pre-scripted reply, his underlying nervousness would have made the jury see him as being rehearsed, unnatural, maybe even cocky. She had to help him avoid that trap, and so she asked him about his health.

"I'm . . . uh, really quite strong, thank you. I feel fit and healthy, and I'm generally happy, but with some obvious concern about this trial."

"That's understandable. You were married recently, were you not?"

"Yes, I was married in December to my best friend, Celeste. I thought perhaps no one was interested in my wedding because I have not seen pictures of it splashed on any tabloid covers, and no one has offered to pay me for photos."

Spectators laughed quietly at Gideon's comment, and Dab did as well. "I'd say you're quite lucky in that, Reverend. The paparazzi have been less kind to you lately, I'm afraid."

"They have their job to do. A free press is one of the cornerstones of our society. As long as they do not invade my home, I'm content with how we are treated."

Dab now switched gears to a question she had disclosed in advance to the Reverend. "Please tell us how you first became a minister, and why."

"I always knew I was going to be a minister. I'm not sure how I knew, but my earliest memory is of watching our family's pastor greet people at the door of the church after service, and how everybody lined up to shake his hand and say something nice to him, and I thought, 'That's a job I'd like!' My parents always went on and on about Reverend Tichenor. They admired him so much, and they made us kids excited about every Sunday. Sunday in our house was a special day, when we put aside whatever troubled us and got dressed up in our best clothes and heard the good news about Jesus."

Gideon talked for another hour, prompted occasionally by leading questions from his attorney. The audience was quiet and attentive, barely moving. Finally, she asked, "In all this planning and praying and learning, did you ever talk directly with God?"

The Reverend Calhoun, who had already been sitting straight and tall in his seat, barely shifted. "No, not in what you might call a normal conversation. I would talk to God, but I never heard voices answering me."

"Did you ever receive any signs or perceive anything you took to be a message from God to you?"

"I'm not sure how to answer you. I saw many miracles that I took to be the Hand of God."

"I mean, did you ever see anything that seemed like a personal message to you from God, as Moses saw the burning bush?"

"No. I never witnessed any such thing. I never felt God was talking only to me."

"Did you ever perform a miracle yourself?"

"I'm a man, not a God or a prophet. I cannot perform miracles."

"I mean," said Dab, "did you ever, for example, heal a person?"

"I have no special healing powers, Ms. Curara. I would speak to people who were sick, and sometimes they would feel better if I spoke to them or touched them."

"Were you invoking the power of God when you did this?"

The courtroom was hushed as Gideon looked at his hands, his five fingertips barely touching each other. He took a long breath, and when he looked up, he said, "No. I am not an agent of God."

This admission provoked enough stirring in the courtroom for Judge Schuster to bang her gavel and ask for silence, one of the few times she'd had to do so. Jerome sat back and looked at Mac, whose gaze remained fixed on Calhoun. Lacy turned in her seat to observe the reaction in the room, and when she did, she looked directly at the old woman who had been slowly shuffling out of the room when she had scolded Mac two weeks earlier. The old woman smiled and waved.

When the spectators settled down, Dab continued. "What do you mean when you say you are not an 'agent of God'?"

"I mean I cannot invoke God. I cannot make God come and do my bidding like some genie out of a lamp." Nearly all spectators laughed at that notion, as if they were at a late-night talk show.

Dab said, "We have seen videos in which you claim to be the agent of God. You say now you are not God's agent. Were you ever the agent of God?"

Gideon said, "I always felt I was an accurate interpreter of God's laws as I understood them. That was what I meant when I said I am God's agent here on Earth."

"Do you still feel that way? Or are you God's agent in some things and not in others?"

"I talk about God, not for God. He has never directly authorized me to speak on His behalf."

"You are saying you are not God's legal representative?" asked Dab.

"That is correct."

The questioning went on in this vein for quite a while, citing Judge O'Neill's earlier testimony about agency. Gideon then was asked to talk about his fundraising efforts and speeches specifically designed to appeal for financial support from viewers. He was asked how his in-person appeals differed from his televised pulpit appeals and then from his televised pleas recorded in a studio. He patiently went over the script development for each situation.

Inside, Gideon was dying a little with each question, putting himself more and more in the shoes of a casual listener, or even in Jerome's shoes. He thought, as he answered Dab's friendly questioning, *Listen to yourself, Gideon! It looks like everything you say is carefully scripted and calculated. What happened to speaking from the heart? How can they know you're not a phony? What if they're right that you are?*

Dab finally ended her questioning by asking Gideon about his relationship with the Lights, whether he had ever met them or had any previous connection with them or their family, or even with the town of Marshfield, Ohio. She wanted to give Gideon a chance to show his sympathy and compassion for the Lights while distancing himself from any cause for ill will coming from Jerome or Lacy. She wanted to make Gideon seem like the victim, which, of course, would have been Mac's strategy, too, had he been working for the Reverend. "Before this case, I never met the Lights and was never in Marshfield," he said truthfully.

And so, when Dab concluded interrogating the witness, Mac took over, knowing he had his work cut out for him, and that this witness more than any other could make or break his case.

Judge Schuster interrupted. "Excuse me, Mr. MacConnell, but I realize that the hour is getting late, and I believe we can all benefit from adjourning for the night. Court is adjourned until 9: a.m. tomorrow."

Just like that, the air went out of the balloon that had been this tension-filled day. Each person there went emotionally limp. Mac's shoulders betrayed his sudden withdrawal from the adrenaline high he had felt when Dab said, "Your witness, counselor." Gideon outwardly appeared as the calmest of the major players in this drama, but inwardly, he was a wreck, and it was only his years of public appearances that saved him from making a fool of himself.

That night, back in his hotel room after a silent dinner with Celeste and his defense team, Gideon received a phone call from Morgan Cheney, the Congregational Services Director at CFS. She spoke fast, as though she could not wait to deliver her message and split. "The phones here are ringing off the hook," she said. Gideon briefly reflected on what an anachronism that expression was becoming. "A lot of people are upset by what you said today, and a lot of them are withdrawing their support. We've lost fifteen hundred subscribers in the past two hours!"

Gideon wondered what the evening newscasts had said and what soundbites of his they had used. He had not thought to watch the network news, but if he had thought of it, it's likely he would have passed on the opportunity. He said to Morgan, "Calm down. Calm down. Have you spoken with Ebenezer about the numbers?"

"Yes. He's very concerned. We haven't been able to enter the cancellations yet, but when we do, he thinks we may be down almost a million dollars already, and the phone calls and emails are still coming in."

Gideon said softly, "It will slow down in an hour or two as people go to bed. Those who sleep on it tonight will probably stay with us. We'll be okay. You'll see."

Celeste looked quizzically at Gideon when he got off the phone. He did not notice her right away, but absentmindedly took off his clothes and put on his pajama bottoms. Only then did he hear her call his name. "Gideon, what is it?"

"It's the beginning of the end," he said.

"It'll be good when it's over," said Lacy, giving Jerome a half-hearted neck massage as he sat in the standard-issue blue-and-yellow hotel easy chair facing the flat-screen TV above a dark brown chest of drawers.

"I can't wait," said Jerome, bending his head forward, encouraging a more robust massage.

"What are we going to do next?"

"If we lose?"

Lacy looked around the room. "Either way. I guess it'll be different if we win."

"No kidding, Lace. There's no telling how much money they could give us, but I'd settle for one dollar at this point. If we win, our lives are gonna change. We're going to be swamped by the media for a while, and you can bet Gideon will appeal if he loses. He'll have to."

"Mmm. This could drag out for a long time. A really long time."

"You got that right."

She stopped her massage and rubbed hand lotion on her hands. "What about if we lose? You're not going to appeal it, are you?"

"Mac wants to, for sure," said Jerome, and he stood up and walked to the kitchenette to make some tea.

"I don't," said Lacy, turning to watch him.

Jerome filled the generic teakettle with enough water for two cups, and said, "I don't either, really. I don't think I could go through this anymore. I don't care about winning anymore."

Lacy turned away when he spoke, and she folded her arms as she walked towards the two-seat sofa with the gaudy heavy-duty fabric. Before she reached it, she wheeled and faced Jerome again. "I can't believe you said that. Didn't I ask you to stop two weeks ago?"

"A lot has happened. Was it only two weeks? We couldn't quit then. We can't quit now. Whatever happens, happens. Maybe it's what God wants."

They watched some TV, looking for something that would not require them to think or learn. When the show ended, Lacy stood and looked at Jerome. He turned off the TV, and she said, "Maybe this whole thing had to happen. Maybe we had to be a part of it. Maybe our house was chosen. Maybe something good will come out of it."

"You know, I really like Gideon," answered Jerome. "I admire him. Heck, the whole country admires him. I'd like to be Gideon Calhoun right now. He's going to win, you know."

† † †

"It's too soon to say that, Brother Gideon," Dab Curara said outside the courtroom early Tuesday morning. "I feel confident that we are doing very well with the jury. The best thing we have going for us is you. You will remain calm and serene no matter what MacConnell tries to do. He won't be able to twist you as he did to some witnesses. You just have to get through this next day or so, and let me take it from there."

Gideon brushed imaginary sweat away from his brow with the butt of his hand. "I wish I were anywhere but here, to be honest."

"I believe God wanted you to be here, Gideon," said Celeste, taking his other elbow with both hands. "You represent what's good and decent."

"No one knows that," Gideon replied. "They see another television preacher on the take. They think I'm a phony, like you-know-who."

"You are the sacrificial lamb, atoning for their sins."

"I'm not atoning!" Gideon cried. "I'm trying to save their asses. If we win, the others get to keep doing what they're doing, taking money in God's name from people who can't afford it."

"Gideon, no! That's not right. The bad ones are only a small minority, they—"

"But how do you know who's good and who's bad? That's the problem. It's so easy to fool everyone. Heck, I can't always tell the phonies. The good ones and the bad ones, they're all selling the same medicine."

"It's good medicine, Gideon," Lindsay Meier, Dab's assistant, broke in.

"How do we know that, though?" protested Gideon, exasperated. "I've never talked with God. How can I say I know without a doubt what God wants? What if Jerome Light is right? He's a decent person, not some monster. What if he's right?"

Dab Curara clapped her hand over Gideon's mouth and looked around to make sure no one had heard. The small conference room in which they had taken sanctuary should have reassured her, but her client's words were incendiary enough to throw off her judgment. "You are *not* going to say that on the stand today!"

"Of course not, Dabria. I'm not stupid."

"Let's all calm down, shall we?" said Celeste.

Chapter 57

God Made Flesh

It was time for court to reconvene. The defense team left the small room and crossed the corridor to Judge Schuster's courtroom. Reporters, who were not supposed to ask questions inside, couldn't help themselves. When one of them called out a question to Gideon, they all did. The bedlam was repeated when the plaintiffs made the same journey.

Gideon appeared composed and confident—his TV face—as he took the stand again. Mac, of course, would not be the sycophant that Dab Curara had appeared to be. Mac said, "Good morning, Reverend."

"Good morning."

Mac had carefully considered his strategy for questioning Gideon, both in terms of how best to elicit the answers he wanted from Gideon, and in terms of what would play best with the jury. He determined not to fawn over the minister, but not to bully him either. He had to keep Gideon from being too comfortable while preventing the jury from developing any more sympathy for him. So, the attorney avoided any pleasantries, but threw a series of softball questions at Gideon to help establish the rhythm Mac desired, as if they were opposing basketball teams. He asked seemingly relevant questions that had no purpose other than to lull Gideon into complacency. If that worked, Mac might be able to get the usually brilliant minister to slip up and say something damaging.

To that end, Mac asked about the history of CFS, why it was located in Stonecrest, how he met his first wife, how she died, and a dozen other questions that were almost meaningless to his case, but to which he knew Dab Curara would not object.

Finally, without changing his rhythmic delivery or trumpeting his intent, he said, "Reverend Calhoun, yesterday you told the court that you talk about God, that you interpret God's laws. Is that a correct summary of your remarks?"

"Yes, I'd say so. I represent what God stands for."

Mac pounced, but softly like a kitten, "And how do you know what God stands for?"

Gideon tried his best not to hesitate, but a tiny hitch entered his speech nevertheless. "I, uh . . . I have studied God's word, and I've also read extensively the writings of the great theologians and philosophers."

"So your theology comes from others? You have no thoughts of your own?"

"Of course I have my own thoughts, Mr. MacConnell. I have never—"

Mac interrupted, "You have, in fact, made a very considerable fortune by convincing, or trying to convince, others that you have some unique insights, have you not?"

"Have I made a fortune?"

"No, Reverend, I don't need you to confirm that you have profited handsomely. We've already heard quite a lot about the money you bring in. But have you not tried to convince others—and by 'others' I mean basically the entire country—that you speak for God?"

Gideon began to say, "In the first place—"

But Mac again cut him off, speaking more rapidly now, changing the tempo to keep Calhoun off balance. "Wouldn't you say that repeating a phrase such as 'God's agent' over two thousand times qualifies as an effort to convince people?"

"In a sense, it does, but—"

"How can you say otherwise? The very essence of marketing an idea—"

Dab Curara had seen and heard enough. She knew MacConnell's tactics all too well, and she knew she had to blow the whistle. "Your Honor!"

"Mr. MacConnell," said Judge Schuster, dryly, "You will please allow the witness to answer one question before you submit another."

"Yes, Your Honor," said Mac, backing off like a basketball player who had had no intention of committing the foul and was shocked one had been called. "Reverend Calhoun, in general would you say that the constant repetition of a phrase or idea can instill it in the minds and memories of listeners?"

"Objection, Your Honor," said Dab. "The witness has no expertise in the field of marketing and psychology."

Mac rebutted, "He most certainly is an expert in public speaking and audience metrics."

"Overruled. The question does not call for expert testimony. Please answer the question, Reverend."

"I would say that is generally accepted as a fact."

"Regardless of whether the phrase that is repeated is itself true?" asked Mac.

"Yes, I suppose."

"So, in repeating the statement two thousand, four hundred, and eighteen times that *you* are 'God's agent here on Earth,' what was your intention, sir?"

"To glorify God. To say that there is no higher serving than serving Him."

"So anyone could be God's agent?"

"Yes, I suppose so."

"But not everyone *is* God's agent, is that correct?"

"Of course not. Not everyone even believes in God."

Mac said, with slightly grander gestures than before, to emphasize the importance of his words, "So, if you are one of the few people who serves God at this highest level, then aren't you claiming to be in some way special, some way exalted above those who don't perform this higher service?"

"I feel blessed, Mr. MacConnell, not special. I am certainly not exalted above anyone."

"Your humility is commendable, Reverend, but so is your bank account, and so—"

Dab said, "Objection."

"Overruled."

Mac continued, "So, it seems that you are asking people to support you financially because you are special, unique."

"It's not me that's special, though. It's the theology I espouse. It's the message I bring. Why would they go to a church that did not bring them comfort?"

"It's the message you bring . . . from whom, Reverend? Is it your own message that you made up? Or is it a message from God?"

"It's a universal message of love from God about His only son Jesus!"

"And you bring this message from God, this Good News!"

"That's my job."

Mac said, "So then you, sir, *are* God's agent, precisely as you told us two thousand four hundred and eighteen times in the past five years."

"Yes and no," said Gideon as he adjusted himself in the chair, finally beginning to lose his cool under Mac's disruptive assault.

"You are or you aren't, Reverend. I hate to sound like an old song, but first you say you do, and then you don't!"

"All due respect to counsel's knowledge of old songs," said Dab to hearty laughter in the room, a sort of collective sigh of relief after the tension of the last few minutes, "but counsel is badgering the witness. The Reverend Calhoun intends to answer each question fully, but needs the opportunity to do so."

"I agree, Ms. Curara," Judge Schuster said sternly. "Mr. MacConnell, I want you to speak at whatever pace you want, but do not intimidate the witness. Allow him to answer."

"Yes, Your Honor, and once again I apologize for the passion I bring to this subject, because it is the very heart of our case, Your Honor." Mac managed to turn an "apology" to the court into a tiny nudge of the jury. Judge Schuster considered telling the jury to disregard that last remark from Mac, but she decided that the damage was already done and she could only make it worse.

"Please, Reverend, answer my question. Take as long as you wish. Did you tell the truth when you told the world over and over again that you are God's agent, or are you telling the truth now, when you say that 'no,' you're not God's agent?"

It came, at last, to this moment. Mac knew that if Gideon said he is not God's agent, his empire would crumble, and his contributions would dry up. He also knew that if Gideon insisted that he is, in fact, God's agent, the jury would have to find in the Lights' favor. Either way, Mac would win.

"I'd like to explain," Gideon said calmly. Dab's small interruption had been long enough to allow him to catch his breath and collect his thoughts. "The theology I present is not something I made up, but it's also not something I got directly from God. I'm only special in that I have taken the time to learn the messages that others claim to have received."

Mac knew the die had been cast at that point. Gideon was prepared to see his ministry end. On the one hand, Mac respected him for that honesty. He had incorrectly predicted that Gideon would be more protective of the money he was earning than in living his principles, but he had clearly underestimated the Reverend Gideon Calvin Calhoun. He felt, for the first time, a tiny twinge of guilt that he would be the instrument of Calhoun's downfall. He could ease up on the throttle, at least for now, and let Gideon commit occupational suicide. "Please share the basis of your theology with us, Reverend."

"My view is not solely a religious view. It is the view of scientists and scholars, academicians and philosophers. Bill Bryson wrote in *A Short History of Nearly Everything*, 'There needn't actually be a universe at all. For the longest time there wasn't. There were no atoms and no universe for them to float about in. There was nothing—nothing at all anywhere.'"

"So, you are saying, Reverend, that before there were atoms, there was 'nothing anywhere.' Is that your testimony?"

"Yes. There was nothing until God made it."

By golly! thought Mac. If Gideon was determined to fall on his sword, Mac was determined to help him, in the hope that the minister might catch himself and still decide to save his own career. "If there was nothing at all, as you said, then God must have been part of the nothing. God *was* nothing. So, what created God?"

"Nothing created God. God was not created."

"Wait a minute. 'God was not created?' There was nothing at all, and God was not created. So, God just came into existence, out of the nothing. Is that a fair way to put it?"

"I suppose it's as good as any."

MacConnell rubbed his chin and stepped slowly away from Gideon and towards the jury. "God just existed. Nothing created God. God could exist without any creator. Yet you wanted us to believe that all these atoms that weren't there before could not exist without a creator."

Dab Curara rose again. "Is there a question here, Your Honor, or merely a tirade about nothing?"

"Of course there's a question," Mac said. "The question is, what changed in the cosmos? How could there be nothing and then something. You said, Reverend, 'For the longest time' there was nothing. What does that mean, 'for the longest time'?"

Gideon said, "It means forever. From the beginning of time, until God decided to create Heaven and Earth and all the living things."

"God 'decided?' What was God doing before He . . . or She . . . decided to create Heaven and Earth and all the living things?"

"How can I possibly know what God did before? God simply was.

God doesn't have to do anything to be God."

Mac now played it cool, like a curious student asking a professor a profound question. He did not want Gideon so be seen as a man under attack and gain the jury's sympathy. Quietly, earnestly, he asked, "If there was nothing, and God did nothing, then how can you possibly say God existed? It seems to me that if there has been nothing forever, as you said, from the beginning of time, and through these infinite ages God did nothing, then there is no evidence at all that God existed. Please tell the court how anything can exist—something with the intelligence to make a 'decision' to create things—for an infinite number of years in the middle of absolutely nothing, *doing* absolutely nothing, and be said to exist?"

Gideon was angry. "That's a preposterous question!"

Mac strode close to Gideon. "Not at all. Because if there were a time when God did not exist, and nothing created God, as you testified, then how could God exist today?"

"But God *DOES* exist!"

Mac pleaded, "And how do you know that? Has God talked to you or appeared to you? Remember, you are under oath, Reverend Calhoun."

"I know because I know. Hebrews 11 says, 'Faith is the assurance of things hoped for, the conviction of things not seen.' I have complete faith in the Lord."

"You have faith, which is a way of saying you *think* it's true, but you have no proof. So, I'll ask you again: Has God spoken to you? Has God physically appeared before you?"

"No. God does not need to resort to such theatrics to be the Lord of everything that is. God does not have to explain Himself to me or prove Himself to me! I am His Servant, not His Judge. I am nothing to God."

"You are not God's agent here on Earth?"

"No more than any other righteous person."

"Yet you have repeatedly said, on television and radio and everywhere else, that you *are* God's agent? Was that a lie?"

"Not a lie, a . . . a . . . metaphorical truth!"

"So you *are* God's agent? You told the truth!?

"I am a truthful man, Mr. MacConnell. I am God's agent, but my only contract with God is in my heart. I serve the Lord my God with all my heart."

Mac paused before his next question, giving the spectators an opportunity to whisper among themselves, a chord that the judge quickly diminished with her gavel.

Mac returned to his desk and retrieved a glass of water. He took a slow drink while regarding Gideon, and said, "We are here because of what has been called an 'Act of God.' Do you believe there are such things, such Acts of God?"

"Of course."

"Did God destroy the home of Jerome and Lacy Light?"

"You're ascribing human qualities to God. You're trying to hold God responsible, but God doesn't have human qualities. God transcends human qualities. God does not plan or control events. God is not thinking."

"You said a few minutes ago that God 'decided' to create Heaven and Earth, but now you say God does not think; God does not control; God does not plan. Essentially, your argument, Reverend, is that God is *not*. If this sinkhole was not an Act of God, what was it then?"

"It was an act beyond the control of God," said Gideon.

"There are things beyond God's control?"

"God is not omnipotent. God does not control everything that happens. In fact, I don't think God controls anything that happens, unless you count creation as 'happening.' When we say something is an Act of God, it's an expression, not literal truth. God did not make the hole open beneath Mr. Light's house. God didn't even create the sinkhole exactly. God is *in* the sinkhole *and* the earth it passed through *AND* in the house, and in everything and everyone, but God controls nothing and no one."

"God does not control you, Reverend?"

"No."

"Are you beyond God's control?"

"I am . . . not."

"You just said God controls no one. Now you are saying God could control you. Which is it?"

"God is not in control."

"Who is?"

"Each man. Each woman. We each control our own lives."

"And God? Where is this God?"

"God is everywhere. God is everything. God is us."

"We are God?"

"We are God's image. We are God made flesh."

"Is there a God out there?" asked Mac, gesturing both arms out broadly.

"I don't know."

"Thank you, Reverend, for your testimony," said Mac. He returned to his seat next to Jerome at the plaintiffs' table as the spectators burst into dozens of private conversations.

Chapter 58

Pessimism

Moses Light fidgeted in his cap and gown as he stood between Joe and Marty among his fellow seniors, posed for their final class picture. He was aware that one senior was missing. Sylvana would never be a part of that scene of happy young faces—faces that, when wrinkled and old, would look at that photo and recall only some of the names. Those names and those faces would unlatch a brainful of memories and stories. Classmates, forever-frozen contemporaries, would meet at reunions and by accident in unexpected places, and say, "Do you remember that girl who died our senior year? What was her name?"

These thoughts flooded Moses's mind as he mingled with his fellow seniors, each of them looking like slightly goofy penguins, and each of them comfortable because they looked, in their final moment together, the same. Todd Fox had called Moses last night and invited him to join the family at church on the Sunday before graduation. Sylvana's father said there would be a special remembrance of Sylvana, and then they'd like Moses to join them for Sunday dinner.

When he'd gotten off the phone with Todd, Moses found his sister in her room and told her about it. "What do you think I should do, Miriam?"

"What did you tell them?"

"I told him I'd probably go, and I'd call him later."

"Are you gonna ask Mom and Dad?"

"Should I? I mean, I guess I should."

Miriam nodded.

"Yeah, you're right. D'you wanna come with me?"

Miriam bit her lip while she considered it for a second or two, and then said, "Yeah. I do."

At the class photoshoot, Rebecca Crane, Sylvana's best friend, who at one time loved to tease Moses, now came over and grabbed Moses's arm, pulling him away from the guys.

"What do you want?" asked Moses, feeling awkward with Rebecca but more kindly towards her than before. His words were not angry.

"I miss her. Nobody knew her better than you except me. When I'm with you, it's kind of like she's here again."

"Yeah. I miss her so much, I can't stand it. I want to be able to see her one more time, to tell her I'll always love her."

"She should be here, graduating," said Rebecca, choking up.

Moses leaned into her. "Please don't cry." He was far taller than Rebecca, and as he cupped the back of her head with his palm, he ended up pulling her cheek to his chest.

She spoke into his shirt. Her voice was muffled. "It feels better when I do."

† † †

"Then I won't let you," said Gideon to his lawyer.

"We have no choice," Dab Curara replied. "We are about to lose. If we settle now, we have a better chance of avoiding some horrible outcome. The Lights aren't asking for that much money. There's too much at stake if we lose."

Celeste said, "And there's just as much at stake if we settle. People will find out either way, and there'll be no end of these Act of God lawsuits. We have no choice but to trust in the Lord, that He will guide this jury to the proper decision."

"I wish I shared your faith, my dear," said Gideon. "But I share your opinion. We must trust the jury."

Dab said, "It's too risky."

"Why are you convinced we're going to lose now? What's changed?" asked Gideon.

"For one thing, the judge has ruled against using a questionnaire to help the jury through the intricacies of this case, as we'd suggested. I'd feel more confident if the jury had to answer a sequence of questions to lead them to a verdict."

"There's more though, isn't there?" asked Celeste.

"Gideon's testimony was very damaging."

Gideon bristled. "I don't see how. You told me to distance myself from God, to prove I'm not God's agent."

"Right. Not His agent. I didn't expect you to doubt His existence! The jury is going to see right through that. They'll know you're lying. You went too far."

"I wasn't lying."

"What?" exclaimed Dab.

"My faith has been battered, Dabria. Do you honestly think I would sit up there and lie about that, knowing it will destroy my ministry?"

"I can't believe this! Celeste, talk to him."

"It won't do any good, but I am praying for my husband, and for you, too, Sister Dabria."

"If we win," said the exasperated attorney, "how will you return to your ministry? You're committing professional suicide."

"I don't expect to return to it. It's that simple. I have made more than enough money to retire and take care of Celeste. I don't want to beg for any more money, not once the rest of my life. I can't do it anymore. Whether I am famous or infamous, I can use my celebrity to do good works and inspire others, like Jimmy Carter did."

"You may have no choice. If they win, we're going to be hit again and again until there's nothing left. Even if you leave CFS, it won't matter. They'll come after you *and* the church, like the Lights have done. If you lose, it's all over. You had it in the bag, but you went too far."

"I trust the jury."

"And in my professional opinion, that's a mistake. They could easily swing to the other side now, and I wouldn't blame them. We have to settle!"

"Please calm down, Dabria," said Gideon as coolly as possible. "You need to be composed for this afternoon."

"With all due respect, Gideon, I know how to handle myself in court, better, apparently, than you do. I can't believe what I'm hearing."

"Look at it this way, my friend: if they doubt there's a God, they'll doubt I'm His agent."

Dab fired back, "And the Lights will appeal us to death, and they'll ultimately win. By the time they do, there won't be anything left of CFS to sue."

Gideon looked at his lap, took a deep breath, and then looked at Celeste. He slowly turned his head to face Dab, and said serenely, "I don't share your pessimism." With that, he stood and left the room.

Chapter 59

Hypocrisy

Jerome was too nervous to sit in a stuffy little conference room. As soon as he had wolfed down the sandwiches that Reg Lundin brought in so the team did not have to leave the building, Jerome chose to pace the wide hallway outside the courtroom. Not expecting him to be there, the news cameras stood as silent sentinels because their producers had run to get lunch or to call their editors from a private corner somewhere.

Lacy took a few seconds more to eat, and then stepped into the hall to find her husband. As she approached him from behind, she could see his eyes were following an exceptionally attractive blonde as she walked towards them from a good fifty feet away. Lacy stepped right up to Jerome's ear before he noticed her, and whispered, "Take your eyes off her right now, before I have to hurt you." Then she laughed, breaking the tension.

After the woman had passed, Jerome put an arm around Lacy affectionately and said, "You know all I do is look, don't you? It doesn't mean a thing."

"How can you say that? You were ogling her."

Jerome held up his left hand as if holding a crystal ball. "Imagine you go to a museum and find a room there with a few beautiful paintings. One, in particular, fascinates you. Its style and subject and technique are similar to many other paintings you've seen, but it is somehow unique. As you study the painting, it begins to talk to you, literally talk to you. It reveals a personality, a history of itself, its feelings. Its fascination grows. You no longer want to move on to other paintings. You wish you could stay and revel in this one, adoring its beauty, its depth, its wisdom—even its flaws. *That* is what I feel when I see a beautiful woman."

"You are so full of crap. Didn't you want to hit on her? You were practically drooling."

"You know, I don't think about gorgeous women that way. I wouldn't know what to do with them if they threw themselves at me."

"Oh, you'd figure it out. Something would come up," said Lacy, looking at his crotch and pulling the corner of her closed mouth to one side.

"Very funny. Well, I mean I'd know what to do, but I really don't want to do it. I like looking. And you may not believe it, but I prefer looking when they're dressed, especially like she was."

"Where is this beauty you're talking about?" asked Gideon as he appeared from his meeting with Dab.

Jerome quickly looked around to make sure there were no cameras aimed at them. "She's, uh, well, it's nothing."

"Don't worry . . . I was kidding you," said Gideon, and added more soberly, "How are you, my friend?"

Jerome thought, *Wow! Here I am suing the man, maybe ruining his life, and he can quietly call me his friend?* Then out loud, he said, "Okay, I guess. Strange times, I suppose."

"Reverend!" boomed Dab Curara's voice from down the hall. She could not hear what was being said, but she had no desire to let another word pass between the litigants.

Gideon leaned into Jerome and Lacy as if telling them a massive secret, and confided, "Guess I'm in trouble now, eh?"

Jerome laughed, surprising himself and Lacy, though they both stopped abruptly as the stunning, no-nonsense attorney approached.

"Mrs. Light, Mr. Light. We'll see you inside." She took Gideon's arm and nearly dragged him away. Jerome and Lacy watched them leave, and looked at each other simultaneously. They both stifled an identical laugh.

Back in the cold-sober courtroom, though, the smiles disappeared. Mac joined them, and they all reclaimed the places they'd occupied for nearly four weeks now. In the increasingly mundane fashion to which the Lights had become accustomed, Judge Schuster strode to her bench and gaveled them back into session. "As the defense has now rested and the plaintiffs have indicated that they have no rebuttal witnesses to present, we will now hear closing arguments of counsel. Ms. Curara?"

"Thank you, Your Honor. And thank you, ladies and gentlemen of the jury, for your rapt attention during these past three weeks. You have honored us with your diligence and sense of purpose. You did not become jurors without a rigorous screening process, and that assures me that you are all people of integrity and honesty. Now you will be asked to carry that diligence and that integrity to a new level, as you judge the liability of a man who is known the world over for his sense of purpose, his honesty, and his goodness of heart."

Dab continued, "You are asked to find that, in providing spiritual guidance to millions of people all over the world, he is somehow responsible for all the unfairness of the world, and in particular, the unfair disaster that was visited on the plaintiffs. We admit that the destruction of their house was not their fault, that the Lights did nothing wrong to cause them to lose nearly everything but their lives. The insurance company told the plaintiffs, as they have told so many other unfortunate people before, that this calamity was an Act of God. Please believe me when I tell you, ladies and gentlemen, that insurance companies are poor authorities on religious matters." The spectators laughed lightly.

She was glad that her line got that intended response, but she remained focused. "Insurance companies don't try to be religious experts. They cover everyone regardless of what they believe. So, when they say something is an 'Act of God,' they are not interpreting scripture or passing judgment on the nature of God. They are simply saying that something is beyond anyone's control and beyond the powers of anyone to predict. No one could have known a sinkhole was going to open up beneath a small house in the small town of Marshfield, Ohio. It is a miracle that no one was home at the time, that none of the Lights' family suffered so much as a scratch.

"It is a terrible thing to lose one's house. We don't minimize the magnitude of their loss for one second, but isn't it one of thousands of tragic events that occur every day around the world? How is their suffering any greater than a baby starving to death in Africa because of another 'Act of God' known as a famine? Or any greater than a wife's anguish as she watches her husband washed away in a tsunami? The list is endless, and the unfairness is endless, and yet the plaintiffs would have you believe that this particular Act of God places responsibility on one mere mortal who speaks praisingly of God.

"The plaintiffs' contention is misguided on so many levels, ladies and gentlemen. God does not disclose His plans to anyone. Gideon Calhoun has never claimed to know what God will do next. He knows only what pleases God, and he tries to teach a better way of life to those who would seek it. The Hebrew word 'Rabbi' means 'teacher,' and Reverend Calhoun is a teacher, not a prophet. Nothing Gideon Calhoun could have done would have prevented the disaster that befell the plaintiffs.

"You have heard it said that the Church of the Forgotten Savior, the immensely popular church started by Reverend Calhoun over twenty-five years ago, raises money rather successfully from its congregation. Since when is that a crime? No one gives the church a single penny because they believe Reverend Calhoun is God's agent. They donate what they can afford because of what they get from the Reverend, not what he gets from God. The very fact that so many people support the work of the church is a testament to the importance of its message."

Dab paced within a small area in front of the jury box as she talked. "You heard Judge O'Neill talk about the legal definition of the term 'agent.' It is obvious in that context that Gideon Calhoun is not a legally appointed or contracted representative of God. Reverend Calhoun himself says he is not God's agent in the legal sense of the word, but only in how he tries to communicate God's holy word. If he is not God's legal agent, you cannot hold him responsible.

"There is another reason that this case has no merit. You have heard witness after witness testify that Jerome Light is an atheist. It is his right, of course, to follow whatever religion he chooses, or to follow no religion. That is one of the cornerstones of American democracy. What is not right is for him to say privately there is no God, and then turn around to say that when it benefits him personally that there is a God. It is the height of hypocrisy, and you should not allow him to succeed."

Someone among the spectators said "Amen," and Judge Schuster banged her gavel hard before anyone else could speak.

Dab continued, "Ladies and gentlemen, there is only one verdict you can reach when you examine all the facts in this case. That verdict is that the Reverend Gideon Calhoun bears no responsibility to the plaintiffs for their loss, and that the Church of the Forgotten Savior also bears no such responsibility. I thank you for your service and your honest endeavor."

With that, Dab sat down. Mac was amazed at the brevity of her closing argument. It caught him a bit by surprise, but he hid his astonishment well.

"Mr. MacConnell, are you prepared to deliver your closing argument?" asked the judge.

"Your Honor, Mr. and Mrs. Light would like to take a thirty-minute break before we begin."

"I'm not surprised, Mr. MacConnell. We will recess and be back here in exactly thirty minutes."

Mac knew the press would be lying in wait outside the courtroom, so he decided to remain at the plaintiffs' table and study his notes. Jerome and Lacy stood up to stretch, but seeing Mac remain at the table, Jerome simply threw his arms out wide in a brief paroxysm, and sat down again next to the lawyer.

Lacy was about to join her husband at the table again when she heard someone calling her name, a voice she did not recognize. She swiveled on her feet and came face-to-face with the old woman whom she'd now seen twice before in the courtroom.

"How do you do, dear? I'm Ethel Gitter." She raised her hand to shake Lacy's.

Lacy took the offered hand and realized there was barely enough to shake. She gingerly lifted Ethel's hand up and lowered it, as if handling a rare porcelain plate. "Hello, Ethel. I'm Lacy Light."

"Yes, I know. You're quite famous now."

"Oh hardly," Lacy scoffed. "I'm having my fifteen minutes. It won't last."

"Well, it's good that you recognize that, my dear. It keeps you humble, which is one of the reasons that you're my favorite."

"Your favorite?"

"Yes, my favorite person in this silly trial. It's hard to like your husband, to be perfectly honest with you. And Gideon already has his fans. No, Lacy, I like you!"

"Well, thank you very much. I'm honored." Lacy touched her fingertips of one hand to the middle of her chest, and then felt that surely she looked precisely like a character she'd seen in some old movie and had mocked for this "inane" gesture. "Would you like my autograph or something?" she said, and then she laughed at her own pretension. She'd meant it as a joke, hadn't she?

"Oh, I might need that if we shoot some video of you."

"What?" Lacy's jaw dropped.

"I don't want your autograph, Lacy; I want your interview."

"My interview?"

"If you'd be so kind."

"I thought you were . . . just a spectator."

"Well, in a sense I am. I came here out of fascination, not out of some assignment from a copy editor. And as I watched you and your husband, I thought you'd be a perfect subject for a story I'd like to write."

Jerome had abandoned his own thoughts and had picked up that this conversation behind him was not some trivial exchange. "Write for whom?" he said, directing his gaze at Ethel, unaware, thankfully, that she had insulted him moments earlier.

"I sometimes submit work to various Christian publications. I have my own blog now, too, and I'm thinking of doing a podcast."

Jerome said, "What kinds of 'Christian publications' do you mean? Have you been published?"

"Oh my, yes. Lots of times. It's good work."

"It pays that well?" asked Lacy.

"No, not really. But it's good work. It's the Lord's work. Most of my publishers are evangelical, but not all of them. I was published once in the *Jerusalem Times*!"

"It's very sweet of you, Ethel, to want to do an interview with me, but I really want to let this trial be the end. And I'm not allowed to speak with the press except the few words I might say coming in and out of here."

"I know that, my dear. I don't expect you to talk with me until there's been a verdict. But then I'd like to get an exclusive with you. What do you say?"

"I don't think so, Ethel. I'm sorry." Lacy tilted her head to one side as if to emphasize her regret.

"Well, you know, I'd hate to write what I have so far without getting some context from you," said Ethel, sounding as skeptical as possible.

"You don't mean . . . ?"

"Of course I do, dear. You made such interesting remarks that day . . . what was it, three weeks ago or so?"

"That's extortion!"

"No, not at all, my dear," said the woman, her smile making her look younger than her eighty years. "It's journalism. Some journalists would write what they heard without giving you a chance to explain. I'm not that way at all. I like you. I want to hear your explanation."

"I love my husband, Ms. Gitter. I won't participate in anything that insults him."

Jerome swiveled his head, but not his body, to look at Lacy, deeply in love with her.

"I knew you'd say that," Ethel shrugged her shoulders and gave an impish smile. "That's one of the reasons you're my favorite."

"Will you let us have approval of your copy?" Lacy asked.

"Of course. So, will you think about it?"

"I will. Thank you for asking, Ethel."

"You're welcome. Now I'd better get back to my seat before somebody takes it!"

Ethel returned to the back corner of the courtroom, and Lacy realized that the woman had been there every day, so immobile that she was barely noticeable. Lacy turned and sat next to Jerome, and they both faced away from the gallery of spectators behind them. Lacy leaned one shoulder against Jerome and said, "Well, whaddaya know?"

They talked briefly for the remainder of the break, trying not to disturb Mac, who had seemed intensely focused during the conversations. Only when the door from Judge Schuster's chambers opened and the elegant lady herself emerged did Mac resume his barristerial demeanor.

"Court is now in session" was intoned, and not one second of grace was given to the spectators to settle themselves before Judge Schuster said, "Mr. MacConnell, your closing arguments, please."

Mac stood, and magically appeared taller than at any previous moment of his life.

Chapter 60

Joy

Mac eyed the jurors silently for a moment, and then began. "There is one matter not in dispute today, ladies and gentlemen of the jury. It was an Act of God that destroyed the home in which Jerome and Lacy Light lived with their two children, Moses and Miriam. A heavily mortgaged home, I might add, because Jerome and Lacy are not wealthy. They both work at good jobs. They save what little they can. They are good parents, providing as best they can for their children. Their son Moses is about to go to college after he graduates from public school next month.

"But when a sinkhole destroyed their house last June, they lost everything except, thankfully, their lives. Some people think God was trying to send them a message. Some people think it was a fluke, a random act. The insurance company says it was an Act of God, and no one has disputed that. In fact, the law of this country says there are such things as Acts of God, and that it is perfectly legal and acceptable to attribute certain events to God. The United States, whose motto is 'In God We Trust,' legally recognizes the existence and the abilities of God. Think about that for a minute as you deliberate. Our laws say that it is perfectly acceptable for an insurance company to blame catastrophes on God in order to protect themselves from paying a claim. If the Big Rock Mountain Mutual Insurance Company says that it was God who destroyed a house, then by golly it was God! Well, we agree, ladies and gentlemen. We agree.

"It probably seemed odd to you at first that Mr. and Mrs. Light would sue a famous evangelist and expect him and his church to pay for their loss. After all, as far as we know, Gideon Calhoun did not direct God to destroy their house, nor did God tell Reverend Calhoun what was going to happen. So, we readily admit that it is unlikely there is anything the Reverend could have done to prevent this tragedy.

"How, then, can we hold him responsible? It is his own words that prove our case, his own words, repeated again and again and again . . . 2,418 times or more. And each time he repeats these words—'I am God's agent here on Earth'—his coffers fill up with money. Millions of dollars come pouring in because people believe Gideon Calhoun is God's agent, His representative, someone who has the authority to convey God's word. Millions of people believe that! You may not believe it, but that doesn't matter, because millions of your fellow Americans think he's God's agent, and they are willing to send every spare dollar they have to him and to his church because of it.

"Gideon Calhoun trades in people's fear. He is a multimillionaire because people fear the Lord their God and want someone to protect them and tell them how to live. Yet when that God he serves acts to destroy someone's life, Gideon Calhoun says it has nothing to do with him! And then he asks for more money. In fact, he had the temerity to mention the sinkhole hitting the Lights' house and then ask for donations to his church! He would reap benefits from someone else's tragedy, and yet he says he has no responsibility. That's just wrong. That's just wrong."

Mac let that sink in for a brief moment, and members of the jury were clearly contemplating his words. He did not let them ruminate long.

"Lots of people will tell you that Gideon Calhoun is a great man, a famous man, a well-respected man, and we have no argument with that. We do not doubt his appeal. We do not doubt the sincerity of his congregation in Arkansas and on television. The people who support him are good people, but they have been taken advantage of by a man with a Bible and a lie. The Reverend Calhoun now admits to you all that he does not talk with God, that he's not really God's agent after all.

"And so you now have no choice really, ladies and gentlemen. If you believe that he is telling the truth now, then you must recognize that he has been amassing a fortune based on a lie. And if you believe that he told the truth before when he said 2,418 times that he is God's agent, then you must recognize that he bears the responsibility of that claim! He cannot collect millions in income and then walk away from his debts because they are inconvenient."

Thaddeus MacConnell drew his first long breath since he began his diatribe. He had never turned his body away from the jury for even one second the entire time, but used his height and his voice to draw them in, to mesmerize the jury. Now he dramatically turned his back on them and walked several feet away, then turned again to face them.

"Spare me your sympathy for Gideon Calhoun. Find him financially, if not physically, responsible for this tragedy. Tell him that he cannot balance his books on the backs of struggling Christians and then turn his back on people who suffer at the hands of his God. We ask you to order Gideon Calhoun and the Church of the Forgotten Savior to pay Jerome and Lacy Light the sum of $325,000 for the loss of their house and possessions, and to award punitive damages in whatever amount you feel will properly show him that good, God-fearing people will not put up with his charade.

"Let there be no mistake what we are asking. We are not asking you to condemn religion and the respectful worship of God; we are asking that you condemn those who would exploit that respect and manipulate the public for personal gain.

"I thank you, ladies and gentlemen, for your attention, and I trust in you to make the proper decision."

Mac bowed slightly towards the jury, then turned to Judge Schuster and said, "Thank you, Your Honor. We are done." He sat down again next to Jerome.

The people watching were absolutely quiet for a long moment, and then all began talking to their neighbors at once, as if some invisible conductor had waved a baton and cued them. Judge Schuster banged her gavel several times, and the room was silent again.

"Thank you, Mr. MacConnell," she said, then pivoted slightly towards the jury. "Ladies and gentlemen, you have heard the testimony of both sides in this dispute, and you have heard the closing arguments of counsel for both sides. Shortly, I will ask you to begin your deliberations."

For the next half hour, she instructed the jury in the finer points of their process and in some points of law that had been raised. There were no surprises for Mac or Dab; they both had been well briefed by Judge Schuster on how she intended to instruct the jury, and which of the points they had requested would be made and not made. At last she said, "I ask you now to retire to the jury room and consider your verdict. Court is adjourned until the jury returns."

As the jury filed out, Jerome could not move. His legs did not want to help him stand. The end seemed to come so abruptly. He looked to the defense table and saw Gideon similarly glued to his chair. Gideon saw Jerome watching him and smiled, though it was not his usual "TV" smile.

Gideon made the first move. Jerome saw Dab Curara lean over and say something to the minister, who then stood and walked past her into the aisle. He mouthed "Good luck" to Jerome as he stepped towards the exit, with Celeste, Dab, and Lindsay right behind. Jerome nodded as if to say, "You, too."

Mac hustled them out of the courthouse and straight to the hotel. "I'll be paged when the jury returns. We shouldn't expect them today, though."

"Do you think we could head back to Marshfield for the evening, then?" asked Lacy.

"No. You need to stay here in Columbus, in case they decide quickly."

"How long do you think it'll take?" asked Jerome, knowing that the answer would be vague.

"Impossible to say. Do your best to relax."

Jerome laughed. "Yeah, right."

"I'm going to work on getting the appeals papers in order in case we don't catch a break with the jury."

"You think we're going to lose?" said Jerome.

"No, I feel pretty good, but you never know. I think we'll win, but we have to be prepared for any contingency."

Jerome looked up and swiveled his head back and forth as if scanning the skies for alien spacecraft. "No, we don't."

"Of course we do," said Mac, a bit annoyed. "We don't want to fumble around later.”

“There won’t be an appeal if we lose.”

“Jerome, you have to. There’s too much riding on it, not just you and Lacy. People are counting on us, and there are rulings we can appeal. We’ll have a good shot at it.”

“No, we won’t. If we lose now, we’ll lose every time. And if I didn’t believe that, then I guess I’d make sure of it. I don’t want to win. I hate what I’ve done.”

Lacy took Jerome’s hand and intertwined her fingers with his, and then squeezed. “I . . . don’t want to appeal, either,” she said.

Mac was aware that his anger and frustration would amount to nothing. It was best at this point to appear cooperative. He said, “You know I’ll have to try to change your minds, don’t you?”

† † †

“You won’t succeed, Dabria. I’ve made up my mind,” said Gideon, having a nearly identical conversation with Celeste in their hotel room.

“Did the Lights talk with you about this?”

Gideon smiled. “No one talked with me about it, my dear. It’s time for it to end, though. I think you’re wrong about one thing. I think we will win.”

“God will protect us,” said Celeste.

Gideon said nothing. He stepped into the bathroom and washed his face.

After Dab went to her room, Celeste went down to the lobby to get some toiletries. There she ran into Lacy. They hugged and both looked around, checking for “spies.”

“Let’s get a cup of something in the lounge, okay?” asked Celeste.

They ordered two coffees and sat in a quiet corner. “This trial has been hard on you, hasn’t it?” Celeste said.

Lacy gave her coffee an extra, unnecessary stir and watched the ripples slide around the cup. “I don’t always love Jerome. When we’re with my parents, I feel torn trying to keep everyone happy, to pay enough attention to Jerome and to my parents, so no one feels left out. It’s so hard. My parents never wanted me to marry Jerome. They thought he wasn't good enough for me. But I could never have found anyone who would love me more or be more devoted to me."

"Isn't that a wonderful thing for you to be able to say?"

"I think so . . . and I think my parents realize that now."

"And you know what? Jerome would say the same about you. You never show him anything but love."

Lacy smiled and said, "Loving someone is being able to convince them you love them even during those moments when you don't."

Her cell phone rang; it was Moses. He said he had talked with their teachers when he learned that the jury was now deliberating, and they had said that he and Miriam could miss school the next day. "We're going to come down in the morning, really early, in case there's a verdict," he told his mother.

"Come to the hotel. Do you know where it is?"

"I'll get directions. We'll be there by nine."

Lacy and Celeste finished their drinks and sat in silence, occasionally smiling at each other in some kind of secret conspiracy. "I'd better get back upstairs before they come looking for me," said Lacy.

"Me, too. Can't get caught fraternizing with the enemy," Celeste laughed. The women stood, hugged each other warmly, and left to spend the evening—a quiet, tense, yet comforting evening—with their husbands.

The next morning, one of those perfect May days with which Ohio rewards its citizens, Moses rang his parents' room from the lobby at 9 a.m. sharp. "Should we come up?" he asked.

Jerome and Lacy were packing everything in case the verdict came today. The hotel had agreed to let them check out, but to hold their room open as long as possible in case the jury did not return. The manager extended the same courtesy to Gideon and Celeste, and to both legal teams. Lacy fixed a light breakfast for everyone and took as long as possible to do the dishes afterwards. Miriam watched some TV, and Moses tried his best to study for an upcoming exam. Jerome scoured the Internet for anything to do with the trial.

At 11 o'clock, the room phone rang. "They're back," said Mac. Lacy dried her hands while everyone grabbed the bags. She gave one brief look around the room, grabbed a jacket from the coat closet, and they all scooted as quickly as possible to the lobby. Gideon and Celeste were checking out as they arrived.

"I guess this is it, eh?" said Gideon, trying to look upbeat for everyone, but knowing that one of them was about to be crushed, their lives changed forever. *Perhaps*, he thought, *we will both be crushed.*

The two teams walked across the busy Columbus streets and hustled into the courthouse, paying no heed to the throng of reporters, one of whom failed to notice his napkin still stuck in his trousers. Lacy went over to him, and he thought for a fleeting moment that she was going to answer one of the questions he had shouted at her above the din. Instead, she silently reached for his crotch, snatched the napkin there, and handed it to him, not waiting to see the stunned and perplexed look on his face.

It seemed as if all of Columbus had heard that the verdict was in; people Jerome and Gideon had never seen before were trying to get seats. One man was offering $1,000 cash to get in. The two legal teams squeezed and pushed the last few meters into the courtroom. Jerome was acutely aware that he might never see this place again, and he tried to memorize the moment as he held Miriam's hand and stepped through the crowds in the hallway, looking like he was in some weird Iditarod, crossing mountains covered with people instead of with snow.

The courtroom was louder than it had ever been. It reminded Moses of the stands before a baseball game. He was tempted to look for the hot dog vendor.

When everyone was seated, the deputy clerk announced Judge Schuster for the last time, and she entered the room with great purpose as the spectators stood. As she sat, the jury was brought into the room and took their customary seats. The chairs in the jury box seemed to creak extra loudly, as if complaining about the entire affair.

"Have you reached a verdict, Mr. Chairman?" the judge asked the quiet jury foreman who had betrayed not one emotion during the past four weeks.

"We have, Your Honor," he said.

"How say you?" she asked. Jerome mused that this expression was never used anywhere in the English language except in a court of law. He held his breath, afraid to move.

"In the matter of Jerome and Lacy Light versus the Church of the Forgotten Savior, we find in favor of the defendant and see no liability owed by the defendant to the plaintiffs."

The crowd stirred. Was there any chance that the Church would be forgiven but Gideon held liable? Nearly everyone in the courtroom thought they'd both get the same verdict. *But,* Jerome thought, *sometimes the film that wins Best Director loses the big prize.* Could it happen this time?

Judge Schuster paused dramatically, letting the first verdict sink in for a moment. "And in the second matter?"

"In the matter of Jerome and Lacy Light versus Gideon Calvin Calhoun, we find in favor of the plaintiffs and award them $325,000 plus punitive damages of $2.5 million."

Jerome's heart was pounding. He'd expected to lose, but he hadn't expected to react this way. "What if I had a heart attack right now, right here? Which would be the bigger news story?"

Vera Schuster banged her gavel, but the room was beyond control. She thanked the jury for their service, declared that court was adjourned, and disappeared into her chambers.

At Gideon's table, there was shock. Dab slammed her notebook shut, not so loud as to be heard by anyone but those immediately beside her. Terre Béliveau, the Chairman of the Board of CFS, was trying to shake her hand with more gusto than she felt was acceptable. He was thrilled that the Church had been exonerated, yet horrified at Gideon's loss. Celeste had rushed to hug her husband, but Gideon barely showed any emotion.

Reg Lundin had a broad smile and was heartily congratulating Mac, whose demeanor had barely changed from his usual stoicism. Lacy looked at Moses and Miriam. No one smiled. Jerome tried to smile, but it was a feeble attempt. "I can't believe it," he said to no one in particular.

Dab said to Gideon, "We need to talk, but it can wait until Monday. I'll start working on the appeal this week."

"I suppose you have to, don't you?" asked Gideon, clutching Celeste's hand.

Dab looked perplexed. "What do you mean?"

"I don't have much appetite for any more of this. I wish we could just walk away."

"You'd be ruined. There'll be other lawsuits if we don't challenge it. Anyway, we'll win on appeal; I guarantee it."

Gideon nodded. "Call me on Monday." He steered Celeste, who tried her best to smile bravely to all who watched them, towards the exit.

Reg pulled his right elbow up from his side with his open palm facing down in a too-jubilant attempt to shake Jerome's hand. The only other time Reg had felt this excited was when he'd gotten into law school. Mac stuck his right hand out and Jerome grasped it. "Thanks a lot, Thaddeus. You've really been amazing. I'm glad it was you."

"Me?"

"You who took the case. Another attorney might've blown it, but you did the best anyone could have done with it. I mean that. But there's one thing I want to know."

"What's that?"

Jerome said, "Why did you take the case?"

Mac smiled. "Let's just say I admire you and your wife, and leave it at that. I'm glad you won."

"I don't feel like I won. Weird, huh?"

"We'll appeal the CFS verdict. We might get that one, too."

Jerome said, "I told you I wouldn't. Can you appeal without me?"

"Not without your consent," Mac said. "I wish you'd reconsider. They're sure to appeal the verdict on Calhoun, and it would help if we counterattack."

"I'm done, Mac. If they appeal, you can fight it without me."

Lacy, too, came over and shook hands with the two attorneys. "I guess we won't be seeing you again, Mr. MacConnell. Thank you for everything you did."

Mac leaned over and kissed Lacy's cheek. "The pleasure has been mine. Good luck to you both." He grabbed his briefcase, wheeled on one foot and strode toward the exit.

Jerome looked at Lacy and said, "Time to go, eh? Come on, kids," he called to Moses and Miriam, and the four of them followed Mac and Reg out.

Jerome again understood why they are called the "press." There were microphones and arms being thrust at him and the others from every direction. Mac had not progressed far with his few seconds' head start, and he was surrounded by a crush of people. Dab and Gideon, off to another side, were similarly trapped.

Questions were fired at Jerome in such a torrent that it was impossible to catch all of any single question. "What was the . . ." "How did you . . ." ". . . planning to appeal . . ."

A voice—it could have belonged to any one of a dozen people— shouted above the din at Jerome. "Why do you think you won?" Jerome realized that the jury had issued a verdict and did not have to explain its reasoning. He had no idea why, and the question made him want to run over to the jury and ask them, but they had been spirited out a side door. He wondered if any resourceful reporter had already found a way to corner one of them.

"I think we won because . . . because I guess the jury could sympathize with our loss." It was amazing how the reporters were able to quiet themselves when Jerome began to speak. Jerome wondered how they could all shut up like that, as if he had pushed a button he didn't know he had. As he paused for breath, it was as if the button had been released, and the shouting at him renewed.

"Do you think they ignored the fact that you're an atheist?"

"I'm not an atheist. I'm . . . not an atheist."

"Then what are you?"

"I can't really answer that question." And fortunately, he didn't have to, because ten other questions were immediately thrown at him, and he could choose something less incendiary.

Gideon was enduring the same treatment across the hall. He was tempted to stun the mob of journalists by announcing his resignation from CFS, but he knew that the proper approach was first to tell his Board of Trustees privately, instead of letting them hear it on TV. He knew, as sure as he knew that his faith had turned a corner, that his ministry was over. But taking the ministry away from the man does not mean removing the minister inside. One reporter had asked if he had anything to say, and Gideon replied, "This coming Sunday is Mother's Day. I want to quote Julia Ward Howe, who founded Mother's Day not as a day of maudlin sentiment, but as a day of peace. She said, 'We, the women of one country / Will be too tender of those of another country / To allow our sons to be trained to injure theirs.' Go in peace, ladies and gentlemen, and please allow me and my wife to do the same."

Jerome, who had been making his way to the elevator along with Lacy and the kids, heard Gideon's final remarks and was stunned by the caliber of the man he had sued, the man he had almost certainly brought down. The Lights got on the elevator, and as the door began to close, Gideon suddenly reached out and forced it to open again. He and Celeste got on and the door closed, sealing out the rest of the world.

Gideon shook hands with Lacy and Miriam and Moses, and finally with Jerome. "Good luck to you. The road ahead of you is difficult and long, I'm afraid." He pressed a piece of paper into Jerome's hand.

"What's this?" Jerome said, looking down as he opened a personal check from Gideon. "What? Are you *crazy*? This is huge! Why would you give this to me now?"

"I thought you were going to lose. I had it ready to go, something to get you and your family on your feet again."

"I can't take this."

"Yes you can . . . but you had better remember to declare it on your income tax."

Jerome showed the check to Lacy, who said, "Oh my goodness … Gideon! And Celeste! But . . ." Words failed her.

"Please. Take it," said Celeste. "The thing is, you're going to need it now; the appeal is going to last for months or years. Anyway, you're going to lose eventually and get nothing."

"It's a personal gift," said Gideon. You don't have to share it with your lawyers. You can always . . ." and then the elevator doors opened on the ground floor and Gideon stepped out, anxious to take Celeste and avoid the public. "Oh, just . . . take it and good luck."

Jerome said, "We'll get by, thanks. Thank God for you, Gideon Calhoun."

Gideon took Celeste's hand. Looking straight ahead as he led her away, he said quietly, "What God?"

⤳ ★ ⤶

Author's Postword

This story of Jerome and Lacy Light, and their legal battle against the forces of religion, is a story I hope will entertain, provoke, and inspire you. It is not an accident that I say "entertain" first, for above all, this book is an amusement.

My story, like my religion, does not provide answers to all of the questions it raises. For example, why does the sky appear an unnatural yellow on the morning and evening of the sinkhole? Is it just a coincidence? There are several possible answers, including supernatural ones. You, dear reader, are invited to provide your own answer. It is not my intention ever to tell you whether you are "right," because I have no desire to try to mold your religious beliefs. I doubt you'd let me even if I did try. You might want to ponder other unexplained events. (See Discussion Points next.)

Having read this story, you can now solve its mysteries yourself. Don't look for pat answers.

To my friends and family. If you saw your name—first, last, or both—in the book, please know that it is my homage to you, but the character is not meant to be you. It is entirely coincidental if any of the person's characteristics or actions resemble you. Each name was chosen carefully by me to honor you all. No name was chosen accidentally. So, yes, you can honestly tell your friends that you are named in this book.

Discussion Points for Jerome v. God

General topics

Jerome and Lacy live in a place called Marshfield, and Gideon lives in a place called Stonecrest? What might those place names signify?

What are MacConnell's possible motives for taking the Lights' case? Are there clues to his mindset? Do you consider Mac to be a good person?

Chapters 1 and 2

What is the significance of the "jaundiced sky" that Jerome sees before the sinkhole strikes? What might it portend?

Chapter 12

Lacy is the "worry eater," in that she takes on everyone else's worries and anxieties. How else does Lacy take care of her family? What do you think of her role in the trial?

Chapters 16 and 17

How did your preconceptions about Gideon change during the entire story, and especially in these chapters, where so much of Gideon's formative years is revealed? What expectations did you have for Gideon? Did he turn out to be better or worse?

Chapter 24

Look at the exchange between Gideon and Celeste while she is still at the rehab clinic. Celeste asks the name of Gideon's first wife.

"Julie. Julie McElwain when I first met her. We were very young. I was just 23 when we got married."

"How old was she?"

"Let me see. She was 21. I was just out of seminary. It was a mistake. She wasn't prepared to be a minister's wife. She had no idea."

At this point, the dynamic between Celeste and Gideon begins to change. Although she is physically injured, she recognizes that he is the one in need of comfort. She becomes someone to whom he can confess his feelings, ultimately ending with his feelings for her. What does Celeste do to show Gideon that she is willing to comfort him? What else might she have done?

Chapter 27

Mac says he will answer Jerome's question about whether Mac believes in God, but refuses to do so during their first meeting. In fact, he never does answer the question. What do you think Mac believes? Why is Mac so interested in this case? (This is the one great mystery built into this story.)

Chapter 33

Celeste wonders if she might have been called to be Gideon's companion, confidante, and "helpmeet." What, to her, are the implications of this last word, and of the idea of being called?

Chapter 44

Lacy has a new attitude towards Angie O'Graham, the TV reporter. How has Lacy's attitude changed, and why?

Chapter 45

At the end of the chapter, Miriam reveals to her friend Jessica that Sylvana had asked her (Miriam) if she knew anyone who had had an abortion? Isn't that a strange question for Sylvana to have asked Moses's little sister? Why did Sylvana do that? (Another mystery.)

Chapter 51

In the middle of the narrative of the trial, the reader is suddenly transported outside, where "everything seemed quiet and normal." Mundane, everyday events are described. What is the author trying to say here?

Chapter 51

Dab cross-examines Jerome and, when she finishes abruptly, says she reserves the right to bring him back to the witness stand. But she never does. Why do you think she decided not to interrogate him again?

Chapter 58

Dab has established herself in the jurors' minds as a bit aloof, even a bit cold, perhaps with a slightly arrogant and imperious air. Suddenly, as she questions Gideon, she wants the jurors to see even this cold, businesslike woman consider this holy man to be special. She hopes it will create sympathy for Gideon and also show her to be a person who can be warm and compassionate with the "right" kind of people. Is this a good strategy? Could it have worked?

Chapter 59

If you were on the jury, how would you have voted? Why?

About the Author

Jeffrey Melvin Hutchins has been honored as one of the pioneers of the closed-captioning service that makes television accessible to people who are deaf or hard of hearing. He was responsible for the development of the technology to caption live programs.

Born in New York City, Jeff grew up in Saudi Arabia and attended high school in Beirut, Lebanon, before earning a degree in broadcasting & film from Boston University, where he met his wife, Diane. In the 1970s, Jeff was a TV producer at WGBH in Boston, and later was a founder of VITAC, the captioning company.

Since retiring, he has been the creator of a collection of children's stories, songs, and videos about Denton the Dragon. In 2022, *Denton the Dragon the Musical!,* a stage show he wrote with Matthew Gould, debuted.

His dystopian novel PERPETUONICS was published by Pisgah Press in 2024.

ABOUT PISGAH PRESS

Pisgah Press was established in 2011 in Asheville, NC, to publish works of quality offering original ideas and insight into the human condition and the world around us. If you support the old-fashioned tradition of publishing for the pleasure of the reader and the benefit of the author, please encourage your friends and colleagues to visit www.PisgahPress. com. For more information about Pisgah Press books, contact us at pisgahpress@gmail.com. All Pisgah Press releases can be ordered from Amazon.com, B&N.com, and through local bookstores.